MEET ME *under*
THE KISSING BOUGH

MEET ME *under* THE KISSING BOUGH

A CHRISTMAS ROMANCE COLLECTION

JOSI S. KILPACK   ANNEKA R. WALKER

SARAH L. McCONKIE

Covenant Communications, Inc.

CONTENTS

MEET ME *under* THE KISSING BOUGH

JOSI S. KILPACK

CHAPTER ONE

Bingham, Nottinghamshire, England, 1819

DEBORAH TOOK A BREATH AND forced her smile a bit wider as the first carriage turned into view, the frozen gravel crunching beneath the iron-banded wheels. When she recognized Mother's set of four grays pulling the carriage, she felt herself relax. Mother's presence would go a long way to setting the other guests—and Deborah herself—at ease as the party gathered throughout the afternoon.

Her daughter, Jane, shifted on the step beside Deborah, pulling her wool shawl tighter across her shoulders while letting out a dramatic sigh, as though they'd been waiting in the cold for hours, not less than a single minute. Deborah ignored her daughter's angst, mostly because her own angst demanded the majority of her attention. It was not an easy thing to step back into a life she had set in a corner for five years, but what better time to do so than at Christmastide?

New beginnings.

Letting go of the past.

Redemption and laughter.

All these things were the wishes she had for her three children. And herself.

Jane shifted again as the carriage stopped in front of the house, and Deborah straightened her spine so as to appear confident and capable.

"Ah, there are my two favorite girls," her mother, Lady Affington, said after the footman helped her down from the carriage. She and Deborah pressed cheeks, kissed the air, and squeezed hands.

"I am so glad you could come, Mother," Deborah said, feeling a lump of gratitude rise up in her throat. She could never have done this without Mother's encouragement. "Thank you."

"You must assume I am invited to far more house parties than is the case," Mother said, her green eyes smiling. She could have had her choice of warmer climes, but she was here because, as always, she was Deborah's best support. "Besides, your cook makes the best Christmas pudding."

"You are a terrible liar, Mother," Deborah said. Her cook, though dependable and skilled, struggled with puddings, an ongoing joke said in whispers. Deborah had hired a woman from the village to come in to make the Christmas puddings and pastries this year, and Cook felt too overwhelmed with the other demands upon the kitchen to be offended. Deborah wanted—needed—everything to be just right.

Mother laughed, causing the small golden bird that trimmed her hat to quiver as though it, too, were enjoying the joke. The bird was nestled among faux berries and fresh evergreen that trimmed the rest of the bonnet. Mother loved any chance to dress to a theme, and Deborah felt sure that every item packed in the three trunks now being unloaded from beneath the carriage would be perfectly coordinated to the season. Mother had even talked Deborah into ordering half a dozen new dresses, including a red dress made from a lovely damask satin she'd set aside for Fifth Night—her favorite evening of the twelve-day celebration. The dress currently hung in her wardrobe, but Deborah was not yet sure she would wear it. She'd been out of mourning for over a year now but felt conspicuous when she wore anything other than her grays and purples.

Today she wore a new rich purple muslin with ivory lace and a double-ruffled hem. It felt ostentatious, and she'd wondered a dozen times if she should change into something more subtle. But she was the hostess of a Christmas house party and needed to set the tone.

It was time for double-ruffled hems and red damask satin.

Deborah looked past her mother to the open carriage door. "Where is your mystery guest?"

"They will arrive in a few days," Mother said, then looked past Deborah to Jane still standing on the step. "Ah, there is my beautiful granddaughter."

Jane's sour expression did not change. "I am freezing to death, Grandmama."

Mother laughed and gave Jane the same air kiss and cheek press she'd bestowed on Deborah.

"Now, where are my grandsons?" Mother asked, looking around as though Nicholas and Ashley might have blended so perfectly into the brick that she'd missed them upon initial inspection.

"In the nursery," Jane said, shooting another glare in Deborah's direction. At thirteen years old, Jane was proving herself a master at the role of disgruntled adolescent. "Mother did not make *them* greet the guests."

"Which is exactly right," Mother said with a crisp nod.

Deborah sent a grateful smile for the support.

It was time Jane learned how to conduct herself in company, even if she was still more girl than she was young woman. However, realizing that Jane would have her Season in only a few more years had been only one part of the motivation behind Deborah's inviting Society back into her life.

Deborah looked down the drive and felt her stomach flip in anticipation.

Was it right to have invited him?

Was she ready?

"You are the eldest child, and a daughter no less," Mother said to Jane, drawing Deborah's attention back to the moment. "How should you ever become a hostess if you do not learn at the knee of such an expert? Besides that, those boys are bedlam personified; they'd as likely get run down by a carriage as not if your mother left them uncontained. Now, Jane dear"—she looped her arm through Jane's and turned her toward the house—"come with me to the parlor and enjoy a cup of tea until the other guests arrive. I am positively frozen in my shoes!"

Lady Constance and her ward, a quiet young woman with dark hair and green eyes, were the next to arrive, then Nigel's sister and her family, then three carriages at once. Deborah enjoyed reuniting with family and friends, but she remained alert for the sound of the final carriage to arrive. Just before it was time to dress for dinner, she at last heard the wheels upon the drive.

Deborah excused herself from a conversation with her brother, Lord Affington, and nodded at the footman to open the front door when she reached it, glancing over her shoulder to make sure no one noticed her departure. She had insisted Jane join her to greet the other guests, but this one she wanted to greet alone.

The temperature was colder now than it had been that morning, and the setting sun cast an amber glow upon the winter landscape as she stepped onto the porch and pulled the door closed behind her. The naked trees, stripped of their glamour by winter's icy hold, stood as stark sentries against the firelit sky.

The flip of Deborah's heart as the carriage got closer brought a flush to her cheeks, and she doubted her decision another two hundred times in the moments that it took for the flush to travel down the length of her body and into her toes.

New beginnings.

Letting go of the past.

Before Nigel had fallen ill, Phillip Dempsey had attended their Christmastide celebration every year with his wife, and then, after Lois died some nine years ago now, he'd brought their sons to stay in the nursery with Nigel and Deborah's sons. The four boys had been thick as thieves and almost as much trouble from their very first Christmas together. As Nigel's condition worsened and he no longer socialized or received visitors, he would still see Phillip, who would come for cards or brandy or just to talk, refusing to be refused entry into the sickroom based on his position as Nigel's oldest friend.

After Nigel's death, Phillip had continued his visits, bringing his boys to play with Deborah's sons for a few days at a time and helping her with estate management or talking to the boys about some matter of etiquette for which they needed a man's teaching. Sometimes they spent hours in the study discussing one topic or another. During other visits he spent most of his time fishing with the children at the fishing hole he and Nigel had favored as boys or walking to the village to call on old acquaintances from his boyhood. Phillip's compassion for Deborah's loss, born of having experienced the very trial himself, was different from the compulsory sympathy shared by those who did not know what it was like to lose the future you had always expected.

It had taken several of these visits over the course of nearly two years before Deborah first considered that perhaps Phillip wasn't simply checking to see how the family was faring.

Might he be coming to see *her*?

The thought had embarrassed her, but once considered, she could not stop considering it further. Did he purposely seek her out, or was it coincidence that he would appear in the garden when she was cutting flowers or the upstairs sitting room she preferred? Did he hold her gaze a bit longer than necessary? Did he compliment her out of good manners or something else? Did what she had begun to feel toward Phillip reflect how much she missed Nigel, or did it have nothing to do with Nigel at all?

No sooner did the carriage come to a stop than its door burst open and two boys tumbled out in a flurry of buckled shoes and flapping shirttails. Michael and Thomas were thirteen and eleven, respectively, but retained the energy of much younger boys. They were so much like Deborah's own boys that they could all four be brothers. The thought made her face catch fire.

"W-Welcome to Winfrey House," Deborah said with practiced measure.

"Where is Nicholas?" Michael asked, or was he Thomas? She had never been good at telling them apart since they looked so very similar to one another. Blond hair and blue eyes, like Lois. Phillip had darker coloring, with more silver in his hair each time Deborah saw him. It seemed he was always in need of a haircut, but the outgrown style looked well on him.

"Where is Ashley?" one of them asked.

"Did we miss dinner?"

"Can we stay in the green room?"

"It is haunted!"

"It is not; that was just Nicholas playing a trick."

A heavier timbre prompted them to stop talking over one another. "Boys, where are your manners? Mrs. Winfrey just extended you a welcome to her home."

Deborah looked from the fidgety boys to Phillip, who now stood behind them. Their eyes met and held.

One, mistletoe.

Two, mistletoe.

Three.

"We are starved!" one of the boys said, pulling Deborah from the moment she felt sure she could have stayed in for a very long time. She looked away from their father and smiled at the two boys.

"Let's get you boys settled in the nursery—dinner will be brought there soon enough."

One boy groaned. The other ran ahead. Phillip came up behind her as she ushered the lads through the front door. He put his hand on the small of her back, and the absolute thrill of his touch washed through her. Fourteen more days of this, and then . . . well, that was the point, wasn't it? For the next two weeks, they would see one another every day, watch how their children interacted, enjoy the company of mutual friends and family. By the end of the house party, she felt sure they would know what the future held for them.

She could not wait to see how it all played out.

CHAPTER TWO

As the hostess, it was Deborah's responsibility to assure the comfort of her guests, and thankfully, she had not forgotten how to do so in the years since she had served in this capacity. In appreciation of the travel each guest had endured that day, she had not planned evening entertainment and began saying good night to her guests around ten. A few of the men, including Phillip, stayed to continue their card playing, and although she would have liked to stay on hand until the last of the guests had retired, her day would start early the next morning. Deborah parted company with the retiring guests at the bottom of the staircase so as to steal into the kitchen and confer with Mrs. Fisher, the housekeeper. She had not remembered that Mrs. Lund disliked potatoes and wanted to make sure there would be alternatives on hand for the other meals.

After reviewing the next day's meals with Mrs. Fisher, Deborah headed toward the nursery. She wanted to believe the children would be asleep, but of course, they wouldn't be, what with cousins and friends here to stay for two full weeks—nine children, if you did not count the four young women who were staying together in Jane's room. The children did a remarkable job of faking their sleep when Deborah first entered.

She took her time walking between the cots and sleeping mats that had been arranged in the nursery until, eventually, one child could not suppress his nervous giggle, which set them all off.

"What? You are not asleep?" she said in feigned surprise, putting her hands on her hips as she looked from one giggling child to the next. "I am completely shocked."

She reassigned a few of them to different beds in hopes it would dispel the energy, then kissed each of the children on the forehead.

"Do keep in mind that any children who do not settle down now that you have been officially tucked in shall be thrown out the nursery window. You can ask Nicholas and Ashley to confirm that it is not an empty threat."

"It is true!" Nicholas said eagerly, familiar with her threat, as she used it on her sons regularly, though of course she had not actually followed through. "She throws Ashley into the snow nearly every night!"

She pulled the door closed on the renewed giggles, smiling to herself at the joy of having a full house, then turned and stopped.

Phillip stood in the corridor outside the nursery-room door, one shoulder leaning against the wall as he watched her with a soft smile. He pushed himself upright while she swallowed the nerves bursting through her like exploding chestnuts.

"I was just checking on the children," she said, as though that weren't obvious.

"I believe I heard something about windows and headlong dives into the snow." He cocked his head to the side, and she felt a warm sort of rumble settle through her stomach, strong enough that she placed a hand over her middle.

There had been a time when she had never imagined she could be attracted to another man. When Nigel had died, the loneliness and regret had felt like bricks in her chest that she would never be rid of. And then she had begun managing the estate, connecting with other village leaders to coordinate charitable efforts and support the parish, and taking walks with Phillip when he came to visit. The bricks had begun to lift. The future had stopped looking so dark and cheerless. She was only thirty-five years old, comfortable and confident in ways she'd never been before, and ready to start living again.

But to feel the physical and emotional stirrings with someone other than Nigel?

The thoughts had felt wrong . . . until they hadn't. Nigel had been ill a long time, and he'd said more than once he wanted her to be cared for. She had put off the more detailed conversation of Nigel's wishes for her future because it had been too painful to consider at the time, and then there had been nothing to talk of except how to manage his comfort as the end drew near. She wished now that she'd allowed those discussions to play out. He would want her to be more than just cared for, wouldn't he? Would he want her to love again and be loved in return?

Would he approve of Phillip fulfilling that role?

She had come to believe that he would.

During Phillip's last visit two months ago, they'd gone for a walk to see the autumn leaves, and when the boys had run ahead, he had slipped his hand around hers as easily as if he'd done it a hundred times before. She hadn't known what to say, so she'd said nothing and simply enjoyed the thrill until the sound of the boys fighting over who'd found the bigger stick first had sent Phillip running ahead to break up the fight before someone's head met up with the stick at the heart of the argument.

Phillip had been unable to visit since then due to business he'd needed to take care of in London before snow threatened his ability to travel.

But here he was now.

In her house.

Just outside the nursery, where their children were pretending to sleep again.

He looked at her in a way that turned the air between them warm and sharp, like the first bite of a crisp ginger biscuit.

"I am very glad you came, Phillip," she said in a soft voice.

"I am very glad that you invited me." He paused to smile a bit wider. She smiled too. He moved half a step closer. "I know your duties as hostess will keep you occupied a great deal, but I do hope we might find time to have a conversation, just the two of us. Do you think it possible to schedule such a conference?"

It was not as though they hadn't had private conversations before. But this was different. For one thing, he'd made a specific request, and for another, the air was getting even warmer and sharper. "Y-yes," she said. "I believe the lamps in the study are lit right now if you—"

The sound of men's voices coming up the stairs sent the invitation skittering like schoolgirls trying to balance on their skates.

They both straightened as though on command. He reached out and brushed her arm with his hand, sending chills up and down her spine. "Perhaps another day."

She nodded as Phillip went left toward the guest rooms, and Deborah went toward the family wing and the unwelcome interruption. After she rounded the corner and startled her brother and Mr. Lund, she stopped to speak to them, then went on to her room, where she reviewed the corridor exchange with Phillip a hundred times as she readied for bed.

A private conversation.

Just the two of them.

Surely it would not be too difficult to arrange such a thing.

CHAPTER THREE

It proved to be extremely difficult to arrange such a thing.

Deborah was up before the sun, conferring with her staff and making sure everything was in order for the first official day of her Christmas house party. Per tradition, Christmas Eve was devoted to decking the halls—quite literally—with the greenery of which it was bad luck to bring indoors before this day. The task required sleds and axes and plenty of warm cider. Phillip took charge of the children who wanted to participate in the hunt for holly and ivy and fresh evergreen boughs. The party went into the woods and returned some hours later with bundles of greenery that those who had stayed behind fashioned into bows and draperies and winding chains they wove throughout banisters and wired up on the fireplace mantels with the help of the staff. The entire main level was brought to life and smelled like the heart of a forest. With all the senses now on alert, Deborah felt Christmastide truly upon them.

She and Phillip crossed paths a dozen times, sometimes with a brush of the arm or a gaze held a moment longer than necessary, but time for a private conversation did not present itself. There was something rather delicious about the postponement, however, a building tension that Deborah found invigorating.

Christmas Eve was the night the local gentry came to Winfrey House for dinner, filling out the party to nearly fifty persons. The young ladies, as Jane and her friends and cousins were now referred to, joined the adults for dinner, and Deborah could not be more pleased by how well they conducted themselves throughout the meal. The hall had been cleared to accommodate dancing, and though Deborah did not participate, the majority of the other guests did, while others visited or played cards in the parlor while enjoying ginger punch and spiced wine. All in all, the evening was a grand success, and by the time the last attendee had departed in the early-morning hours, the other house guests—Phillip included—had gone to bed.

When Deborah checked on the children, they were actually asleep, and Phillip was not there to greet her when she came out of the nursery. She felt a prick of disappointment but understood that he, too, was likely worn out from the day. Through the evening he'd given particular attention to some of the older guests whom he had known in his youth when he'd lived nearer the village. Such attention had both been a credit to Deborah as hostess and a great help to her responsibility to ensure each guest had an enjoyable night. She'd have liked the chance to thank him, yet her own fatigue quickly quashed any lingering disappointment.

She was asleep before her head managed to make a dent in her pillow and awake before dawn the next morning.

Church services and the annual visit to the vicarage were first on the agenda for First Night, and her guests mingled with other parishioners and left behind generous donations. When they arrived back at Winfrey House in the early afternoon, the Yule log, which had been cut months earlier so as to be seasoned in time for tonight's burning, had been set upon its braces in the yard, the branches long since trimmed so that it presented as a twenty-foot log ready to be fashioned.

The party enjoyed a cold luncheon before the guests departed to their rooms and changed from their church clothes to attire more suitable for either the exertion or the observing of the exertion, depending on each guest's particular interests. The children spilled onto the grounds several minutes before the adults arrived, and their energy quickly grew into a frenzy so that by the time the full party was gathered, rubbing their hands together and stamping their feet to ward off the cold, the children had nearly worn themselves out with games of hoodman-blind and general chase-and-be-chased.

Because Winfrey House lacked the sort of grand hearth that could accommodate an entire tree over the course of twelve nights as it slowly burned through the symbolic regrets and hardships of the past year, the Winfrey House Yule log was always cut into twenty-five sections: two to be burned each night and one to be saved for next year's lighting.

The guests were invited to join in the cutting using two-man saws, as was the Winfrey House tradition. Deborah sportingly took one side and her brother the other for the first competition, which they lost to Mr. Lund and Mr. Carrington. By then, the rest of the guests had decided whether they wanted to take a turn, and Deborah was able to take the more comfortable position of a spectator. Timid beginnings turned into a fierce competition after a bit more ale, and though the team of Noel—Nigel's younger sister—and her lifelong friend Mrs. Lund cut through two rounds, they threw up their hands once the men began making wagers.

Coats and cravats were tossed to the side, sweat and banter mingling as teams competed against one another to cut through their section fastest. The children were impervious to the cold, but the young ladies and women began going inside when their toes went numb. Deborah stayed with the hardier guests, laughing and cheering at the sight of usually proper men working the saws. As the hostess, it was her duty to fully support the activities of her guests, but Phillip had been one of the first to throw off his coat, and she'd felt her commitment to stay increase as the log shortened and the sweat of his exertion began to dampen his linen shirt. Phillip helped manage his uncle's large estate in Derby, and it seemed he might physically participate in the work more than she'd realized. His physique reflected neither the unworked leanness nor the doughy fatness of most noblemen his age.

"Gracious," Deborah heard someone say from behind her.

She looked over her shoulder to see Mother standing a few feet behind her, also staring at Phillip. When Mother met Deborah's eyes with a curious look, the subsequent blush drove off a bit more of Deborah's chill; she had not considered that anyone else would notice her notice. She faced forward as Mother stepped up beside her, keeping her voice low. "I had thought you invited Mr. Dempsey in an attempt to balance the numbers. It seems there might have been an additional reason I had not considered."

"Oh, Mother, do not be silly," Deborah said, forcing herself to look away from Phillip. The goal of this activity had nothing to do with admiring the male physique set to advantage with the effort taking place, but as that had become her sole preoccupation, she found it difficult to turn her thoughts toward any other factor.

"Seat me beside him at dinner tonight," Mother suggested.

The men were on their final measures of cutting, and Deborah swallowed as Phillip wiped the sweat from his face with his sleeve before planting his feet and taking hold of the two-handled end of his saw. He stood opposite Mr. Lund, his eyes bright, his outgrown hair wet with sweat around his face, and his smile as wide as the winter sun. Goodness, but he was handsome.

"Deborah?"

Deborah blinked and forced her eyes to her mother again. "I'm sorry?"

"Seat me next to Mr. Dempsey at dinner tonight."

"The seating arrangement was decided weeks ago, Mother, and—"

"Circumstances change," Mother cut in, a determined look on her face that sent Deborah back in time to the years when Mother had managed every aspect of her life and brooked no argument. "Change the arrangement."

Deborah had not mentioned her curious feelings about Phillip to anyone, not even Mother, with whom she talked about everything else. To love again was deeply personal, and she had not felt ready to take on anyone else's thoughts on the matter. However, she had invited him to a house party made up of her family and friends and had agreed to a private conversation at some point during this visit. Perhaps it was time to talk to Mother and reveal what was quickly becoming an important topic in her own thoughts.

Having Mother share a meal with Phillip might very well be the perfect way to broach the subject. Mother's blessing would be encouraging and could help Deborah set her own concerns to rest. She still felt butterflies when she agreed, however. "Yes, Mother."

"And go inside before anyone else notices your particular attention."

Deborah scanned the other guests watching the scene—had her attention been so very particular? She would need to be more guarded.

Deborah nodded, then turned to the house. At the door, she looked back in time to see Phillip and Mr. Lund cut through their side of the log ahead of the competition. They dropped their saw and raised their arms to the cheering spectators in triumph. Phillip scanned the faces until he met Deborah's eyes, held her gaze, and then winked.

The gesture moved through her as she slipped inside and closed the door behind her. Yes, she needed to talk to someone about what was happening between her and Phillip. She needed Mother's help sorting through exactly what it meant for her future and her family.

CHAPTER FOUR

AT DINNER THAT NIGHT, DEBORAH tried to concentrate on her own conversation but found her attention straying to the other side of the table, where Mother's every attention was upon Phillip. Twice he looked up and caught Deborah watching. Both times she quickly turned her attention to her plate in hopes of not betraying her interest.

Perhaps her anxiety was because she was wrestling with whether it was appropriate to feel what she felt for Phillip. Perhaps because her mother's approval was so very important to her. Or perhaps she was nervous because Mother had been the one to encourage young Deborah toward Nigel Winfrey all those years ago. Inviting Mother into this new possibility with Phillip felt . . . profound.

Deborah had found Nigel silly and overbearing when she had first met him in London back when she was but eighteen years old. Mother had known the family, however, and encouraged Deborah's attention, then prodded and finally demanded Deborah take advantage of his company anytime she could. In the beginning Deborah had complied in order to avoid an argument with her mother, and then Nigel's easygoing nature, deep-blue eyes, and quick wit had drawn her in. Their happy marriage was a personal success her mother often took credit for securing, and Deborah was very grateful to have followed Mother's counsel. It was in part because Deborah had loved Nigel so deeply that she believed she could love again. The opportunity to discuss how she felt now with her mother was like the first bit of sugar on a child's tongue.

If Mother did not approve, however . . . Deborah looked across the table in time to see her mother laugh at something Phillip had said and smiled in relief. She turned back to Noel to ask after her eldest daughter, who was preparing for her first Season in the spring.

The evening entertainment for First Night centered on music—Mrs. Carrington was a lauded harpist, and Mrs. Lund played the pianoforte with a skill that ten years of lessons had not earned for Deborah.

The parlor was well situated for gatherings—the main room was large, with seating areas interspersed throughout and a rounded alcove raised a single step, where the pianoforte and harp were set apart from the open space. On the west side were two sets of double doors. One led to a cardroom that, when the doors were opened, felt as though it were a part of the parlor. The second led out to a small balcony that looked over the gardens. Deborah had always lamented that the balcony was not larger, as it accommodated only a few people at a time and therefore did not lend much additional space for parties in the summer. In the winter, however, no one bothered to take in the view of dormant vines and cut-back shrubbery when inside the house there were evergreen boughs, a cheery fire, and the sort of holiday delights to be enjoyed only this time of year.

The children had been practicing some carols that they performed quite well for having only had three days together. They were allowed to stay for another hour and enjoy some wassail with the adults, and then the evening fell to cards and conversation. The young ladies of Jane's entourage stayed until eleven, an hour past their usual bedtimes, and giggled in the corner over whatever it was that set young girls to giggling. The other guests began wandering toward their bedchambers near midnight. The very last guest to leave the parlor happened to be Phillip.

The Lunds' laughter faded up the stairway, and Deborah turned back to the room as Phillip stood with the box of playing cards in his hands. Their eyes met and held.

One, mistletoe.

Two, mistletoe.

Deborah watched Phillip cross the room and put the box of cards on the mantel. She used the time to gather her courage. This was the first time they had been alone since those few moments in the corridor outside the nursery two nights ago.

"I hope you won that last round," she said.

His triumphant laughter throughout the evening had been consistent enough to give the impression that he'd been doing well.

Phillip shrugged, staying near the mantel, which kept some twenty feet between them but was close enough for her to see his coy smile. "I daresay winning was not my motivation."

"Is there another motivation in playing at cards?" she asked, raising her eyebrows and daring to take a few steps closer to him while remaining mindful that the parlor door was open. They were not precisely alone.

"I admit that is usually my primary objective, especially in company with such deep pockets. However, tonight was different." He glanced toward the door as she had a moment earlier, then met her eyes once more. "My goal was only to outlast the others."

"And why is that?" Deborah asked. They were only about six feet apart now, and her entire body was aware of the proximity. She felt silly, and yet, to experience sensations and awareness she'd thought she would never feel again . . .

Phillip continued. "Because I had hoped that the lady of the house would be the last to retire, and it seems my Christmas wish was granted."

She tried to think of a witty response but could find no words.

His grin slowly stretched across his face, showcasing the lines that life had left upon him. The features that betrayed his age were not unattractive. Dare she admit they were the opposite? She herself had made peace with the changes in her looks as the years moved forward, taking a sense of pride in the smile lines she'd earned despite tragedy and the more rounded figure and softened skin brought on by motherhood and maturity. It was only right that she would appreciate the same things on him: life lived and the wisdom, patience, and resilience that came with it.

She heard footsteps in the corridor and held her breath, thinking that once again they would be interrupted. When the footsteps disappeared, however, she suddenly wanted absolute privacy. These last few days had proven that hard to come by in a house full of guests and servants bustling about to meet their needs.

"It is snowing," she heard herself say, then waved toward the double doors that led to the balcony. "Did you see?"

Phillip turned to look as she crossed to the doors and pulled them open, a rush of frigid air causing her to shudder, though nerves may have been a contributing factor. She stepped out onto the balcony too small for socializing but just the right size for two people trying to carve out a few minutes of solitude.

The reverent hush of the snowfall contrasted with the rushing beat of her heart when Phillip stepped out behind her. His hand touched hers, and she was startled, then looked down. He threaded his fingers through hers just as he had those months ago when they'd been walking amid the autumn leaves. She looked up into his brown eyes, full of the same things she felt—energy and longing and hope. The resistance she'd felt in fits and starts these last months melted away as calmness took over. Rightness. Joy.

He touched her face with his hand.

She closed her eyes to fully savor the sensation.

His lips met hers and she was lost.

His kiss ignited within her, and his arm went around her back as she eagerly stepped closer, the feeling of being wanted, of wanting in return, moving through every part of her. She moved her hands to his shoulders, felt the strength of him beneath her, and found the fantasy of his attention pale in comparison to the reality.

CHAPTER FIVE

When planning this house party, Deborah had followed the well-proven template Nigel's mother had used over the forty years she had been the hostess at Winfrey House. The late Mrs. Winfrey had started the tradition the first year she and Nigel's father had married and over time had honed a schedule of activities and events that coincided with each day's focus of traditional Christmastide observances, save one minor change.

As the story went, Nigel's father had tried to talk his wife out of the celebration the year she was within a few weeks of delivering their second child, whom they planned to name Noel if it was a girl and Joseph if it was a boy since it was due so near Christmas. Mrs. Winfrey had refused to cancel the event—it was the tenth year of the tradition, after all, and she was determined to make it the most magnificent. She began having labor pains during the musical performances of First Night, and by noon of Boxing Day, she was in her bedchamber with a midwife and biting on a leather strap to keep from disrupting her guests with her screams.

Thus, Boxing Day was moved to the twenty-seventh instead of the twenty-sixth, which had thereafter become Noel's Day. As she'd grown, Noel had become quite taken with the idea of planning the day herself. After Deborah had become the established hostess, she'd always been relieved to turn the responsibilities over to Noel for the day. She was especially grateful today. Though she and Phillip had been together on the balcony for only a few minutes, Deborah had spent the better part of the night reliving the encounter. When she'd finally fallen asleep, she'd dreamed of it, and therefore, her mind was not as centered on her hostess duties as it should be. Sharing the responsibility of keeping the household entertained and adequately festive today was a welcome reprieve.

The guests trickled in for breakfast, and Deborah visited with this guest and then that one until Phillip came into the room. She'd worried that she would feel embarrassed or shy upon seeing him again, but she felt neither. She stood from her place at the table she shared with three other guests, the eagerness to be near him proving impossible to resist.

"I simply must have another cinnamon bun," she said by way of excuse to the company at her table. Then she joined Phillip at the sideboard and picked up a clean plate from the stack.

"Good morning, Mr. Dempsey. Did you sleep well?" She kept her tone as casual as she could manage and resisted leaning in and letting their shoulders touch.

"*Very* well, Mrs. Winfrey," he said with equal ease. "I wish I slept so well every night."

She pressed her lips together to keep from smiling too overtly and perused the display of breakfast wares. What was it she'd told the guests at her table she simply must have?

If the footman had not come into the parlor to begin dousing the candles last night, surely they'd have had a conversation about what their kiss meant for them going forward. She'd nearly scared the poor footman out of his skin when she'd stepped into the room he'd thought empty. She'd explained that she'd wanted to watch the snow upon the gardens. There had been no choice but to leave Phillip to his own means of escape after the footman cleared the room.

"I hope you did not catch a chill," she said, adding sausage to her plate as a way to extend the layered conversation.

"Thank you for your concern; I stayed quite warm, I assure you."

She dared look up at him and then could not look away, even though the room was full of guests who could notice.

"I hope it will snow again tonight," Phillip said, giving her a quick wink. She appreciated that he was willing to play along with keeping their liaison a secret—everyone here was a friend or family member of Nigel, and though she had not lent a great deal of thought toward their opinions, she was not ready to share such personal information just yet. She was eager to discuss her options with Mother, certain that would give her the insight and direction she so desperately needed.

Noel entered the breakfast room, and the guests erupted into birthday wishes and congratulations on another year lived well. Noel fairly beamed as the women came one at a time to kiss her cheek. Phillip and Deborah finished their breakfast selections and made their way to separate tables.

"What shall be our celebration?" Mrs. Lund asked once the guests returned to their chairs. In the past Noel had chosen snowman-building competitions or performing plays, and once she'd invited a local milliner to help all the women decorate their own holiday bonnets while the men went shooting.

"Well," Noel said, clasping her hands together. "I would like to have a kissing competition."

The room erupted into laughter, distracting each guest enough that they did not notice Phillip and Deborah freezing in place for a moment. Deborah caught Phillip's eye, felt her cheeks heat up, and looked back to her plate that contained a sausage link and a bun.

"Or, rather, a kissing-*bough* competition," Noel added.

More laughter. Deborah forced her hand to pick up her fork and knife and slice up the sausage on her plate. She did not even like sausage, but she ate it in six bites while Noel explained her choice of birthday activity.

The group would break into smaller parts, four or five together, then retire to different areas of the house that right now were being outfitted with the wire, greenery, ribbons, and colored paper each group would use to make their kissing bough. After sufficient time for each group to craft their creation, the boughs would be displayed in the hall, and every person in the party would vote for their favorite. The winning bough would be hung in the parlor, where it would remain for the rest of the house party. Deborah remembered having done this activity once in the early years of her marriage to Nigel, and the memory helped reassure her that this was not some pointed reference to her and Phillip's late-night tryst. She took a deep breath to further calm her racing heart.

No one had seen them.

No one knew.

She realized amid her anxiety, however, that if people did know, it would change the emphasis of this house party, detract from the holiday and from Jane's first foray as hostess. The attention would become directed toward Deborah and Phillip. The thought made her feel even more anxious. She was not ready for that sort of distraction. She was not ready to carry the weight of so many eyes and ears.

"Must we all participate?" Mr. Carrington asked. He looked at the other men as though appealing to them directly. "Surely the other men of the party would agree that this is an activity inconducive to our abilities."

The women protested, and some of the men fell in with Mr. Carrington, but a surprising few thought they might try their hands.

"I suggest we men form a party all our own—show the ladies what we are capable of within the more artistic skill set," Phillip offered, also looking around the room at the men. "What an opportunity to prove ourselves."

Mr. Lund agreed with him, and within a few minutes the other teams were nearly arranged. Someone touched Deborah's arm, and she looked in that direction, paused, and then smiled.

"Good morning, Mother," she said with a smile. She always felt more settled when Mother was on hand. "I did not expect to see you so early."

Mother usually preferred a breakfast tray in her room and an unhurried preparation for her day. It was therefore unusual to see her before noon, but Deborah was glad she was here. She was ready to talk about her feelings and let Mother help her sort out what her next step should be, just as she had helped Deborah sort out so many other steps in her life.

"Might I have a word?" Mother asked.

Deborah paused, for the first time taking in her mother's lack of exuberance. She felt her mood instantly matching that of her mother's. "Are you unwell, Mother?"

"I am well enough." She smiled as though to prove it, but her eyes did not reflect her usual merry temperament. "Meet me in your bedchamber in a quarter of an hour; this entire house is set up with ribbon stations, and that may be the only place for such a conversation."

It was nearly half an hour before Deborah could separate herself from the party, after reviewing with Jane how to move from one station to another to see if the guests needed anything. Deborah passed a kissing-bough station set in the parlor and one set in the library and could hear the sounds of another in the study as she passed by—it was impressive that Noel had made such detailed arrangements without needing to involve Deborah in the preparation.

Mother was already in Deborah's room with a tea service set up in the small sitting room off the main. Deborah sat on the settee opposite while her mother began to pour. It was all so very formal and unexpected.

"Goodness, Mother," Deborah said with an insincere laugh after being handed her cup without a word having been said. "You have me quite concerned."

Mother looked up and held her gaze directly. "I need your promise that you will not give Phillip Dempsey another thought."

Deborah felt the blood drain from her face. Mother saw the reaction and put her half-filled cup on the tray with a snap of porcelain. "Oh, good heavens. Have you given yourself over?"

"Of course not!" Deborah said, her defenses rising. "What sort of woman do you think I am?" Because surely some balcony kissing did not mean she'd given herself over. Had she?

"Why did you not share whatever thoughts you have been having with me before now?" Mother asked, a crease between her eyebrows.

It had been some time since Deborah had been the recipient of Mother's disapproval, and she was out of practice having to defend herself to the woman who was almost always her ally. What had happened at dinner last night? Had Phillip said something offensive?

Deborah took a breath, centering her thoughts so that she did not say too much. Or too little. "Am I not a grown enough woman to have thoughts I do not share with my mother?"

Mother huffed a breath as she stood and began pacing in front of the fireplace, a decidedly male habit that Deborah had seen her mother perform only a handful of times in her life. And never because Deborah had done something to warrant the reaction.

"Be reasonable," Mother said, an edge to her voice. She stopped and turned to stare at Deborah. "You are not seriously considering Phillip Dempsey as a match, are you?"

Feeling trapped and unsure of herself, Deborah said, "And if I were?"

Mother froze momentarily, then came to sit next to Deborah on the settee, taking both of her hands and softening her tone. "Deborah, my darling child, I understand there is a familiarity between you and Mr. Dempsey that must bring a great deal of comfort; he was Nigel's closest friend, after all, and therefore a connection to the man you loved so well."

Deborah nearly choked at the thought that her feelings for Phillip were a representation of her feelings for her late husband but could not dismiss it as easily as she'd have liked. *Was* that a factor in her attraction to Phillip? He was the only single man with whom she'd interacted in the years since Nigel's death, and there *was* a comfort in his having known and loved Nigel.

The thought was incredibly uncomfortable, and Deborah felt like a box of jacks, shaken and poured out upon the ground, as she tried to sort the feelings from last night, this morning, and this moment.

Mother continued. "I acknowledge that he has looked in on your family and shown you deference, but please do not let those things eclipse the reality of your situation. You are a woman of privilege and class he will never understand, and—"

"Phillip is a gentleman," Deborah protested.

"Barely that," Mother said with a shake of her head, though some compassion had entered her expression. "His father was a solicitor, his mother a gentleman's daughter who betrayed her parents' wishes when she married him—it happened in my very Season, and I am well aware of the shadow their scandal still casts. It is only the station of Mr. Dempsey's uncle on his mother's side that has given him a place in our circle—and Nigel's friendship, I daresay. When his uncle dies, the line will pass to Mr. Dempsey's cousin, who is a buffoon. The man may keep Mr. Dempsey on to help with the management, but Mr. Dempsey will gain no place in life beyond what he has now. He could as easily be turned out as kept on. He is little more than a steward for his uncle, living in—"

"That is not true," Deborah said, but she did not exactly know. The fact of it was that she knew very little about Phillip's family and situation. She did know he lived on land owned by his uncle, a landholder of some significance in Derby, and helped with its management. But she did not know what that work entailed and what of his situation was independent of his uncle's grace. He had been Nigel's friend and then her friend—she'd had no reason to dig about his history, and even now she did not particularly want to. What did she care of his parents' marriage fifty years in the past? Why should that affect the way she felt toward him?

And yet she was not so simple as to misunderstand the implications of an uneven match—not the least of which was her mother's disapproval.

"How do you know all of this?" Deborah asked.

Mother rubbed her soft thumbs over Deborah's knuckles. "I am nearly seventy years old, my dear; I know a good many people and am well versed in how to ask the necessary questions to learn what I do not know. He was more forthcoming than he realized when we spoke last night, but I have known his history for years. If I'd had any idea you were giving him particular attention, I'd have suggested you not invite him to the house party at all; he is certainly not the caliber of the other guests."

"His situation does not detract me," Deborah said, wishing her voice sounded stronger. "I am established in my own place."

"Your establishment changes if he makes you his wife—I assure you he is well aware of how you shall elevate him even if you are not concerned with how he will diminish your place."

Deborah shook her head. "You do not know him, Mother; that is an unfair cast."

"I would propose that you do not know him either, or I would not need to fill in these details." She paused and took a breath. "Deborah, there is not another person in the world who loves you as much as I love you. I have given you the sound advice of a loving mother all of your life. Has it ever led you astray?"

Deborah refused to agree or deny it, but she knew the answer she'd have given before this conversation was no. Her mother had always guided her well. She'd guided every step of Deborah's life, even to knowing Nigel would be a good husband before Deborah had been able to distinguish him in a crowd. Mother had been at Deborah's side when Nigel became ill, encouraging and advising her on each step—including this holiday party as a way to help Jane become comfortable in Society. Deborah had trusted her opinion above her own many times and had never regretted that decision.

She stared at their clasped hands, without words, as feelings of foolishness and defiance warred within her. She jumped when she felt Mother's kiss upon her forehead and then felt emotion rising in her chest at what it would mean to make a decision her mother did not endorse. Less than an hour ago she'd been nearly giddy with the joy of standing beside Phillip at the sideboard. Now she felt reduced to the insecurity of a child who could not know her own mind.

Mother spoke softly. "My heart broke right along with yours when Nigel became ill, Deborah, and I understand the loneliness you have felt since that time. You have proven yourself a remarkable woman and mother through the years that have followed, and I could not be prouder." Deborah blinked back tears, her heart absorbing the words like bread and milk.

Mother continued. "There is life left for you to live—I know this is true, and I shall help you find that happiness any way I can, but Phillip is not the man who will bring you the happiness and security you crave. I know it in my bones."

CHAPTER SIX

DEBORAH KEPT TO HER ROOM as long as she could after Mother rejoined the party, mulling over her mother's words, reliving the moments with Phillip last night, and examining her own motives. Were her feelings real or an expression of loneliness? Would Phillip as her husband be a detriment to her children's social potential?

It was maddening and overwhelming, and she could not reach a conclusion. In the past, such matters of confusion could be sorted with either Nigel or her mother. This time, there was no one but herself to sort the facts. She did not know how.

Finally, she forced herself to join her guests—if she were gone much longer, people would worry.

She passed a few different groups putting the final touches on their kissing boughs and then, as an excuse to buy herself a few more minutes, explained to Noel that she needed to talk with the housekeeper. Surely her brain would cobble together a solution if she could have just a bit more time.

Time, however, was not on her side, and though she drew out the discussion with Mrs. Fisher, having taken Jane with her to stay up-to-date on the arrangements, eventually Deborah was fetched to the hall, where the completed kissing boughs were on display on a line of tables covered with bright-red tablecloths. There were eight boughs in total, each of them a wire ball wrapped with holly and ribbons. Each included additional details, such as figures depicting the nativity shaped from paper on one and golden flowers crafted from paper trimmings on another. All the guests were allowed to cast one vote and were cautioned against campaigning for their own creation.

Deborah pretended not to be mindful of Phillip speaking with Mr. Carrington on the far side of the room as she moved past the table amid the other guests, who were all oohing and aahing over the display. She took extra time to inspect the last bough in the line.

Where the other creations were the size of small melons, this one was huge—easily double the size of the others—and not precisely round. The wires made to form the spherical shape were bent in places, and the paper decorations were not limited to the traditional gold, white, and red but included pink and purple, even orange for good measure. While small apples were an expected adornment, there were six large, slightly wrinkled, apples fastened to this globe and a huge blue bow that looked as though it were from a child's dress. Deborah thought it must be the men's creation but then looked to the side, where a group of five children stood deceptively still, bouncing on their toes and unable to hide the attention they were paying her inspection.

Deborah smiled to herself and wrote in her vote without much hesitation. How could she not vote for the children's offering? Especially when her own Ashley was one of the assembly? Nicholas was nowhere to be seen, but she would not have expected him to catch the spirit of the contest.

She talked with the children as the rest of the votes were tallied and then cheered when their kissing bough was announced the winner. The children exploded like popcorn, unable to contain their excitement of having beaten all the adults. Two footmen worked to secure the monstrous creation to the hook in the ceiling above the music area of the parlor. The other boughs would be added to the other decorations about the house.

"The official kissing bough is the only one to sport the mistletoe, however," Noel announced, stepping forward to hand over a sprig of mistletoe tied with a thin red ribbon. The footman standing on the stool took the mistletoe and used a bit of wire to attach it to the base of the bough.

"Now, there are several berries upon this mistletoe," Noel further explained to the group, directing her comments primarily to the children for whom this activity was entirely new. "Each time a kiss is shared beneath the bough, the couple may remove a berry and toss it into the fire. When the berries are gone, the game is finished."

The boys made gagging sounds until their mothers sufficiently shushed them; then Mr. Lund pulled Mrs. Lund forward and kissed her soundly beneath the bough. Deborah laughed to cover her sharp feeling of jealousy and dared not look in Phillip's direction. A grinning Mr. Lund plucked off one of the berries and tossed it into the hearth. It was so easy for the Lunds, and she admired that they were so equally yoked within their marriage— but were they always thus? Hadn't one of them been above and one of them below station when they married? Yet they'd found happiness in their lives together. Why could Mother not see that possibility for Deborah and Phillip?

Betraying her resolve not to look at him, Deborah glanced up and met Phillip's eye for just a moment before turning away and joining others in urging the Carringtons not to let the Lunds be the only ones to take advantage of the game. Did she dare discuss her mother's concern with Phillip? Doing so would hurt Phillip and create tension between him and her mother. But to not talk to him felt wrong. If they were going to build a life together, they had to be able to talk about hard things . . . but things were just getting started between them.

"Unlike Mr. Lund," Mr. Carrington said, lifting his chin and straightening his cravat, "I do not need to remove a berry to confirm that my wife welcomes my affections."

"Are you so certain?" Mrs. Carrington said, raising her eyebrows and folding her arms across her chest to the roar of laughter from the other guests. Deborah did all she could to keep a distant proximity from Phillip and busy herself with her duties, which did not prove too hard. What was more difficult was ignoring the pit in her stomach.

Dinner was of Noel's choosing—she always chose lamb—and complete with her favorite rum custard followed by a pantomime performance she had worked out ahead of time with a few of the other guests. After the performance, numerous conversations sprang up and made a comfortable end to the day that, for everyone except Deborah, had been very nice. She considered leaving before the last of the guests so that she could hide in her bedchamber but knew that would do nothing to resolve the turmoil she was feeling.

She managed to keep a smile on her face and interact as a good hostess should through the remaining evening, then found herself alone in the parlor after Albert Sharps finally ran out of jokes to tell about the Royal Navy. She had not noticed Phillip leave, but then, she had avoided him all day. Had he noticed? How should she act tomorrow?

She straightened a pillow on the settee and then picked up a book from where it had been set upon an end table, admitting that even amid the discomfort, she was disappointed he had not waited for her as he had two nights ago. She did not know what to say to him, but she wanted to be with him.

Phillip was standing in the doorway when she turned, startling her and causing her to press the book to her chest as she let out a squeak of alarm. He smiled as he stepped into the room, closing the door behind him and ensuring they were quite alone together. The blood in her veins began to warm, and the heaviness seemed to melt away, allowing her to relax for the first time since her conversation with Mother.

Did the physical reaction mean that being with him was right?

Or did it mean she was letting her loneliness overtake her good sense?

"Are you all right, Deborah?" he asked as his smiled changed into a look of concern, a line appearing between his furrowed brows. "You seem troubled. Not yourself."

Not yourself, she repeated in her mind as she turned and walked to the bookshelf, where she replaced the book.

Who had she been instead?

A hostess?

A daughter?

A frightened woman?

A former wife?

"I think it is only the duties of hostess taking their toll," she dodged, taking a moment to straighten the other books as her body attuned itself to being alone with him. *Confront this,* the grown woman part of her personality demanded. The rest of her, however, did not trust that was appropriate. "It has been some time since I have borne such responsibility, and I am so afraid of not fulfilling my part as well as I should." As she said the words, she noticed that they did not apply only to her role as hostess. There were decisions to be made and paths in need of choosing. Could she trust herself? Or should she rely on Mother's confidence instead of her own?

Mother seemed to think she should.

That thought frustrated her—why wouldn't Mother trust Deborah to trust herself?

Why would Deborah not trust herself more easily than this?

"Is there anything I can do to help?" Phillip asked.

She turned and smiled at him for having made a sincere offer. "You are always looking for a way to help, aren't you, Phillip?"

"I do try to find ways to help, but you never ask."

"Because I do not need to; you lend a hand before I even realize I need one."

He was watching her closely, his eyes upon her face like the caress she longed for. "I want to make things easy for you, Deborah. I hope you know that is my intention."

She looked at him on the other side of the room and forced herself to see what Mother saw. Phillip did not adhere to fashion and wore the same evening clothes tonight that he'd likely owned for twenty years or more. His cravat was tied in a simple knot and had no gemstone pin as many of the other men sported. His shoes were plain, though well kept, and his waistcoat was unadorned black satin somewhat lacking in sheen. None of this had bothered her before—but should it have? Mother was right that his place in Society was determined by his friends and family connections . . . but then, wasn't hers as well? Had she not been born into the family she'd been born into, married into the family she'd married into, she would not have the place she took for granted in social circles. But would she not still be herself?

Deborah thought of how Phillip had naturally led the children to collect greenery and how he had been the first to throw off his coat when the men had cut through the Yule log. She'd admired the initiative both actions displayed, but they did reflect what he lacked in both mannerisms and elegance when compared to the other men of the party—all of them wealthy and established in the upper circles of the noble class and never eager to do something out of place. *Did* Phillip do the work of a steward? Certainly, his shoulders attested to more physical labor than Nigel had ever endured. Would that bother Deborah in time?

"Phillip," she said, even though she already had his full attention. She walked forward and placed her hands on the back of a chair now set between them.

"Yes?" he replied when she did not continue. He quirked a smile.

She lowered her voice. "What are we doing?"

He leaned in slightly and glanced first to one side and then to the other in an exaggerated attempt to ensure they were alone. He met her eyes again and spoke in a conspiratorial whisper. "Standing apart in your parlor and avoiding telling one another good night."

She smiled but could not allow the jest to distract her entirely. "I believe you know what I mean, and if I might be so bold, we are in no position to be coy with one another. What are *we* doing? What are our expectations? What do we want to have come of this?"

He held her gaze for a few seconds as his expression changed from playful to serious. He walked forward until he stood on the opposite side of the chair, then clasped his hands behind his back. "I have no desire to be coy with you, Deborah, and I pray your forgiveness if I have not been clear in my intentions. I have long admired the woman you are, but in the course of the last year I have felt such things as I never expected to feel again. Upon my last visit to Winfrey House, I felt confident I was not alone. Was I wrong?"

Deborah took a breath and then shook her head slowly. "You are not wrong, Phillip."

He relaxed somewhat, betraying the tension she had not noticed. What a difficult conversation this must be for him. In her fine house that she'd lived in with Nigel, surrounded by her fine friends and family. As much as she wanted to bask in the confessions they had both just made, she could not afford to be derailed from this subject. "But I am not a debutante with a wide-open future and only my own interests to consider."

His face fell slightly, and she bit her tongue to keep from retracting her words. If they were to make something of the attraction they felt, they would have to have uncomfortable conversations. They would be blending two families, merging two cultures and lifestyles into one. Thinking of that made her tired and made Mother's warning louder in her ears: *Phillip is not that man. I feel it in my bones.*

"As you were with Nigel," he said.

Her husband's name moved through her, as did her mother's concerns that her interest in Phillip was due to his connection to Nigel. Oh, there was so much to consider! How was she to make sense of it all?

"Yes, as I was with Nigel," she said, nodding.

"And as I was with Lois," Phillip added with a nod of his own. "Our situations were markedly different the last time we had this sort of choice before us, but I do not think that means we cannot make a new decision based on how life has brought us together."

Was that what had happened? Had life brought them together? She liked the sound of that, the feel of it upon her weary shoulders. But still the conversation was not finished.

"Should you and I . . . continue," she said, "what would that look like?"

He took a breath, and she was relieved that while she could see he was taking this seriously, he wasn't angry. "There is a great deal for us to discuss," he said. "Neither of us is without considerations of the logistics of a relationship between us—am I taking liberty in using that direct a term?"

"No," she said, shaking her head. "I would hope that this . . ." She paused as she looked for the right word, making a looping gesture with her hand as though that might stir the word from a metaphorical pot at her feet.

"Attraction?" he said, lifting his eyebrows and smiling slightly. "Connection? Regard? Dalliance?"

"Not dalliance," she said with another shake of her head and an answering smile at this exchange that was as silly as it was important. "This is not a dalliance. Let us settle on connection."

"All right, so you hope this *connection* between us is intended for marriage."

Her cheeks went hot, but she nodded and ran her fingers along the back of the chair. Marriage. To Phillip. It did not frighten her to have it said out loud. Rather, it encouraged her to be able to admit it, consider it, discuss the particulars.

"I am glad to hear it," he said. "As that is my intention."

She looked up at him. "It is?" Her voice was light and hopeful.

He cocked his head to the side. "Did you think otherwise?" He took a step to the side as though to come around the chair that separated them.

"Stay where you are," she said, putting up a hand in a way that was not quite teasing. "I must be able to think clearly as we discuss the particulars."

He stopped and ran a hand through his hair, casting a look to the side as he chuckled. "Very well. Particulars." He cleared his throat and loosened his shoulders as though he were about to start chopping more wood. "Where would we live?"

"We would have to live here in Winfrey House," Deborah said, her mood settling a bit now that they were back to rational discussion. "Nicholas is to inherit, and I am essentially his regent until he is of age." She realized as she said it that it could be very much to her benefit to have Phillip's help with that responsibility. She was doing a fair job of the work but often felt overwhelmed by the responsibility and worried constantly that she might make a mistake that Nicholas would one day pay for. Phillip had been managing his uncle's lands for nearly twenty years.

"I have no complaint against living in Winfrey House until Nicholas is of age, at which point we could return to Derby, if you were of a mind, or find something nearer to here, if you would rather. I am not particularly determined on where we live and understand your responsibilities."

We.

She crafted her next question carefully, not wanting to offend him. "And what is in Derby for us to return to?"

"My house." He paused. "You have never been to my house, have you? Well, it is nothing as fine as this, but my uncle has separated it out with a few dozen acres so that it might sustain itself. I manage it myself, though it is not much of a thing, and I would rent it out in the meantime."

"You own the land?"

Phillip nodded. "I will. When I agreed to help with the management of my uncle's estate, I wanted security past the time when my cousin will inherit—he is . . . limited in his abilities, and my uncle and I both fear what will come of the estate once he is at the head. Not all the land was entailed, which was why my uncle was able to bequeath me a portion. Again, it is not Winfrey House, but it is not so poor as to cause me any embarrassment."

"You will be a landowner. It is a legally bound inheritance?"

"That is what I just said," he said with a smile.

"Yet you manage your uncle's land as well."

"He prefers to live in London. I am quite comfortable in the country, so I oversee the estate much as he would if he were here: coordinate with the steward and other managers, assist the tenants, and settle squabbles. I could continue in that capacity if the boys and I lived here, though I may need to turn some of my duties over to the steward." He hesitated. "I hope it does not frighten you to know I have given this a great deal of thought. It is not so much being presumptuous on my part as it is my own attempt to resolve the complexities of blending two households into one. And I am in no hurry, so please do not misunderstand my direct delivery of my thoughts. You just seem . . . concerned, and I am trying to be open about how I have mitigated the anxiety for myself."

She wanted to ask why he hadn't told Mother these details but did not want to divulge her mother's disapproval. "I am glad to know you have given this such consideration." She looked down again. "A-And how is your position in the society in Derby?"

Phillip pulled his eyebrows together for a moment, confused at the question.

"I only mean," she clarified, "would you be comfortable in the society here?"

"Do I seem uncomfortable amid your friends and family here at the party?"

She thought on that for a moment without feeling the need to see things Mother's way. Right now, Mother felt very far away. "No," she finally said as she considered that he'd been particularly comfortable when they'd visited the vicarage on Christmas Day and on the evening that the local gentry had joined them—he'd grown up here in Bingham, after all. "You seem quite comfortable."

"Even though my station is lower."

She had to look away again and prayed he could not see the color in her cheeks at his objective observation that was the root of Mother's concerns.

"If my situation is unacceptable for you, Deborah, I would appreciate being told now, before I make a fool of myself."

"It is not," she said quickly, meeting his eyes. "And I do not feel you are below myself or the society here; forgive me for implying as much. I ask because, again, there are many people affected by the choice you and I make, and we have to be able ask these sorts of questions."

"Understood," he said with a nod. "So let me ask you a few questions, Deborah." He crossed his arms over his chest, which rather set them off to a distracting advantage. "How shall you like having the last name Dempsey?"

What an odd question. "I have no objection."

"Good," he said with a nod. "And what about blending our families—how do you foresee that coming about?"

"Our families have got on well for years, though we may need to hide the more expensive ceramics if all four boys are going to live together year-round."

"Do you foresee that any of our children will be negatively affected by a marriage between us?"

"I do not."

Mother did. She felt Phillip would lower the children's prospects in marrying persons of higher rank, but that felt insignificant to Deborah. Deborah's family was well connected even if Phillip's was not, and there was no question as to whether Jane would have a Season or that the boys would go on to school regardless of who Deborah's husband was. What felt far more significant for her children's future was seeing a good marriage, like the one Deborah had seen between her parents growing up, and having a stepfather they knew, loved, and trusted.

Phillip nodded and took the step she'd prevented before. She caught her breath as he placed his hand over hers still on the chair back. A shiver of energy traveled through her at his touch. "I shall build a shed specifically for things we do not want broken and do all I can to ensure happy and successful futures for our children. But perhaps I should ask how you shall feel about an extra man at your dinner table every night."

"Phillip," she said, shaking her head as the air began to crackle between them. It was truly remarkable how that happened. "Do not make this into a game."

He was beside her now and lifted a hand to cup her chin as he leaned in for a soft kiss that felt like fire on her lips. "I understand the concerns, Deborah," he said when he pulled back. "And I know that there will be complexities, but I also believe that the most important element of a good match is accord. Do you agree?" He leaned in again and this time planted a kiss just below her ear.

"Y-yes," she said, fighting to keep her wits about her.

As though he could tell what his attention did to muddle her thoughts, he turned suddenly and walked several feet away before coming to a stop and turning to face her. "I think you are right. We need distance when we are having serious conversations." He folded his arms again, glanced at the floor, and then looked at her once more, one eyebrow cocked. "What are your other concerns?"

She thought about that.

And thought.

And thought.

She had no other concerns; in fact, the concerns she had already brought up were not her concerns at all—they were Mother's. Except perhaps one detail she had not mentioned yet.

"I am uncomfortable making our . . . connection a public one just yet." She hurried to clarify. "I am hostess to this party, which is made up of many people particularly connected to Nigel, and the culmination of our feelings is a very new thing. I want time to find my own way to talk about this, and I need you to respect that, even if you do not feel the same way."

He was silent a few moments, then nodded. "Of course I respect that, Deborah."

"But you are disappointed."

"I am not disappointed," he said, shaking his head, glancing at the floor and then looking at her so directly she could feel it on her skin. "I am eager." He pointed above his head, and she looked to see that when he'd moved away from her, he'd placed himself beneath the kissing bough. When she looked back at his face, he was grinning.

Had she ever been as warm in the dead of winter as she'd been these last few days? She considered for a moment what was proper and right in this situation, but she had expressed her concerns, and he had resolved every one of them. Yes, she would need to find a way to help Mother understand her position and determination, but she *was* a grown woman. She *did* know her own mind, and she wanted this. She wanted Phillip. She wanted to be loved again.

With nothing left to hold her back, she crossed the room, went up on her toes, and let herself become completely lost in his kiss. Again.

CHAPTER SEVEN

"One of the berries is missing since last night," Lady Constance announced the next afternoon when the party had finished taking the food boxes to the parish poor around the village and returned to the parlor, where a high tea had been set for them to enjoy.

"Goodness," Mrs. Carrington said as she pulled off her gloves. "I can assure you Mr. Carrington is not the man who earned it."

"Hey, now," Mr. Carrington sputtered as the other guests laughed.

Deborah risked a glance in Phillip's direction, and he winked in response. She hid her smile and quickly returned her attention to the speculation of who had earned the right to remove a berry, glad that Mother was not in the room.

Gentlemen did not wink.

Gentlemen did not kiss a woman breathless in her parlor in the late hours of the night and then triumphantly pluck a berry from the mistletoe that would surely be counted the next day.

Perhaps being a gentleman at all times was not such an essential feature.

Mother came into the room then, bringing up the tail end of the return party. "Now, what is this?" She surveyed the group still taunting Mr. Carrington. "What have I missed?"

While another guest filled Mother in on the joke, Deborah felt her mood shift; though she felt confident of having sorted her feelings for Phillip last night, she did not know how to handle Mother. To tell her would cause increased conflict that would interfere with the remaining nine days of the house party. To not tell her . . . well, Deborah had never withheld something important from Mother.

The reason Mother was determined against him was because she did not know the truth of Phillip's situation. Perhaps simply sharing what Deborah now knew would resolve her concerns.

Mrs. Greyfield pulled Deborah from her thoughts as she talked of her Christmas traditions growing up in Scotland. Deborah was a solid twenty minutes into learning about Hogmanay when a footman appeared in the doorway, cleared his throat, and announced, "Lord Anthony Clampton, Earl of Minset."

The entire room turned to the doorway at the announcement, fell silent, and then rose to their feet as Lord Clampton stepped into the room. Deborah blinked in surprise, then realized she was waiting for someone else to welcome him when that was her responsibility.

"Lord Clampton," she said as she hurried to cover the awkward pause that had infected the room. She crossed the floor and stopped a few feet in front of him, dropping into the curtsy that was expected in such company—no one could accuse her of poor manners. Once she returned to standing, however, she narrowed her eyes playfully and put her hands on her hips. "I do believe you have come to my party without an invitation, Anthony. I would expect better from one such as you."

Anthony smiled widely before giving an elaborate bow, one highly polished boot pushed forward in order to make the most of his display. When he rose, he put a hand to his chest in mock surprise. "Arriving uninvited is beneath me, Mrs. Winfrey. We have your very own mother to blame for your misunderstanding. Where is that little minx?"

A trickling laugh paved the way for Mother to join them near the doorway. Anthony bowed over her hand and then kissed it with flourish. When he had finished, Mother turned to Deborah, though she waved to include the rest of the group situated around the room. "This is my surprise guest, a day late but very much invited, I assure you. I think some of you already know him. For those who do not, please let me introduce you. Lord Anthony Clampton is an old family friend, and it is an honor to have his attendance."

Deborah smiled, happy to see her old friend—then stood back while her mother made the introductions to the man who now outranked every other person in the room. Deborah had agreed to the unnamed guest weeks ago, even if she had forgotten these last few days, and was not annoyed by the addition—it was Anthony, after all, and he was always welcome and enjoyed. Having a midparty guest of rank join the party was a rather big complication, however, and the hostess within her was feeling a bit panicked. Until now, her brother, Charles—the current Lord Affington, Baron of Hollbridge—was of the highest rank, which meant he had led into dinner each night and sat at the head of the table. Anthony would now take that place. Charles would understand, but would he still not be a bit put out? The group would naturally defer to Anthony. He would be the lead in any conversation, and yet, as a single man, he would need female accompaniment more or less assigned to him.

Wait. Did that mean . . . ?

Deborah looked at her mother, laughing with Anthony and the other guests who had moved toward him. Mother had not invited Anthony as a prospect for Deborah, had she?

Deborah had only to remember their conversation yesterday to feel even more unsure. Anthony was younger than she and lived an entire county away. But he had an excellent reputation and . . . no wife. Deborah looked away from her mother to Phillip, who was in conversation with Mr. Lund and seemed unaware of the shift that had occurred in the room.

"Well, then," Anthony said, suddenly standing before her and therefore drawing her attention back to him and only him. She shifted but then raised her chin as she accepted that she was now the center of his focus. "Am I to have a tour of Morning Glory's fine house," he said, "or will I be left to my own devices as I try to find my way about?"

Morning Glory had been Deborah's nickname when they were young, due to her continual flower picking, but the endearment felt out of place in this company—an intimacy she did not want shared. Of course, she couldn't show her discomfort; the worst thing Deborah could do was spread unease to the other guests.

"I would be honored to give you a tour of my house, King Anthony the Great," she said, using the nickname he had insisted upon during the time in their lives when they had been as close as cousins. She hoped that remaining playful with him would allow her other guests to relax in his company. She turned to the doorway of the parlor amid the chuckles of the guests not used to seeing such banter with someone of his level. "I only hope your head will fit through some of the more narrow doorways," she said with a smile over her shoulder as she led the way out of the room. "Portions of this home date back to the twelfth century, which means some of the passages are rather small. Mr. Carrington only just made it through."

After the tour of the house, which several of the other guests joined them for—though, not Phillip—Deborah fetched Jane from the upstairs parlor and scrambled to the kitchen. Despite feeling out of sorts with her mother right now, she was relieved Mother followed her to the housekeeper's office, where the four women revised every seating chart and reassigned bedchambers since the one previously set aside for Mother's mystery guest was unacceptable. Deciding which of her guests—who had been here for four days already—would be displaced made Deborah feel terrible. They settled upon Albert Sharps, who was currently assigned the Brighton room, done in shades of purple and gold, with its own sitting room, two fireplaces, and grand views over the west gardens. Poor Mr. Sharps was being moved to the third level, where he would have a single room with a stove and a view of the barn. Phillip had already been placed in one of the smaller rooms when he'd first arrived, which at least meant she did not have to consider putting him at a disadvantage.

The cook fetched Mrs. Fisher to help resolve a problem with the butcher, who was demanding payment ahead of terms, and Jane asked to be excused back to the company of the other young ladies. Mother and Deborah were left alone with the charts and diagrams and notes spread upon Mrs. Fisher's desk.

"Why did you not prepare me for this, Mother?" Deborah said quietly, a slight hiss to her words that she didn't intend but did not necessarily regret. "If I had known it was an *earl* joining the party, I would have reserved the Brighton room from the start and arranged the seating charts in a manner that would be easier to resolve."

"I did not want to give away my surprise," Mother said rather easily. "Besides, I was not entirely sure he would come."

Deborah looked at her with narrowed eyes. "You asked me weeks ago if you could invite a mystery guest. I thought you meant to spring Cousin Beth on me or Mrs. Thurston and her dogs."

"I did ask Cousin Beth first, but she was otherwise engaged, which is when I thought of Lord Clampton. Of course, I knew that a man in his position very likely made his Christmastide arrangements last July, as the Season was coming to an end, but I thought to try all the same, knowing it would be such a grand distraction. When I sent my request, he found the idea of surprising you delightful, but he warned me his arrangements may not come together in time. As of last week, he said he thought he might be able to arrive by Fifth Night but was still unable to confirm." She looked up at Deborah and smiled as though this was the only hard thing between them. Deborah wished it were but had no room to return to the topic of Phillip even in her own thoughts right now. "Do you know, I think he did that on purpose so he could play as good a joke on me as I was playing on you." She laughed and shook her head. "What a clever man."

"Mother, I hope that—"

Mrs. Fisher returned, preventing further conversation on the topic, and they spent another forty-five minutes making the necessary changes—companies assigned to each carriage were rearranged, evening entertainments were improved and expanded, and Mother suggested a day trip to Mattersey Priory since Lord Clampton enjoyed medieval architecture. Never mind that it would be mostly covered in snow.

When they finally finished, it was past time to get ready for dinner, and all three women hurried to make up the lost time. Deborah was still feeling flustered when she came down the steps half an hour later and just in time for the party to go in to dinner. Anthony approached her and put out his arm—it was appropriate that he would lead her in, as hostess, and yet she was well aware of Phillip watching as she crossed the hall at Anthony's side. She had been taken into dinner by a different man of the party every night, but it had not yet been Phillip's turn, and if Lord Clampton chose to, he could appropriately lead Deborah to the table each evening.

Once the first course was served, Deborah felt herself relax, at least in part, because she had a clear view of Phillip and he seemed nonplussed as he conversed with Mr. Lund, who seemed equally engaged with him. The men had been friendly at past parties, which was the only time their paths had crossed, but they seemed particularly well matched this year. It was a relief to further acknowledge how well Phillip got on with the other guests, despite his lowered circumstances. Then again, Mr. Lund, though the son of a viscount, ran a fleet of merchant ships out of Liverpool, which essentially put him in trade. Mrs. Lund had been good friends with Noel since their Season together some twenty years ago but did not have a great deal of family connection herself—Deborah thought her father had been a vicar. It was increasingly irritating that Deborah, who did not put stock in rank and position equating the measure of a person, was being put in the position of adjusting her entire party to support the heraldry. Anthony, for his part, was oblivious to the scurrying taking place on his behalf because such things had always been his right.

Oh dear, Anthony, she thought, hating that his appearance was anything less than a welcome addition. The Clampton family had been close to her own for generations, as they had estates in the same county. Deborah and Anthony had grown up much like cousins due to their parents' close association, even though Anthony was some four years younger than Deborah, which had felt like an unnavigable gap back then. He'd gone to Eton and then Cambridge, while she'd married Nigel and set up house here in Nottinghamshire. She had not seen him for years, though she could tell easily enough that he had not changed much. Affable, handsome in that tall, slightly gangly way, and secure in himself. The age difference did not matter so much now that they were both in their thirties. The lack of attraction to him on Deborah's part, however, and her very strong attraction to Phillip, made the balance in age with Anthony unimportant. He was her friend, and she was glad to see him, but she did not imagine that their connection could ever be different than friendship born of youth.

"You were surprised by my arrival, I think," Anthony said once they had completed their updates of life and situation through the first two courses.

Deborah cut a bite of her fish. "Of course I was surprised," she said with a laugh. "I have not seen you since Charles's wedding— what?—eleven years ago or more." She'd been pregnant with Nicholas when she and Anthony had laughed over their childhood memories and made empty promises to stay better connected.

"It is a good surprise, I hope," Anthony said.

She smiled. "Of course it is a good surprise."

"I am relieved to hear it," he said with a sharp nod as he, too, speared a bite with his fork. "I worried you would be cross."

"With you?" Deborah said, shaking her head. "I could never be cross with you." Her feelings toward her mother, however, were not so easily remedied.

With a sinking stomach she accepted that she and Mother would have to have the conversation about her feelings for Phillip before the end of the party. To put it off now that she suspected Mother had an agenda would only complicate the situation. Fortunately, Anthony had behaved as the old friend he had always been, leaving Deborah to conclude that the agenda was only on Mother's part.

The evening entertainment was supposed to be another musical revue, but Mother suggested charades, as it had been a favorite of Anthony's family years ago. It turned into a contest of performance that, when combined with brandy and sherry and even some scotch, became a raucous party. It was well after midnight before Deborah called an end to the game, certain the noise was keeping the children and the staff awake at this point. Additionally, though it was always lovely to laugh and be extreme, she had only so much fortitude for the intensity. There were a few other guests she could see who were uncomfortable.

"And that is the end of the night," she said as she clapped her hands and walked onto the area that had played as the stage. "We are all in danger of forgetting our manners entirely if this goes on much longer, so off to bed with all of you."

A handful of guests whined like children, which allowed Deborah to behave even more like a taciturn nanny. "The next person to complain will get no sweets tomorrow, mark my word!"

"Well done," Mother said as she gave Deborah a good night kiss on the cheek on her way out. "The tides would have turned inappropriate at any minute, I fear."

The compliment helped ease Deborah's fears of upsetting her guests as they continued to file out of the room, and she smiled her thanks to her mother while deciding that the necessary conversation they needed to have would best be taken on tomorrow when they'd all had rest and Deborah had planned what to say and how to say it.

Phillip left with some of the other men, sharing the same sort of good night the others shared with her—he and Deborah had enjoyed very little interaction today. She longed to call him back, enjoy a few minutes of his company, and talk to him about the chaos of her mother's unexpected guest. She could not ask him to stay behind after telling everyone to go on up to bed, and she did not want him to share the anxiety she was feeling. If she were to admit to him her suspicions of Mother's motives, would he guess that Mother disapproved of his attention? Would it further complicate this party?

Lady Constance had had far more to drink than she usually did, and helping her to her room was the final reason for Deborah not to linger about in the parlor in hopes Phillip would return. Lady Constance's ward supported her on one side, while Deborah supported the other—they practically carried her the final length of the corridor. By the time Lady Constance's maid had taken over for Deborah's side, the candles were being doused in the main-level foyer, and Deborah decided against going down to the parlor to see if Phillip was waiting. He'd given no indication that he expected them to meet . . . but then, he'd given no indication on their prior meetings either.

It is just as well, she told herself as fatigue drained into her shoes, making her feet incredibly heavy.

She slept soundly and was up before dawn finalizing the arrangement for today's sleighride. Originally, they were going to take a quick turn around the northern meadows, but the priory was not so much farther, so at noon they headed out, piled into the three sleighs she'd borrowed from neighboring estates, complete with heavy blankets and heated bricks at their feet. The snow was deep, keeping most of the guests in their sleds once they arrived at the ruins, but most of the children and a few of the men—including Phillip and Anthony—gamely jumped out and spent a solid quarter of an hour throwing snowballs and making snow angels. Then it began to snow again, and the party shivered all the way home. When it was Deborah's turn to descend from the sleigh, Phillip was waiting, and she smiled as he put his hands at her waist and lifted her to the ground. Most of the group had already gone into the house, where a large pot of wassail awaited them, but a handful remained, preventing more privacy.

"Thank you, Phillip," Deborah said.

He reached out and pulled her fur collar tighter around her neck, letting his gloved thumb rub against her cheek. "My pleasure, I assure you."

They held one another's eyes another moment before Phillip turned and hurried forward in order to make a snowball he then lobbed at a group of children hiding behind the sleigh. Mrs. Lund took Deborah's arm and thanked her for the wonderful party so far.

Fourth Night was when the house party celebrated the children, so the evening was full of games and merriment in keeping with the youngest members of the party, who, thankfully, were worn out come eight o'clock. Ashley was not feeling well—likely due to too much wassail and mincemeat pies. Deborah kept to the nursery until past ten, when he finally fell asleep. She did not mind being isolated from the party as she rubbed his back and enjoyed the solitude. Another day had passed without her having talked with Mother about her feelings for Phillip. Another day of only group interactions with Phillip. Would he be waiting for her tonight?

When she returned to the parlor, the footman was dousing the candles. She wished him good night and headed to her room, removing the pins from her hair as she made her way up the stairs to her room—the pins had been wearing heavy for well over an hour now. Rumpled locks of her chestnut hair draped her shoulders, and she had a handful of pins by the time she entered her bedchamber.

"Good evening, ma'am," her lady's maid said as she turned from where she'd laid out Deborah's nightdress. "Sounds that everyone had a fine day today."

"Indeed, they did," Deborah said as she handed over the pins. Lucy put them in the tin on the vanity, and Deborah raised a hand to her head, closed her eyes, and massaged her aching scalp.

"A note came for you a bit ago."

Deborah paused in her ministrations and looked up to see Lucy holding out a folded piece of paper. "When?"

"I cannae be sure, ma'am; it was under the door when I came in a few minutes ago."

Deborah took the note and unfolded it.

Meet me under the kissing bough.

Despite feeling dead on her feet, a fresh wave of energy washed through Deborah. She refolded the note and closed her hand around it as though it were a piece of jewelry. "I shall be back shortly," she said. "I, ah, need to confer with one of the guests for a few moments."

It was an imperfect lie—Lucy would go belowstairs and gossip of it in hopes of determining which guest Deborah was conferring with, and she'd likely solve the mystery. Ignoring the note was not something Deborah had the restraint to do, however. She missed time with Phillip.

As she hurried down the stairs, she relived the sensation of his hands at her waist as he'd helped her out of the sleigh upon their return this afternoon, and combed her fingers through her hair in hopes of relieving some of the tangles. What would Phillip make of her state of not-quite-done? There was something intimate about it, the sharing of something that was usually kept behind closed doors.

She'd forgotten a candle in her haste and had to slow her steps as she reached the darkened main level so as to see her way. It would not do to take a tumble right now.

She could see a glow coming from the parlor, reassuring her that Phillip had thought ahead and provided light.

Even though the house was dark and still, she looked about her as she crossed the hall and slipped inside the parlor, turning immediately to close the door behind her just in case some servant had seen her. Better to leave them suspecting her motives then seeing her and Mr. Dempsey end the evening with a good night kiss . . . or two.

"I had nearly given up on you."

Deborah froze, still facing the door, as she realized two things in a single moment:

One, in her anticipation, she had not thought to consider whether or not the note was written in Phillip's hand.

Two, she had completely misinterpreted Anthony's attention after all.

CHAPTER EIGHT

"ANTHONY!" SHE SAID AS SHE spun to face him, pressing her back to the door.

"Deborah!" he said back in the same energy, then laughed as though her exclamation had been a joke.

He was standing, just as the note had indicated, directly under the kissing bough that looked more garish and out of place than it had before. He was in nearly the same place Phillip had been two nights earlier.

She had to think fast, despite the muddle of thoughts in her head.

"I am glad you came," he said, lowering his voice in a way that made her shudder inside.

It was not just the unwelcome advance but that the man making it was *Anthony*. Considering him as a romantic hero was like hearing a rabbit bark like a dog or seeing a Maypole on Christmas Eve.

"I had hoped that you and I—"

"Anthony," she said quickly as a way around the situation presented itself quite starkly in her mind. The coals of the fireplace still glowed, and she moved toward it, throwing the note she'd crumpled in her hand into the hearth, where it quickly burst into flame and then went out, much as she hoped Anthony's intentions would also disappear. "I must tell you straightaway that I came only to settle the misconception in your invitation."

She turned back to find him walking toward her, his expression unchanged in the way of a man used to getting his way who could not believe he would not get it now. She moved to the side so she could keep distance between them.

"You need not be coy with me, Deborah. We have known one another for too long to warrant such games."

"I am not being coy, Anthony. I am being quite forthcoming." She moved behind a chair, much as she had the night when it was she and Phillip having a conversation in this room. She'd needed the distance from Phillip to preserve her ability to think straight, however, not because she objected to his nearness the way she objected to Anthony's. "I came only so I would not leave you waiting and wondering—I wanted to be a good hostess."

"Which is why you closed the door to afford our privacy?" He finally stopped coming toward her, which allowed her to take a deeper breath than she had managed so far. He cocked his head to the side and folded his arms across his chest, looking smug. "It has been such a pleasure to become reacquainted with you these last two days, Deborah. You are as witty as ever but more beautiful than I remember. Motherhood and maturity look well on you."

"That is very kind of you to say, Anthony," she said with a demure nod. "And I enjoyed becoming reacquainted with you as well. However, when you mentioned the . . . kissing bough, I realized I may have given the wrong impression." She remembered his comment about the door and hurried to include that in her explanation. "I closed the door in order to make sure no one overheard."

He was still grinning at her in such a way that she knew he was hearing none of this. "Very well, Deborah, I shall play along. What is it a woman wants in love? To be the pursuer? To feel she is the one making the choice?"

"Neither," Deborah said, shaking her head. "I have no desire to hurt your feelings, Lord Clampton, but—"

"Then, do not dismiss my invitation," he cut in, a bit of the joviality dropping out of his tone. "It is no small thing that I am standing before you and allowing you such insight into my heart and my plans, Deborah. To not take me seriously in this moment would be a mistake. I am ready to marry, and I feel you would make an excellent countess—is that too bold for an old friend to say?"

She swallowed and prayed at the same time. "I do not mean any offense, Anthony; only I am being up front, as I believe our friendship deserves." Her brain was racing for what she could say that would not be offensive or dishonest. It was a fine point to land upon and felt decidedly unsteady. "In the area of marriage, I have more experience than you and know that, for myself, the essential ingredient for a match is accord."

His expression softened again, and he smiled, tipping Deborah off that she'd said the wrong thing. "You and I have accord, Morning Glory. Decades of it."

"A different sort of accord," she said, thinking how to explain what she felt when she was with Phillip without actually saying anything about him. "An energy, an . . . excitement that, while I value our friendship, I do not feel toward you." For an instant she imagined being the recipient of such words, and she withered inside. Perhaps if she'd had more time, she could have crafted an explanation that would not be hurtful. Being caught in a room with a kissing bough late at night, however, had created a situation in which urgency outweighed tact.

His smile fell again. "Are you telling me that you would put attraction above all other aspects of what I can offer? I can give you security, Deborah—position, rank, and title. Your children would be presented to the upper echelons of Society, and *our* children would have every advantage in the world. Surely you would not make a choice based on energy and excitement alone?"

He made a scoffing sound and shook his head. Deborah blinked, stunned by how closely his stated advantages aligned with her mother's. And also by how quickly he could ignore her feelings. She opened her mouth to counter his arguments but remembered that Anthony was a powerful man; telling him off would be foolish and unkind. She, too, had always believed affection and love followed promise—so why had she forgotten that when she was with Phillip? Why did being with Phillip feel so very right and the idea of entertaining Anthony's regard feel so decidedly wrong?

"Anthony," she said in an even and calm voice. "I am glad to have you here; however, it is not your place to tell me how I ought to evaluate a potential match between us. I am a grown woman, independent, and not one to be bullied."

He paused, and then his expression softened as he looked at the floor. "I am sorry, Deborah."

She let out a breath of relief but kept her bearing strong as he looked up at her once again, his expression neither smug nor angry.

"I had thought . . ." He looked to the side and took a breath, looking vulnerable and embarrassed enough that she felt a prick of sympathy for him. "I had thought there was more than renewed childhood friendship between us these last two days. When tonight came to an end I simply felt the overwhelming desire to step past the usual societal restrictions and protocols and go to the heart of things. I am ready to marry; I find you to be an engaging and accomplished woman who would make an excellent countess. I see now that I have not gone about things in a way that might earn your trust."

Gracious, to have him go from so arrogant to so humble in such a short period of time made her dizzy. Had he heard her after all?

"It is very late, Lord Clampton." She gave a gracious nod to show that she did not want tension between them. "I believe we are both past our best behavior and should get some sleep. Maybe tomorrow we could have a more reasonable conversation."

His expression fell even more markedly. "Lord Clampton? Have I damaged our friendship as much as that?"

She looked at the chair before her, uncomfortable meeting his eyes. "Perhaps my familiarity before is part of what put us in this awkward position with one another."

"Forgive me, Deborah. I did not mean to upset you."

"I am not upset." She lied out of a true desire not to hurt him and raised a hand to her head, only then remembering that her hair was down. What had seemed a thrilling intimacy to share with Phillip now made her feel very foolish. She massaged her temple. "But I am very tired. Let us put this to rest for the night."

"Only if you shall consent to call me Anthony again." He put a hand to his chest. "I simply could not abide the idea that I shall be Lord Clampton to you from now on." He offered a petitioning smile in the dimly lit room—a single candle did not give off much light, but the ambiance was not romantic for Deborah.

She returned an accepting smile of her own. "All right, Anthony, I shall honor our friendship in this way."

"Very good," he said, nodding and turning back for the candle he'd put on a small table near the piano. "Let me walk you to your room."

She did not know how to appropriately refuse what was a kindness after she'd already set him back. Besides, the house would be dark once she left this parlor. She nodded and took his arm as he led her up the stairs and into the wing where the family rooms were.

"I am the second door, just there," she said when they turned the corner. When they reached her door, she said, "Thank you. I shall see you tomorrow." *And hopefully have some idea of what to say by then.* "Good night."

She released his arm and turned toward the door.

"Deborah?"

She turned toward him and had no time to react before he pressed his lips against hers, held them there for a moment, and then released her. He grinned while she stood frozen in disbelief.

"I shall see you tomorrow, Morning Glory. Sleep well." He gave one of his elaborate bows, turned, and left her standing in the corridor.

CHAPTER NINE

MOTHER WAS STILL ABED WHEN Deborah let herself into the rose room, the guest bedchamber Mother always used when she came for visits and had decorated herself a few years ago. Deborah looked about for the maid but quickly determined that Mother was alone.

Good.

She closed the door behind her and turned to face her mother.

"Well, good morning, Deborah dear. Are you all right?"

"What are your intentions in bringing Anthony here?" She looked hard at her mother sitting in the bed with a mahogany tray set over her lap. Deborah had stewed half the night over Anthony's kiss and awoke in a fit of nerves and emotion.

Mother paused for a moment in her action of putting marmalade on her toast, then continued as though this were not a fraught conversation. "He is an old family friend," Mother said as her knife scraped against the toast.

"Whom I have not seen in more than a decade."

"Then, I would say it is about time. The two of you got on so well when you were young."

Deborah shook her head in frustration and paced to the window in an attempt to gain some calm. It had snowed again last night, and it made her think of standing on the terrace with Phillip's arms around her. But then Anthony's words from last night came back to her, and she turned to face her mother once more. "By young, I am sure you realize that I was twelve and he was only eight years of age the last time we spent any substantial time with one another. Did the two of you conspire together to present him as a prospect at this house party?"

Mother held Deborah's gaze and then looked back at her toast, now properly marmaladed.

"You should be flattered to have the interest of a man of such esteem," Mother said softly, setting down her toast and brushing her hands with a serviette. She met Deborah's eyes with an expression of undeterred confidence. "It is a credit to you that he came at all."

Deborah turned back to the snow-covered lawns outside the window and took a breath. "That is why you are set against Phillip. Because you want me to become Anthony's countess and have tried to set a course for that to happen without any consideration of my feelings."

"I am set against Mr. Dempsey because he is not worthy of you and can give you nothing in way of position and security. That opinion has nothing to do with Anthony."

"The devil it doesn't!" Deborah turned back sharply.

Mother's eyes went wide at Deborah's cursing, but Deborah spoke before she could be reprimanded or lost her nerve. "This is beyond the extreme, Mother. I have no feelings aside from familiar affection for Anthony, and—"

"Much as you felt for Nigel in the beginning."

Fire crested in Deborah's chest to have Nigel and Anthony put in the same place. "I have known Anthony well enough to know I do not and will not feel for him anything like what I felt for Nigel." She almost said "And Phillip" but stopped herself because . . . it was an atrocious thing to say.

"It is all about context, Deborah. The context in which you have known Anthony is not the context you can know him now. He's a fine man with a place in Parliament, and he is ready to settle down and have a family—past time, really. His mother was telling me that—"

"No," Deborah cut in, shaking her head and making a slicing motion with both hands. "No, Mother. I will not take your direction on this. I am—"

"And you have a duty to your children, if not to the rest of your family, to make a decision that benefits the whole. With Lord Clampton as her stepfather, Jane will find every door open to her. The boys can have their pick of university and marry into ranked households themselves, which further secures the Winfrey line. This preserves not only their security but that of the generations that follow. Nigel would want this for them, and he would want it for you. You are blinded with infatuation for Mr. Dempsey, Deborah, and that will steer you into a path of mediocrity and regret if you do not check yourself and use your head. Mr. Dempsey does not measure to any portion of what Anthony has in spades; surely you can see that."

Deborah's chest was heaving. "You do not know Phillip's position half as well as you think."

"If his position were worth considering, I would know everything I need to know; he is nothing. A no one. He will give you no advantage."

"I do not need advantage!" Deborah's hands balled into fists at her sides.

"That is a selfish choice for you to make," Mother shot back.

"It is not selfish for me to want to be happy, Mother." She placed a hand on her chest. "You make no place for my feelings. Anthony stirs nothing in me, whereas Phillip makes me feel . . ." She stopped herself again from saying something she ought not to say, something that would only make Phillip look worse in her mother's eyes. Phillip was good. He was kind. He was helpful and handsome and devoted, and . . . he drew her to him in every way a woman can be drawn to a man.

"You are lonely, Deborah," Mother said, lifting the tray to one side of the bed and turning to put her legs over the other side.

Deborah did not want her mother to come to her, embrace her, try to talk her out of how she felt. "You truly think I would make a decision out of loneliness, Mother? Have you no faith in me at all?"

Mother stood, and Deborah shook her head, taking a step away from her. "I have needed your counsel for many things, Mother, and I will always be grateful that you saw in Nigel what at first I did not see, but that does not mean the success of my marriage was because of only your recommendation. Nigel and I had our struggles too, but we made it work and we found happiness that I want to find again. I will make my own decision."

Mother gave her a hard look. "You will destroy your future and that of your children."

The words fell like ice between them, and Deborah felt a sudden rise of emotion at the separation taking place between them in this moment. Choosing Phillip would be choosing against Mother. Could a man—any man—be worth that kind of sacrifice? The realization seemed to leech the strength from her bones. Could she stand half so well without Mother holding her up as she had always done? Could she trust her heart over her mother's judgment?

They were not such easy questions to answer, and yet interestingly, Anthony's liberties from last night had helped firm Deborah's resolve. She did not feel anything romantic for him, which made what she felt for Phillip all the more powerful in comparison. Anthony's being here also showed Mother's willingness to manipulate, something Deborah had never considered in all the years Mother had advised and directed her in what she should and should not do.

Deborah took a breath and made her decision. "I am not planning to make any public announcements before the end of this party, Mother, but Phillip and I are going to build a future together."

"Oh, good gracious," Mother said, leaning against the bed. "Tell me that is not true."

Deborah looked at the floor, emotion rising up in her throat. *Dear Lord, give me strength to hold my ground.* "Whether you support it or not is your decision, just as who I share my life and my love with is mine."

She glanced up enough to see that tears had welled up in Mother's eyes. Deborah had to look away.

"Deborah, do not be hasty. Take time to think this through. Think of your children."

"We will talk no more of this, Mother," Deborah said, turning to the door while Mother pushed herself back to her feet. "I love you, Mother, and I want your blessing, but I am a woman of my own making, and I will take my own course."

Still in a heightened state of emotion, Deborah reached the main level and followed the voices to the breakfast room. She froze for a moment when she saw Anthony and Phillip seated at the same table but did not let it detract her from her singular focus.

"Mr. Dempsey."

Phillip looked up, realized that it was her addressing him, and stood, which caused all the other men to stand up too. That was not quite the attention she wanted, but she was too far in to back out now. She could feel Anthony's eyes on her and resisted the urge to squirm beneath his gaze.

"Yes, Mrs. Winfrey?" Phillip said, his eyebrows lifted. She had never addressed him so directly in front of the other guests.

"Forgive me for interrupting your breakfast, but there is a situation involving one of your horses; I told the groom I would fetch you to the barn as soon as possible."

Phillip quickly put his serviette on his plate and asked his tablemates to excuse him.

"I know a fair amount about horses," Anthony said, putting his serviette on his plate as well. "Let me accompany you, Mr. Dempsey."

"Do not bother yourself," Deborah said, fixing him with a hard stare for a moment before following Phillip, who was halfway across the room and looking anxious, as well a man would if one of his two horses had fallen ill. She truly hoped lightning would not strike her for the deception; then again, if it did, she would be spared from what had become a most uncomfortable party.

"What's happened?" Phillip asked when they were in the hall, Deborah walking ahead of him toward the front door of the house—certainly not the quickest or most convenient route to the barn, but it was the one that steered them clear of servants they would encounter if they went through the kitchen.

She didn't answer him, because her heart was racing and it was not safe to speak while they were still inside the house. She was acting in a fit of madness and passion and need for verification that choosing Phillip was the right decision.

"Mrs. Winfrey," he said, running two steps so that he was even with her. He took hold of her arm and stopped her. "Should we not take the route through the grounds?"

"Just come with me," she said under her breath, feeling as though there were eyes and ears everywhere. "Please."

His eyes held hers for only a moment before he nodded, taking a step back so she could lead the way once again. They reached the front door, and the footman opened it for them to pass through. Once outside she stayed near the edge of the house as she tracked in her mind the windows they were passing until they turned the eastern corner and reached a portion of wall between the parlor and the library. She then took Phillip's hand and pulled him to the wall, a bit harder than she needed to, causing him to stumble into the stone.

"My word," Phillip said as he caught himself. "Whatever is the matter? You act as though—"

She stopped his words by stepping up to him, putting her arms around his neck, and kissing him soundly, desperate to feel something other than anger and resentment and fear. And it worked. Her heart rate did not calm, but her mind cleared and the assurance she needed moved through her. What had started as fierce and passionate softened and melded them together until she finally pulled away, out of breath and feeling eased of the intensity. Though she did not feel fully calmed, she felt softer as she leaned her head upon his shoulder. His arms wrapped around her, keeping the shivering at bay. And then she began to cry.

His embrace tightened, and after a few minutes, he lifted her chin to look up at him, their breath clouding together. "What is wrong?"

"Nothing," she said, shaking her head as though that would be convincing.

"That certainly is not true, or you would not be here with tears freezing upon your cheeks."

She snuggled back into his chest, wishing she could just stay there. "I am so afraid of doing everything wrong," she said into his jacket.

"What things?"

It would be unfair to burden him. She just needed to get through this party, fulfill her responsibilities, and put it behind her. Then she could think about the big, wide future and the best way to step into it.

"Deborah, tell me what is wrong. Let me help. Trust me."

Trust him.

Trust Mother.

Trust herself?

Could she truly trust any of them?

"Just stay with me here a little longer," she said, closing her eyes and ignoring the cold that was beginning to bite and snap. "Then I will be all right."

CHAPTER TEN

WHEN SHE AND PHILLIP PARTED company, him going around to the back doors and her going in through the front, she hurried to her room to both repair and prepare herself. She splashed water on her face and freshened her hair, then paced the length of her bedchamber until she could feel her toes again and felt capable of the day ahead. Phillip was the man she wanted a life with; she knew it, he knew it. Whatever difficulties that created, she would work through them as needed. For now, she needed to care for her guests, let Anthony and Mother realize she would not change her mind, and keep her confidence.

It was Fifth Night, the night when scraps would be collected from the house and set outside as a symbol of putting away those things of the past that were of no use. The Winfrey house party had adapted the traditional observation to a day activity, in which they went through the linens of the house, collecting those in need of replacement. In the evening the vicar and his wife would join them for dinner and take the linens with them as donations for the poor. Fifth Night had always been one of her favorites, and she was determined not to let anything interfere with that enjoyment. She squared her shoulders like a brave little soldier and went back to her guests.

The women began going through the closets and cupboards with the help of Mrs. Fisher and the upstairs maids. The men set about building wooden crates to hold the donations, overseen by the groomsman since many of the men did not know how to wield a hammer.

The party filled nine crates with linens and serviceable clothing donations, and Deborah thanked each person for their help before they dispersed to ready themselves for dinner. Her maid helped her into the red gown she'd had made for tonight's dinner, then fashioned her hair into an elaborate twist into which she set tiny silver flowers. It felt rather too much once Deborah could see the full effect in her looking glass, but she hoped that perhaps the boldness of the color would add to the confidence she felt so in need of. She had not had the private conversation with Anthony that she had promised him they would have. She had not confessed to Phillip that Anthony had kissed her. She was not reconciled with her mother or with herself.

But she had made a decision and felt a great deal of peace about that.

The vicar was a rather long-winded man, and he participated in dinner conversation as though he were delivering a sermon. By the time the women left the men to their port, Deborah had noted that he was already wearing on several of the guests. She quite liked the vicar's wife, and the women enjoyed their personal visiting time until the men joined them earlier than usual. The children were brought down, and the vicar took full advantage of having a captive audience as he recounted the Christmas story. What should have taken twenty minutes stretched to forty, then an hour, until Deborah could take it no more and stood while he paused for breath just after having described the three gifts of the Wise Men.

"That was excellent, Mr. Jacobs. Thank you so much for this presentation—a perfect reminder of the reason we celebrate each year. Mrs. Lund, I wonder if you might play the Sussex Carol for us as you did a few nights ago. I, for one, would love to hear the children perform it again, and it has such poignant ties to the wonderful words the vicar has shared with us."

"I would be happy to play," Mrs. Lund said, popping out of her chair as though pinched in her hurry to keep the vicar from starting up again.

As soon as Mrs. Lund finished her performance, Deborah invited the men to load the donations into the vicar's carriage while the women endured a long good night on the front steps. The other guests drifted back to the parlor until only Deborah and Noel were left with false smiles and tapping toes beneath the long skirts of their evening gowns. Finally, the vicar and his wife stepped into their linen-laden carriage.

"We may need to rethink this particular tradition," Noel said as she and Deborah waved from the front step. "Unless you think he was trying to make up for the five years he did not get to play this part."

Deborah laughed, her first laugh of the day. "I quite agree," she said, taking Noel's arm as they turned back to the house. "Too many renditions such as these and we shall all hate the very idea of reading from the Bible."

Noel laughed as they removed their capes and handed them to the footmen. Once the servants had departed to hang the outer garments, Noel stepped forward to block Deborah's return to the parlor and took both of her hands. "I am so glad you had this house party, Deborah. I know it cannot be easy."

"I have been glad to have everyone here," Deborah said, wishing it were more a full truth than it was. "And *very* glad that you are here with me. I am sorry we have not had a chance to visit more intimately. I'm afraid my duties have kept me rather busy."

"Ah, but those duties look well on you," Noel said, giving Deborah's hands a squeeze. "You are alive and energized in ways you have not been for some time. Nigel would be glad of it, you know."

A lump rose in Deborah's throat, and she felt a sudden longing for her husband and friend. "Do you think so?"

"I *know* he would," Noel said, and then she leaned in. "And he would approve of Phillip too."

Deborah's face flushed hot, and Noel laughed. "Do not worry; I have not told anyone—well, except Mrs. Lund, but she knows to hold her tongue."

Deborah closed her eyes in embarrassment as her heart began to race. She could find no words but felt her weariness increase. More expectations to manage.

"Deborah," Noel said. "My dear sister."

Deborah opened her eyes again.

"I had left a book in the parlor the night of my birthday; I came back to retrieve it and found rather more than I expected under the kissing bough. It did not upset me to see you and Phillip together, if that is what you are afraid of."

"It . . . It did not?"

Noel shook her head. "Nigel did not want you to live your life alone, and he loved Phillip too. You do not need my blessing, but you have it all the same."

"I do not know what to say," Deborah finally admitted when no other words came to mind. Noel had seen them three days ago and had said nothing? She approved?

"Then, say nothing until you are ready." Noel turned and took Deborah's arm in her own again, moving them toward the parlor. "But keep what I said in your heart and take it out and look it over when the time is right. I know you and your mother share much of the confidence you might share with a friend in other circumstances, but know that you have my ear, too, if you should ever need it."

Deborah stopped, the door to the parlor only a short distance away. "Mother does not approve of Phillip."

Noel was silent for a moment. "I imagine that is very difficult for you."

"It is," Deborah said, barely able to whisper the words.

"Will it stop you from continuing?"

Deborah took a deep breath. She thought of how Phillip had held her this morning, even though she had not confided why she'd needed the comfort. She thought of their boys, so much like brothers already, and the way Phillip always wanted to help. And then she thought of her mother's face when she'd told her this morning that she had already made her choice. "No," Deborah said at last. "But I am not sure Mother will ever forgive me for it."

"Oh, Deborah," Noel said, turning so they faced one another once more. "She loves you, and while Phillip may not be her choice for you, she will not stop loving you for a reason such as that. I am sure of it."

"Thank you," Deborah whispered, knowing Noel was right but all the same being sad for the disappointment her mother would feel. "I cannot tell you how glad I am to have your support."

"Always." Noel leaned in and kissed Deborah on the cheek before continuing their walk into the parlor. She released Deborah's arm and joined Mrs. Lund where she sat at a table looking to start up a hand of loo.

Anthony and Mother—how appropriate—shared a settee on the other side of the room, and every chair around them was filled as Anthony entertained the guests with some story or another; he had always been an excellent storyteller. Most of the children were seated on the floor, also listening with rapt attention. Deborah stood in the doorway, catching her breath and looking about the room until she found Phillip. He met her eyes and gave a small smile and a nod as he took a sip of his wine.

Deborah did not want to base her decisions on the approval of others, but there was validation in knowing that an outside party—Nigel's sister, no less—saw Deborah's need to live a life of happiness. Suddenly, she wanted to be near Phillip, to just be beside him, where she felt more herself than she did when they were apart. She'd avoided conversation with him when they were with the group, but she decided that she no longer cared if people suspected there was more than friendship between them. Such suspicions would be correct. She smiled at Phillip when he caught her watching him, and began to walk toward him.

"Well, there she is right now."

Deborah looked toward Anthony, whose booming voice had cut through all the other softer conversations in the room. He was looking at her. The children and the handful of the adults gathered near him looked at her too, with expressions ranging from discomfort to good humor. Mr. Carrington leaned in to whisper something in his wife's ear. She shrugged, shook her head, and then looked back at Deborah for merely a glance before taking a sip of her wine and pointedly turning away.

"Mama?" Nicholas jumped to his feet, turning to look at her with shock on his face.

"She wouldn't!" Jane chimed in, also looking at Deborah, who felt like she was suddenly on stage in nothing but her shift.

What had she missed?

"I assure you she would," Anthony said. "And she did."

She met his eyes, and though he was smiling, his eyes were hard.

Deborah tried to smile, with every eye on her, hoping against hope that he was sharing some antic from their childhood.

"That is why there is one less berry on the mistletoe than there was yesterday," Anthony continued. "Your mother stole a kiss, and I was the lucky man to lose it."

The rushing that sounded in her ears drowned out every other reaction she might otherwise have heard. She stared at Anthony, disbelieving that he would do anything so awful as to call her out in front of her guests, in front of her *children*, and for something that had not been of her choosing. It was not gentlemanly in any respect; it was revenge.

Phillip!

She looked in his direction only to see him set his glass upon a side table, his expression unreadable as he avoided her eyes. The entire room was now tuned in to what Anthony had said. Deborah tried to swallow the stone in her throat as she looked back to this highly ranked guest, who was using his position like a sword to cut her down.

"I would not believe everything you hear, children," Deborah said, trying to laugh it off. Nicholas looked instantly relieved.

Jane, however, was unconvinced and, to Deborah's surprise, also looked toward Phillip to see his reaction. Deborah raised her voice, unwilling to let Anthony take any more advantage than he already had. "Lord Clampton is known for his wild stories that make him look the part of a hero even when he is the villain."

Anthony narrowed his eyes slightly. "I've no idea what stories you are talking about," he said, crossing his arms over his chest. "Pray tell us what you mean."

"I-I . . . mean . . ." Everyone was looking at her, waiting for her. She glanced at Mother, who raised her eyebrows expectantly but provided no rescue. Very well. She had been wrestling with her independence, her power as a grown woman, for several days now. What would a grown woman do in such a situation as this?

She looked away from Anthony to the children, all watching her. "There is a caution that ought to have been shared when we hung that kissing bough, children, and that is that a kiss only counts if it is agreed to by both parties. I did not steal a kiss— rather, a kiss was taken from me without my permission and without my consent. If Lord Clampton removed a berry for such a thing as that, then he has proven himself double the scoundrel and twice the cad."

The room fell completely silent, save for the Yule log crackling in the fireplace. People like Deborah did not say such things about a person of rank. Awkward glances passed between the adults. Deborah looked to Phillip, only to find the place he'd occupied a minute earlier now empty. His glass was still on the side table where he'd placed it. With a quick turn of her head, she caught sight of him slipping out the parlor door. To follow him would tell her guests more than she wanted to reveal and would be abandoning them to the discomfort she had contributed to by defending herself and turning Anthony's accusation back on him. Everyone was looking at her.

To not follow him, however . . .

Her heart thundered in her chest as she turned to look at Mrs. Lund, who was as frozen as the rest of them. "Mrs. Lund, if you would be so kind as to play something. Please excuse me."

She hurried out of the room as she heard Mrs. Lund invite everyone to gather around the piano. Someone pulled the parlor door shut behind her as Deborah hurried after Phillip. He was already halfway up the stairs.

CHAPTER ELEVEN

"PHILLIP," SHE CALLED AS SHE reached the base of the stairs and lifted the skirts of her red dress so as to follow him. "It is not as he told it."

He did not stop.

She hurried to catch up.

"Phillip, please let me explain."

He stopped without turning to look at her. She stopped a few steps below him, feeling as though it was out of place for her to get any closer without his invitation. "Last night," she said, somewhat breathless, "I had a note in my room that said, *Meet me under the kissing bough.* There was no name, and I thought it was from *you.* I hurried to the parlor and found Anthony instead. I covered my eagerness by explaining I had no interest in that sort of attention from him. He pretended he understood and then offered to escort me to my room. I did not see how I could refuse him." She paused and took a deep breath. "At my door he kissed me, likely for the exact purpose of taking his revenge with that little display tonight." She pointed back toward the parlor. "I did not welcome it."

Phillip had let her say all of this to the back of his coat. Once the silence had stretched to brittle, he turned to face her, looking tired and sad but troubled too. She could not fault him any of those things. "He is an infinitely better prospect for you, Deborah. I see now where your concerns about my situation came from. I shall politely remove myself from the contest."

"That is unfair," she said. "You cannot mistake my preference, Phillip. I have not been guarded in the least about my feelings for you."

"Not when we are alone," he said. "But in company, you treat me with the same polite kindness you extend to everyone else. And you have not been honest with me about Lord Clampton even though you had every opportunity to do so. Why did you not tell me he kissed you?"

"I did not want to burden you."

"You do not trust me?"

She hesitated, then shook her head. "It is not about trust."

"Isn't it?"

Was it? Her face flushed.

Phillip continued. "You drew me from the house this morning, cried upon my shoulder, and still did not tell me what troubled you. Perhaps I am a widow's dalliance after all. A Christmastide flirtation to push out the door along with the scraps and regrets of Fifth Night." He shook his head and turned toward the stairs again. He would leave—could she blame him? If he left, would he ever come back?

Deborah realized in that moment more fully what she had done, inviting him in but then pushing him away. Knowing he would not press her in company but fully enjoying the stolen moments he allowed her to take one at a time like candy from a jar. It was unfair to him. It was not right.

"Phillip," she said as he took another step. He stopped but did not turn back to her. She took hold of his hand hanging at his side as Mrs. Lund began playing a jig for those guests who wanted to dance.

He allowed her to take his hand, looking at their fingers as they intertwined with one another. Then he looked over his shoulder and met her eye. "What do you want, Deborah? Do you even know?"

Deborah had been on numerous journeys throughout her life—the journey of growing up, the journey of being a wife and mother, the journey of widowhood. And yet, through it all, had she not most of all been on a journey of her own development? Becoming herself? Learning what she wanted and allowing herself to have it? Finding joy?

She wanted Phillip to be a part of that. She wanted to be a part of his journey too. When she was with him, she felt that wanting deep in her core.

A handful of seconds passed as he waited for her to speak. An expression of disappointment darkened his face. Once again she had reached for him but not let him know her whole heart.

She took two more stairs up so that she was eye level to him. She leaned in for a kiss that could say all she was thinking, but he took a step down, holding her gaze as he refused the kiss and released her hand.

"I want a life with you, Deborah. If that is not your same objective, do me the courtesy of not taking advantage of my affections."

Her throat was growing tight. "I have not meant to take advantage, Phillip. I just . . . I do not know how to do this."

"Do what?"

"Be with you. Bring our lives together, our families."

"It starts with admitting what you want and choosing happiness over the judgments of others. You are so worried about how you shall be affected by us choosing to be together—have you thought nothing for the effect it has upon me? To leave my uncle, who has given me so much opportunity? To leave the land I have worked hard to procure and manage all these years? To uproot my children in order to be with a woman who kisses another man and allows me to hear of it as part of a crowd in her parlor?"

"He kissed me," Deborah said, though she knew it was a feeble defense.

He paused. "You have struggled to trust me or trust choosing me—I have seen it in your eyes more than once—but can I trust you? Can I be confident you mean what you say when you say you want to be with me yet behave in ways contrary?"

She looked at the stairs and wished she could stop time for just a few minutes, think through what he'd said and what she felt.

"If you want us to be together, then you should be willing to act the part all the time. You should be comfortable confiding in me when a man takes liberty," Phillip said.

"You make it sound so easy."

"You make it sound so difficult."

She lifted her head and met his eye again. "You do not understand, Phillip. I have never chosen my happiness over someone else's. I have . . ." She stopped herself upon the realization that what she'd said was not entirely true. While she'd put her husband's and children's needs first for many years, she had not suffered for having cared for them, and she had not missed out on joy of her own. These last several days she had relished the sensation of being wanted and of wanting something for herself. She had put herself and her desires first, and it had been . . . marvelous. She had been happy.

"Phillip," she said in a whisper. "I do believe I am in love with you. How is that possible?"

Phillip quirked the tiniest of grins. "Why must it be impossible?"

It was such a difficult thing, to trust one's self.

Unless it was not so difficult.

Unless it was only fear of the unknown that stood in her way.

Fear of disappointing others.

She felt such responsibility for the future, yet when had she ever known the future? Why did she think it was all up to her? She had not planned to be swept off her feet by the dashing Nigel Winfrey when she was eighteen years old, but he had entered her life with a whirlwind and left with a gasp. She had not planned to have three children who were all so different from one another and yet so very much like herself. She had not planned to manage an estate or to have her mother as her best friend through all those unanticipated changes. Or to have fallen in love with Phillip Dempsey.

Attempting to control her future had never worked. Loving the people in her life and doing her best by them, on the other hand, had always come through.

She looked into Phillip's face, his patient smile, his gracious eyes. She felt things combining in her mind, clarifying, becoming solid.

Phillip let out a breath, misinterpreting her delay. "I shall leave in the morning, Deborah. Finish your house party; enjoy your time with your family and friends. It was never my desire to complicate your life, and I shall spare you trying to explain it as anything other than that. You are not ready. I will not press you for something you cannot give."

"You . . . you will leave?"

"I am making you uncomfortable. That is the opposite of what I want for you."

"I do not want you to go."

"But you do want me to keep pretending there is nothing between us—I cannot do that any longer."

She pulled on his hand, bringing it close to her chest. "Wait!"

It was Fifth Night, the night when the leavings of the past year were put out the door and traded for the invitation of new adventures and fresh joy. The people she loved best in the world, and who loved her back, were here at her invitation, enjoying one another, wishing one another well. Phillip had been patient through the entire house party, and she had taken full advantage of that. Would she now cause him pain and deny herself the joy he brought into her life?

The answer was a resounding no, and it reverberated in her chest like a bell.

"You want to be in my life, Phillip?" she whispered to him. "Every part?"

He took a step up, putting them eye to eye again. "Every part, Deborah. All or nothing."

She leaned in to kiss him . . . out here in the open, where anyone could see them. His face had softened, and that he did not pull away this time helped the hope grow in her chest that he was—if not convinced—willing to believe her. Trust her. The kiss was full of promise and a sensation of rightness. They were good for each other, *to* each other. They had years ahead of them to enjoy and live out in comfort and security . . . assuming she did not ruin this chance.

She took his hand and descended the stairs, pulling him with her. He did not resist or ask questions—that beautiful curiosity of his working in her favor. She did not pause upon the threshold of the parlor, and she avoided Mother's eyes as she crossed the room. Mrs. Lund's hands on the pianoforte stilled.

The monstrous kissing bough the children had made, complete with bent ribbons and apples beyond their prime, hung over the music stage, a few berries left upon the lock of mistletoe. She felt the slightest tug of resistance from Phillip when he must have realized her intention, but she tightened her grip and he did not pull away, which he certainly could have if he were entirely against this course.

She stepped into place and turned to face Phillip, who looked surprisingly embarrassed and terribly surprised. Had she done badly with this? She had meant to make the very public display in order to convince him, and everyone else, that she was serious in her feelings and willing to endure whatever . . .

His lips upon hers stilled the thoughts racing in circles through her brain. The same rush of rightness that had accompanied their stolen kisses washed through her, and her arms went around his neck as his tightened around her back. Had it been only a minute ago that she'd admitted to herself that she was in love with this man? She knew now that she'd been in love with him far longer than she'd dared admit.

She did not remember their audience until two hands began to clap, then four, then six. Phillip lifted his face from hers, and then they both turned to look upon the guests. Mother had stood and was walking from the room, which caused Deborah a pang. But she had to believe they could build again, stronger, perhaps, now that they both knew Deborah was a woman of her own mind. Anthony pushed back from his chair and followed Mother out—Deborah felt little pang over his exit. Her children looked confused, which she understood but felt capable of explaining now that there were no more secrets.

Everyone else was smiling and celebratory.

Phillip put his arm around her and pulled her close. She leaned in, took a breath, and let go of past expectations and heavy fears of what the future held. She was here, now, with a man who loved her and wanted a future with her. What a beautiful start to a new year.

EPILOGUE

JANE SHIFTED HER WEIGHT FROM one foot to the other and let out a dramatic sigh as the first carriage turned the corner toward the house. "It is even colder this year than it was last year," she whined.

"And you will survive it again, just as you did the last," Deborah said.

A full year had passed, but the thirteen-year-old girl with two wild younger brothers was not so different from the fourteen-year-old girl with four of them. The front door opened, and all four of the monsters spilled out, with Phillip behind them, issuing orders and barking commands. It had been his idea to have the boys join the welcoming party for the reason that they would all need to join Society one day, and they might as well start practicing company manners now. Plus, with two parents to help manage them, there ought to be strength in numbers.

"This is stupid," Michael said—Deborah was embarrassed to have ever not been able to tell him and Thomas apart.

"My face is going to freeze off!" Ashley added as he went cross-eyed in an attempt to watch himself wrinkle his nose.

"If you keep complaining," Phillip said, stepping beside Deborah and putting an arm around her shoulders, "we shall make you stay to greet the first four guests instead of only the first three."

"Stop complaining," Thomas said, elbowing his brother.

"Thomas is hurting me!" Michael whined.

"It's Grandmama," Jane said, causing Phillip and Deborah to turn their attention to the carriage being pulled by the familiar set of four grays.

Mother had left last year's house party the morning following Deborah and Phillip's kiss beneath the kissing bough. Anthony, however, had stayed, and after a few days of avoidance, he and Deborah had talked through the situation and determined that their friendship could continue as it had before.

Mother had not come to the wedding, nor for her usual summer visit in August, but she had responded to Deborah's letter in September and finally come for a one-week stay in October. Things had been awkward at first but had improved as the days built upon each other. Perhaps because Mother saw how helpful Phillip was with the children and the management of the estate. Perhaps because Jane talked about how Phillip was helping her learn to dance. Or maybe because Deborah had told Mother that she would have a new grandchild in the spring. By the time Mother's trunks were being loaded into the carriage at the end of the week, she had committed to come to the Christmastide house party. Last year's scandal had become this year's celebration, and though Deborah and Phillip's marriage had, as expected, presented a great deal of complexity and conflict management as they joined two families together, there was much to be said of new beginnings and second acts.

Mother's carriage came to a stop, and the footman stepped forward to open the door. Mother descended carefully, this year's bonnet trimmed with golden ribbons and real pine cones.

"Welcome, Mother," Deborah said, stepping forward to share a kiss in the air and pressed cheek. "Thank you for arriving early enough to help greet the other guests."

"Of course," Mother said with a smile. "I wouldn't miss it." She turned her attention to Phillip and stepped forward to greet him.

"It is wonderful to see you again, Lady Affington," he said, bowing slightly.

"As it is to see you, Mr. Dempsey."

Deborah and Phillip shared a look over her head, a silent reminder that it took time to build relationships that mattered. Mother moved on to cluck over the children as another carriage turned the bend.

The six white horses betrayed its occupant, and Deborah gave Phillip's hand a squeeze. Anthony *had* come to the wedding, where he had discovered a connection with Lady Constance's ward, who had escaped his notice last Christmas. They had married in September and graciously accepted the invitation to attend the house party this year.

"Well, I hope you children will join me for tea in the parlor," Mother said, shooing them toward the door as the first snow-flakes began to fall. "I am nearly frozen in my shoes; thank goodness I beat the snow."

"We should wait to welcome the next set of guests," Jane said with a proper nod.

Mother smiled. "As is exactly right and proper. What a fine hostess you are, Jane."

They greeted Lord and Lady Clampton, and then Deborah found herself alone with Phillip on the step as everyone else gave in to the promise of hot tea and warm cinnamon buns. She stepped toward him and brushed a few snowflakes from the shoulder of his cape. "That was not so bad," she said.

"Not half as bad as I feared it would be," Phillip said. "Your mother still frightens me though." He looked toward the interior of the house and gave a dramatic shudder.

Deborah laughed, then put her arms around his waist and laid her head against his chest as she had for the first time almost a year ago. She closed her eyes as his arms wrapped around her.

One could never know the future—not the heartache, nor the joy—and perhaps that was for the best. There was learning and struggle to be had for everyone, but there was also joy when a person allowed their heart to trust in possibilities.

New beginnings.

Letting go of the past.

Redemption and laughter.

All these things were the wishes Deborah had for her children. And herself.

ABOUT THE AUTHOR

Through the course of her writing career, Josi has written in a variety of genres, won several awards, and been an active part of the writing community. Josi also loves to travel to beautiful places and cook delicious food. She is the mother of four adult children and lives in Northern Utah.

To Shawna, Hilda, Elaine, and Marie—my grandmothers
Your influence made all the difference.

OTHER COVENANT BOOKS AND
AUDIOBOOKS BY ANNEKA R. WALKER

Love in Disguise

The Masked Baron

"Lord Blakely's Gift" in *A Hopeful Christmas*

Refining the Debutante

Brides & Brothers

PRAISE FOR
ANNEKA R. WALKER

"Healing, forgiveness, and the spirit of Christmas combine in this love story that involves generations and reminds us what matters most."
—Josi Kilpack, author of the Mayfield Family series

"Torn between their love for each other and their love for their fighting families, Walker's dynamic characters will keep you hoping and dreaming until the very end. Be prepared for a meaningful, enjoyable reconciliation that will satisfy all of the Christmas season feelings."
—Sarah McConkie, author of *The Promise of Miss Spencer*

ACKNOWLEDGMENTS

As always, I am grateful to my loving Heavenly Father and my family for their love and support. Thank you, Jenny Rabe, Jamie Bartlett, and Jennie Goutet, for your help in polishing my story. And special thanks to the team at Covenant Communications for giving me so many opportunities to share my stories with the world!

HEALING HEARTS
for THE HOLIDAYS

ANNEKA R. WALKER

CHAPTER ONE

Northamptonshire, 1812

JULIA HUNT THOUGHT THERE MUST be something magical about the charming little town of Amorwich. When she arrived at her grandmother's estate with her family to celebrate the holidays, she felt brave for the first time. Brave enough to ignore her father's edict and visit the forbidden manor house Fairmore Hall, where her sister lay sick and with child. All too soon, their visit was at an end.

"I have to go, Ivy, but I know Lord Blakely will see to your needs," Julia said. "He is a good husband to you, is he not?" She knew the answer, but she mentioned it simply to make her sister smile before she departed.

"He is the best sort of husband," Ivy said, though her smile was small and her voice weakened with fatigue. "I wish Papa would read my letters so he would know just how good Curtis is to me."

Everyone had thought the wedding between Ivy and Lord Blakely would end the decades-old feud over a land dispute between their families, but the past could not be shaken from the minds of their parents long enough for them to forgive. Although Papa had given his blessing for his eldest daughter's marriage, in the year since then, regret had hardened his heart once more, and he had banned any mention of Ivy or her wretched new family. This meant there had been no opportunity to tell him about the baby. Julia had hoped returning to Amorwich would soften his heart, but she'd been wrong. And now Ivy was ill, and Julia refused to risk her chance to visit and care for her sister by telling her father.

"Someday Papa will forgive the past," Julia said, hoping her words were true. "I'll do my best to return tomorrow." Julia hated to leave her sister forced to her bed, but time waited for no one—certainly not for their father.

Ivy shifted in her bed, her auburn hair strung across her pillow, and reached for Julia's hand. "Do be careful and don't let anyone see you. Maids talk, you know."

"Of course." Julia pulled away and slipped the hood of her purple cloak over her chignon and low over her eyes. She hurried out of her sister's room and down the corridor, glancing around her as she did. She wasn't worried about the servants seeing her, but rather the family Ivy had married into. She stopped at the end of the passage, hugging the wall with her back, and peered around the corner. Why had she stayed so long? Surely, the family would be home by now from their house calls.

Grandmother had given her strict instructions on the routines of Lady Blakely and her two sons. This way she still avoided the family should her father catch her and question her. Julia had successfully visited twice already without any repercussions. However, her plotting with Grandmother could not help her now. It was Julia's own fault she had lost track of the time. When she saw no one in the corridor, she hurried to the staircase.

"Psst." A whisper from behind Julia bound her feet to the ground. "I know a better way." The baritone voice was oddly familiar.

Julia slowly pivoted. A crack in the door revealed Esmond Park, Ivy's brother-in-law. The man she had spent a year trying to forget. Julia's pulse raced. Why did she have to be caught by him?

Footfalls on the stairs doubled her panic. It was surely Lady Blakely coming to denounce her and send her away. Esmond reached forward and snatched Julia's arm. His strong grasp yanked her toward him. Before she could so much as squeak, she was in Esmond's bedchamber. He quickly shut the door but did not release her from his grasp. He put his ear to the door and pulled her close so she might do the same.

Julia's ear rested against the cold wood, but she could not hear anything over the deafening sound of her heartbeat. She was too near Esmond to think at all. Never had she been so close to a man besides her father—they were nearly embracing. She was mesmerized by Esmond's firm touch on her arm and the masculine scent radiating from him. His warm breath tickled her forehead, causing her to nearly miss a muffled sound as it neared the door. Fear seized her, and she forgot to pull away. The soft footfalls passed, and Esmond finally stepped back. But not before she had a good long look at his profile—his strong jaw, long dark side-whiskers, and the way the cowlick above his forehead made his hair flip back. She'd missed him.

Warmth seeped from her arm as he released her.

"You're safe." He turned his light-brown eyes on her.

"No," she said, inhaling sharply. "I'm far from safe." The intensity of his gaze was too much for her comfort, and she looked away, allowing her reason to slowly overcome her nerves. "Why am I in your bedchamber, Mr. Park?"

He gave her a sheepish smile. "I'm protecting you from my mother."

Esmond's easy, open manner reminded Julia of the time she'd spent with him at Ivy's wedding. Together, they had played mediator between their families and had not left each other's side. No matter how hard she'd tried, she had not forgotten him or his kindness. Though, it would have been better if she had. After today, her memory wouldn't stand a chance. How could she erase what it felt like to be in close proximity to him?

"A generous thought, sir. Or it would be, had I not been avoiding you too."

He laughed, surprised. "Me? So you plan your visits when only your sister is home?" He tsked while shaking his head. "That will not do, Miss Hunt."

Why was he not at all flustered that they were sealed together in his room? Her own heart raced inside of her. While his intentions were likely innocent, their current situation was not.

"You know it's better for all of us this way," she said and tried to walk around him.

He stepped in front of her, his tall form blocking her way. Did he think to detain her until they were caught? She thought him much too good for such an idea.

"Have our months apart brought you to hate my family as much as your father does, or is there another reason for your avoidance?" His voice was playful like it had been at the wedding, but she knew he was in earnest.

"I do not hate anyone," she said, dropping her head. There was interest in his eyes, and she needed to squelch any ideas in his mind. "Though, I find some hard to tolerate." Oh, why could she not make her words sound compelling? She went the opposite direction than the one she'd initially tried.

He blocked her again. "How do you know if you cannot tolerate us if you don't give us a chance?"

"Delaying me for another moment could prevent me from seeing my sister again. Please."

His smile slipped, though there was understanding in his eyes. "My apologies. I will let you get on your way."

"You won't tell your mother?" Julia wasn't sure Esmond's mother held as strong of a grudge as Julia's father, since in the past year Lady Blakely had reconnected with Grandmother, but she couldn't risk jeopardizing her opportunities to visit.

"No, of course I won't tell." He shifted away from the door. "Let me send for our carriage. It's been raining off and on all morning."

"I cannot delay. My father knows I am fond of long walks, but he does not know I have come to Fairmore Hall. I usually keep my visits brief, but I lost track of the time."

"Still, you should consider your health."

His eagerness did strange things to her insides. She took in his tidy room, the stack of books on the bedside table, and the deer antlers above his headboard while she searched for an excuse. "My cloak is heavy enough. I thank you for your concern, but I really should hurry."

"Let me show you to the servants' staircase. It is a far more discreet method of coming and going." He took one last long glance at her before opening the door. Together, they hurried back toward Ivy's room. Before reaching it, they turned, and Esmond led her to the secluded stair. He stayed with her all the way to the front door, where he extended her an umbrella from a rack in the entryway.

"Here, at least take this. I see you do not have one of your own."

Julia pushed it away. "I forgot mine, but—"

"Please," he said, placing the umbrella in her hands. "It will set my mind at ease. I do not like the idea of you being drenched."

"Thank you." She gave him a tentative smile.

She was several steps past him when he called after her. "If you feel brave, I shall be home during calling hours tomorrow."

She turned to give him a tight smile, but the last of her courage had fled at the sight of him. She would forgo visiting on the morrow simply to avoid Esmond. Julia ached to be near Ivy while visiting Amorwich for Christmas, but Esmond's presence would complicate everything. Ivy had written several times expressing her brother-in-law's interest in Julia, but her father had already lost a wife prematurely and now a daughter through strained relations. He did not deserve to lose another child, which was precisely what would happen if anything of a permanent nature developed between her and Esmond. She could not encourage what she could not accept—even if it meant holding Esmond at arm's length. Her father was her only living parent, and the last thing she wanted was to forfeit his affection.

A swirl of wind lifted the bottom of her cloak, propelling her forward. She took one last look at the three-story manor house with its dozens of windows and cream-colored limestone, opened the umbrella, and hiked her dress up just enough to lengthen her stride. As soon as she was out of sight of Fairmore, she ran.

When she reached Ravencross, her grandmother's estate, Alice, her younger sister by a year, eagerly opened the door and helped her remove her cloak and bonnet. Their butler stepped forward and took the wet articles from their hands. Julia suspected Barnes knew more than he let on, and the strain of secrecy filled her with worry.

"I shall have to return this umbrella later," she said to him. "Please put it somewhere safe for me."

He gave her a curt nod and hurried away. Even the butler was wise enough to disappear before Papa could find him.

Julia turned to Alice. "Is Papa angry?"

"At you?" Alice scoffed and pushed back her strawberry curls. "He thinks you can do no wrong."

Apparently, their father did not have the same level of imagination as Esmond Park. Julia blushed even thinking about her time with him in his bedchamber.

Alice's words broke her from her reverie. "When he asked about you, I fibbed and said you were napping."

"Alice!" Julia's attempts to chasten her sister were rarely effective, but she had to try. "You mustn't get yourself into trouble."

"Why not?" Alice asked. "I can't seem to do anything right, so I might as well cover for you. How is Ivy?"

"She is still quite unwell." Julia recalled Ivy's pale features and sighed. Ivy was refusing food, and what she did eat she couldn't keep down. It did not bode well for either her or her baby. "She sleeps more than she eats. I wish I could have stayed longer."

"Shh!" Alice whispered. "I hear footsteps. Quickly, to the library."

Julia groaned. *Not again.* The library was more of a wide corridor lined with books near the back of the house than an actual room. At the end of the passage was a small nook with two chairs and a lamp, both framed by a large oval window. Alice pushed Julia toward a chair and practically threw a book at her.

Julia caught the volume right as her father rounded the corner.

"Julia?" Her father stopped, eyeing her strangely. "Your cheeks are bright red. Are you ill?"

Guilty? Flustered? Both of those emotions came to mind, but she was not ill. "I was on a walk, Papa."

Alice gave her an accusing stare.

"Not napping?" Papa's gaze darted back and forth between her and Alice.

"No, Papa." Julia could not bring herself to lie to him—not when she was already filled with remorse for betraying his wishes.

"Next time bring a scarf and don't walk too far. While you were gone, the doctor arrived. You recall the little tumble your grandmother had yesterday? Well, it seems she was hiding her pain very well. The doctor said her ankle is broken, and since her balance is not good, she must stay down. I'd hate for you to catch a cold and join her in the sickbed."

"Poor Grandmother!" Julia said. "I cannot imagine she will enjoy staying in her room."

Papa shook his head. "I fear her recovery will be just as hard on her mind as her aging body. Alice." Papa turned to face Julia's sister. "Do not think that I have forgotten you. Why did you lie to me? Or are you going to tell me you were simply mistaken . . . again?"

"These scenarios seem to choose me, not the other way around." Alice shrugged off his concern.

"And you try so very hard to avoid them." Papa lifted his eyes to the ceiling in exasperation. "We have come this Christmas only for me to meet the new land steward and to address your grandmother's health. Since your aunt Morris is not here to guide you, I expect your best behavior while I see to these tasks. Not that we will be entertaining, because we won't be. Neither will we be accepting invitations. The last thing I want is for either of you to attach yourselves to anyone in Amorwich. We have too many ties to this cursed area as it is. If my own mother did not live here, I would insist we never see it again."

Julia looked at Alice. Neither of them brought up Ivy's name. It hurt to know their own sister wasn't welcome. Ivy was Lady Blakely now, and the very title set Papa on edge. Perhaps he'd let her visit if they begged, but with Ivy so ill, and feelings so raw, attempting such a feat might make the situation worse.

Papa did not say anything more, but his rigid stance and the grim set of his mouth sealed his words with finality.

CHAPTER TWO

Two days later, Julia and Alice sat for tea with Papa and Mr. Harvey, Ravencross's new land steward. Mr. Harvey was an easily excitable man. Julia was sure he could convince a cat to skin itself after the way his smooth tongue had convinced Papa there were riches to be made if he invested his money just as Mr. Harvey instructed him. She was not surprised when the two of them stood from their matching elbow chairs in the drawing room and disappeared into the study, with nary a word to her or her sister.

Julia set down her teacup and saucer on the floral porcelain platter and turned to Alice. "Let's finish our tea with Grandmother."

Alice nodded, and with the help of the maid, they were soon sitting at Grandmother's bedside.

"How is your ankle today?" Julia asked. She had assisted the doctor in changing the dressings early that morning to bind Grandmother's foot, but Julia could only imagine the pain that accompanied the bruising and swelling around the broken bone.

"Never mind my leg." Grandmother tucked her long white braid behind her small shoulder. "You'd better hurry if you are to walk to Fairmore today. I am sure you missed seeing Ivy yesterday."

"You think there is still time?" Julia looked at the clock on the mantel. "I'm anxious to know if she's kept any food down since I saw her last."

Alice didn't let Grandmother answer. "You're not going to leave me here alone again, are you?" Her lips curled down into a pout. "What am I to do while you are away?"

"I requested a book on Greek mythology you might like," Grandmother said to Alice.

Alice's pout marginally softened. She loved stories of all sorts.

Julia put her hand on her sister's arm. "I promise to bring you with me when I know Papa will not miss you. One more incident and Aunt Morris will not let you accompany the family to London."

"Why is everyone always supposing I will do something wrong?"

Julia's gaze connected with Grandmother's in shared amusement. Just yesterday, while Julia prepared a poultice for a sore on Grandmother's injured calf, Alice had insisted on helping. She was supposed to soak bread in milk while Julia crushed herbs. Julia had expected her to use a single slice of bread, but Alice had used all the milk and bread in the kitchen and made enough poultice for a small army. Cook had not been very happy. Julia knew her sister always meant well, so she tried hard to play the peacemaker between Alice and their aunt. Thankfully, Grandmother found Alice to be amusing. Aunt Morris, on the other hand, was too strict to let such mistakes go.

Julia squeezed her arm. "You need only keep Papa from passing any stories to Aunt Morris. He will see how responsible you are, and it will be those accounts she will hear."

Alice folded her arms and grumbled, "Must you continually remind me of her? I am on holiday, if you remember."

Julia could sympathize with Alice since she herself was relieved to have space from her aunt too. Neither of them enjoyed the expectation forced upon them. "It's imperative we keep you out of trouble until we return to Peterborough. I will never survive a London Season if Aunt doesn't let you go with me."

"Very well. I shall write Ivy a story," Alice declared. Her sister had a wonderful imagination that Julia envied. "I'm going to use

Mr. Harvey as the model for my villain. Doesn't our steward have such a wicked look about him?"

Julia hid her laugh. "I do think Ivy could use a story to cheer her up. You'd better make it a comedy."

"I am sure every highwayman I have ever heard of has Mr. Harvey's thick, dark brows and the same deep scowl. I would be wary of him if I were you."

Grandmother frowned. "I told your father he ought to ask the locals for a recommendation before he hired a land steward."

Julia stood, happy Alice was not begging to join her and that Grandmother would have her companionship. "Do be sure to get his physical description just so. Ivy will want every detail so she can envision him herself."

Alice sighed. "You'll kiss her for me?"

"And me?" Grandmother asked.

"I will kiss her twice." Julia said goodbye with a salute. While she hated disobeying Papa, it helped to know Grandmother and Alice supported her.

The walk to Fairmore took nearly thirty minutes. Julia's toes were numb by the time she arrived, and the wind bit at her cheeks and nose. She stepped through the gates and noticed two men talking just outside the front door. She quickly concealed herself behind a nearby tree and peered around it.

Lord Blakely—Ivy's husband—and, of course, Esmond.

This was Lady Blakely's away hours when she usually called on her friends, but it was harder to plan around the men. Their schedules were not always known to Julia and could change without her awareness. The tree she stood behind was one of many bordering the property. She moved slowly behind one and then another, hoping the men would leave and she could make it to the house unseen. It was much too long a walk for her to simply turn around.

As she followed the trees, she saw a brick gazebo draped in brown clematis vines on one side. It was an easy walk from there to the house, and she could wait comfortably without being seen.

She stepped inside and sat on the edge of one of the wooden benches encircling the space, fatigued from her walk. The benches were damp from the morning frost, so when the cold seeped into her from her seat, Julia stood and leaned against a pillar while absently fingering the vines. This spot would be lovely come spring and summer.

She set her hand on the half wall, but the brick beneath her hand gave a little when she shifted her weight. The mortar around the brick had broken, and the brick did not seem to fit well. She attempted to wiggle it back into place, but it felt as if there was something in the way underneath it. Debris, perhaps?

She lifted the brick and drew in her breath. A small box rested in an alcove carved into the half wall. Curious, Julia set the brick aside and pulled the box out. It was cube-shaped with a hinged lid. She popped it open and blinked at her discovery. A half dozen letters were tightly tucked inside. As she riffled through the stack, she noticed each one was addressed to Miss Young. Who was Miss Young, and why did Julia feel a burning desire to read the woman's letters?

��� ��� ���

Esmond stepped outside Fairmore House with his brother, Curtis, for a private word.

"What is it?" Esmond asked. "Did the doctor say something more about Ivy?"

Curtis rolled his shoulders back. "The doctor says not to worry; Ivy's condition is perfectly normal. Mother, on the other hand, says she's never seen an expectant woman this sick and insists I go for the doctor in Northampton and get a second opinion."

"You'll make the right decision," Esmond said, shivering when a gust of wind brushed past them.

"I am not so sure," Curtis said. "I have reason to doubt Mother's fears since despite Ivy's illness, Mother thinks it is perfectly acceptable to continue planning for our annual Christmas ball—as if I don't have enough on my mind."

"We are all concerned about Ivy, especially Mama," Esmond said. "But I understand your frustration. Mama has already ordered a large crate of oranges for the party. Every year she must outdo herself from the year before. Still, the planning is good for her. She has had little to think about since Father died. Especially now, with her heart wrapped up in the future heir of Fairmore and Amelia gone, Mother needs the distraction." Their sister was attending a cousin's house party and would not return home for an entire month.

"I see your point." Curtis blew out his breath. "Parties are her thing, not mine. How can I muster a smile when a line of people inquire over and over again after my wife? This whole thing is literally making me ill. If Ivy's condition were contagious, I would feel as if I had been struck."

"Your wife nauseates you?" Esmond asked in an attempt to lighten the conversation.

"I dare you to find a prettier woman in the entire county, even with her being sick in bed," Curtis growled. "I cannot explain it, Esmond. When she empties the contents of her stomach, I am inevitably sick too."

Esmond couldn't help his laugh. He nearly brought up Julia's name as a beauty contestant but felt it wise to refrain. "My apologies. That does sound serious. I cannot pretend to relate."

"Not a word to anyone. It's humiliating. A man is not supposed to be sick without good reason."

"I promise not to tell anyone." Esmond forced his face to be serious, but it was quite a chore.

"If you did, you would have to find yourself a new place to live."

The humor left Esmond in an instant. Curtis might be in jest, but Esmond knew his time to leave was coming. As a second son, there was no large inheritance or title he was born to receive. He had resisted Curtis's offer to buy him an army commission. Esmond would fight to protect his family's freedom, but his heart was not in any effort to build England an empire. The law did not appeal to him; neither did the church.

What Esmond really wanted was what he couldn't have—to run an estate. He loved the land, but farming was not for someone of his station. He also loved interacting with the tenants. Curtis had the ideal lifestyle. Esmond would never admit to his jealousy, as it was petty of him. He truly meant to find something else suitable, but he was at a loss as to what it might be.

Curtis interrupted his reverie. "Ivy has an unnatural love for Christmas."

"Oh?" Esmond had heard this on more than one occasion, but he sensed his brother needed to express something more.

"She would love all the festivities this year, but she is much too ill to enjoy them. Last year, she could not stop giving to all those we met. With such a generous heart, she deserves a special holiday. It would be easier to buy her a dozen new gowns and take her on a tour of the Continent than give her what she truly wants. The one thing that would make her happy I cannot bestow. She wants her family back in her life."

"We would all give her that, if we could," Esmond said. Reuniting Ivy with her family would truly be the ideal gift. "If you think of anything I can do to help, you know I would not hesitate to lend a hand."

Curtis kicked a small rock, and it skidded across the steps. "If I could think of a solution, I would have thought of it by now."

Esmond's mind turned over what details he knew of the feud. Lost in his thoughts, he turned and saw a flash of deep purple—the color of Julia's cloak—just beyond the tree line. He had hoped Julia would come with the obligation to return his umbrella the day before, but she had not. He'd wasted months thinking about her since his brother's wedding. Why, he didn't know. They'd hardly had more than two days in each other's company. When he'd heard from Ivy that Julia was returning for the holidays, he'd been convinced one last look would settle his mind.

He hadn't expected to have to force her to look at him. Her aloofness had surprised him. She clearly did not have the same stirring in her heart that he experienced in her presence. And, dash it all, she was far prettier than he'd remembered. Her voice was soothing with its mildness—never angry, always calm and collected—so unlike his own excited tones. Instead of dismissing her as he'd meant to, his heart had flipped inside his chest.

"I hope Ivy will turn a corner soon," Esmond said, now eager to end his conversation with Curtis. Either his imagination was running wild, or Julia was attempting to evade him again.

"My heart and my *stomach* have the same hope."

Esmond slapped his brother on the back. "Tell Mother I am standing in for you should she have any concerns about the ball. There is no need for you to worry about one more thing."

Curtis gave Esmond a crooked smile. "I appreciate your offer. I could use the help."

Esmond nodded, then jumped over the side of the steps onto the damp grass.

"Where are you going in such a hurry?" Curtis called after him.

"I wouldn't want to catch the illness you've been complaining about. I happen to like keeping my breakfast down." He winked at Curtis, happy to hear his brother's soft laugh in response, then crossed the garden toward the line of trees on the side of the house.

Where had Julia gone? Esmond didn't stand a chance with the woman. He had no future to offer if her father even let Esmond court her. Still, he was drawn to her. He justified that he could still speak to her, enjoy looking at her, and drive her mad with his teasing. Her dainty smile filled him with such pleasure.

He finally caught sight of her standing in the gazebo. She was so intent on something in her hands that she didn't notice him approaching. He decided to sneak up behind her and surprise her. Once he was a foot or two away, he noiselessly removed his gloves and tucked them into his great coat. He reached up his arms and put his bare hands over her eyes.

Upon contact, Julia squeaked and gave a little jump, dropping what she'd been holding. Several letters and a box tumbled to the ground.

Esmond uncovered her eyes, hoping she would find his playful attempt humorous and not bothersome.

"Mr. Park!" Julia put her hand to her heart.

"It's Esmond," he urged. "I thought we were good friends."

"Good friends?"

Why did that idea seem to disturb her so greatly? "Yes." He bent down to pick up the open box, sorry to find it had broken. "We got on so well last time we were in each other's company, or have you forgotten?"

"You mean two days ago, when you locked me in your room and wouldn't let me pass?"

"I was speaking about when we danced the night before the wedding, and you so graciously let me fetch your drink and hold your fan for you. I can be terribly obliging."

"That was nearly a year ago," Julia said without a hint of a smile. "And you know how my father would feel about such a friendship."

"One of the hinges has come free." Esmond examined the box, turning it over in his hands. "It was my fault, and I insist on repairing it for you. Now, as to our friendship, I find the idea of our families at war deplorable. My mother has softened a great deal since the wedding, and perhaps in time, your father will too. I see no reason we can't be friends."

"Papa was anxious at the wedding, but since then he has grown increasingly resentful. I cannot understand it." Julia bent over and picked up a few letters.

Esmond stooped and claimed the others, shuffling them into an orderly pile. He read the name off the top of the stack. "Miss Young? Do these letters belong to my mother?"

Julia blanched. "You mean Lady Blakely?"

"Young was my mother's surname before she married. These are clearly very old since they are addressed with her maiden name."

"Oh, I see." Julia looked at the address once more.

"Shall we ask her? This scrawl is decidedly male." He leaned back and narrowed his brow. "You wouldn't be stealing her correspondence, would you? I will have to report this offense to her right away."

Julia snatched the letters back. "What would your mother think if you presented such an idea? Our families have enough problems as it is."

"Ah, so you *are* capable of anger. I've never seen this emotion on you." He leaned forward and whispered, "Don't worry. I find it charming the way your lips turn in on themselves like that."

Julia immediately relaxed her mouth, likely in an attempt to thwart his enjoyment, but her eyes were still furious. "If you knew how much I love my sister, you would not tease me about this. I found the letters under a loose brick over there. I promise I had no intention of stealing anything."

Esmond gently touched her wrist. "I believe you. I don't mean any harm with my words—only to coax a smile or two."

"Here." She pressed the letters toward him, more than a little flustered by either his touch or his words. "Pretend *you* found them and take them to your mother."

Esmond accepted the letters. "I will. I hope they will bring good memories." The last thing his mother needed was a stack of bad reminiscence.

"Why would you think they might hold unpleasant memories?"

Esmond shrugged. "They have been left unread and hidden out here for a reason. Fairmore Hall has had a great deal to worry about with your sister's health. Everyone seems to be as unhinged as this box. I would hate to give Mother these and upset her further."

Julia stared at the letters. "The only way you'll know is if you read them first."

"I wouldn't want to break her confidence." He might be a tease, but he would never intentionally hurt anyone. He flipped through the letters with his thumb. "Then again, if it would prevent more pain . . ."

"Protecting the ones we love is often all we can do," Julia said softly. "But I would not presume to influence your decision."

"Of course not," Esmond said. "Ivy has told me how you have long carried the role of peacemaker in your home. I cannot imagine you counseling me to do anything to upset anyone. If the letters were new, I would not even consider it. Come, we will sit down and read the first letter. If it's a harmless correspondence, I will deliver them to my mother directly."

Esmond was almost surprised when Julia followed him to the bench. Finally, she had willingly agreed to be in his presence for more than two minutes strung together. Easily breaking the seal, he unfolded the letter and set the others next to him on the bench.

He moved closer to Julia on his other side and put the letter out for her to see as he read.

> *"Dearest Danielle,*
> *I know Lord Blakely is pressing his intention to court you. I thought we had an understanding. Do not cower to your parents' wishes. If we hold strong, everything will work out as planned.*
> *Forever yours,*
> *Jonathan"*

Julia's eyes met his. "Is Danielle your mother's name?"

"It is." Esmond's mind whirled. "Is Jonathan your father's name?"

Julia nodded slowly. "Then . . . our parents used to care for each other."

"So it seems." Esmond folded the letter and set it back in the box. He opened another one.

Julia's eyebrows furrowed. "What are you doing?"

"Well, we have established that these letters are emotionally charged. We had better read them all before we make a decision." He flipped open the second letter and extended it out, gesturing for her to read.

"Dearest Danielle,

I've been waiting for an answer. Does this mean you have thrown away our history so you might marry a man with a title? This is your mother's wish, not yours. I cannot believe you would willingly go along with this. Meet me here tonight. It isn't too late. We can still find a way to be together.

Forever yours,

Jonathan"

Julia put her hand over her mouth. "I'm not sure I can read any more. These are my father's intimate thoughts."

Esmond swallowed, his throat suddenly dry. "We need to know whether or not we should give them to my mother. I cannot willingly bring her pain."

"Then, we will leave it alone. My father's letters, if you will." Julia extended her trembling hand, her palm facing upward.

"It seems to me you would like to get these letters back at all costs. I think a trade might be in order."

"You mean to blackmail me?"

Esmond's eyes widened. "I am no scoundrel. I merely ask that we read all the letters before we act. This could be the secret to finally finding peace between our two families." He thought of Curtis's wish for Ivy and a budding, unrequited hope of his own.

"It would hurt our parents deeply if they knew what we were about." A little scar by one of Julia's blue-green eyes pulled tight as she beseeched him.

"We need to consider who stands to benefit should we resolve the feud." Esmond thought of himself and the chance he might have with Julia should all obstacles be removed, but his personal desires descended to the dark recesses of his mind, where they could not surface to tease him. "Think of Ivy and Curtis."

Julia frowned and sank back on the bench. "My sister is a good person. She deserves the love of both of her families. Very well. But we must agree on when, if ever, the letters come to light."

"Agreed." He thumbed through the letters and picked out another one. He read aloud:

> "*Dearest Danielle,*
>   *Today is to be your wedding day. Please, say your vows to the man you love—the man who loves you. I'll be here . . . waiting . . . hoping.*"

"It's unsigned, but it's the same handwriting," Julia said, leaning over Esmond's arm to see. "My poor father. I never had the faintest idea of his heartache."

Esmond picked up another one.

> "*Dearest Danielle,*
>   *Everyone is talking about the land. This has nothing to do with the land. You must believe I would marry you and forsake all I own. Marry me, Danielle. I will love you until my dying breath, and even then, I am sure my spirit will not cease to love you.*"

Esmond's voice wavered. Reading about such devotion stirred an inner longing for such a connection of his own. Out of the corner of his vision, he saw Julia blink back the moisture in her eyes. He cleared his throat. "They aren't dated, but this one must have been written before the wedding. I'm not sure of the order of any of these."

Julia pointed to the mention of the word *land* in the letter. "Look here. It suggests the feud did not begin because of the land but because of the rift between your mother and my father. But my father always talks about how the land should've been his and how it is only right a Hunt now resides here as Lord Blakely's wife."

"I wonder what prevented him from being considered an acceptable suitor."

Julia frowned and looked at the remaining letters. "Two left," she whispered.

Esmond took one, broke the seal, and read,

> *"Dearest Danielle,*
> *You did not come, but I haven't lost hope. Let's elope to Scotland and put this mess behind us. I know your parents never liked me, but I cannot imagine them being cruel enough to keep us apart. I'll be here again tomorrow. Please come!*
> *Yours always,*
> *Jonathan"*

"Why didn't she come?" Despair laced Julia's voice.

Esmond shook his head. "I've never heard even a hint about a past relationship between Mother and your father. I thought my parents had a love match. Occasionally, there were things that bothered my mother about my father, but he was a good person. I only heard the same old argument from my father, who said time and again that your father hated us because he felt cheated out of our land."

"Better read the last one." Julia pointed to the final sealed letter on the bench.

Esmond picked it up, hesitant. He sought Julia's gaze for courage, but her sad eyes tugged at his heart. He broke the seal and, flipping it open, handed it to her to read.

> *"Dearest Danielle,*
> *Why aren't you reading my letters? Your parents won't let me near you, and I cannot understand what has turned you from me. Have I offended you? I swear on my life I would never intentionally hurt you. Forgive me? My heart is ever yours and always will be.*
> *Faithfully yours,*
> *Jonathan"*

Julia sighed and sank back.

Esmond reached over and clasped Julia's gloved hand. "I know it hurts, but you must remember this was a long time ago. They both moved on, married, and had families."

"And my father was happy in his marriage." Julia said it almost to herself. "He speaks about my mother with such reverence. This feels like a betrayal to her."

Esmond gently squeezed her dainty hand, attempting to remind her she was not alone in her loss and confusion. "What should we do with the letters?"

She looked down at their hands and slowly pulled hers out of his grasp. "I don't know. I need time to think it over."

Esmond was reluctant to say goodbye, but he knew it was time. "Is Ivy expecting you?"

"Yes, but I cannot see her now. She will guess that there is something wrong, and I cannot tell her about this yet. She is carrying enough burdens as it is."

"I will send her your well-wishes." Esmond cleared his throat, suddenly feeling awkward. He felt close to Julia one minute and distant the next. "And I insist you take a carriage home this time. It is going to rain again, and with these temperatures, it could snow."

Julia pursed her lips and nodded. "That would be kind. If the driver lets me out before the turn in the road, I could walk the rest of the way unseen."

"My thoughts exactly." Esmond handed her the letters.

"No, you keep them. They belong to your mother."

"I will wait to give them to her until you have had time to prepare yourself." He had a strong desire to make her think well of him, despite the wedge between their families. "I know I can be a great tease, but I would be angry with myself if you thought I behaved like less than a gentleman today."

She gave him a small smile. "A great tease? You mean an *insufferable* tease."

Esmond chuckled. "You flatter me, Miss Hunt," he said and stood.

Julia stood as well and hesitated. "Julia . . . if you please."

He froze, his heart thudding. "What prompted this request?"

Her smile grew slowly, like a rose uncurling in the morning light. "If we are going to keep such a great secret between us, it is fitting we become friends first."

"You don't know how happy it makes me to hear that." Esmond wanted to be so much more than friends, but this was a step in the right direction. He could stare at her blue-green eyes for much longer than he dared, so he extended his arm to her. The moment she accepted his arm, he pulled his gaze away from her and added, "I was afraid your father would prevent such an opportunity."

"He would gladly prevent it, if he knew." She fell into step with him. "But the more I think on it, the more I realize I should not have to ask his permission for whom I call my friend. That is my privilege."

Perhaps the letters were to thank for making her think about her own situation. Esmond had no idea what to make of their tentative friendship, but he didn't dare press her to pursue anything more. He had more than just the family feud keeping him from exploring a courtship with Julia. He still had nothing to offer, should she want him.

CHAPTER THREE

JULIA ARRIVED HOME TO FIND Alice working on another story and tiptoed past the sitting room door so as not to alert anyone of her presence. She needed time alone to think. Once in her room, she stopped short. There was Esmond's umbrella leaning against her small closet. How was she supposed to forget him and his charming company with this in her room?

She reached out and touched the sleek fabric. Esmond Park was a likable fellow. He had the pedigree to meet Aunt Morris's approval and the determination to meet her father's—if circumstances were different. She wished they were, for Esmond made her feel like she was someone special. The way he looked at her sent warmth racing through her veins. Despite all her father said about Esmond's family, she sensed he was a man who could be trusted.

Such thoughts would lead to no good. With a quick movement, she pushed the umbrella into her closet and shut the door. Not Esmond's sweetness or the way he made her feel could change the past. This morning had painted her a clearer picture of how impossible ending the feud was.

Surely, Ivy had often wished for the same peace Julia did. Beyond the burden of carrying a child, there was an emotional weight Ivy would bear far longer than she deserved.

Now Julia felt as if she carried it too.

A knock sounded on her bedroom door.

"Come in," she said.

The door opened, and Papa stood on the threshold. "When did you get back?"

"A few moments ago."

"Exploring always was a favorite pastime for you," Papa said.

Julia forced a smile. "There is much in Amorwich I haven't seen, but I am content with the beauty here at Ravencross."

Papa looked past her through her bedroom window. "I loved it here as a boy, but I'm not sure why. Peterborough feels more like home now."

Julia's stomach twisted with an ache for her father. He should not have to spend his holidays at Amorwich with his collection of uncomfortable memories.

"I was going to check on Grandmother," Julia said. "How is she today?"

"Improved." Papa fidgeted with his thumbnail. "I was thinking of hiring a companion to stay with her so we could return home sooner than planned."

"Oh?" Julia's stomach clenched.

"Your aunt gets anxious when you are away. You know she feels like you and your sisters are like her own daughters."

Aunt Morris was with them year-round. What about Ivy? Julia could not just abandon her this way. After waiting so long between visits to see Grandmother, and then with Grandmother's injury, it hurt to think of saying goodbye to her too.

Papa rested his hand on the door handle. "No doubt Alice is keen on the idea. She loves the festivities Aunt Morris lines up for us."

Papa was wrong about Alice. Neither she nor Julia were eager to hurry home. The moment they returned Aunt would turn all her attentions to marrying Julia off. It would mean a continuation of being Aunt's puppet—saying what Aunt wanted her to say, wearing what Aunt wanted her to wear, being introduced to those

Aunt deemed worthy. As hard as it was to be in Amorwich under such difficult circumstances, Julia loathed the idea of returning to Aunt's clutches. Her tradition for long walks had begun as a way to escape her aunt's mothering, as well meaning as it was.

"You seem upset," Papa said.

Julia had so many emotions tumbling inside her. Thoughts of her young father—heartbroken—worries for Ivy, forbidden hope for Esmond. Nothing she could speak of. "I do not like leaving Grandmother without her family. Ravencross must be so lonely for her."

Papa nodded. "I don't doubt it. There is a bit of a mess with the land steward too. I had hoped to have it sorted out by now."

"Something serious?"

"Nothing you need worry about. Just a matter of Mr. Harvey's lofty ideas that involve risking my money. He keeps pressing me to invest in—oh, never mind. Let's see how things are a week from now, shall we? I can force myself to push through that long."

"Thank you, Papa." Julia put her arm through her father's. "I had better see to Grandmother. Care to join me?"

"I was just with her. I am sure she will appreciate your companionship." The two of them made their way down the corridor before parting ways.

Julia found Grandmother with her writing table across her lap. "Am I interrupting?"

"It's all right, dear. I am finished with my letter."

"Are you in pain this afternoon?" Julia shut the door behind her.

"Every minute."

"I'm so sorry." Julia thought through the different ways to alleviate Grandmother's discomfort. "Should I request some lavender tea to help you relax?"

"No, your company will do the trick."

"Then, I shall stay as long as you'd like." Julia took a seat on the chair beside her grandmother's bed and noticed a napkin next to it folded in the shape of a swan. "This is beautiful."

"It's from your father. When he was a boy, a kitchen maid taught him the art of folding napkins. All these years later, he has not forgotten. Every day he has been here he has left me a different design. I know being at Ravencross is hard for him, but he still finds ways to show me he cares."

Julia admired the perfect swan. "I had no idea he could do this."

"Your father has had a difficult life," Grandmother said, "but only a good man could face his demons and still produce something so lovely." She squinted at Julia. "You seem flushed. Are you well?"

"Me?" Julia put a hand to her chest. "Of course."

"You've met Mr. Park again, haven't you?" Grandmother gave her a mischievous smile.

"Again?"

"I remember how you two were at Ivy's wedding. I was sure it was love at first sight."

Julia scoffed. "Hardly. Mr. Park is a tease and a—"

"A gentleman," Grandmother finished. "After our last land steward died in that tragic horse accident, Mr. Park and Lord Blakely's land steward came to oversee our harvest. Mr. Park should have been spending time with his own family. Instead, he came here to help an old woman."

"He does have a kind air about him." Julia moved from her chair to the edge of the bed and began rubbing Grandmother's legs, attempting to keep up her blood circulation like the doctor had ordered.

Grandmother adjusted her pillow. "He has been that way since he was a boy. He once brought an injured badger to our stables when his own father had told him to get rid of the creature. The young Mr. Park was more worried for the animal than for his own safety."

What was Julia to say? Even if she agreed that Esmond Park was an admirable man, she could not encourage his attentions. She glanced at the swan napkin. Her father was a good man too, but he was protective of those he loved. She couldn't fathom him letting the offspring of his enemy court another daughter.

✿ ✿ ✿

There was a small snowdrift on one side of the road, and the rest seemed only glazed with white. When Julia stepped onto the road, her boot slipped, but she managed to right herself. At first glance, it had seemed quite passable, but now she wondered if she dared risk a walk. One thought of her limited time with Ivy was enough to spur her forward.

It took longer than normal to make it around the bend in the road. She was surprised to see a carriage waiting just after the bridge. She recognized the driver as the same who had taken her home the day before. Her mood brightened.

The carriage door opened, and Esmond stepped down. "I had a feeling you would be coming this way about this time." The corner of his lips twitched.

"Your reasoning is astounding," Julia teased, surprising herself by how familiar she felt with Esmond after their last meeting. Grandmother's words were getting to her.

His eyes seemed to laugh, and he walked closer to her. "I had hoped you would not find me too impertinent. I merely wanted to save you a cold walk if I could."

"I thank you." She stepped toward him, then paused. "Do you think it quite all right for us to ride together? I've not brought a maid, and if my father happens upon us, he would not approve." It was such a short distance that it seemed harmless, but her aunt's lessons of propriety had her second-guessing herself.

Esmond's expression turned mischievous. "Did you not know your sister and my brother courted this way?"

"What do you mean?"

"It started innocently enough. They would meet right at this very spot and go—quite alone—to search for the owner of a missing purse."

Julia raised a brow. "And look what happened to them."

"Exactly." Esmond grinned.

Julia buried her smile and instead folded her arms across her chest. "This isn't a game, Esmond." His flirtations were likely harmless, but he needed to understand that any thought beyond friendship was impossible. "My father wants to return to Peterborough soon. My elder sister is desperately ill. Your mother and my father despise each other. I am not even supposed to be speaking to you."

Esmond's smile slipped. "What good is it if we always despair and worry? I promise I am as concerned as you are. We will figure this out *together*."

Sighing, Julia took a step toward the carriage. "You won't get the wrong idea?"

Esmond raised a brow. "Will you?"

"Never," Julia said, feeling her cheeks burn a little. "But I will thank you for your kindness."

"That I will accept. Come, I have a proposal for a solution to our problems." He helped her inside the carriage and shut the door after climbing in himself.

Julia rubbed her temples. "I could hardly sleep last night thinking about everything."

Esmond's features softened. "Hoping is a far more useful practice than fretting, which is exactly why I came up with an idea and you did not."

A laugh bubbled out of her mouth before she could hold it back. "I daresay you are overconfident."

The carriage lurched forward, and Esmond leaned toward her. "I cannot help wanting to make you smile. You always seem so hesitant, and I find it my duty to encourage it where I can."

"Hesitant to smile?" Julia shook her head. "I smile."

"You wear a practiced smile. The one you just showed me was a real smile. I can easily tell the difference."

Julia pursed her lips, refusing to indulge him. "Perhaps I'm searching for my purpose, my reason to smile." Everyone seemed to have a passion or interest in something, but she just wanted everyone around her to be happy. Fretting over everyone hardly felt like a purpose.

"Then, I shall help you find it," Esmond declared, his determination making her laugh again.

"I think now would be a good time for you to tell me about your brilliant idea."

"It *is* rather brilliant. I'm happy you have faith in me already." She gave him a quelling look, and he chuckled. "I think we ought to get our parents together. In the same room."

"Impossible," Julia argued. "My father is not accepting invitations or making them. He is isolating himself from the entire community."

"What about ferreting him out? Get him on a horse ride, and we will have my mother at the destination."

"It won't work." Julia sighed. "He would simply turn around and flee the scene."

"What if he had to save her life?"

Although amused, she had to shake her head. "Are you planning on pushing her out of a window? Your love for your mother is touching."

"Tempting," Esmond said. "Are you trying to compete with my brilliance? Never mind. As much as I love your idea, I think mine might be less harmful."

"Pray tell," Julia said, folding her arms and staring in expectation.

"Picture a hunt for mistletoe and a broken sleigh. They won't expect it and will be forced to ride home together."

Esmond was a romantic, but his idea did have merit. "You might be onto something," Julia admitted.

"Do you think you could convince your father to take you on an outing?"

"I can try," Julia said.

"Excellent." Esmond grinned. "Your sister tells me your family has a tradition of gathering fresh greenery together every year to decorate the house for the holidays."

"It's true. We take our holiday preparations most seriously. Christmastide has always reminded us of our mother, and we adore every part of it."

"It just so happens that my mother requires greenery for her Christmas ball. Ever since she was a young girl, she's had the same tradition as your family. I can't presume to say she and your father ever gathered greenery together, but it's a connection that will bring us both to the same location. However, since it's bad luck to have the greenery in the house before Christmas Eve, it's a plan that will have to wait until then."

The carriage pulled to a stop. Julia hadn't noticed how near they were to Fairmore, engrossed as she was in Esmond's idea.

He extended his gloved hand to her. "I will make myself scarce. I know how you like your private time with your sister."

She stared at his hand, knowing he meant to help her out but wishing she could stay in the carriage with him just a moment longer. He did such a beautiful job at helping ease her anxieties. As soon as she was with Ivy, Julia knew her frustrations with her situation would return. Even so, she put her hand in his, and he held it for a moment, not moving. She quickly withdrew it, giving him an exasperated look, and helped herself out.

"Good luck." His words weren't even a little apologetic. "I will have the driver return you home when you are ready."

Julia shook her head as they parted ways. Esmond Park was the biggest flirt she had ever met. He acted like he understood their situation, but he persisted in toying with her. She sighed and made her way in to see her sister.

Ivy was in her bed, her face pale, strands of her hair coming out of her long braid. All three girls took after their father's coloring, with red tones in their hair. Julia's was dark auburn, with more brown than her sisters', while Alice's hair was more of a true red, like that of their father. Julia's worry heightened at the sight of Ivy's normally vibrant auburn hair now matted against her pillow.

"Any better today?" Julia asked, although the answer seemed obvious.

Ivy groaned. "When I hold very still, my stomach almost feels settled. But when I move, I am suddenly on a ship, with waves rocking me back and forth, and there is no hope for the contents of my stomach. I haven't kept down any food since yesterday morning."

"Is Lord Blakely concerned?"

"Curtis is doing his level best to stay away from me. He feels ill when he is near me."

Julia covered her mouth so her smile would be hidden. "Did he tell you this?"

Ivy looked at the ceiling in exasperation. "He nearly pushed my face away from the bowl so he could cast up his own breakfast. I've never heard of such a phenomenon."

Julia sat on the edge of Ivy's bed and smoothed the gray knitted blanket that had been spread over the ivory quilt. "You need something to think about—a distraction."

"Please, if you are to dance for me like Alice does when I am sad, I shall never forgive you. The motion will make me sick again."

"You used to laugh at such antics," Julia said, a smile stealing over her lips. "But I have a better idea. Esmond says your family is to go on a hunt for mistletoe. Perhaps an outing and some fresh air would be good for you."

"I wish it were an outing with Papa and my sisters." Ivy's eyes filled with moisture.

Julia couldn't make her any promises yet, but Esmond had given her a glimmer of hope. "I do too."

Ivy sniffed. "I'm consumed with the knowledge that my father will never see my child, never acknowledge him or her as his own grandchild. My heart aches. I thought that when I married, Papa would soften, but he's been impossibly stubborn."

"We came for the wedding," Julia offered. "And he is here for the holidays, even though Aunt Morris vehemently argued against it. It feels like a small step, but it is in the right direction."

"I suppose," Ivy said. "Whatever you do, don't marry Esmond. He is a good man, but I shouldn't think you would want to curse yourself as Curtis and I have done."

"Marry Esmond?" Julia scoffed. "Do not be ridiculous. He teases me, but that is all."

"Have you seen him since you've arrived? Don't even talk to him. It might give him ideas."

Julia looked around the room for something to focus on besides her thoughts of Esmond. She hurried to change the subject. "Your concern should be on your health. Let me worry about Papa and everyone else, and you worry about keeping your food down. Have you tried eating soup? I know it's your favorite."

A whisper of a smile crossed Ivy's face. "Soup always used to remind me of the comforts and smells of home, but now it reminds me of Curtis. He requested Cook make a white-bean soup for dinner, specially for me. Perhaps it will be just the thing."

"I hope it is," Julia said, wishing someone cared as much about her as Curtis did Ivy. "I should dearly like you to be able to search for holly and mistletoe, as I know it's one of your favorite traditions."

For the rest of their visit, she told Ivy about the new story Alice was writing and regaled her with a few tales about their summer that had failed to make it into her letters. Before long, an hour had passed, and Julia bid her sister goodbye.

Her thoughts strayed to Esmond when she stepped outside and saw that, as he had promised, the carriage was ready and waiting. She stared at the mauve upholstered material inside and shook her head, pushing him to a dark corner of her mind, determined to smother the growing feelings curling around her heart.

CHAPTER FOUR

ESMOND LEANED HIS SHOULDER AGAINST the outside of the carriage as Julia approached with her younger sister.

"You again?" Julia gave him a dry look.

"Me again." He tipped his hat, refusing to believe she wasn't happy to see him. "I see I will be delivering two Misses Hunt to Fairmore today. What a pleasure to be in the company of such beautiful ladies."

Julia's younger sister giggled, and Julia gave her sister a stern look. "Do not encourage him, Alice."

Ah, Alice was her name. He had forgotten. Esmond extended his hand to the redhead. "You had better listen to your sister. I can be insufferable at times."

"I am not very good at listening." Miss Alice grinned and accepted his assistance into the carriage. She took a step up and paused. "The wedding was so long ago, I couldn't remember what you looked like. Julia said you were not at all handsome, but I disagree."

Esmond looked over his shoulder at Julia. She ducked her head, and his lips pulled into a half smile. Despite her claim, he had caught her staring at him a time or two. He was not an expert on the feelings of a woman, but he had never felt such a connection and was sure she felt it too. She looked up, her cheeks pink and her gaze soft. Yes, she had lied to her sister through her teeth.

He released Miss Alice's hand as soon as she was safely inside, and she continued. "How would you like to become a character in my next novel?"

"Certainly, if you are true to my nature in your book. Write me as humble, gallant, and, as you said, incomparably handsome."

Julia snickered as she accepted his hand next. She attempted to move forward, but he tugged her back. With Miss Alice in their company, there would not be a private moment between them. He leaned in and murmured, "Are you well?"

Julia's eyes widened. "Yes, I am well."

"You haven't been worrying about everything, have you?"

Julia shook her head. "Not any more than before."

"Good." Satisfied, Esmond helped her the rest of the way into the carriage, then seated himself across from the sisters. He was glad Miss Alice could see Ivy too, but conversation would not be as easy with Julia as it was when she visited alone.

"So you write books?" Esmond asked Miss Alice.

Alice nodded. "It keeps me out of trouble."

Esmond bit down hard on his lip to keep from laughing. "I see. What does your sister here do to keep out of trouble?"

"Oh, Julia never breaks any rules."

Julia folded her arms and gave him a challenging look. "And what about you, Mr. Park? What do you do?"

He loved getting under her skin. "These days I study, but in my free time, I hide in the gazebo for a bit of light reading."

Julia's brows shot up. Clearly, she had not let Miss Alice in on their little secret. He loved having something that was just theirs, even though he hated what the letters represented.

"Julia likes to read too!" Miss Alice said. "Ever since she was a little girl, you could find her curled up and lost in a book."

"Alice, Mr. Park does not need to know about my childhood."

"I bet you were a darling little girl." He knew his flirting was overt, but he could not help himself when in her company. Her quiet and serious nature practically begged for his help.

Julia shook her head, but he knew she was amused. "What were you like as a child?"

"Truthfully," he answered, "I followed my father around everywhere. I wanted to know everything he did. I loved meeting new people in London and wherever we traveled, but I always loved coming home best." There—the smile he had been waiting for. "I sense you liked being at home best too."

Julia lifted a shoulder. "I don't know. I like it here a great deal. It's peaceful and slower-paced. I can see why you would be eager to return."

He almost forgot Miss Alice was in the carriage with them until the conveyance slowed to a stop in front of Fairmore and his focus on Julia broke.

"Well," Esmond said, reaching for the door. "You had better begin your visit right away. My mother had a headache this morning, and I don't think she will be gone long."

He helped the sisters out and watched them walk arm in arm ahead of him. After a moment, Julia looked back at him over her shoulder. She gave him a little smile—a thank-you, no doubt.

That smile did more for him than she likely meant it to. Even though a relationship was forbidden between them, he had never wanted anything more. He had thought himself too young and unsettled at only three and twenty to pursue a woman for more than just a dance or a few house calls, so he was a little out of his realm of expertise, but it didn't take experience for the heart to recognize its match. Reconciling the difficulties of their unique situation was an entirely different matter. Still, it was getting harder to talk himself out of pursuing Julia.

☀ ☀ ☀

Julia stretched out on the bed next to Ivy. Julia and Alice had managed several visits in the past week since their father was neck-deep in an investment scheme with Mr. Harvey. Or, at least, Papa called it that. But he was intrigued enough to forget he was still in Amorwich. Papa was an intelligent man and would make the best decision in the end; Julia was sure of it. But even as she pulled a feather pillow under her head, she felt the clock ticking. It would be so hard to leave for Peterborough when the time came.

"Thank you for coming again, Julia," Ivy said, rolling over to face her. "Even after the snowstorm."

"Alice wanted to come, but Grandmother does better when one of us is there to distract her. Alice volunteered to read her part of the story she wrote."

Ivy frowned. "I am glad Grandmother's needs are being met. I have neglected her these last few months."

Julia was grateful she could help. There was something rewarding about caring for someone who could not do so for themselves.

Ivy strained her neck to see out the window. "I assume the weather was fair for your walk?"

"There is a blanket of clouds in the sky, but the temperature is fair." Julia wanted to tell Ivy of Esmond's efforts to send a carriage every day for her, but she was afraid her sister would read too much into it—especially the part where Esmond usually came along for the ride. Her time with him had become the highlight of her day. Their conversation was always easy, and she had learned so much about him.

She absently picked at a thread in the blanket, and her thoughts returned to her sister. "I remember after Mama died, you let me sleep in your bed with you for weeks."

"I remember it too," Ivy said. "But it was selfish. I didn't want to be alone either."

"Our beds were two feet apart," Julia said with a laugh.

Ivy laughed too. "Yes, but Alice wanted to sleep in your bed, and she kicks in her sleep."

"I miss those days. Hurry and feel better, will you?"

Her sister smiled and closed her eyes. "Lady Blakely says the worst will be over for me in a few weeks." Ivy had always been thin, but her face had a new hollowness to it that Julia didn't like at all.

"I have an idea." She shifted to her knees on the bed. "I am going to prop you up with pillows and fix your hair. It will cheer you; I promise."

Ivy groaned. "Why does it matter?"

"Because taking care of yourself will give you something to feel good about." Julia reached up and began stuffing pillows under Ivy's head. When she finished, she pulled the bell for the maid to assist her. Between the two of them, they curled Ivy's hair and pinned it up in a loose, comfortable chignon.

Julia stepped back to survey her work. "We need to dress you now."

"Oh, good heavens, Julia. I have nowhere to go. What good is this?"

"Come, I haven't much time left." Julia hurried to the closet and picked out a simple white day gown printed with small yellow flowers.

Ivy leaned away from the pillows into a sitting position. "I might forbid you entrance tomorrow," she grumbled.

When the maid stepped forward to take over, Julia quietly slipped from the room. She did not know Fairmore Hall well, as it was a large house, but she did remember seeing Lord Blakely exit a study near the front. As she made her way in that direction, she caught sight of Esmond exiting the library.

"Esmond," Julia called to him.

"Ah, Julia." His eyes twinkled. "How is Ivy today?"

"She is the same." Julia tried not to react at the thrill of seeing him again. "I am in need of a favor. Could you find Lord Blakely? I would like for him to devise a way to get Ivy out of her room today. She is dressing now and could use a change of scenery."

"I am sure Curtis will have an idea."

"Thank you. I must return before Ivy thinks I have left to return home." Julia smiled at Esmond, hoping he knew how much she appreciated him, and hurried back to her sister's bedroom.

"Where were you?" Ivy asked when Julia slipped back into her room. She was dressed now and leaning into her pillows again.

"Do you think I wanted to witness you getting sick because I asked you to get up? No, thank you."

Ivy seemed too tired to laugh. "I'm not sick this moment, but I do feel exhausted. I forgot how long it takes to get dressed."

Julia chuckled softly and came back to sit by her sister. "You look much improved."

"Thank you," Ivy said. "You were right. Other than the exhaustion, I do feel better. Prettier, at least. Perhaps a bit of rouge for my cheeks and Curtis will forget to be ill around me."

"Remember what Mama used to do?"

"Don't you dare pinch my cheeks." Ivy covered her face with her hands.

Julia would have done it to make Ivy laugh, but there was a knock on the door. Curtis stuck his head inside and paused when he saw his wife.

"Ivy . . . you look . . ."

"Improved?" Ivy asked, hope radiating in her voice.

A large smile crossed his face. "Ravishingly beautiful."

"Darling, please. My sister is right here, and she does not know how incorrigible you can be."

Curtis looked at Julia. "You don't mind, do you?"

Julia giggled. "No, not in the least. If Ivy is happy, so am I."

"Excellent, because my brother and I have a proposal."

"Esmond?" Ivy asked.

Curtis opened the door wider and let Esmond inside.

Esmond bowed to Ivy and then to Julia. "Ladies? We would like to treat you both to a sleighride."

Julia grinned as she observed Ivy's astonishment.

"It sounds like the perfect way to ring in the Christmas holiday," Ivy said wistfully. "I'm just not sure I am up for it."

"Allow me," Curtis said, stepping forward. He scooped Ivy into his arms.

"Wait," Esmond said, leaving the room. When he entered again, he carried a bucket. "In case the unfortunate happens."

Ivy moaned. "Your mother would be shocked."

"She would not," Curtis said. "She would be pleased to know you were out of your room. She worries a great deal about you."

"You will all close your eyes if I get sick?" Ivy asked.

Julia noticed the glint of amusement in Esmond's eye. He chuckled and said, "I will close my eyes when you *both* get sick." Curtis gave Esmond a kick as he passed him. Esmond winced, and Julia smothered a laugh. "My brother is most gallant."

With a few arrangements, they were soon piled into the sleigh.

"Don't worry," Esmond said once seated next to Julia. "We will drive to Ravencross and see you home before anyone can worry." He spread a thick blanket over her lap, further reassuring her that she was in good hands. Curtis did the same for Ivy in the seat in front of them.

"He loves her, doesn't he?" Julia whispered to Esmond, her question more one of wonder than uncertainty.

"Very much." Esmond brought his head near hers. "He wasn't the same after our father died. Ivy resurrected his smile. I think we are all smiling less with her down in bed. She is not there to scold us and tell us to do otherwise."

Julia laughed softly. "You are right. She doesn't like anyone to feel downhearted." She was grateful her sister was appreciated by her new family.

Esmond blew out his breath. "I think if my sister were home from her holiday house party, we might have more to think about. Amelia has a way of distracting everyone."

The air nipped at Julia's cheeks as the sleigh continued forward. "I remember her from Ivy's wedding. Are the two of you close?"

Esmond shrugged. "She is the baby of the family, so we all spoil her. None of us feel at all guilty about it either."

"You have a wonderful family, despite what Papa says."

Esmond looked sideways at her and grinned. "Some of us are even quite charming."

Julia's lips couldn't help but mirror his. "Is it your charm that keeps you unattached? You are simply too much for the ladies?"

She felt her cheeks warm at such a bold question. She had grown too comfortable with Esmond. It was so easy to banter with him in conversation.

She glanced at him, but her words did not have the effect she had intended. His smile had fallen and there was a bitterness in his regard. "It is not my surplus of charm but my lack of income." He cleared his throat and turned his face forward.

Regret knotted in her stomach. She had only meant to tease him a little like he always did her. "Forgive me. It was not my place to pry."

His eyes softened, but his smile did not return. "Nonsense. I am a second son, so it is not unexpected that I will have to find a living."

"Do you have something in mind?"

"I am studying to become a barrister."

"Oh, does that interest you?"

Esmond stole a look at her. "No, not really."

"What does interest you?"

Esmond seemed to take in her intense gaze and chuckled. "The land. I think I would make a very happy farmer."

"My grandfather was a farmer, and he did quite well, but I cannot see your mother being pleased by such a career."

"Yes, but your grandfather was a landowner. I remember hearing that he had earnings from a previous career in the navy. I would need someone to invest in me if I don't want to be stuck living the life of a poverty-stricken tenant farmer."

"So you are considering other options, like becoming a barrister," Julia said.

"I have to." Esmond pulled his hat down lower over his brow. "My first objective must be to establish a source of income. When I am not making sure the carriage is being made ready for a certain lovely young lady, I am studying the law. You would not believe how much there is to learn."

Julia had never seen Esmond even remotely unhappy before, but this clearly weighed on him a great deal. "I am sure you could be successful at whatever you put your mind to."

"Your confidence in me means a great deal. Thank you."

The sleigh avoided the road and took the backcountry toward Ravencross. Everything was laced with white powder.

"I had no idea we were so close to such beauty," Julia said. "I used to explore a great deal on my walks, but now my goal is only to be with Ivy."

"Ah," Esmond said. "So that is why your father does not mind when you disappear for hours."

"In Peterborough, my walks were my only freedom."

"You do not get on with your youngest sister?"

"Oh no, my sisters are my dearest friends. We squabble like every family, but I love them both."

"Then, why did you need to escape your home?"

"I know you are thinking it's because of my father, but he is very good to us. It's hard to explain."

"You don't have to tell me if it makes you uncomfortable."

Julia rubbed her gloved hands together in an attempt to warm them. "Have you ever felt like you have to be a certain way to please someone?"

Esmond scrunched his brows together like he was pondering her question. "I suppose. When my father died, I wanted to be cheerful and helpful to keep up my family's morale. It was exhausting."

"I know what you mean."

Esmond met her gaze, a breeze lifting tufts of his hair beneath his hat. "Do you feel that way at home?"

"Every day. My aunt expects so much from all of us. Forgive me—she means well."

"I understand. Most parents are likely the same way . . . loving but pushy."

Julia nodded. "Sometimes I think my walks are so I might discover myself again."

"To find that purpose you said you're searching for?" Esmond asked.

"Yes." Julia pulled the blanket tighter around her legs. "And I can imagine what I would say if I could express my own opinions without censure."

"You seem to speak freely here. Does this mean you like being in Amorwich?"

"Oh yes." Julia took in the snow-covered branches around them. "I like it very much—especially from the view of a sleigh."

Esmond grinned. "I had hoped you would." His grin froze and he squinted at something in the distance. "Does that man seem familiar to you?"

Julia turned to follow his line of vision. Her hands shook, and she clenched them together beneath the blanket. "I think it's my father."

Esmond leaned forward to catch Curtis's attention. "Does that look like Mr. Hunt?"

Curtis said something Julia did not hear, and the sleigh took a hard turn to the left, away from Ravencross.

"Sink low in your seat," Esmond said. "He shouldn't see you, but I do not want to cause any trouble for you or Ivy if he does."

Julia's heart thudded, and she obeyed him. "I should have been more careful."

Esmond kept his head facing her father. "He is riding along the property line. I do not think he suspects us." Then he raised his voice over the seat. "Curtis, drive toward the road."

After a few minutes, Esmond turned to Julia. "You can sit up now. He is out of view."

Julia obeyed, her heart rate gradually regulating while feelings of guilt and fear remained. "That was far too close. Papa would have been so angry with me!"

Esmond reached over, but she was disappointed when he fell short of taking her hand. "We would not have abandoned you to his wrath. I just wish we could have avoided the scare." He motioned to the bench in front of them. "I don't know how my brother stands the constant fear of confrontation. It must be so hard for him."

Julia mumbled an agreement.

Every time she felt herself being pulled closer to Esmond, reality reminded her of how impossible such a connection was. They both wanted to help end the feud, but it was growing harder for her to be with Esmond and keep other ideas from sneaking into her heart.

CHAPTER FIVE

THAT EVENING AT DINNER, ESMOND sat angled from his mother, who sat at the head of the table. He left a chair between him and Curtis, where Ivy normally sat.

"I do wish Ivy could make it down to eat with us," Mother said, pushing back a long black ringlet by her face as she bent over for a bite.

Curtis sighed. "Remind me: How long does it take to grow a child again? How did you ever do this three times?"

"I did it five times," his mother answered, her tone somber. "Life is unpredictable, which is why I am so terribly upset about her disagreeable father."

Esmond knew about his mother's tragic early losses, but the mention of Mr. Hunt made him choke on his bite of roll. He coughed a few times and took a long swig from his glass. Dare he push the topic? This was a rare opportunity to open a dialogue, so perhaps he should not waste it. "Do you think Mr. Hunt is aware of his future grandchild?" He was curious of the answer, but more so, he knew the two families couldn't keep going on as they had. A discussion would be the first step to change.

His mother looked up from her plate. "I know he is in town after ignoring his daughter for an entire year. I am not as ignorant as you think. I also know Ivy's sister has been to the house several times in the last two weeks."

Esmond sat back in surprise.

"Even now," his mother continued, "with Mr. Hunt staying at Ravencross with his mother, our *neighbor*, he still refuses to visit Ivy. I, for one, cannot stomach such utter rudeness. Why, it's shameful, that's what it is. He might not care to see me, but his daughter deserves better."

Curtis folded his arms. "Since all is out in the open now, I am not sure Miss Julia has told her father about the baby . . . or Ivy's current state of health."

Surprise caused his mother to inhale sharply. "Why ever not?"

Esmond knew why. "Miss Hunt is a peacemaker and is playing a precarious role coming here at all. She hasn't been granted permission to visit Ivy, and speaking to her father would jeopardize all opportunity to do so."

"I see." His mother pushed back her plate.

A daring thought crossed Esmond's mind—one that might open conversation between their families. "Someone ought to tell him about the baby."

Anger flared in Curtis's eyes. "If you think a blow to the face an appropriate greeting, then by all means, I volunteer."

Esmond thrummed his fingers on the table. "Maybe I should be the one to tell him. He doesn't hate me yet."

"Nonsense," his mother said, huffing. "I will tell him."

"No," Curtis and Esmond said at the same time. Esmond wanted the two to meet again, but not with his mother acting like a riled and protective bear. No reconciliation would come from pointing the finger of blame.

"I think it would be best coming from me," she insisted.

"Mother," Esmond began, regretting bringing it up. "A letter from Curtis would suffice."

"I have made my decision," she said. "I will go directly."

Esmond's mouth dropped. "It's nearly eight. Tomorrow would suit better."

"Or never," his brother mumbled as he went back to eating.

Mother shook her head. "I wouldn't want to forget the perfect jab I just crafted in my head." She stood and moved to the door, stuck her head out, and said to a footman, "Have a carriage prepared and send for my cloak and hat. I am going out."

"I'm coming with you." Curtis dropped his napkin onto the table and stood.

Esmond stood too and shoved Curtis back into his seat. "You are under enough stress as it is. Ivy needs a relationship with her father, not a greater rift. You are liable to say or do something you will regret. I will do my best to keep Mother above reproach."

"I am going alone," Mother insisted. "Don't try to follow me. It's been more than twenty-five years since I've spoken to Mr. Hunt, and I don't want him to think I'm hiding behind my grown sons."

"Be reasonable, Mother," Curtis said. "I have seen the man angry but once, and it's seared into my mind. He is not one to be crossed."

Mother's eyes narrowed, and she lifted her chin. "I have tiptoed around the Hunt family long enough. Ivy is my daughter now too, and I will not let her suffer for a moment longer. I was reminded tonight what it was like to be in her condition. She needs us to rally around her. Go be with her, Curtis dear. I shall see to this on my own."

Esmond stepped forward.

Mother raised her hand to stop him, her posture resolute. "If I am not back within the hour, you may come, but not a moment sooner."

Rooted in position, helpless to do more, Esmond watched his mother leave the room with more determination than he had ever seen in her. So much for the plans he and Julia had made for their parents to meet in an unobtrusive setting. He rubbed the tension from his neck. He hoped Julia would forgive him.

"What have we done?" Curtis asked, staring at the open door.

Esmond swallowed hard. "We've sent a tornado to put out a wildfire."

⚘ ⚘ ⚘

"Mr. Harvey was about to kiss the frightened Lady Helena," Alice read to Julia and their father in her best voice, "but in his eagerness to reach her, he tripped over his cane. His body fell hard, his face crashing through the wall, rendering him dead on the spot. Lady Helena was finally safe. They say that when they removed his body, his head had gone through a painting of a dog on the other side, adding an interesting appeal to an otherwise boring rendition. Alas, the Bow Street runner would not let them keep Mr. Harvey's body in the wall even for the sake of art. The end." Alice swooped into a deep curtsy.

Julia giggled. "I hope the real Mr. Harvey never *stumbles* upon your story."

"You told me to write a comedy and so I did." Alice shrugged and took a seat beside her.

Their father chuckled too. "I don't know where these strange stories come from, Alice, but they are better than the theater."

"Really?" Alice leaned toward him. "If Aunt Morris ever deems me worthy of London, then I shall see for myself."

Papa pulled a book off an end table and flipped it open. "You must trust your aunt. She knows more about this sort of thing than I do. Julia, see what is keeping dinner."

Julia stood from where she'd been curled up on the sofa. "They are likely bringing Grandmother her dinner first, but I shall check." She stepped into the corridor the same time the butler opened the front door not ten feet away. Julia gasped. She ducked back inside the drawing room with the door parted enough for her to hear.

"I should like a private audience with Mr. Hunt," Lady Blakely said.

"What is it, Julia?" her father asked.

Julia's eyes darted between him and Alice, her words lodged in her throat, as she stepped toward them.

The drawing room door opened behind her, and their butler entered. "Lady Blakely to see you, sir."

One side of the book slipped from her father's hands. Julia caught a slight tremble in his movements as he closed the book and set it back on the end table. When he looked up, his eyes were hard.

Barnes cleared his throat. "She is requesting a private audience. Said it is of utmost importance."

"Ivy!" Julia put her hand to her throat. "It must be Ivy."

"Julia, Alice, to your rooms," Papa barked.

Alice jumped to her feet and hurried to Julia. The two of them scurried from the room but stopped short in front of Lady Blakely in the vestibule. Julia had not seen her since the wedding, and she had forgotten how beautiful and regal she was. Her dark hair and high cheekbones were complemented by her fine green evening gown. Julia curtsied, followed by Alice. Without a single word passing between the three of them, Julia pulled Alice away.

When they reached the top of the staircase and rounded the corner, Julia froze.

"What is it?" Alice said quietly.

"I have to know what they say to each other," Julia whispered. The irrational but forceful idea surprised her.

"Papa would be livid." Alice cringed and shook her head. "You have grown too brave since your visits to Ivy."

"Wait for me. I shan't be long."

"Julia! This is not the sort of thing an intelligent girl does. This is the sort of thing an impulsive, thoughtless girl does—like me. Please think this through."

"I'll be gone but a moment." Julia turned and hurried back down the stairs. Barnes lowered his head, pretending not to see her, and stepped away from the front door to give her privacy. She would have to thank him later. The drawing room door was cracked open, and she stepped closer to it, pressing herself against the wall and peering carefully inside. Lady Blakely and her father stood facing each other, several feet apart.

"I know I am the last person you expected to see tonight. I can scarcely believe I am here myself."

"Then, why *are* you here?"

"A family matter," Lady Blakely said. "I thought you ought to know that Ivy is expecting."

Silence.

"Don't you have anything to say about this?"

Papa cleared his throat. "I assume she will have the best care."

"Certainly. When shall we expect your visit?"

Papa's laugh of derision caused Julia to step away from the door, her heart racing. "You don't belong here." His voice was low and gruff. "You've said what you wanted to say, and now you may leave."

Julia knew she should run back to her room, but her feet were frozen to the floor.

"Your temper has not improved, nor your manners." There was a moment's hesitation before she said, "I haven't finished saying what I came to say."

"Save your lecture for your children. I don't have time for this."

"You were only ever interested in what benefited you." Lady Blakely's voice started even, but it began to rise with each word. "I thought a grandchild would be significant enough, but forgive me, why would your own flesh and blood matter? Love was never your strong suit."

Julia flung a hand over her mouth.

"What?" Papa folded his arms. "I can't imagine a more cold, loveless house than the one Ivy is in now. If anything goes amiss with my Ivy, it shall fall on your shoulders. Blast, woman! Are you going to leave, or do I need to pick you up and carry you to the door?"

Hot tears stung Julia's eyes. She hurt for her father and yet feared his words were creating deeper roots of hatred. Her feet finally stumbled away from the door toward the stairs. There was never going to be a reconciliation between the families. Never.

Once upstairs, she turned the corner and slumped against the wall. The coffin on Papa and Lady Blakely's past seemed to shut with the thud of the front door. When the drawing room door slammed moments later, it was like a mound of dirt covering up their history as if it had never existed. Her dear sister seemed further from her than ever.

She pressed her eyes closed, and there was Esmond. The image of his smile calmed her and yet made her ache with a longing she had never experienced before. Without her permission he had become her new dream, but how could such a dream come to fruition when it was choked by their own families?

CHAPTER SIX

ESMOND DRUMMED HIS FINGERS ON the arm of his chair while Curtis paced before the fireplace, a steady flame licking the back of the grate.

"I can't wait another minute," Esmond said. "My horse should be saddled by now. I'm leaving."

Curtis crossed to the window and pushed the drape back. "Wait. Mother's back."

Esmond shot to his feet, and he and Curtis hurried from the room. Murray opened the door, and the brothers darted into the dark, cold evening. A footman was already helping their mother down from the carriage, but Esmond and Curtis quickly flanked her sides.

Tears pooled in her eyes.

"What happened?" Esmond demanded.

Curtis growled, "Will it be pistols, swords, or fisticuffs?"

"Boys, stop this!" Lady Blakely took a deep breath and hurried toward the house. "He is a horrible man, and our Ivy is better off without him. There will not be a duel, because we will have no reason to ever see that wretched man again."

A punch to his gut could not have affected Esmond more. This was it, then. All his hopes for a match with Julia gone with a single blunder on his part. He never should have pushed a conversation about Mr. Hunt. He should have waited to set them up in a carefree search for mistletoe.

Mother insisted she was well but excused herself to go to bed. Esmond kissed her on the cheek, his heart contrite. Curtis disappeared to be with Ivy, leaving Esmond to take up his brother's position in front of the fire, pacing.

Part of him wanted to rescue Julia from a man such as Mr. Hunt. However, he couldn't bring himself to hate the man, not after the way he had poured his heart into those letters. There was a reason behind Mr. Hunt's anger, and it was because of Esmond's mother.

He knew what needed to happen. Mother needed to read the letters. Tomorrow, when Julia came to see Ivy, he would tell her it was time to deliver the letters to their rightful owners. It was the only thing left to do.

※ ※ ※

Julia quickly dressed in heavy layers for her walk to see Ivy, worried Papa would stop her but determined to visit her sister, despite that she'd woken with a sore throat. She and Alice had talked the night before and decided this visit could very well be Julia's last before they were whisked back to Peterborough. Alice had dearly wanted to come, but after Father's talk with Lady Blakely, she feared her ability to attract trouble would curse their efforts, so instead she had stayed up late to finish her comedy and had slipped it under her sister's door sometime before Julia woke in the morning. With a heavy heart, Julia now packed the story into a basket.

When no one impeded her progress, she stopped in the breakfast room, which was blessedly empty, and surveyed her food choices. She stared at the muffins, heavy with dates, and frowned, her throat protesting the offerings. She could not bring herself to eat them. She slipped out of the room and made her way to the vestibule. Barnes opened the front door in time for Julia to see her father riding up in the distance. Gulping, she turned to the butler.

He closed the door, shutting Julia back inside. "The servants' entrance might be safer for you, miss."

"I think you're right. You have been so good to look out for me."

"I've worked here for thirty years," Barnes said, lowering his voice. "Not always as a butler, mind you. But I know a thing or two about the history between Mr. Hunt and Lady Blakely."

Julia drew in her breath. "You know, then, that they were—"

"Once smitten, bound to be married?"

Bound to be married? "What happened?" she asked. "I have been trying to piece it together, but there is so much I am left to guess at."

"I wish I could tell you, miss. But, like you, I can only hope things will work out for the best."

Before last night, she had harbored the same hope. Now she expected Papa to say they were leaving the town of Amorwich at any moment. She gave Barnes a sympathetic smile. "Can you show me to the servants' entrance?" Julia needed to hurry if she was going to get a chance to say goodbye to Ivy.

Just beyond the kitchen was her freedom. She thanked Barnes and hurried around the back of Ravencross toward the road. Her head whipped in every direction until she was out of sight. She half-slid, half-ran to the bridge.

No carriage.

It was a sign. Did Esmond know about Lady Blakely's trip to Ravencross the night before? Had his mother's distress upset him enough for him to forget Julia? Sighing, she pushed forward. What else could Esmond have done? He needed to support his mother, not worry about Julia. Disheartened, and now a bit hungry, she was tempted to have a good cry. Then it dawned on her. She was out walking earlier than normal. She shook her head. Her silly thoughts were distracting her from her true purpose, which was spending one last visit with Ivy. It was for the best that Esmond hadn't come yet—then there would be no awkward goodbye with him. The thought made her stomach tighten. Could she really leave without seeing him again? Her eyes began to water.

She turned at the fork in the road toward Fairmore. After a few paces, she saw a carriage coming toward her. Against the white, bleak winter backdrop, the arrival of the stark black conveyance breathed hope into her. A small laugh escaped at the same time as an errant tear. The carriage was a small gesture in the grand scheme of things—unexpected, unrequired—but, oh, how the simple service warmed her heart. She brushed her tears away and stepped aside as the carriage closed the distance between them and pulled to a stop.

The door opened, and Esmond stuck out his head. "It's freezing outside. Hurry." He stepped down and practically scooped her into the carriage, saving her from the bite of the wind on her cheeks. Once seated, Esmond covered her lap with a blanket.

"How did you know to come early?" Julia asked. She wanted to memorize his features—the dimples on his cheeks that only appeared when he smiled, the way his hair waved in front in a swoop off his forehead. But would she remember the different shades of brown the light brought out in his eyes?

"I decided I would wait here all morning for you." Esmond gave her a lopsided grin.

Julia shook her head, trying to hide the sheen of moisture in her eyes. "You've been too kind."

His face fell. "Perhaps my eagerness to please you has caused me to overstep."

Was this where he told her that she had imagined more to his generosity than he'd meant to imply? Esmond moved to sit next to her, his hip and leg pressed close to her own, but he did not grab her hand or even look at her. His expression was somber. "It was my fault my mother came to your father last night. I thought I could rush their reconciliation. When I brought up how Ivy deserved to see her family, I hadn't the faintest inkling my mother would volunteer to be the voice of reason." Esmond sighed. "She ruined our carefully laid plans, and I am completely to blame."

It took a moment for Julia to realize he was apologizing, not telling her he didn't want to see her again. With this realization, she could breathe easier. As much turmoil as she was in about their families, she was not ready to hear Esmond tell her of his disinterest in her.

She met his gaze. "Our plan was made with the best of intentions, but we cannot force them to forgive each other." She hated telling him the rest, but she didn't want to simply disappear, never to see him again. "And I can't force my father to stay here. I have every reason to believe he will want to take us back to Peterborough as soon as tomorrow."

Esmond sputtered. "What about your grandmother?"

"He has already suggested a companion care for her during our absence." She wanted to be the one to do it, but right now keeping the peace seemed far more important than making demands.

"You must beg him to stay." Esmond's desperation filled her with hope for something she had begun to crave between them.

But it didn't matter. It was too late.

"Esmond, I overheard them talking last night. There is no chance he will listen to me."

"Not even for a harmless trip to the woods to search for holly or mistletoe to cheer up your grandmother?" His eyes begged her to consider.

"I have deceived my father enough by coming here," Julia argued. "My relationship with him is important."

"What is deception when you have his best interests in mind?" Esmond's ambitious expression melted into one of resignation. "I don't want to be like your aunt and tell you what to do. This must be your own decision."

Julia pushed her head back against the soft upholstered seat. "I simply want everyone to be happy, especially at Christmas." She had desires for herself too, but she could never please just herself at the expense of her family.

"I understand." Esmond turned to look out the window. "It is your nature to feel this way. Curtis says Ivy is always happier after you leave. I know I am happier after I see you." She stilled at his words. Did she really make him happy? Esmond turned back to face her, his smile sad. "I want the same for those I love. Which is why I have come to a decision. I was up half the night, but no matter how much I deliberated, the answer is the same. I must give my mother the letters."

Julia exhaled slowly. She knew this must happen eventually. "Are you sure the time is right?"

Esmond ran his hands down his thighs. "The truth might not bring immediate happiness, but it can bring peace."

"Peace?" Julia nodded. "After the tempest our families have been caught in, that ought to count for something."

"Yes," Esmond agreed. "But before we can enjoy the calm after a storm, we might have to stir up one last lightning show."

Julia shivered at the thought. "I don't like the sound of that. We are causing a great deal of trouble, aren't we? Are you sure we shouldn't just put the letters back and let her find them naturally? What if the past is better left alone?" She stared at the floor of the carriage, wondering how best to handle everything.

"It's an opportunity to heal, and that is what we are offering . . . no more, no less. It will be up to my mother if she wishes to address the issue with your father."

Julia glanced up and found Esmond staring intently at her. Their connection seemed to soften Esmond's features, and he reached over and brushed his thumb against her cheek. "I can't stop thinking about you."

Warmth shivered down her back and arms. She shook her head slowly, reminding herself it couldn't work. "I'm leaving, remember?"

"Not if I can help it." His mouth screwed tight.

Whether he cared enough for her or was motivated to help Ivy, the result would be the same. Pitting Esmond's will against Papa's would serve no good in the end. The thought of pushing him away when she wanted to please him now more than anyone hurt, but doing so would prevent more heartache in the long run.

"Some people simply cannot get along." She willed him to understand. "Your optimism does you credit. It'll serve you well in your future. I imagine you'll find a career you love working the land, and you'll have a home to support your wife and children. I will hear all about it from Ivy, and I will be so proud of you."

Esmond drew back in his seat to look at her, his expression strained. "Don't give up on us yet, Julia. Don't even think it. While you talk to Ivy, I will give the letters to my mother."

Don't give up on us. The words made her heart ache. He did care for her, or perhaps she was beginning to wish for it so greatly that she imagined more depth of his feelings than was truly there.

"Very well." Julia ducked her head, her cheeks warm. "I wish you luck."

"I will have the carriage ready for your ride back. I might not be finished speaking to Mother by the time you leave." Esmond slid ever closer to her, and his hand gently turned her cheek so she faced him. "Tell me this is not goodbye."

"I . . . I don't know."

Esmond's look intensified, his eyes imploring hers.

She wanted to just tell him what he wanted to hear, even if she could not make it true, for staying was what she wanted too—with all her heart. But she couldn't promise what she could not control. "We shall have to wait and see." It was the best she could offer either of them.

CHAPTER SEVEN

Ivy was dressed, with her hair fixed, and sitting in bed when Julia came in.

"You look well," Julia said, shutting the door behind her. "Are you feeling better?"

"I kept dinner down last night and slept deeply. This morning I had more energy than I've had in months. I admit I am feeling exhausted after dressing again, but I think I might venture downstairs today."

The news was a great relief, but Julia's smile was tight. While Ivy felt better, Julia did not. Her throat burned, and her body ached. Was her worry making her sick?

"Your scar by your eye pulls upward when you are upset," Ivy said. "What is it? Did something happen with Esmond?"

"Ivy," Julia began, ignoring the insinuation. "There is something I need to tell you."

"You and Esmond are engaged?!" Ivy jumped off the bed, only to sway and lean back against it. She put her hand to her head and moaned. "Fear not. I simply need a moment."

"Stay still, you goose!" Julia waited as Ivy blinked a few times and smiled.

"You forget I am the older sister," Ivy reminded her. "And I command you to tell me every detail."

"I am not engaged," Julia's tone came out more annoyed than she'd intended. "I daresay there has been no reason for you to form such a conclusion."

"How can you say that? Remember, I was in the sleigh with both of you, and I saw how easy you were in each other's company. Despite my warning, which I have not relinquished, I must admit you'd make a fine couple. And while you might not have come to that conclusion, Esmond certainly has. Curtis told me his brother sends the carriage for you every day to bring you here. If that is not a romantic gesture, what is it?"

"Kindness?" Julia offered. Then she shrugged. "Oh, I don't know. He is very good to me, and I cannot deny he makes me wish for something between us. However, he has been most clear about his situation. He requires a position before he can afford to marry. Besides, Papa would be adamantly against it, as we both know." That was an understatement, but Julia needed to explain the circumstances first.

Ivy sighed. "You are right on both counts. My marriage was a Christmas miracle. Perhaps we should start praying for one for you. Or should we pray that you both forget all about each other? I am torn and know whatever you choose will be a difficult path to follow."

How could Ivy tease her about Esmond, then warn her about him in the next breath?

The bed dipped as Julia sat down next to Ivy. "There is a far more serious matter at hand, and I must tell you about it before I depart." She took a deep breath and began. "I found some letters addressed to your mother-in-law. They were old and still sealed. Esmond did not want to worry his mother . . . so we read them."

Ivy gasped. "Julia! This is not like you to be so . . ."

"Troublesome?"

"Yes. This is something Alice might do, but not you!"

"Ivy, they were love letters from Papa. He wanted to marry Lady Blakely."

Ivy's eyes widened, but she sat silently until Julia finished telling her about the surprise visit the night before.

Ivy's mouth formed a firm line. "It was not right for you two to meddle. This is not a romantic play in which everyone will end up happy, no matter how we wish it were. Trust me, I know."

"You are right, of course." Julia sighed, muffling her urge to cough. There was no reason to make Ivy worry about her too. "It's simply been awful watching this wall go up between you and Papa."

Ivy stared at the ceiling. "It hurts having Papa silent in my life, but I could never be happy thinking of you jeopardizing your relationship with him too. It's why I advised you against forming an attachment to Esmond." She faced Julia once more. "Thank you for telling me about the letters. It helps to know why Papa despises the family so."

"There's more," Julia said hesitantly. "Esmond is giving the letters to Lady Blakely as we speak."

Ivy shook her head. "You should have given them to her right away. I know you want to protect everyone from getting hurt, but sometimes being hurt is the only way to heal."

"You are making me quite ashamed of myself." Julia dropped her gaze to her lap. "Aunt Morris would be mortified. Perhaps I need more of her guidance than I thought. I never should have touched the letters, let alone read them, but it made sense in the moment. Esmond and I were motivated by our desire to unite our families. Is that wrong?"

"Oh dear. You love him, don't you?"

Julia's solemn expression cracked. "Love him?"

"I can see it in your eyes and hear it in your words."

"Maybe. No." A self-deprecating laugh tumbled out of her mouth. "Yes, I suppose I do."

"Oh, Sister."

Julia covered her eyes with her hands. "I don't think I have admitted it to myself until this moment. What if he does not intend to ask for me? He is a terrible flirt."

"Stuff and nonsense. He is a good man—as kind and sincere as they come. Curtis has never seen him pursue a woman as he has you this past month. He told me so just yesterday."

Julia looked at Ivy between her fingers. "It does not make me feel at all better knowing you and your husband have discussed this. What am I going to do?"

Ivy pulled Julia's hands down. Her smile lessened the paleness of her features. "Do nothing yet. Just enjoy the feeling. We will know soon enough how Lady Blakely reacts to the letters."

Julia groaned. "Even if the letters manage to fix this impossible feud, they cannot put Esmond in a position to marry any sooner."

Ivy squeezed Julia's hand. "You always worry more than your share. Bide your time, and for heaven's sake, have a little faith."

Julia bit her lip. "Is it too much to believe that our whole family could be together for the holiday?"

"I've been hoping for the same thing." Ivy pulled her feet up onto the bed and leaned back against her pillows. "I fear this conversation has worn me to shreds."

"It's time for me to return anyway," Julia said.

"Until tomorrow, then?" Ivy yawned and burrowed under her quilt.

Julia's shoulders fell. She didn't want to upset Ivy, but it was inevitable. "I might not be able to come tomorrow."

Ivy's brows drew together. "Why not?"

"I don't think you realize how eager Papa is to leave." Julia fingered the quilt.

Ivy's eyes filled with frustrated tears. "I must have been in denial. I've come to depend upon your visits."

Julia moved to embrace her sister. "I will be anxious for news of the baby."

Ivy squeezed Julia tightly. "I will be anxious to tell you." When Ivy pulled back, her frown deepened. "Oh, Julia, poor Esmond."

Tears swam in Julia's eyes now, blurring her vision. She could tell Ivy wanted to assure her that all would be well, and Julia wanted to say the same to Ivy, but they were both anxious for their futures. Sometimes, no matter the efforts made to the contrary, a person's path was chosen for them.

CHAPTER EIGHT

ESMOND STOOD OUTSIDE HIS MOTHER's door, pacing. He'd given her the letters, explained where he had found them, and with panic in her eyes, she'd sent him from the room. He pushed his hand through his hair and sighed for the tenth time. Had an hour passed? This was madness. He needed this to work. It had mostly been about Curtis and Ivy before, but now all he could think about was what this meant for Julia. And she could not even commit to seeing him again. Would she ask her father to take her to the woods to search for Christmas greenery?

What Esmond wouldn't do to find some mistletoe himself. He knew just where he would hang it. During the Christmas ball, he would sneak Julia away and . . . and what? Kiss her? Without any promise of a future together? He blinked a few times, clearing the all-too-tempting image from his mind. Why had he not spent more time dedicating himself to his studies so he had a stable future to offer her? More than one door was metaphorically shut to him.

He leaned against the wall opposite the door. One thing at a time. The letters needed to be dealt with first.

With a creak and a rush of air, the door he faced suddenly opened. His mother stood on the other side, her eyes red and puffy.

"Mother?"

She held a handkerchief to her nose. "Did you read these?"

He clasped his hands together, his posture guilty but resolute. "Yes."

"All of them?"

"Yes."

Her brow furrowed, turning her petite features into a fierce scowl. "If you think you are getting an explanation, you are wrong. I owe you nothing."

He stalled for a moment, then blurted, "Of course not."

Before he could say another word, the door shut in his face. He stood there in shock, needing a moment before he could drag himself away. Whether his mother was embarrassed or angry or both, he had nothing concrete to tell Julia. Well, he did have one thing to say, as much as he might regret it. The thought urged him with purpose toward the front door, as he hoped to catch Julia before she left.

A footman opened the door just as he reached for the handle. The man dipped his head. "If you are looking for Miss Hunt, you might still catch her."

Esmond could see the carriage just over the man's head. *Blast!* He pushed past the footman and darted down the path, just as the carriage started rolling forward.

"Wait!" he called to the driver, but there was no response. He reached the carriage and smacked his hand against the side, finally catching the driver's attention. "Hold up a moment."

The driver pulled back on the reins, and the black conveyance slowed to a stop.

Julia stuck her head out the window. "Esmond?"

He took a second to catch his breath. "My mother read the letters. She won't speak to me about them." Julia stared down at him, concern written across her face. "Julia, we must try one more time to get them to make peace before your father takes you all home."

"What if it only makes things worse? We would be responsible."

"Julia, I beg you to consider it. Tomorrow is Christmas Eve, and I have already convinced my mother to search for fresh greenery at ten in the morning. We will go just after breakfast to the pine grove that borders both our properties. Do you remember it from our sleighride?" When she nodded, he continued. "If there is any way to convince your father, you must bring him there."

Julia put her hand on the windowsill. "I will try. I promise."

He reached up and put his hand on top of hers, wishing he could offer for her then and there, but he was not at liberty to do so. There was so much to overcome before he could declare his feelings.

"Goodbye," she said, her features laced with discouragement.

"Goodbye," he repeated. He ached to see her on the verge of tears. With a wave of his hand, the carriage tugged back into motion. Esmond bounced his fist against his sides. He hated this powerless feeling. Here he was, stuck watching the back of a carriage while the girl he loved rode out of his life. He *loved* her. The realization of such a feeling should have filled him with euphoria. Instead, his heart sank in his chest.

❁ ❁ ❁

Julia made her way from the bridge back to Ravencross with careful, deliberate steps across the icy patches. She had to hurry, despite the pull she felt in the opposite direction. Admitting she loved Esmond, as much to herself as to Ivy, was like setting her heart on paper and hiding it in a box much like her father had. It was useless. No one could see evidence of it, and no one besides Ivy could know. Under such uncertain circumstances, she could not even tell the one person who truly mattered. Her throat constricted with emotion, causing her to fall into a coughing spell.

She finally managed to gain control of her breathing again as she climbed the stone steps to Ravencross. The front door flung open before she reached it. Julia's breath caught as she stared at the woman in the doorway, framed like a great portrait. Her medium brown hair was piled high on her head with an elaborate bow, as if she were much younger than she was, and in her hands she held a small white Pomeranian puppy. Beyond her opulent dress and style, which clashed with the rustic country setting, it was her commanding stance and disapproving frown that caused Julia to miss her step on the last stair.

Aunt Morris had come to Ravencross.

"Julia, darling, where have you been?"

"How do you do, Aunt Morris?" Julia steadied herself and curtsied to her, which seemed a strange way to greet her closest relative after nearly a month apart. Aunt Morris insisted on the precise social protocol for every situation. Although, on closer inspection, Julia could see a faint hint of rouge on Aunt Morris's cheeks, which Aunt would never admit to. And Julia would never be permitted to wear such a low neckline without a fichu, had she ever wanted to, where Aunt seemed perfectly comfortable to set a different set of standards for herself.

"Hurry inside before you catch your death. Amorwich is a forsaken little hole in the middle of England, and it's shocking to have my relations visiting here. I can see why my sister, God rest her soul, chose to stay in Peterborough instead."

Julia walked past her and inside the house. She had not finished untying her bonnet before her aunt demanded again where she had been. Julia sighed. "You know I am fond of long walks."

"It's the weather that has me upended, Julia. Where is your common sense? Come, your papa is in the drawing room with Alice, and we've been waiting for your return."

Julia wanted to ask why Aunt was there at all, but such a question would be deemed impertinent. She followed Aunt into the drawing room and found Papa standing by the window.

"Where did Alice go?" Aunt's voice went up a notch like it always did when she was annoyed.

"What?" Papa asked. "Oh, I did not even notice her leave the room."

Julia crossed her fingers behind her back. Alice couldn't get herself into trouble so soon again in Aunt's company. All the sisters avoided Aunt in their own way, but Alice was less tactful, which usually led to a greater number of punishments.

"Jonathan, what has you so distracted this morning? I came all this way, and no one seems very happy to see me."

"Sorry, Fanny," Papa said, his attitude somber. He motioned for her to sit down. "We are indeed happy to see you."

"It is a good thing I came," Aunt Morris said with such firmness that even her puppy knew not to squirm on her lap. "No one here seems to be able to take care of themselves without my help."

Papa had more patience than a saint when around Aunt Morris. The fact that she could even keep him in line—temper and all—actually made the woman's imperfections easier to bear. Papa crossed to Aunt's side and sat beside her, while Julia sat opposite them. "I wish you would have written. I was hoping to have our trunks packed so we might return tomorrow, weather permitting."

Even though it was an expected announcement, Julia's shoulders slumped with disappointment.

Aunt's pout pulled into a pleased smile. "That is exactly what I hoped too. My goal is to help arrange care for your dear mother and bring this family back home for the holiday celebrations. I have planned engagements for us all the way up until Twelfth Night."

Julia's knee started to bounce. She could feel Esmond's words urging her to interrupt. Convincing Papa to participate in an outing seemed even more unlikely with Aunt's presence.

Papa put his hands up and rested them on the back of his head. "I already sent inquiries out about a companion last week and have had a few responses. The staff here does well enough, but my mother's condition requires constant attention. I am to interview a candidate in an hour or so. We should know soon enough."

"Good. I cannot imagine staying here as long as you have. You must be eager to return home."

Papa did not respond. Julia searched his features for clues to his feelings. His depressed posture could mean so many things. She ached to cheer him and fix everything.

"Julia, when we return, there will be no more of this walking business." Aunt Morris's eyes widened to emphasize her words, and her lips pulled tight, making her expression an almost perfect match with her dog's. "I have put up with it long enough."

Julia's knee froze, and a sickening sensation formed in her stomach. "Yes, Aunt."

"Really, Fanny," Papa said. "They are harmless enough."

"How long was she gone this morning? Hours, no doubt, and in these wretched temperatures."

"Julia has a strong constitution. Even after hours in the cold, she always comes back revived in spirit. She has an adventurous nature. I really had no idea until we came here."

Twisting her hands in her skirts, Julia could barely refrain from admitting the truth about her walks, but if she opened her mouth, she would surely cough again, which would fuel Aunt's argument.

"It isn't seemly for a young lady to be out of doors in the winter. You are not raising three boys, Jonathan. How many times have I urged you to let me advise you in all things right and proper for young ladies?"

Julia's cough finally escaped, but she muffled it in her sleeve while the others spoke. Now that her throat was free, she could bring herself to speak. "Papa, Grandmother ought not be left without family for the holidays. She's already suffering from melancholy." Caring for Grandmother and Ivy had made Julia feel truly useful. It gave her purpose she'd not had before. In that moment, she realized that nursing the sick and helpless was what she wanted to do more than anything. The thought of educating herself to be better qualified brought her a rush of excitement.

Papa shifted uncomfortably, and Julia held her breath while he stewed over his decision. "I am sorry. It cannot be helped."

Julia shook her head. "Leave Alice and me to be her companions. Or just me."

"Your kindness does you credit," Papa said. "But the answer is no. Sending Ivy to act as a companion was a mistake I have regretted for the last year."

"Julia, I am surprised at you!" Aunt wrinkled her nose. "You shouldn't interrupt a conversation between your father and me." She stroked her puppy a little faster. "Here I thought you'd have missed me and would be eager to return home."

Julia loved her aunt, but she loved Ivy, Grandmother, and Esmond too, and they needed her. Feeling useful was part of why Amorwich suited her best. Her gaze darted to her aunt, then to her father, and she jumped in again. "What about collecting boughs of greenery for the house to leave it with a bit of cheer in our absence? You know it's my favorite Christmas Eve tradition, and I noticed a grove of pine trees not far from here."

"Julia," Aunt said, a bit exasperated.

Papa held up his hand to subdue her. "A wonderful idea, dear, but the servants will have to manage the task this time. We will continue the tradition next year."

Julia bit her lip. How could he so easily dismiss an activity that was so dear to her? To all of them? The situation pressed all the air from her lungs, leaving her feeling defeated. "Excuse me," she said, standing. "I should look in on Alice."

Aunt Morris's voice followed her from the room. "Julia is clearly unhappy. I never should have let you bring the girls. I do hope the parties I have planned will cheer them up again."

Julia picked up her skirts and rushed up the stairs. As she went to pass Grandmother's room, her feet seemed to stop of their own accord. In the short time she had been at Ravencross, she had bonded with her grandmother and couldn't pass up a single opportunity to be with her before they left. Julia turned and cracked the door open.

Grandmother smiled at her from her bed.

"Am I intruding?" Julia asked.

"Never. Come in."

Julia stepped inside and shut the door behind her.

"Your hesitancy just now reminded me of when Ivy was here last Christmas." Grandmother pointed for Julia to sit down. "She carried the weight of the world on her shoulders, and I was too wrapped up in dying to notice."

"Did you really think you were going to die?" Julia sank into the seat by her bed.

"I still feel like a woman of eighty years with a hole in my heart from losing your grandfather, but then I thought death was a few breaths away. At the time, I had to look past my own struggles to address the needs of another. But you seem to do that rather easily, don't you? I daresay it's far more difficult for you to give your own needs much credence."

Even now Julia knew she was suppressing her own desires for happiness. So many others were worse off than her. "Ivy told me how you were the bridge between her husband and Papa. She never would have married without your help." Julia wanted to tell her about the letters and her growing feelings for Esmond, but it seemed so selfish.

Grandmother chuckled. "Ivy forgot to give credit to the One who matters. She prayed for a miracle, and she got it. I shouldn't have lived, but I did. In the end, all that matters is what God wants."

Her words were hard to swallow. "I often want to be the one taking care of everyone, but I need to trust that God also cares for me."

"Trust is important, but you can't just sit around waiting for things to happen. I can tell you from experience it never works. You need a good dose of action with every ounce of faith."

Action? Julia scoffed inwardly. Esmond wanted her to act, but how could she? She could never cross Aunt Morris, and how could she convince Papa to change his mind about their outing? "Thank you, Grandmother," she said, even if she wished the advice had been different. "I will miss you when we leave. I wish you were well enough to come home with us."

Grandmother smiled. "I know you are worried about me, but once your father is gone, Ivy will be permitted to visit again. She won't let me spend too much time on my own."

The thought offered minimal comfort. While Ivy had once cared for Grandmother, now Ivy needed the caring.

"I hope you heal quickly. And I hope Papa lets me visit again soon." She glanced at a folded napkin in the shape of an orchid on the table by Grandmother's bed and sighed. Papa would be so disappointed in her traitorous thoughts.

Julia said good night and made her way to find Alice. Grandmother's words kept echoing in her mind. Faith and action. Faith and action. But what action? She whispered a heartfelt prayer and opened Alice's door.

Alice was dressed to go out.

"What are you doing?" Julia asked. "You cannot go anywhere, or Aunt will be livid."

"I don't care," Alice said, shoving her hands into her gloves. "I regret not saying goodbye to Ivy in person. If I am going to leave with that wretched woman, then I will have my freedom while I can."

"You know Aunt means well," Julia said. "Remember all the new dresses she bought us? In the height of fashion too. We have all the ribbons we could ask for and invitations to parties at the best homes in our small society." Julia sighed.

"Aunt Morris hates me," Alice said, her face crumpling. A tear dripped from her eye. "I cannot find joy in a party or a dress when she said I must put aside my writing to become a real lady."

"She said that? I fear she is in one of her moods." Julia shut the door so no one would overhear them.

Alice swiped at her eyes and mimicked Aunt's tight voice. "Quality books are written by educated men for men, and everything else is fanciful drivel."

Julia rubbed Alice's arm. "Aunt has always permitted you to write in the past. I don't understand it."

"It's as I said. She hates me," Alice said, collapsing onto the bed.

"This is more proof of her lack of patience than of her feelings for you," Julia reassured her as she sat on the bed next to her. "You and I do things when we are angry too. I know she won't say she is sorry, but I'd wager when we return home, she will buy you something as her way of apologizing."

Alice sat up and leaned against Julia. "I don't care about her presents. I don't want to go back to Peterborough. Can't we just stay here with Ivy and Grandmother forever?"

Julia wrapped her arm around her sister, feeling bone-deep tired. Her cold had sapped all her energy. "I am wishing for the same thing."

CHAPTER NINE

Julia tossed and turned trying to sleep. *Act. Act. Act.* She shifted to her side and fluffed her pillow. *Act. Act. Act.* She heaved a sigh and crawled out of bed. She had to do something. She had to act. She went to her writing table and pulled parchment and pen toward her.

> *Dear Papa,*
>   *I have so many things I want to tell you, but I cannot find the courage to do so. Please meet me in the grove of pine trees on the border of our property. I will be collecting greenery for Grandmother. I will explain everything there.*
>   *Yours,*
>   *Julia*

Her hand trembled, and her head felt heavy with fatigue. She folded the note, sealed it, and went back to bed. Sadly, writing the note served to increase her anxiety, and her muscles refused to relax. She tossed in her bed for hours before dawn finally came. Ignoring her pounding headache, her aching limbs, and the fire in her throat, she alerted the maid to help her dress. The house was quiet when Julia slipped into Alice's room with her cloak pinned at her neck.

"Alice, wake up." Julia gently shook her.

"Are you going to see Ivy again?" Alice pushed up into a sitting position. "Please let me come. I want to say goodbye."

"No, I am going to see Esmond."

"You mean Mr. Park?"

Julia coughed into her shoulder, embarrassed by her mistake. "Yes, of course."

"Why now?"

"He and I have devised a way to help Papa talk with Lady Blakely. Give this note to Papa but not until after breakfast." Julia put the folded paper into Alice's hand. "It is imperative he receives it around ten o'clock. Can you help me?"

Alice studied her for a moment before answering. "I will."

Julia grimaced. "I don't want you to get into trouble."

"It happens often enough with little effort on my part," Alice said with a sigh. "I can take care of myself."

"Are you sure? I don't want Aunt Morris—"

"Julia," Alice interrupted, "I promise not to do anything rash like run away."

Thank heavens, since Julia was the one running away. Having two daughters turn up missing would cause pure mayhem. "I'll see you this afternoon."

The sun had just started to stretch forth its first beams of light on the horizon when Julia slipped out the front door. Not even Barnes was awake yet. It was paramount she leave before anyone could ruin her plan. As reckless as her decision might seem, she felt strongly that she was taking a stand of courage for the sake of her family.

The cold air outside shocked her and triggered a coughing spell, leaving her chest aching. Julia pulled her cloak tighter around her. The wind seemed to pierce through her layers and permeate her body. Her cheeks burned, and she burrowed her chin into her cloak as she made her way around the house. The pine trees were more than a mile away, and trudging through the snow instead of along the road made her steps slow and labored.

When she finally arrived, she was exhausted. The trees created a little wind barrier, but even so, Julia had hours to wait. She felt foolish and scared and began to question her decision. Was this a worthwhile sacrifice to bring two families together? She shivered. So much could go wrong. Fatigue forced her to her knees, and she huddled up against a tree. She closed her eyes and prayed harder than she had ever prayed before. Did God care about her and her family? She had acted, but now she needed to remember to have faith. She said amen right as the snow started to fall.

❀ ❀ ❀

While Christmas Eve was generally a quiet day for many families, as the real festivities would take place in the coming days, Esmond's family turned it into bedlam. Both the servants and the family scurried around every inch of the house in preparation for the annual Christmas ball. With the sudden snowstorm, there was more than just a mountain of tasks weighing on everyone's minds.

Things had been awkward since Esmond had given the letters to his mother, and he had been tiptoeing around her ever since. However, there was no time left to mince words. He had his mother cornered in the drawing room, and he would not take no for an answer. "You can't change your mind. Think how enjoyable it will be to gather our own greenery this year. You know we grow the best mistletoe in the area."

"Look at the snow, Esmond." His mother pointed at the window. The snow outside was piled several inches high on the ledge, and large flakes whirled through the air. "A game of chess would be far more preferable. I know how fond you are of it."

They had been arguing about this all morning. "Can't you brave the weather for one hour?" Esmond gritted his teeth beneath his smile. "It would mean a lot to me."

"I feel as if I am talking to Esmond the child. I haven't seen you get this into holiday preparations since . . . well, ever."

"Exactly." Esmond snapped his fingers. "Shouldn't it mean something to you?"

His mother scrunched her face in thought. "I have a better idea. Why don't you hurry and pick us some, and then I will help fold the boughs and tie ribbon on them after you return? While you are out, I will be in my room, praying the weather lets up so my ball is not ruined."

Esmond caught her arm as she turned to leave. "This was supposed to be time spent with you, Mother. It won't take but an hour."

"Really, Esmond?"

"Really."

She sighed. "Very well. Let me go put on every stitch of clothing I own and hope I survive this storm."

"Wonderful. I will send for the sleigh." Esmond watched his mother leave the drawing room. When he turned to the window, he cringed. It would be a miracle if his sweet, soft-spoken Julia had convinced her father to take her out in this weather. They could not have asked for a worse turn of events.

Once in the sleigh with his mother, Esmond flicked the reins, and the pair of mares began a slow trot toward their destination.

"Look how big the snow flurries are," his mother said. "I forgot how beautiful they are up close."

"You've been far too busy to notice such things," Esmond replied.

His mother tucked her arm around his. "You're right. And it might all be for naught if we have to cancel our plans. Even the Christmas after your father died, our holiday did not feel so bleak. All this underlying contention with the Hunts has me upended. Add to that if the snow does not let up soon, there will be no Christmas ball, and poor Ivy will have nothing to look forward to."

Esmond could tell his mother was nigh to tears. "I'm disappointed you're not more excited to spend time with me. You have underestimated my ability to cheer you with a sleighride and a hunt for mistletoe."

His mother smiled at him. "You have your father's sense of humor."

"Do I?"

She nodded. "His enthusiasm eased me into our marriage."

Esmond batted a snowflake from his eyelashes. It was the worst possible weather to plan a rendezvous. "Um, you and Father. Did you love each other?"

"Very much."

"In the beginning?" Esmond stole a glance at her.

"I respected him, which led to admiration, which led to love."

Esmond knew such an order was what was hoped for in a match. Love was a luxury for the upper class. If he had any less self-respect and had never met Julia, he might be tempted to set himself up with a rich wife. Julia wouldn't likely come with a big dowry, but he couldn't find it in his heart to care. He would find a way to support her—if given the opportunity.

It was not long before they were in the grove of pine trees. Esmond reined in the mares, pulling the sleigh to a stop. The grove was not very thick, but it was big enough that they could not see anyone else in the vicinity. Esmond climbed down, then helped his mother do the same. He scanned the area. Would Julia come? The morning was already growing late. He pulled a saw out of the back of the sleigh and with his free arm escorted his mother through the trees.

"See anything that catches your eye? I know you have particular taste." Even as he said it, his eyes searched again for any sign of Julia.

"The higher, shorter branches are easier to bend, unless we find some younger trees."

"Let's walk this way." Esmond knew he could not ask his mother to delay any longer than necessary in this weather. He would have to cut some branches quickly and get her out of the elements.

His mother clung to him as she took slow, careful steps deeper into the trees. He saw a small clump of purple at the bottom of a tall pine, and the color reminded him of Julia. Had she been here already and left her cloak over a shrub? He'd be beyond frustrated with himself if that were the case.

"Just a moment." He released his mother and set the saw down. He jogged over to the cloak, and his heart stopped. What he'd thought was a shrub was Julia. He bent down and cupped his hands on her shoulders.

Her eyes flitted open. "Esmond, you came." Her words slurred together, and her eyes shut again.

"Julia!" He lifted her shivering body, one arm going under her legs and the other cradling her head against his chest, and turned back toward his mother.

"Who is it?" His mother gasped. "Is that Ivy's sister?"

"Yes, and she's half-frozen."

Out of the corner of his eye he saw movement. He turned and recognized Mr. Hunt on horseback. "Over here!" he yelled. Dash it all! This was all his fault. "Mother, wait here and inform Mr. Hunt about his daughter. I need to get her to the sleigh."

He pulled Julia tightly against him as he half-ran, half-stumbled through the drifts of snow. "Don't worry, Julia. We will get you home and warm." She opened her eyes momentarily, and they shuddered closed. "Stay awake, darling."

He had barely managed to get her into the back seat of the sleigh when Mr. Hunt came up behind him on his horse. He dismounted and raced up behind Esmond.

"Let me see her!" Mr. Hunt pushed Esmond out of the way. He took one look at his daughter and swore.

Esmond moved around him and climbed up. He pulled Julia close and dug in her cloak for her hands. He rubbed them with his free hand. "Quick, help my mother up and drive us to Fairmore."

"To Ravencross, you mean." Mr. Hunt scowled.

Esmond did not get angry easily, but blood pounded in his ears. "I don't care where you take us—just get us out of this blasted snow!"

Mr. Hunt huffed and turned to help Esmond's mother inside.

"Put my mother back here with us. She can help me warm Julia." Esmond pulled Julia onto his lap to create room for his mother.

Mr. Hunt grabbed his horse's reins and tied them to the back of the sleigh, then scrambled in and brought the reins down hard. Sleighs were slower than carriages, and the initial pace infuriated Esmond. And, of course, they were headed toward Ravencross. The last thing he wanted was to be on Mr. Hunt's land.

"Turn her so I might rub her legs," his mother said.

Esmond obeyed, desperate for help. He removed his glove and put his warm hand to Julia's cheek. "It's going to be all right," he told her. "Your father is here, and we are halfway home already." Her eyes fluttered open again but closed when a coughing spell nearly stole all her breath.

Mr. Hunt turned back and shot Esmond a withering glare. "I should call you out." His nostrils flared. "I should have known there would be a Blakely involved."

"Just drive . . . sir." Esmond had no tolerance for this man who had treated his family so poorly.

"I'm sorry," Julia whispered, her voice hoarse.

"You have nothing to be sorry for," he assured her.

His mother leaned forward to catch his eye. "What is going on, Esmond?"

"I'll explain everything once we get Julia cared for."

Ravencross came into view, and Esmond shifted to block the change in wind when the sleigh turned up the drive. Mr. Hunt jumped down first and reached for Julia.

"I can take it from here," Mr. Hunt said. "Get your mother home."

"I'm not leaving her," Esmond said even as he lifted Julia in his arms and placed her in her father's.

"Didn't you hear me, boy? You're not welcome. You almost killed my daughter!"

"I did no such thing," Esmond argued. "I can explain every-thing, but not until I know Julia is out of danger."

Mr. Hunt grunted. He turned toward the house, his footfalls heavy on the path, leaving Esmond standing by his mother.

"Help me down," she insisted. "We aren't going to let that man boss us around."

Esmond raised a brow but did as he was told. "I hope this won't be too awkward for you, Mother. I swear I would never put Julia in danger."

"I had no idea you knew *Julia* so well." Mother emphasized her given name, and he cringed.

"I might have helped in her secret visits to see Ivy while you were making house calls or running errands in the village," Esmond said while he pulled Mother's arm toward the house, wishing he could explain at another, less desperate, time.

"And you just happened to fall in love with her in the last few weeks?"

They stopped short at the door, and Esmond cleared his throat. "She caught my eye at the wedding. Respect led to admiration, which inevitably led to . . ."

"Love?"

Esmond nodded and slammed the metal knocker a few times against the wooden door.

"I said something similar about how I fell for your father."

Esmond gave a short, humorless laugh. "Let me rearrange my words, then. I admired her first, and then I respected her. But what does it matter? I fell in love with the wrong person. And now her life is in danger."

The door opened, and by some miracle, the butler let them in. A woman his mother's age with wide-set eyes and a feather in her hair stepped out of a nearby room. Esmond had never been inside Ravencross, but he thought he would have heard if yet another gently born woman was in residence.

The woman stood there, blinking back tears. "Well? Will someone please tell me what happened?"

Esmond put his hand on his mother's back. "Has a doctor been sent for?"

"We are sending a footman for one now," the woman said, bringing a handkerchief to her nose.

Mr. Hunt came down the stairs. He looked at all of them, then focused on the stranger. "The maids are going to start a warm bath. Alice is with Julia."

"Perhaps you should see to introductions, and I will call for tea for our guests."

Mr. Hunt rubbed his forehead. "Right. Tea." He glared at Esmond before sighing and giving a sweeping gesture. "This is the family Ivy married into, Lady Blakely and her son, ah . . ."

"Mr. Esmond Park," Esmond supplied.

Mr. Hunt motioned to the stranger. "This is my late wife's sister, Miss Fanny Morris."

"I would have been at the wedding, but I caught a dreadful cold," Miss Morris said with a stiff curtsy. When she lifted her head, her eyebrows furrowed with wary curiosity. "The drawing room is just here. Make yourselves comfortable, and I shall ring for tea. I am certain you will understand if I do not join you, as my niece surely has need of me."

"Please, see to Miss Hunt," Esmond said, speaking for his mother. "Her well-being is most important to us."

Miss Morris tipped her head and left.

Esmond entered the drawing room with his mother and was surprised when Mr. Hunt followed them inside.

"I'm ready for that explanation, Mr. Park," he growled.

Esmond walked to a chair and stood behind it, gripping his hands on the back to steady himself. The panic from discovering Julia had not quite worn off. "The last thing I want is to cause any trouble for anyone."

"A little late for that, isn't it?" Mr. Hunt snapped.

"Let my son speak," Mother said rather forcefully.

Esmond swallowed, steeling himself for what he was about to say. "As you now know, Ivy has been quite sick with child.

Miss Hunt has been walking to see her several afternoons a week. We discovered . . ." He glanced at his mother and then changed tactics. "We thought getting our families together would help soften past circumstances. Miss Hunt and I only want what will help Ivy. She's suffering a great deal physically, but we also believe her spirits are low because she is parted from her family, sir."

"So Julia risked her life and hid in the woods because of some harebrained idea of yours?"

Esmond kept his tone even. "We were to meet at ten on the hour. From what I can tell, Miss Hunt has been out there all night, which, I assure you, was not part of our plan."

Mr. Hunt ran his hand through his short red hair. "After the maids dress her in dry clothes, I will ask her directly."

"Esmond," his mother said. "Will you give Mr. Hunt and me a moment of privacy?"

Yesterday such a meeting was all he could have asked for. Today he knew a little more of Mr. Hunt's character, and he did not want to leave his mother alone with the man. "You don't have to do this, Mother. I was wrong. I—"

"Esmond," Mother said again. "I require only a few minutes."

Mr. Hunt went to the fireplace and rested his arm on the mantel. Esmond walked by him, trying his best not to glare, and left them alone. Instead of shutting the door all the way, he left the smallest crack and stood as close as he could to the opening.

Mr. Hunt began. "If this is to be a continuation of our last discussion—"

Mother cut him off. "Enough, Jonathan. I let you bully me last time, but that was before I knew the whole story."

"What are you talking about?"

"I found a pile of letters you wrote to me. They were from before my wedding."

There was silence for so long that Esmond felt sweat gathering on the back of his neck. How would Mr. Hunt respond?

"In all these years, you never looked in our secret place?" the man finally said, his voice hoarse.

"For twenty-seven years, I have not stepped foot in the gazebo."

Esmond traced back through the years in his memory. He realized his mother was telling the truth. He had no recollection of ever seeing her inside the gazebo.

"Why not?" Mr. Hunt asked.

"You know why," Mother said, her voice softening a notch. "I couldn't very well go there after what happened."

"So you believed the rumors about me?"

"I was confused by the accusations, I'll admit, but it was more than that. My parents wanted me to marry Garret. They needed to sell Fairmore Hall quickly so Father could relocate to Bath and attend to his health. Lord Blakely was wealthy, titled, and in the market for a summer home. Everything fell into place. For two months, I waited for you to return from London and save me, but you were simply gone."

Mr. Hunt scoffed. "You knew I was attempting to gather funds to buy the land. When I returned, you were engaged to Lord Blakely, and I couldn't get close to you. Why didn't you check our place to see if I'd written?"

"It was too late," Mother said. "The land and estate were sold to Garret, and I was engaged without my permission. My whole life was planned for me before I could fathom what had happened. Truly, my parents did a masterful job at painting your character. They said you'd invested your money poorly and lost everything. I didn't want to believe them, but it didn't matter. They had always thought us wrong for each other. Why have a gentleman son of a farmer for a son-in-law when they could have a baron? It wasn't personal for them, though it was very personal for me."

Esmond leaned his head as near as he could to the doorframe.

After an uncomfortable pause, Mr. Hunt finally responded. "Your father promised me that land if I had the funds. It was meant to be mine. I only ever wanted it to please your father, to elevate myself in his eyes and finally receive his permission to marry you." Esmond gripped the door handle with unease. "But they were right about me losing my merchant-shipment investment. I went to London, and the bank said my funds were gone. All the cargo had burned up in some blasted warehouse fire; it was completely out of my hands. I was determined to salvage my losses, but when I returned, it no longer mattered. You were already engaged to that man. After you married, I couldn't bring myself to come back again."

Footfalls sounded from within the room, and Esmond stepped back. When no one opened the door, he carefully resumed his position to eavesdrop, praying there would be some way for these two to finally make things right.

"It was better for both of us," Mother said. "I would have had a difficult time making a life with Garret with you around, and you had a family of your own to start."

A quiet moment passed, and then Mr. Hunt began the conversation again. "I knew you didn't read the letters right away since the seals were unbroken. After your wedding, I never returned to the gazebo to check again. I assumed eventually you'd read them. I was convinced you would instantly believe me and regret your choices. At least, I wanted you to regret what you'd given up."

"I've had a good life," Mother said. "I did care for you . . . once. But I was happy with Garret."

"I was happy, too, until my wife died." Silence permeated through the door to Esmond, but finally Mr. Hunt spoke again. "I never forgot you, Danielle. There was a time my life ceased to matter because you were not in it."

More silence. "The girl in me mourns for what could have been, but none of it matters any longer. Our children need us."

Mr. Hunt chuckled. "After our messy past, our children have married. Fate has a strange sense of humor."

"Yes, and now Esmond is in love with Julia. I can't help but think this is not fate but a divine hand leading us down a better path."

"I can't keep my girls apart," Mr. Hunt said. "Julia could have died today."

"And I will not wound Esmond by forbidding him to follow his heart."

Mr. Hunt groaned. "Such reasoning is what got me trapped into agreeing to the first wedding."

Esmond's heart soared. He wished Julia were standing beside him to witness this. Their parents' hearts were softening, and more so, they were considering him as a candidate for Julia's hand. How he wished her better this moment so he could tell her what her sacrifice had bought them.

"Let's not speak of the wedding just yet," his mother said. "You have a daughter to see to, and my son is quite beside himself with worry."

"I will go to her now if you are all right here."

"I am perfectly capable of seeing to my own needs, thank you."

Esmond stepped back several paces. He bowed his head and waited for Mr. Hunt to come out. He had sorely misjudged Julia's father. His gruff facade hid a tender, devoted man.

Instead of seeing Mr. Hunt first, he was surprised when Alice came down the stairs at great speed. She tumbled down the last few steps. He reached out and grabbed her.

"What is it?"

Mr. Hunt stepped out of the drawing room. "Alice?"

"It's Julia. She has a terrible fever."

"A fever? From the snow?" Esmond could not understand the correlation.

"Perhaps her body is in shock," Mr. Hunt surmised, gripping the banister. He propelled himself up the stairs, taking them two at a time.

"How bad is she?" Esmond asked Alice, wishing he had the right to follow Mr. Hunt.

Alice shook her head. "I don't know. I've never seen her like this. I'm frightened."

Mother reached out and took Alice's hand that Mr. Hunt had dropped. He had not realized she had been behind them. "Oh, dear girl. Come here. We mustn't assume the worst. The doctor is on his way." She motioned to the stairs. "Show me to her room. I know a thing or two about fevers."

Esmond watched them go up and did not know what to do. Was he welcome in the sickroom? He had no claim on Julia to justify breaching propriety—in fact, he could only hope she loved him in return—but staying put made no sense either. Anxiety pushed his feet upward, step by step. A corridor lined with rooms extended before him. Ravencross was not large, but which of the doors led to Julia?

He stopped at the first door and, with a deep breath, knocked.

"Come in." He recognized Mrs. Hunt's voice.

Esmond hesitantly pushed the door open. Inside, the elderly Mrs. Hunt was propped up with pillows.

"Mr. Park?" she said.

"Yes, ma'am." He bowed his head, knowing he owed the woman an explanation for interrupting her privacy, and stepped closer to her. "I beg your pardon. I had hoped to find Miss Hunt."

"There has been a great deal of rushing around, but they have failed to inform me of exactly what has happened."

"Miss Hunt is sick."

"Julia?"

"Yes."

"And if you are upstairs searching for her, I can only guess you have attached yourself to her in some way."

"Precisely." Despite his worries, he cracked a smile. Mrs. Hunt was a kind woman, but she did not mince words.

"Have you considered the bulwark between you and Julia?"

"You mean your son?" Esmond felt his lips tugging farther upward. "I have reason to hope where he is concerned."

"This, too, is news." Julia's grandmother looked at him shrewdly. "And do you deserve her?"

Esmond's smile faltered. "Actually, I will not be able to ask for her hand until I secure employment."

"What are you studying?"

"I, um, graduated from university and am studying the law."

"Why did you look away when you said you are studying the law? You are not the dishonest sort."

"I am endeavoring to find a passion for the subject. It is laborious at the moment."

"Why not study something different if it displeases you so?"

"I find farming appealing, but I care for Julia and want to provide her with the comforts she is used to."

"Yes, I remember your help with our harvest. My husband was a farmer, you know."

"I hope I have not caused offense. I have the highest respect for those who work the land."

"After the way you and Fairmore's land steward stepped in here, I believe you know much about the stewardship of land."

"I accompanied my father on his estate business more than my elder brother did. Our steward is like an uncle to me. It is perhaps his passions that have ignited mine. But without an inheritance, I must seek another path." He cleared his throat. "Forgive me. I must excuse myself. I will be sure to send word as soon as I discover news of Miss Hunt."

Mrs. Hunt chuckled and closed her eyes. "Julia's a sweet girl. You make sure she is well cared for."

"I will." He dipped his head in farewell.

CHAPTER TEN

THE DOCTOR CONFIRMED THE FEVER not an hour later, and they were told to wait it out. Julia thrashed in her bed and pulled at her nightgown. Esmond had been allowed to see her for a few moments, then ushered out so she might rest. None of this should have happened. She had the purest intentions, so why was she being punished? He grappled to understand why she had been out in the woods for so long.

Ravencross was a quarter of the size of Fairmore, and had Esmond not been so restless, he would have found it surprisingly warm and comfortable. He rotated rooms to stay busy, starting with pacing around the pink-and-blue oriental rug in the corridor. Then he sat on the settee in the drawing room and stared into the bewitching flames of the fire. He'd even tried reading in the house's small library, but though his eyes roved over the pages, the story did not register.

"You are still here?" Mr. Hunt entered the drawing room, his face lined with worry and fatigue.

"I sent a footman to take my mother home a few hours ago, but I couldn't bring myself to leave."

Mr. Hunt sank into a seat. "I have enough to worry about with my mother's recovery and a ridiculous land steward, but if I lose Julia . . ." He rubbed his eyes with the bottoms of his palms.

Esmond had never imagined seeing such a tough man in such a humble state. He folded his arms tight across his chest. "What is this about your land steward?" There was no reason to ask, except for a strange desire to distract the broken man across from him.

Mr. Hunt sank lower in his chair and stretched out his legs. "Mr. Harvey thinks I should cut down all the timber on the north of Ravencross and try to farm it. He also thinks I should sell my best ground and use the money to invest in a farm in the West Indies. He is willing to take the funds there himself and says the returns will be far greater than would be possible in England."

Esmond's brow rose. "You do realize that the north part of Ravencross's estate has not been farmed before for a reason. It's rocky, and the soil is not suited for anything beyond trees."

Mr. Hunt's tired gaze met his. "You seem to know a lot about my land."

"I know a lot about land in general, sir."

"Tell me, then, what do you know about the West Indies farms?"

Esmond looked back at the fireplace. "Some do very well. But your ground here is already profitable, sir. Investments are like relationships. They take time to research and produce results. Those who take shortcuts often lose what they put in. If you cannot cover the risk for a new endeavor, then you must rely on what you already know will work. Is this Mr. Harvey someone you trust?"

Mr. Hunt sat up. "I am beginning to think he is not."

Esmond was uncomfortable advising Julia's father—especially when he knew Mr. Hunt blamed him for his daughter's illness. He shifted his feet.

"Go home, son. Borrow a horse and get some sleep."

He couldn't think of an excuse to prolong his stay. "You'll send word if anything changes?"

Mr. Hunt gave him a curt nod. "I've never seen her this way, but she is strong. She'll pull through."

If that was supposed to comfort Esmond, it did not. However, he knew he had overstayed his welcome. "Good night, sir." Esmond reluctantly pulled himself out of his seat and dragged his feet to the door.

He was home before he knew it and found his way to his room. He had no desire to eat or sleep. He went to his desk and, without even realizing what he was doing, began composing a letter.

Dearest Julia,

I never told you about the first time I saw you. I thought you were lovelier than the bride. You were standing by your sister like a beacon of support, calming her nerves and smiling at everyone. I've asked myself many times why I could never shake this memory. When I saw you again, it became abundantly clear. You walk with an air of goodness, you seek to build others up, and you don't turn from a challenge.

As the storms of life have shaken your sister, you've naturally responded by spreading your light and piercing through her darkest days. I've watched in awe as your presence brightened the walls of my home too. Every man ought to wish for such a woman by his side—I know I do.

I cannot ask for your hand now, as I am not in a position to marry just yet. Never have I been more anxious to secure a living. Never have I had such great motivation to be a better man and rescue my family as you have done yours.

Julia, I beseech you to fight this illness with every fiber of your being. I am begging God to grant you and me a chance at a life together. Just as you have softened the hearts of our parents, my own heart will never be the same without you. I love you, dearest. The letters we found brought you to think of me as a friend. I pray this letter will help you think of me as so much more.

Your devoted servant,
Esmond Park

The letter was more a prayer than anything he could say to Julia. Even as he expressed the depths of his feelings, he knew it was far easier to write them than to say them. What good would it do to pour his heart out to her if he could not even court her yet? Her father would laugh at such a proposal. And Julia . . . what would she think? If they, like their parents, were not meant to be, then Esmond would try to endure it. All he truly cared about right now was that she lived.

CHAPTER ELEVEN

HEAT SUFFOCATED JULIA, AND WAVES of cold chilled her. Sleep was a comfort and a curse. One minute she was at Ravencross, in her room with Alice and Papa, and the next she was back home in Peterborough. She even thought she saw a glimpse of Esmond. His sad expression surely proved his disappointment in her. Julia had failed to bring peace to their families. She'd ruined Christmastide for everyone.

"I'm sorry, Esmond. I tried."

She closed her eyes, and a restless sleep carried his image away. She tossed and turned and lost track of time. Finally, she saw Ivy, as if resurrected from a dark recess of her mind. Ivy lay in her own bed, heartsick and so very alone.

"I gave everything I had, Ivy. Nothing worked."

A voice soothed her. She couldn't recognize it, but it was decidedly motherly.

"Hush, child. Ivy is well. She is happy."

"No, she's lonely." Julia shivered. "And I let Esmond down."

"Esmond is coming, dear. He loves you."

Julia's eyelids were like paperweights. She wanted to open them to identify the voice, but she was so tired. Sleep overcame her, and she could not resist the pull.

✹ ✹ ✹

Esmond did not remember falling asleep, but when he opened his eyes, it was morning. He arched his back and rubbed the knot in his neck. Why had he not gone to bed? Oh yes. He'd fallen asleep after writing Julia a letter.

He glanced down, and his heart stopped. Where was the letter?

His desk was empty and the floor clear. After a moment of searching, it appeared the entire room was in its usual state. He pulled at his already loose cravat and hurried into the corridor. Pine branches the servants had procured draped the staircase, and a large evergreen bough tied with ribbon hung on the front door.

It was Christmas Day.

Tonight would be his mother's annual ball, and he'd forgotten all about it. He stepped into the breakfast room utterly surprised to find Ivy there with Curtis. She stood from her seat, much thinner than her normal self, still not even showing her condition, but with a bit more color to her cheeks than in recent days.

He gave her a quick bow. "Any word of your sister?"

"Your mother has gone there this morning to check on her. We should know soon enough."

How could any apology be sufficient for being the cause of Julia's illness? "I . . . I'm so sorry."

Ivy gave him a warm smile. "Your mother told me everything. You and Julia have sacrificed much for me." A tear dripped down her cheek and then another. "Thank you, Esmond."

"Sit down, dearest." Curtis glanced at Esmond and shook his head. "My wife finally makes it down for breakfast, and you have to go and make her cry."

Esmond sighed and ran his hand through his disheveled hair. "I feel like a mess."

"You look like one too," Curtis said. "Sit and eat. You can't help Julia if you don't help yourself."

Esmond could appreciate the logic. He filled his plate and sat.

"Julia is rarely ill," Ivy said. "We must remember everyone gets a fever now and then."

Esmond did not want to worry Ivy by describing how Julia had looked the day before. Ivy was finally making progress herself. "Neither of you found a letter I wrote, did you?"

Both of them shook their heads.

"I will ask the housekeeper." This was one letter he did not want passing from hand to hand through all the servants. His heart was on that paper, and he felt vulnerable having it out of his possession.

A door shut somewhere outside the dining room, and there were voices before Murray stepped into the room. "A messenger came from Ravencross requesting Mr. Park's presence."

Esmond pushed his chair out so quickly it fell backward. He glanced at Curtis, whose expression mirrored his own worry. He reached down and righted his chair, flustered by his clumsiness.

"I am sure everything will be all right," Ivy said. "If my father did not kill Curtis for loving me, he will not hurt you for doing the same for Julia."

Esmond blinked. Apparently, Ivy had not needed to read his letter to know exactly how he felt. It wasn't Mr. Hunt he was worried about anyway. All he cared about was Julia. He prayed she was still alive.

CHAPTER TWELVE

Dreams of cold and snow haunted Julia. She kept repeating in her mind the words spoken to her by an unfamiliar voice: *Ivy is well. Esmond is coming.* A wet mound of snow fell on her head. She tried to shake it off, but it dripped down her cheek and neck. Julia gasped and opened her eyes. She saw Edith, her maid, replacing a damp cloth on Julia's forehead.

"Papa?" She tried to sit up. Why was she in bed? What was happening?

"Get her father," a woman said.

Julia turned and found Lady Blakely by her bedside. "Lady Blakely? Why are you here?"

"Because of your courage, we've decided to put the past behind us once and for all, and our families are once again friends. I just sent for your father. He will be so happy to see you are awake." Lady Blakely leaned over and felt Julia's head. "Oh, blessed child! Your fever has broken."

Julia took in Lady Blakely's tired posture, her hair falling loose of its pins. "Are you well, my lady?"

Lady Blakely met her gaze and laughed. "Me? Yes, dear. It is you who have been sick."

Julia coughed several times. She put her hand to the wet cloth and sighed. "I do feel awful. Please . . . tell me what has happened."

"We went out to pick mistletoe and found you half-frozen and barely conscious. When we returned you home, we managed to warm you, but then your fever set in."

"I remember having a cough, but I thought it no more than a cold."

Aunt Morris slipped into the room, and upon seeing Julia awake, hurried to her side. "Dear girl, this whole house has been upended with you ill. I fear my words about your winter walks drove you from the house."

"I—"

"Don't bother to deny it. I shouldn't have tried to take away what brings you joy. Can you ever forgive me?"

Julia nodded, even while knowing that Aunt would continue to hover and caution her, but only because it was the way she showed her love.

Aunt Morris picked up Julia's hand with both of hers and sighed. "I know I haven't been the best substitute mother, but I do want your happiness." Her eyes widened. "Oh, your father. He will want to know you are better!" She dropped Julia's hands, grabbed her skirts, and rushed from the room. Her aunt wasn't normally so confusing or affectionate, but perhaps the severity of Julia's illness had warranted the reaction.

Papa entered a few moments later, and with him was a very somber and disheveled Esmond. Papa came to her and took her hands, as her aunt had done, in his much larger ones. "What a relief! God knew we couldn't manage without you."

Julia started to smile but began coughing again. Papa's strong hand cradled her head and lifted her. A cup was brought to her lips, and she drank deeply. He gently lowered her back onto her pillow and then reached for her hand once more.

"Alice told us how you woke her before dawn to leave for the pine grove," he said. "Why?"

Julia took a long, slow breath. "I did it for Ivy . . . for all of us. I only wanted you and Lady Blakely to finally end the feud so we could be a family again."

Papa cleared his throat, barely holding back his emotion. "You must stop trying to carry this burden alone. Things are going to change around here. As your grandmother would say, it looks like another Christmas miracle." He turned to Lady Blakely. They shared a look—one slightly uncomfortable but amiable nonetheless. There was peace there, beyond what Julia had ever thought possible. Her father turned back to her and smiled. "There is a young man here eager to speak with you. Mr. Park?"

He moved aside so she could better see her visitor. Esmond's head was bowed, but at the mention of his name, he raised it. Gone was the confident, playful man Julia knew. His face was lined with fatigue, and his demeanor was serious. She realized he must have taken the brunt of their parents' anger, maybe even the blame for her sickness.

"If you'll excuse us," Papa said. "We will give you and Mr. Park a moment alone." Papa turned to Esmond. "I don't have to remind you that you aren't married to my daughter and to behave, but it's my duty. So there, I said it."

Esmond nodded. Julia watched him follow their parents to the door and shut it behind them. When he turned to face her, their eyes finally connected. What must he think of her? She surely resembled a half-drowned kitten. She fiddled with the collar on her nightgown and smoothed the damp curls on her forehead.

"Julia," Esmond said, his voice low.

She ceased fidgeting and looked at him. He moved to her bedside and stood there looking over her as if she were lying dead in a coffin.

"What is it?" she said. Esmond was never this serious. She relied on him to be a source of joy and encouragement. "I know I look a fright . . ."

Esmond shook his head and knelt down by her bed. He wiped at one of his eyes and attempted a smile. "You sure know how to bait a man and dangle him by a hook."

"I'm too tired to decipher the meaning behind your metaphor."

Esmond gave a strangled laugh. "You don't even know what you have done to me. What you have done *for* me. Not an hour ago I was summoned to this house, afraid you were going to die. Then my mother confessed she had stolen a love letter I had written to you."

"What?" Did he say *love* letter?

He smiled more with his eyes than his mouth—a look so loving, so cherishing that one would think he was gazing at a princess. "My mother brought my private letter to your father. They plotted against us—which I thought was quite juvenile of them. Your father took my hand, looked me square in the eye, and gave his permission for me to court you. That is . . . if you're willing."

Julia's words were lodged in her throat, but she nodded.

His lips spread into a wide smile. "There is more," he said. "I've been hired on as the land steward here at Ravencross. Your father dismissed the last one, who tried talking him into some poor investments. I can hardly believe he took the advice I offered him and turned the position over to me, but your grandmother went on and on about my service during the past harvest. It came down to you. Your father wants his daughter cared for. The position comes with a good-sized cottage on the grounds." His voice choked. "Your grandmother said the home should go to a man who . . . loves the land . . . like her late husband."

Julia wiped at her eyes, which were now streaming tears. "Oh, Esmond."

He pulled out his handkerchief and handed it to her. "Their only request is that we care for Mrs. Hunt during her last years on earth."

"I wouldn't want it any other way. Remember when I said I was searching for a purpose—a reason to smile? I believe taking care of those who cannot care for themselves is what brings me joy. Nursing Grandmother will be a true honor."

The smile he shared with her told her how happy he was for her. "She claims you are better than a companion, although she will be happy to have one in her employ so you are not overtaxed."

"She is too kind to me." How Julia loved her sweet grandmother.

"You deserve it." Esmond squeezed her hand. "Would you like to read my letter to you now?"

Julia would rather hear the words from his mouth. "Why don't you skip to the good part and just tell me."

He chuckled and leaned over so he was close to her face. He lifted one of her hands in his and rubbed it affectionately with his thumb. "There once was a boy who loved a girl so much he thought his heart would wither and die with her when she became sick. I sense you are keen enough to decipher that I am that boy, desperately in love, and you are the girl I cannot be without."

Esmond's gaze landed on her lips. To her utter horror, her throat went dry, and she began coughing. He propped her up with one arm and held her until she finished. His warmth soothed her more than any tea or medicine.

She rested her head against his firm chest, exhausted. She lifted one hand to finger a button beneath his cravat. "I promise I didn't do that on purpose."

His eyes softened along with his words. "What? Avoid receiving my kiss?" His finger grazed her bottom lip.

Her cheeks burned with the thrill of his touch, but she was nervous too. "I would never do that," she breathed.

"Truly?" He tucked her hair behind her ear, making her skin erupt in gooseflesh. "You should have told me weeks ago and put me out of my misery." His somber expression faded into one quite mischievous and familiar. "Miss Julia, you have brought two families together, paved the way for your sister's happiness, and managed to capture my heart." He grinned before he swept down and pressed his lips against hers. If she was sick before, she could no longer remember. His kiss was gentle at first, but as his lips moved over hers, she could feel the emotions he had built up over the last several days. She kissed him back, reassuring him that she wasn't going anywhere.

Julia curled her fingers around the hair at the nape of Esmond's neck. Someday this man would be her husband, and this kiss would be the first of many.

And finally, her entire family would be whole again.

A satisfied sigh escaped Esmond as he slowly released her. Julia sank against him, her strength utterly exhausted.

"Happy Christmas, dearest."

"Christmas?" She turned her head to meet his very near gaze. "It came without me even knowing."

"So it seems."

"You must leave so you can prepare for your family's ball." She glanced at the window. "The weather has been dreadful, hasn't it? It is a good thing I never returned your umbrella. You must take it now."

"Whoever braves the roads will come, but I doubt many will make it tonight." He grinned at her. "I do have another bit of news to share. Your father and aunt have been invited to lead out the first dance at my mother's ball."

"You must tell me every detail!" She wished she were well enough to see it.

Esmond shook his head. "I cannot go, so you can keep my umbrella. You see, I will be reading you a certain story Alice has been writing in secret to give you on Twelfth Night. She feels you should have it now so you are not sad to miss the dancing."

Julia looked at her hands. "You mean, we will be spending the evening together? Alone?"

Esmond tipped her chin up. "You will have to restrain yourself. I cannot kiss you all night long and expect you to regain your health. I promised we would be well-behaved and the door would remain open. I will read to you and no more."

Julia grinned. "I shall have the happiest Christmas, for I have everything I could have asked for."

Esmond moved his hand along her cheek and brushed away her hair. His fingers played with a curl by her ear. "When we are as old as your grandmother, we will look back to see Christmas as a day of miracles—a day of love." He dipped his head and kissed her once more.

CHAPTER THIRTEEN

THE DRAWING ROOM AT RAVENCROSS glowed from the burning
Yule log in the fireplace and the soft haze of lamplight. A sweet
pine fragrance permeated the air from several boughs of holly. The
red berries were barely noticeable in the evening light, but Esmond
was rather proud of the decor. In the days while Julia recovered, he
had taken it upon himself to bring the house some holiday cheer.
He hadn't been permitted to visit Julia in her room again after
Christmas night, and he ached to see her again, to reassure himself
that Christmas hadn't been a figment of his imagination.

Curtis nudged him. "I'm not sure how you convinced Mr.
Hunt to throw a holiday party. I find I have competition for the
role of favorite son-in-law."

"As long as I am Julia's favorite," Esmond replied, "that is
all that matters. When do you suppose she will come down for
dinner?"

Curtis gripped his shoulder. "I've learned the wait is worth
the end result."

His brother stepped away, and Esmond pivoted in a slow circle
to see if anything was amiss in the drawing room. His mother
was visiting with Miss Morris on the settee. Ivy was looking less
green and quite happy to be back at Ravencross. Mr. Hunt had

carried his mother down to join in the celebrations. Her ankle was propped up with pillows, and Mr. Hunt was fussing over her. There was Twelfth-cake and wassail to celebrate, and Esmond had even organized a few games. He knew how special the holidays were to Julia, and he wanted the party to be perfect. Blast! Why was he nervous?

When he turned back, Julia stood framed in the doorway with Alice behind her. He smiled with his mouth open, making him feel like a gaping buffoon. He clamped his jaw shut and hurried over to her. Tonight Julia's hair was twisted up, and curls cascaded out of the top. Soft ringlets hung on either side of her face, and her complexion had finally restored to a healthy pink. Her dress, a pretty lavender, reminded him of Julia's personality—elegant and gentle.

She put out her hands as he approached, and Esmond clasped them in his own.

"It's beautiful!" Julia gushed. "Alice said this was all your idea—even the decorations. What a thoughtful surprise!"

"You might have missed the Christmas ball, but we will make up for it with a memorable Twelfth Night."

Julia released one of his hands and stepped aside so her sister could pass. As soon as Alice was a few feet away, Julia took a small square piece of paper out of the top of her glove and discreetly placed it in Esmond's hand.

"What is this?" Intrigued, he kept his voice low.

"You shall see." Julia dropped his other hand and crossed to greet Ivy, leaving him alone.

He turned his back to the group and unfolded the note.

Meet me in the library after dinner.

Esmond's brows launched skyward. A clandestine meeting? This was not like his sweet and proper Julia. His stomach knotted with a sudden pang of worry. Surely, it wasn't anything negative. Not after the way she'd just received him.

All through dinner Esmond stole glances at Julia. She met his gaze a time or two, and there was nothing suspicious about her manner. He pulled out his pocket watch, wishing the time would fly faster, and did his best to patiently finish his meal. After the ladies were excused, Esmond pushed himself to the edge of his chair. He could not wait for port. "Excuse me while I see to the necessary."

His brother's gaze darted to Mr. Hunt and back to Esmond. Curtis would be on his own until he returned. Esmond stood and slipped from the dining room into the corridor. He followed the passage until he slipped into the narrow library. Julia's smile greeted him.

"What is this all about?" Esmond held up his note. Julia beckoned him closer. He stepped so near her that his legs touched her skirts. "Is everything all right?" he whispered.

Julia brought her hands up around his neck. "I haven't had a moment alone with you since Christmas. This was the best I could manage."

Esmond was not one to blush, but he felt his cheeks color. So this *was* a clandestine meeting. "Where has my shy little Julia gone? Your victory over your illness has made you most impressively brave."

Julia grinned and looked upward.

Esmond did the same. Directly above them was a kissing bough. His gaze lowered to meet Julia's. He encircled her waist and pulled her tight against him, relishing the feeling. "Apparently I wasn't the only one planning a surprise."

"We are even now." Julia's breath danced across his mouth. "I decorated for you with this kissing bough, *and* I wrote you a love note . . . albeit one line with only a meeting destination."

Esmond chuckled. "I'd say there never was a better love letter." He closed the gap between them and captured her lips with his own.

ABOUT THE AUTHOR

ANNEKA R. WALKER IS AN award-winning author raised by a librarian and an English teacher turned judge. After being fed a steady diet of books, she decided to learn about writing. The result was a bachelor's degree in English and history. When she isn't dreaming up a happy ending for a story, she's busy living her own together with her husband and adorable children.

Subscribe to Anneka's newsletter at https://mailchi.mp/a278fdec4416/authorannekawalker and follow her on social media.

Facebook: @AnnekaRWalker
Instagram: @authorannekawalker

OTHER BOOKS AND AUDIOBOOKS

BY SARAH L. McCONKIE

The Promise of Miss Spencer

Love and Secrets at Cassfield Manor

A CHRISTMAS CORRESPONDENCE

SARAH L. McCONKIE

PROLOGUE

December 1838

THE DOOR TO THE STUDY crashed open, startling Caroline in her seat in the nook by the fire. "There you are, Caroline!" her father, Jacob Morleigh bellowed at her. "Put down that stupid book. When will you start behaving like a young lady?"

Caroline looked down at the book's worn pages. It was a beautiful edition with fading gold-leaf edges and a soft leather cover. She did not respond to her father. It was better to stay silent during Lord Marchant's rages.

At thirteen Caroline had grown up far more than most girls her age. Losing her mother a year earlier and living with her father's mourning anger had caused the light of her childhood to extinguish. Father would never understand that the fairy tales in her books were her only escape. They reminded her of better, lost times. They reminded her of her kind mother and of a father who hadn't yet forgotten how to smile. They reminded her that there had been happiness once.

Her father stepped toward her, swaying a bit. "Hand that book of nonsense to me—now!" he yelled.

She rose from her chair, defeated, and surrendered her dearest possession.

"Return to your governess. A young lady of your status and rank must fill her head with every kind of appropriate knowledge, not this rubbish." He shook the book in her face for emphasis.

Caroline felt her father's eyes bore into her back as she turned and silently left the room. He held his ever-present flask in one hand and clutched her book in the other as he slammed the door shut behind her. He would never again be who he once was. How long could she endure life in this house?

CHAPTER ONE

December 1843

THE FACT WAS THAT JOHN Charleston felt dead. Dead as a doornail, really, whatever that meant. After a nearly sleepless December night, he arrived in the center of London. He had traveled by the new train route, the train's sooty ash leaching into his lungs at every stop, until he finally pulled up to his platform around midafternoon. As he hurried from the train, he glanced down at a scrap of paper, where he had scrawled an address and time. He was almost late for his appointment or, rather, his father's appointment, which was now his obligation to keep.

His appointment proved a chatty one. He had a feeling the old woman may not have a lot of visitors. After almost an hour of polite conversation, John knew it was time for him to excuse himself and set out on his next errand.

"Thank you again, Lady Loresetter," he said as he stood, "for allowing me to call and for all of your insights. I will be sure to seek out your niece this evening and inform her of our discussion." He bowed toward the old lady.

The woman's bushy gray eyebrows wrinkled. "Thank you, and good luck," she said with a warning grin. "Until we meet again."

Though still curious about the woman's cryptic words, John hurried to the town house where he would be staying with his good friend Timothy Lennox. There remained just enough time for him to deposit his things, freshen up, and complete the promised errand before it would be too late in the evening to visit a young gentlewoman. He'd brought no man with him, for he employed no such person. Though he was a gentleman and anyone knowing his character would verify such claims, his purse and his pockets were much leaner than those of almost all men of his station.

As soon as John had deposited his traveling case in Timothy's guest room, his friend questioned him. "Whom exactly did you come to visit?"

"An acquaintance of my father's." John looked down at the scribbled address and walked toward the front door.

"I see." With puppylike eagerness Timothy trailed behind him. "Is this acquaintance, by chance, a young lady?"

John smiled and smoothed his light-brown hair and threadbare navy jacket. "Yes, actually. My father was her father's steward, and his dying charge was for me to deliver something to her." John cocked an eyebrow. "But what is that to you?"

A toothy grin spread over Timothy's face. "I possess monetary endowment, as it were, but my build"—he pointed toward his belly and his thick thighs—"does not automatically make me of any interest to females. However, you—a strapping twenty-four-year-old with a handsome face—will draw her in. When she learns you have nothing, she will realize that although my stature may be lacking and I am slightly older, I am a worthy target." Timothy let out a bounding laugh. He always had lacked a little confidence with the ladies.

"Ah, I see," John said, managing a tired chuckle. "I would help if I could, old friend." The truth was he did not wish to make any connection like that with the lady—or any lady, for that matter. Not after what had transpired last summer. He would have nothing to do with this woman beyond his duty. More importantly, he must focus on improving his sister's health. He would deliver the letter, then devote all his time to helping Sophie care for their younger sister, Isabel, back home in Thornton Heath. Timothy gazed at John unrelentingly. John sighed. "You are welcome to come along, and perhaps she will find you charming." He gestured his hand in front of him, inviting Timothy to join him.

"I'd be delighted." Timothy bounced a little on his toes as they walked out the door. "What is her name?"

John smiled at his silly friend. "Lady Caroline Morleigh."

Timothy's beaming face fell, and his bounce ceased. "Actually, I think I'd prefer to stay here." He crumpled his suit tails in his hands and edged back toward his town house.

John raised an eyebrow curiously. "Why the change of heart?"

Timothy let out a laugh and gesticulated widely. "I know Lady Caroline, and there is nothing that would induce me to voluntarily call on her, ever. Last time I attempted a conversation in her presence she mocked me in front of my entire party. She was so patronizing that no one dared speak to me the rest of the evening."

"I am only delivering a letter," John said, knowing his friend was often overly dramatic. "Surely she will be cordial about a simple delivery."

Except it wasn't just a letter he was delivering. If this woman was as rude as Timothy described, did he really want to go through with what the letter said he must do? No one would know if she never received it.

But he stood straighter and brushed his hands together. "Thank you for your warning." He felt for the letter in his ticket pocket.

"Good luck, friend. You'll need it," Timothy said under his breath and skirted inside.

John entered the carriage, exhausted from his travels, and wondered how much Timothy had exaggerated. When the carriage stopped at his destination, he exited quickly and strode without pausing to the lady's door, its large gargoyle-shaped knocker daring him to grasp it.

No matter what the lady did or said, he had promised his father—and now the old woman, the lady's aunt—that he would find her, even if it meant he must do so when he was as tired and pale as a ghost at her door. The ordeal would be over within a day or two at the most. He would do as he had promised.

Caroline Morleigh sat perched behind thick velvet curtains in the parlor when a quick succession of knocks sounded from the front door in the entry hall.

She didn't move as she listened to her butler question the visitor. "May I help you?"

"I am here to see Lady Caroline."

She was not expecting any visitors, although her dancing had been unparalleled at last night's ball. Perhaps Lord Parry had chosen to call. She wouldn't blame him.

Pulling the curtain back, she peered down the corridor into the vestibule as the butler closed the door slightly and tilted his head.

"I presume I have the right address." It was a male voice. He paused and then said loudly, "Lady Caroline's aunt, Lady Loresetter, gave it to me."

Her butler straightened, then opened the door widely. "Well then, do come in."

Who could the man be? He hadn't even mentioned his name or how he was connected with Caroline's aunt.

The butler quickly approached her and handed her the strange man's card. "Show him in." She stood, her chin at the perfect angle of pride and indifference.

The man entered behind the butler, hastily walked past the long curtains, then stopped once he noticed her. He gave a bow in her general direction. As his head lifted, he studied her from her gown upward until he met her eyes.

The butler cleared his throat. "A Mr. John Charleston to see you, my lady."

Keeping her voice uninterested, she asked, "Oh . . . a Mr. Charleston . . . of where and whom?"

The man himself spoke up. "Of Thornton Heath and Mr. Wallace Charleston, my father." The name sounded familiar.

She clenched her jaw. "And why exactly should I entertain a visitor such as yourself?" She raised an eyebrow at him, trying to intimidate him, but he took one step closer. Most men seemed to stare at her face, impressed, but strangely, he appeared unaffected.

"I have a connection with your family through our fathers." His voice was a low, agitated whisper.

She stepped toward him and pursed her lips. Some unpolished stranger would not intimidate her.

"I have something important to deliver," Mr. Charleston finished.

She finally placed his surname—something to do with her father's holdings. Why hadn't her eccentric aunt warned her such a visitor would call? Not that they had spoken lately. Still, it was just like the mad, meddling old woman.

Mr. Charleston's eyes met hers again. "I think there might be a glimmer of curiosity in those steely eyes of yours."

She let out a mocking laugh. "Do not attempt to challenge me, Mr. Charleston. You call here, unannounced and unconnected, and then try to bait me with some mysterious package surely of no consequence to someone of my position?" Just what exactly was he about? Clearly, he didn't comprehend her superior standing. She was not to be trifled with and ought not to be bothered by someone of such obviously low circumstance. He was handsome, to be sure, but his coat was starting to fray, and his white shirt was almost beige.

She tilted her head and brushed her hand toward him, dismissing his words. "Shall we point out your flaws? When dealing with someone of my situation, do you not think it wise to write and ask if you *might* come? Especially as someone of your"—she gestured to all of him—"status? What could you possibly have to deliver to me?"

She thought she saw his jaw tighten as he took one step closer. His voice remained low. "If I had come for a pleasure visit, I *might* ask your permission, as I am sure your gentleman suitors do. But I am here, Lady Caroline, on business."

He had imitated her tone precisely. How infuriating!

"Is that so?" she said, plastering on a false smile. "Then, pray, make yourself comfortable. I am sure you are not used to such fine furnishings in your situation."

She gestured to several overstuffed couches. Finally deciding on a claw-foot armchair, he seated himself. He reached into his coat pocket and withdrew a letter, holding it between his fingertips. "I came to deliver this."

"Ah, a letter." She settled onto the velvet couch across from him. "What scheme have you concocted with such a note?" She jutted out her chin and narrowed her eyes. "Let me warn you—I am not to be trifled with. You would be wise to eschew any beggarly requests for charity."

He said nothing and maintained a steady gaze across the room. Caroline disliked his indifference as he waved the letter in the air.

"Have you read it?" Caroline asked, leaning forward an inch. "You can read, I presume?" She stared at him with a pitiful, mocking pout.

"Perhaps," he said. She wondered if he meant to answer the first or second question. "It is a letter from your father to mine, giving instructions to carry out, written nearly five years ago. Due to my father's long-lasting illness, he never accomplished the task. He wished to regain his health and deliver this himself, but instead he gave me the charge upon his deathbed."

Her father, who even when living had never wished to speak to her, had asked a stranger to deliver a letter? Impossible.

Caroline scanned his face. "It appears we have both lost our fathers."

Mr. Charleston gave a short nod, and Caroline looked away. Something in his eyes felt inviting and too trustworthy. She would not give them purchase any longer.

"How long has your father been deceased?" she asked, watching the falling leaves tumble down outside the window.

"It will be a year this Christmas Eve."

Caroline swallowed. Dreadful to lose a loved one on such a beautiful holiday. She thought about asking more but masked her interest. "Death affects us all," she said, devoid of emotion. It had been nearly five years since her own father's passing. She did not allow herself to dwell on that day. Too much had happened; too much had surfaced. She tried to ignore Mr. Charleston's wrinkled brow. After a quiet pause, he handed her the letter. "I am afraid you will dislike the contents."

"Let me set you at ease," Caroline said, steeling herself again. "I determined from the very moment you decided to thrust your undeserving person into my home, to find whatever you say disagreeable."

He heaved a short sigh and shook his head. "Naturally. I am just the messenger."

Ignoring his comment, Caroline unfolded the letter, exposing a single page.

My Dear Wallace,

There was a time when I was happy. When I was kind. I am all too aware this seems like a distorted memory, but it is the truth. My wife's death ruined me, and because I was consumed by grief, I poisoned everyone within my grasp. Only now do I ashamedly realize how abominably I treated the world—especially you and my daughter.

Oh, how I wish I could amend my ways and return to my younger self! I deserve no mercy. Instead, justice requires that I die in my shame.

I will be dead before I can amend what I have done to Caroline. She never could abide my company for long. I plead with you to find her, tell her I love her. And if she still insists on traveling, you must bring her home. Our housekeeper, Mrs. Horne, will

speak with Caroline. Mrs. Horne will know what
to do next.
 For this service, I thank you more than I can
express.
  Your indebted friend,
  Jacob Morleigh

Her father was right—she had run away, always finding some
way to travel with her cousins rather than stay at home. Yet, for
one moment, she wished to clasp the letter to her heart. He'd
said he loved her. She scanned that line again. Perhaps she ought
to thank Mr. Charleston for finding her and bringing this last
message from her father.

The smile that had formed fell as awful memories suddenly
haunted her. Her father's silence, his distance. The way he
pushed her away, banished her to her governesses as though she
were invisible.

No, one line of a letter was not enough to overcome the pain he
had caused her. As Mr. Charleston said, he was only the messenger,
on duty from his own father. He did not deserve thanks, especially
with his assuming attitude and decidedly low station.

He studied her as she deliberately met his stare with a blank
face. "I believe your business is finished," she said as she rose
from the couch. "I wish you a good day." She gestured toward
the door.

After a dreadful, motionless pause, he turned his head but
did not move. "My task is not finished, Lady Caroline."

"Excuse me? You are ridiculous. Do you not understand that
I have dismissed you? You have delivered your note, so I release
you from all obligation." She wielded a deliberate glare. "Leave."

Mr. Charleston did not move.

Caroline fought the urge to stomp her foot. She was not
accustomed to people disobeying her orders. He needed to leave so
she could sort through the mess her father had made of her heart
and mind.

"Perhaps you should read it once more," he said. "The letter states that I am to take you to your childhood home."

He couldn't possibly believe she would agree to travel with him, a complete stranger of absolutely no consequence. Besides, she lived in Town now and found it much more agreeable than the manor of her childhood—fewer memories haunted her here.

"If I write to the housekeeper, I am sure she will tell me what I need to know, whatever it is." She shifted and continued. "I hope you don't think there's money in this for you. I do not have time for charity cases. I am the heiress to my father's account, and I refuse to conduct business with pond scum." She laughed and clasped her hands behind her back, distancing herself from him. This man needed to leave. "I will not be led on some wild-goose chase. Personal gain is the only reason someone like you would come here, and I intend to guard every pound of my father's legacy."

Mr. Charleston's jaw tightened again. "I assure you I want none of your wealth." He took a breath. "Lady Caroline, there could be more to this than money."

She wondered what he could possibly mean, but she turned her back to him.

He spoke slowly. "My father's soul will never rest until I finish what was promised."

Though she couldn't see Mr. Charleston's face, he sounded resolute. Would her father haunt her too if she disregarded his letter? Would he care enough? All he'd ever cared about were his bank holdings. Now the fortune was hers, and she would not give one shilling away to past acquaintances who came clawing at her gold.

But in the letter her father had said he loved her. Did that carry any weight? If she hadn't been avoiding home—traveling so far away with cousins—would she have made it back in time to see her father before he passed? If only he hadn't died the day before she'd made it back home. Was it her fault he could only write a letter instead of seeing his daughter's face one last time?

Mr. Charleston spoke again. "Your father is pleading with you. With me. You see that, don't you?"

She turned toward him. "Mr. Charleston, I must ask you to leave. You cannot force me to go."

She gestured toward the open door.

"I feared you might say that." He angled toward her.

"Thank you for understanding. Get out."

"Which is why I asked your aunt if she might accompany us as a chaperone. She assured me she would be ready to travel by week's end."

"Excuse me?" Caroline scathed, unable to keep her voice in check.

Mr. Charleston smiled, undeterred. "Your aunt, your father's sister? Lady Loresetter? She wishes you to go and will accompany us. I think she is looking forward to it, and if you deny her this trip, she told me you might just send her to the grave prematurely."

Caroline clamped her eyes shut and let out a gust of air through her nose. "You can't be serious. My aunt is nearly deaf. I doubt you could have had such an extensive conversation with her." Heat rose on her cheeks as her tone swirled out of control.

Why must he bring Aunt Ebby into this? As a child, Caroline was close to the old woman, but as Aunt Ebby's hearing had deteriorated, Caroline had stopped calling on the old bat, who was not only Caroline's only close relative but also possessed a large amount of money Caroline was to inherit. If she stayed in the woman's good graces, that was. Obligation pulled at her, and the sensible part of her told her not to misstep against her aunt's wishes. She didn't wish to send the woman to her grave prematurely, especially if in the process, she was written out of the will.

Mr. Charleston swallowed, and the smile on his face irked Caroline. "I will have time to explain more, Lady Caroline, when I return on Friday at ten." He bowed, giving an infuriating tip of his hat. "With Lady Loresetter, of course."

"I will still refuse," she said, but he was nearly through the door. The quick clip of his boots echoed in Caroline's ears.

She stood in the entryway and read the letter one more time. Her childhood home. With this slippery, coercive, low-class Mr. Charleston, no less.

He simply did not understand. Her mind raced back to her thirteen-year-old self, just months before her father had died. She had come upon him in his study—again—glazed eyes staring at the fire, an empty wine bottle on the table.

"What is it, Caroline?" he'd barked.

"I just wished to ask, Father, if I might spend a week with Eliza." She'd fumbled with the fine trim on her gown. "She has invited me to stay with her—"

"Out of the question, you stupid girl. How many times must I tell you that anyone associated with that family is beneath us? If you spend time with them, people will think you are like them."

She'd held her head high, determined not to cower this time. "She is a good person, Father. Her brothers, too, are respectable, and her father and mother—"

"Don't get me started on her brothers. You, with your weak mind, might fall for one of them and ruin everything with an attachment to an untitled man. Can't you see the empire I have built for you? I was no fool when I married your mother. You must marry someone who can improve your situation and rank."

"You can't mean that. Mama had a fortune and was the daughter of an earl, but you can't tell me you didn't love her."

"Oh, I loved her, but even love can't save a person. Now I am left without her." He'd reached violently for his wine bottle but, in his drunken stupor, missed, sending it rolling until it crashed to the ground. A shard of glass had landed next to Caroline's feet. As she'd reached to pick the piece up, it had sliced her hand, and she'd let out a small cry.

"Now look at what you've done," her father had said, dazed and glassy-eyed. "Get out!"

Caroline blinked, bringing herself back to the present. If she went back to Croyden, she'd have to step foot in that house. In that study, perhaps.

How could she endure all the memories?

❀ ❀ ❀

Based on Timothy's descriptions, John had expected a cross, ugly shrew of a woman, but Caroline Morleigh was utterly beautiful. At least, until she'd opened her mouth, exposing her viperous tongue and heated temper. Her dark-brown curls had framed her face, and her gown had perfectly suited her porcelain skin and thin waist. But when he had brought his eyes up to her face, she had glared at him.

It had only gotten worse from there.

He would not dwell on her beauty. Being blinded by a woman's looks had ruined him before. He had deliberately postponed this meeting, waiting months after his father had given him the task to deliver the letter. First, he had mourned his father's death and been wary of leaving his younger sisters. Later, when his relationship with Anna developed, he'd told himself they could deliver the letter together, after they were married.

In the end, Anna had proved untrustworthy. More than that, she was downright deceitful and two-faced. If a woman like her couldn't be trusted, who could?

He would perform only the task required with Lady Caroline and give her the wide berth and stoic detachment she appeared to crave so much. Luckily, he'd have for company the elderly Lady Loresetter—thank goodness for her—who had assured him she could placate Lady Caroline.

Running his fingers through his hair, he sighed. The only women he cared about now were his sisters, and it would stay that way.

CHAPTER TWO

FRIDAY MORNING CAME TOO QUICKLY. Caroline hoped with every part of her soul that the cunning, pushy Mr. Charleston would not show his face. She had been blunt with him but wondered if it was enough to scare him off.

At exactly ten, a knock came at the door.

Blast! The nerve of him, coming back here.

However, when the butler opened the door, it was not Mr. Charleston but a thin young woman who stood there. The woman hovered near the butler, speaking in hushed tones. She looked as though she had tried to improve her hair and grooming, but despite the vast effort Caroline supposed it had taken, a smudge of soot across her cheek belied her status. Her dirty nails showed as she clasped her dress, and her tattered hem hung all too visible above her feet. When she noticed Caroline, she abruptly turned from the butler and curtsied.

"Beg your pardon, miss," the young woman said. Caroline had expected more of a lower-class accent from the girl. "I wish to see the housekeeper."

"I hope my butler has been telling you that you should have called at the servants' entrance. But I can tell you right now our housekeeper is too busy for someone like you."

The woman cleared her throat, holding her ground. "You see, I am looking for work, and one of the teachers from the ragged school suggested I try here. She showed me the advertisement, my lady, that you needed someone for your kitchen. I can read, I'm very clean, and I have a character reference from—"

Caroline raised her hand and cleared her throat loudly to make her point. "I employ only the highest caliber of person, and although I am sure you think yourself among them, your presentation denotes otherwise." She shooed her fingers toward her. "Apply at some other, less-established house that takes in the surplus population."

The young woman said nothing, curtsied, and turned away. Her gaze was so far buried into the floor that she nearly bumped into the tall man who was being let into the house.

"Oh, excuse me." Mr. Charleston smiled at the young woman. "Begging your pardon, miss."

The young woman looked at him and held Mr. Charleston's gaze for a moment. Caroline could see tears streaked down the young woman's cheeks, leaving glimmering paths on her dusty skin. How pitiful. The girl would never get anywhere if she couldn't learn to take rejection. Caroline scoffed and lifted an eyebrow at Mr. Charleston. He must be one of those types who apologized to everyone.

"Always so kind?" Caroline asked him with mock solemnity. His eyes followed the poor girl as she scurried down the front steps like a frightened mouse. "It is a wonder you didn't give her your handkerchief."

"She might have deserved it more than some gentlewomen I know," he whispered, flexing his jaw.

Caroline glared. How dare he make such a comment! "You decided to come back, then?"

"I am a man of my word."

"So I see." She pursed her lips and looked him up and down. This coat was even shabbier than his last. "And I am a woman of my word, Mr. Charleston," she said, not moving. "I am not going."

"In that case, let me quote your aunt. 'If she refuses, tell her I will never forgive her.'" He said it in a nasally voice, a near-perfect mimic of her aunt. It almost made her want to smile. Until she remembered what would come with her aunt's disdain. No part of her inheritance.

Did he know what he implied when he recited such a declaration? A part of her remembered, too, how Aunt Ebby had been one of the few people who seemed to care about her after her mother's death and her father's anger and eventual silence.

If her aunt hadn't been so definitive and demanding, Caroline would have left Mr. Charleston standing alone in the entryway. But as firm as she wished to be in her resolve, she knew there was too much at stake. If she were to have her inheritance, she had to appease Aunt Ebby. She had to go with Mr. Charleston.

She wouldn't let him off easy though. "Am I forced to travel with you dressed so? Whomever we meet will surely think you are my servant."

He blew a gust of charged air toward her. "I am, in every way, prepared to leave, and these traveling clothes serve as a shield against your barrage of rude remarks."

He was far too plucky. Someone of his status ought to cower, yet he seemed to say whatever he wished—it unnerved her.

He stepped closer. "Your aunt is in the carriage. I know you could keep me waiting all day, but for her sake, we really ought to go."

She heaved a sigh. "I cannot believe I am being subjected to such coercion and conspiracy. You must give me a few moments."

She turned and begrudgingly called her lady's maid, Edith, to help her change into a traveling gown.

When she came back down, Mr. Charleston offered her his arm. She looked narrowly at it, then back at him. She scooped up her skirt in both hands and walked on, adding a mocking laugh. She had perfected that laugh.

They walked side by side to the carriage, Caroline trying to ignore the man there and the fact that she had just capitulated to his absurd plan.

"Good day, Aunt," Caroline said after she warily allowed Mr. Charleston to hand her into the carriage. She sat next to her aunt, who nodded, a slight smile across her lips, her cane resting against her skirt.

"Lovely to see you, my dear. It has been far too long since you have visited. I am very pleased Mr. Charleston here was so good as to arrange some quality time for us."

Her aunt was already siding with the pond scum? Unbelievable.

As the infuriating man entered the carriage to sit across from the women, Caroline turned her attention to the window. Heavy clouds threatened rain in the gray weather outside, but inside the carriage seemed even more dismal.

❋ ❋ ❋

John had expected that Lady Caroline's company would prove unpleasant, but the first hour of the carriage ride was utterly intolerable. The time passed in complete, horrible silence. As they drove on, with him stuck with near strangers and so few shared topics of interest, the silence ate at his nerves, and he wondered exactly how much conversation was needed. He wished the whole ordeal were already over. His sister needed him to find her a better doctor, and soon.

But Sophie and Isabel would expect better manners from him. It was a burden having such upstanding, wonderful siblings. Their good influence always tugged at him, their expectations silently whispering in the recesses of his mind. This Caroline Morleigh was the task in front of him, and he should at least make some effort at conversation, for that was what a good person would do. If his sisters were here, they'd know what to say.

He swallowed. "Has it been a long time since you've been to Croyden?"

Lady Caroline, who had been reading for the better part of the last half hour, put down her book. "I see you have done your research." She avoided answering the question, but at least she was talking.

"My father, along with your aunt, have supplied me with all necessary information." He left out the warning given to him by Timothy Lennox. "We shall travel directly to Elbury House, for Mrs. Horne is still employed there."

"It seems your father knew much of my father's situation," Caroline said as she looked away, "though my father almost never mentioned yours."

"I understand my father managed all Lord Marchant's shares in the manufacturing plants and spent much time with him in the month before he died." The sun shone through the window and onto Lady Caroline's beautiful face, but John thought he saw a storm cloud roll across her blue-gray eyes. He had little experience with such openly taciturn women. His most recent experience had been with Anna, who had appeared so kind and had turned out to be something else entirely. If he hadn't such wonderful sisters, he would have sworn off all females.

John was sure the aunt could not hear them, though one eye twitched open every so often as she dozed.

"Perhaps you ought to tell me about your childhood home. I have never traveled through that part of Surrey."

She huffed. "I hardly know where to start. Elbury House is quite large and beautiful. Although, when I moved to Town, I turned its management over to my solicitor, who has filled the estate with renters since my father's death." She shrugged and continued. "I don't know who lives there now, for I think it turned over again. I receive a handsome rent for it, not that I left Elbury House for want of money—I was just tired of living there." She picked at the intricate trim of her bonnet string.

"You have not been back since your father's death?"

Her slender neck tightened as she swallowed. "Not since a few months after the funeral, no."

The expression on her face seemed to convey more than annoyance. Had she really never gone back, even to visit old friends or her father's grave?

Her gaze settled out the window, and John felt himself wincing. Why had he insisted on a journey to a place that seemed to cause her so much pain? Not understanding a female's history and motives had never boded well for him and most definitely would not now.

"It must be hard to return, but thank you for . . ." He searched for the right words. "For allowing me to follow through with my promise."

"Do not thank me for anything." Her eyes tightened as she continued to avoid his gaze. Her aunt roused a little, shaking her head. Lady Caroline continued. "I knew I could not be rid of you until you had finished your duty. I just pray whatever you are getting at will be over more quickly this way."

Lady Caroline jolted forward a bit, casting a glance at her aunt, who seemed to have inadvertently elbowed her.

Lady Loresetter stirred herself awake. "You know, Mr. Charleston, as a girl, my niece was always prided on her impeccable manners. Such a precision of language. As I have become hard of hearing these past few years, you will have to be the judge of how she has maintained her skill."

John held back his laughter at the aunt's ironic timing.

Lady Caroline scowled at the old lady, who soon settled again into a decidedly loud snore, and returned to dutifully studying her book.

John looked out the window. After a few minutes of turning over Lady Caroline's unpleasantries in his mind, he muttered, "It doesn't have to be this way."

Lady Caroline lowered her book and stared at him. "Excuse me? What did you say?" she prodded a bit louder.

John watched as she raised her voice, wondering if Lady Loresetter might stir and watch them closer. "It . . . was nothing."

Lady Caroline's gloved fists clenched. "I believe I heard you say it doesn't have to be this way. On the contrary; since you forced me to ride in this carriage, I believe it does have to be this way."

"I wasn't talking about the carriage ride, Lady Caroline." He blew out an exasperated breath.

Her lips pouted, and she lifted her chin. "Then, what exactly did you mean?"

"I meant . . ." He tried not to stumble over his words and endeavored to keep his voice low. "You do not need to treat every living, breathing human being with malice. The world is not quite as bad or as threatening as to merit your complete rudeness."

He had barely spoken above a whisper, but he thought he saw the half-open eye of Lady Loresetter quiver.

Lady Caroline pushed herself away from the squabs, her hands going white as she gripped the edge.

"Do not presume to understand me." She articulated each syllable. She held his gaze for a long moment, until John bowed his head, pulling back toward the window. She pushed herself into her own corner and said nothing more.

CHAPTER THREE

As they drove up the park, a flood of memories swirled through Caroline's mind. The recollections began pleasantly: carefree summers, strolling near the streams with her mother, the times she would hide in the hedges and wait for a servant to find her, the walks she used to take with her father—before he changed. She had been happy there until her mother died and everything fell apart.

She pulled herself from her reflections as she stepped from the carriage. The air was a perfect cold, and the smell wafting from the kitchens reminded her of the wassail the cooks always made with the harvest apples just before Christmas. The scent made her feel like a girl again.

Seeing the front door brought back memories of the last time she had shut it, when she was full of anger, grief, and pain. She had fled for what she had hoped would be forever.

Caroline turned to her aunt. "I cannot believe I am doing this," she said loudly and with enough emphasis for her aunt to recognize her displeasure.

"You will manage well enough." Aunt Ebby looked straight forward.

Caroline swallowed and begrudgingly knocked, with Mr. Charleston and Aunt Ebby flanking her.

How many of the servants from her childhood were still here? Perhaps she could request seeing the housekeeper right away and then be gone before too many servants gossiped about her visit.

A handsome, tall butler opened the door. "May I help you?" He was new.

"I have some business to conduct with Mrs. Horne, who knows why I call. Is she in?"

"I am afraid she's gone until tomorrow morning, preparing something for my master. May I tell her who called?"

She gave him her name, expecting to be let in immediately to the house, which still belonged to her. It felt strange being left on the doorstep. Caroline scoffed at the man's incivility. He must be *quite* new.

"Allen, who is there? Do not keep them waiting in the cold!" He looked over his shoulder toward someone who seemed to be the mistress of the house.

"Oh yes, forgive me," the butler said. "Come in and warm yourself."

Caroline was scrutinizing the awful window coverings when the mistress of the house stopped and let out a squeal, clasping her hands in delight.

"Caroline Morleigh? Is it really you? So you have not forgotten us! I was just thinking about you the other day. Oh, how lovely. I am so grateful to see you, for it has been ages since we've been together!"

"Sylvia Felwig? I am surprised to see you here. And may I introduce my aunt, Lady Loresetter, and Mr. Charleston?" Caroline tried for a steady tone, feeling more excitement at seeing her old friend than she was willing to let on. She could not believe Sylvia was the new interim mistress of Elbury House.

Sylvia cleared her throat and smiled. "I beg your pardon, Caroline, but it is Lady Sylvia Hartley now. I wrote to you about the happy news and invited you to the wedding, but you must not have received the letter." Her smiled faded slightly.

Caroline felt her tongue go dry. The letter had been to tell of her marriage . . . to Lord Hartley? She hadn't even opened it, sticking to her resolve that Sylvia had been beneath her. "And you have now rented Elbury House? Or are you visiting its current occupants?" Caroline hoped against reason the latter was the truth.

"Oh yes. You see, after you left, Lord Hartley visited our assembly again, and I fell for him. I have always loved Elbury, so when the last renters quitted it, I begged him to apply. We have made it our own. Of course, Mrs. Horne was happy to stay on, and she is quite a wonder, I daresay. She knows everyone and everything. But here I am, gabbing on. Please make yourself comfortable."

They walked a few paces away from the others, and Sylvia leaned closer. "You said his name is Mr. Charleston, correct? Are you engaged to him, my dear?" She peered behind Caroline with a studying eye.

"Heaven forbid," Caroline said in a low voice. "We are on business, settling a small matter of my father's. Aunt Ebby"—she gestured toward the old woman—"is here as chaperone."

"I see. That is too bad. He's quite handsome, although probably not enough to tempt you. You were always so particular in those matters." She stopped speaking and gave a quick smile. "Do be seated."

Caroline felt herself paralyzed. She should not stay. Happy memories of the two of them came crashing into her mind. Their matching dolls, the hours of dress-up, the secret tunnel out of her room—but now this was Sylvia's house. And if Caroline were to see Lord Hartley . . .

"Why, thank you," she found herself saying, "but it has been a trying day of travel, and we must find our way to Deer's Cross Inn. I merely wished to speak with Mrs. Horne and then we were to be on our way."

Sylvia did not press the matter. "I am so sorry she is out. As Allen mentioned, she is gathering the last of the supplies for tomorrow. We are having dinner and dancing here, and I insist you come. There will be only a few couples, and we would be delighted to have you. Tell me you will attend."

Mr. Charleston had lagged behind the two young women for most of the conversation but came quickly up to them now. "I think I may speak for the whole party. We would be delighted."

The nerve! Caroline wanted to put him in his place right there but quelled the urge to berate him in front of her old friend. Sylvia would see through her false pleasantries then, and Caroline's pride would not let herself fall in her former friend's eyes. Instead of speaking out she sent a decided glare toward Mr. Charleston.

"I am so glad," Sylvia said. "Mrs. Horne will be thrilled to see you."

Caroline hoped that would be the case. She had been quite rude to the older woman the last few years she'd lived in Elbury House. It was then she had learned to be defensive, mistrusting, and self-preserving. After all, if her father had shut her from his life, who else would do the same?

She thanked Sylvia and quickly took her leave. She made it back to the carriage, where Mr. Charleston handed her in. He said nothing, and she waited until he was fully settled to accuse him.

"I am not prepared for a social event, Mr. Charleston. This was to be a quick trip. I have not the correct gowns, gloves, etcetera for an evening of dinner and dancing." Her jaw clenched twice. "I hardly expected us to stay longer than one evening and had planned to return tomorrow. It is *not* your place to accept invitations for our party."

He only smiled. "With all due respect"—she suspected he thought very little due—"I said yes because Lady Hartley sounded excited to see you. To turn down her invitation would have been quite rude."

She had been known to turn down more illustrious invitations. "Do you not understand my social status? I accept dinner and dance invitations from only persons who will increase my standing and connections. Of course, you wouldn't think of such matters." She smoothed her skirt and lifted her eyebrows patronizingly. "My father instructed me in the ways of good breeding, and I am sure you were given no such education." She sighed and then glowered at him. "Dining with Sylvia does not help me in any regard."

Aunt Ebby's wiry eyebrows drew upward. "Caroline, can you not just try to enjoy yourself? You and Sylvia *used* to be the best of friends."

That had been when she was weak, when she'd thought she needed friends. She had no time for them now, not unless they increased her connections. She blew out a gust of air.

Aunt Ebby continued to look pointedly at her. "It wouldn't do to strain any relationships unnecessarily."

Was she sending a roundabout warning for Caroline to keep in her good graces? That blasted inheritance always hung between them.

"If you say we must attend, I suppose we shall," Caroline conceded, glowering at them both until they reached the inn.

Her thoughts spun out of control, and anger came bubbling up toward them all—first at her father for not letting her marry Lord Hartley and then at Sylvia for snatching him and the house when Caroline should have had them both.

Then there was this John Charleston. What right did he have to barge into her life and cause her to remember so much from her past? He was slippery, like a fish, maneuvering his way into everyone's good graces and always out of hers.

🌸 🌸 🌸

"This will have to do," she said to her borrowed maid the next evening. She wore a dark-maroon silk gown, perfectly tailored with intricate lace dripping from the collar. The skirt could not possibly be as full as those she usually wore, and although the maid had procured a few flowers, her hair and jewelry remained remarkably dull compared to her London trappings. She reminded herself she ought to always be prepared for lavish events, no matter how quick the trip was meant to be. People always extended invitations to her, and when one was wanted so frequently, one must be ready. She had always been taught that rank was preserved through fine dress.

Mr. Charleston waited in the front parlor of the inn and stood upon her entry.

"Good afternoon," she said to him. He gave a small bow, and she held her chin high, not meeting his gaze.

"You surprise me." He offered his arm.

"Why is that?" She clutched her fan as they moved toward the carriage.

"You are not nearly as drab as you insinuated yesterday that you would be."

Caroline's mouth fell open, something she normally made sure never to do. She finally closed it, clenching her jaw. "I assume you mean that as a compliment, sir?"

"Naturally," he said, a smile turning up his lips.

"You ought to work on your delivery."

He handed her into the carriage. Aunt Ebby was already perched on the bench, a shawl gathered about her shoulders, her eyes on her niece. Caroline settled herself next to her, trying to ignore her searching gaze, when Mr. Charleston cleared his throat. "You could too." He drew his lips into a tight line.

Aunt Ebby seized a long breath and exhaled, smiling. "I trust we shall all enjoy the evening. I, for one, plan on it." Her eyes lingered on Caroline, who said nothing. Her aunt had always been so different from her father. Didn't she understand how beneath them it was to be with Sylvia in their own home? Caroline huffed and turned to the window, choosing to ignore them both until they pulled into the drive and exited the carriage.

"Let us not stay long," she said when they walked toward the house. "We need only make an appearance, not seem rude, and then speak with Mrs. Horne."

"As you wish." Mr. Charleston raised his eyebrows as he led her and Aunt Ebby, one lady on each arm, to the front door.

✿ ✿ ✿

To Caroline's dismay, they had not gone directly to Mrs. Horne and had been prevailed upon to stay for dinner. She tried to ignore Mr. Charleston altogether, thankful his seat at the table was farthest from hers. As the meal began, she could not help but enjoy herself.

"The mincemeat pies are incredible." She smiled at Sylvia. "Do you still keep the same cook?"

"We do," Lord Hartley said, his voice low. He smiled politely at Caroline, employing a businesslike tone. "It would have been foolish to let go of such wonderful staff. I believe your mother found the cook years ago."

Caroline nodded, grateful for the respectful ease between them. It felt like they were old friends, nothing more. Proper and easy. She turned to Sylvia. "Did you tell Cook to make all my favorites? Blood pudding, delectable tarts, and this bread!"

Lord Hartley and his wife exchanged a loving glance, and Sylvia smiled. "Of course, though she had already planned some of them. Your mother made so many excellent choices here at Elbury." She patted her husband's arm as he nodded in agreement. They were well suited, Caroline had to admit, and very clearly in love.

She snuck a glance or two throughout the meal toward Mr. Charleston, who seemed quite enthralled with his dinner plate, but when he looked up, it was in her direction. Twice she studied Sylvia, jealous of her happiness, realizing the pleasure that might come from having an intimate confidant in a good husband.

🌼 🌼 🌼

As the party moved to dancing, John kept waiting for Lady Caroline to crack—to snap at someone or deliver a cutting comment—but she never did. What surprised him more was how happy she appeared. Could it be possible that this unfeeling shrew of a woman had taken her aunt's advice?

It was fortunate they hadn't been seated closely at dinner, for it was surely his proximity that exacerbated her temper. He did seem to have that effect on women—driving them mad, angry, or simply away.

What he didn't understand was why Lady Caroline bristled so easily. If Lady Hartley truly had been one of her closest friends, the woman seemed an excellent influence. Though, he realized, associating with wonderful acquaintances didn't mean a person always turned out well. If that *had* been a true principle, Anna would have been much kinder on account of her having associated with his sister so frequently. He shook his head and hoped too late that no one noticed his movement. Why did he still think about Anna? No doubt being in the same place as Lady Caroline didn't help. Too many eerie similarities between the women.

Coming out of his musings, John realized everyone was clearing away from the table, dinner now over. Wanting to be busy, he escorted Lady Loresetter to a comfortable chair, where she could watch the dancing. He hadn't danced since the last time he and Anna had taken the floor months ago, but the air held such an inviting atmosphere that he found himself searching for a partner. That was a good sign. He wasn't so injured from Anna that he'd never consider dancing again.

If only his sisters could be there with him . . . if only Isabel could still dance at all. It had been two years since she'd stopped, her feet growing too stiff and full of pain. But when she had danced, she had been glorious.

John missed the first set, not asking a partner quickly enough. As he studied the dancers, he noticed Lady Caroline among them with a partner decidedly below her station, and yet she smiled. John couldn't believe it. He had been sure that she would not dance at all. When she accepted a partner for the second dance, he had to look twice, as this companion was even shabbier than the first.

John had been introduced to Lady Hartley's sister at dinner and asked her for the second set. It felt good to dance again. Anna had always hinted at his need for improvement, but Miss Elisabeth Felwig smiled willingly and even complimented him.

When the music ceased, John thanked her and returned her to the edge of the dance floor. He was moving toward the drinks when he heard Lady Caroline laugh for the first time. It was enough to make him turn toward her in surprise as she leaned toward Lady Hartley.

"Do you remember when we used to practice our dances? You always forced me to be the man," she said.

Lady Hartley raised her eyebrows. "Well, it certainly has not hurt your abilities—perhaps knowing the men's part has made you more the expert. I heard several of the young men of our party praise your skill."

Lady Caroline beamed. "Thank you. To be on this floor, actually dancing—it is what I always dreamed of as a child. It is what it should have been."

"I am so glad you feel that way," Lady Hartley said. They moved away, and Lady Hartley introduced another willing partner to Lady Caroline.

Lady Caroline was more beautiful than John had realized, which scared him. What was it about a pleasant female dancing that made him lose his senses? His resolve? He had sworn off the ladies forever. Better to turn to serve the older lady of the party and ignore all else. He brought Lady Loresetter some refreshments and found himself following her gaze as she watched her niece carefully, a slight smile playing on her lips.

"Are you going to dance again, Mr. Charleston?" she asked.

"Are you seeking an invitation, madam?" He swooped his hand across his waist and bowed. "I would be honored to stand up with you." His eyes wrinkled as he looked at her shaking head.

She chuckled softly and jutted her pointed chin across the room toward her niece.

The waltz ended, and John observed Lady Caroline clap and smile widely—a genuine, unaffected smile, her cheeks rosy. Gone was the bored expression, her eyes sparkling in a way he had never seen before.

She was . . . mesmerizing.

Without letting himself analyze too much, he nodded to her aunt and immediately made his way to Lady Caroline. It was only one dance, after all. What harm could come from that? He felt he must capitalize on her good mood. Who knew when it would be gone again?

Weaving through the crowd took its toll, however, for when he reached the place Lady Caroline had stood, she was gone.

To his left was a small corridor. Perhaps she went there for some fresh air. He followed the passage to an exquisite library. Or, more likely, it once was exquisite. Only half of the floor-to-ceiling shelves now contained books. Apparently, Lord Hartley's book collection was not even a third of what Lord Marchant's must have been.

As he walked farther into the room, he noticed an ajar door with a filigree handle. Curiosity propelled him forward through the library toward a small porch overlooking the gardens.

He pushed the door open imperceptibly farther, to the back of a maroon gown.

Lady Caroline didn't notice him at first, but the space was too small, too intimate for that to last long.

Best to take the offensive role and speak first. "I cannot help but think you and I missed a most enjoyable set just now."

She showed no surprise as her hands gripped the railing firmly, but she did not turn.

He ventured again. "I saw you dancing before, and I thought I saw you enjoying it too."

Her straight nose almost came into view as her head shifted a degree. "So you admit to watching me?"

She was trying to bait him.

"I admit I was, Lady Caroline, along with several other young men, I am sure. I don't think you have the power to go unnoticed anywhere."

She looked out again at the garden and gave a dry laugh. "How wrong you are."

Now she appeared to want flattery—but she had seemed so happy, in such a new mood, that he was willing to give it. "Tell me honestly—everyone gravitates toward you, or at the very least watches you . . . when have you ever been left alone?"

"More times than I can count. In this house, at least." Her voice left her in a choked escape. She looked down, and something urged him one step closer. The air turned vulnerable, and for the first time, he feared her porcelain frame might shatter. The silence was unbearable.

"Lady Caroline," he said with a softer tone, "I came to ask you for the next dance. The music is so merry, the couples so cheerful. If you'd be willing . . ." Drawing close behind her, he placed a few of his fingers lightly on top of hers. Through gloved hands their fingers brushed, and she did not move away. His breath caught, and he was as much surprised by his action as by her acceptance of it.

He thought he heard her draw a breath to answer when she turned and pushed away from him. Her eyes were red and swollen. Tear rivulets forged their way down her cheeks, and her face was drained of its color.

"Why did you have to bring me here?" She drew her hands behind her. "I forgot how much joy I *used* to feel. Sylvia was my best friend; she was like my sister. She used to come here every day. Lord Hartley, too, in the summers, long before he was a lord or anyone of consequence. The three of us were thick as thieves, not worrying so much about decorum, holdings, rank, or title, and definitely not romance. Now they are married, and where am I? I knew myself to be above them. I found new friends. I thought Eliza would be better, that my father would at least approve of her, but no. No one proved worthy, and then I saw what my father saw. I didn't need them. Instead I fell in love with my father's money and furthering my status. If I had thought . . . if I had known my memories of Elbury could be even more painful, I would have never come." She flung her hand back toward the open door and inhaled. "I would have sworn to never see you again."

She looked to dart past him then, but her skirt was too large, and he purposefully edged toward the doorframe to block her. "Wait." He had to speak to her here. He had brought her here, and if he had broken something, if he had broken her, he would be the one to fix it.

She seemed to realize she could not run, or perhaps she recalled that she should not, with the signs of her tears so evident across her face. Defeated, she sat on a nearby bench and wilted onto the railing.

"I am sorry," he said. It was a weak phrase. It had not gotten him out of many scrapes before, but he felt he ought to at least try it one more time.

An unimpressed eyebrow raised at him. "You do not understand."

He cleared his throat. "You . . . are right," he said.

Lady Caroline's eyes went wide, and she stared at him.

"I don't understand," he continued. "And I can't understand unless you choose to tell me." He heaved a sigh and took a slow step closer. "I am willing to listen."

He kept her in his gaze, the beauty of her face for once appearing kind. The tears had turned her irises almost cerulean, and the moonlight illuminated her face. Her voice dropped to a whisper. "The study's shelves lie nearly empty. When I lived here every inch of that room was covered, floor to ceiling. There I would steal away to imaginary islands and faraway castles . . . and now does anyone enjoy it?" Her eyes winced shut, and her arms curled around herself. She turned away, gripping the railing, and gestured toward the shrubs. "And just look at this garden. Surely you can imagine that we did not keep it in this kind of disarray."

He hesitated, a new gentleness in his voice. "Perhaps, Lady Caroline, they do not have the means you had at your disposal when you lived here. Your father was surely able to employ more groundsmen . . . buy more books—"

"No! That is not what irks me so!" Her voice dropped to a scathing, tight whisper. "What irks me is that they are . . . happy." Her eyes turned dark and hollow.

What he saw there was deep and painful. She blinked back more moisture and turned away from him once again. How could someone hate that others were happy? Could she really feel that way? He stepped behind her, offering his handkerchief over her shoulder.

She batted it away and faced him. "We ought to go."

"As you wish, Lady Caroline." He tucked his handkerchief back into his pocket.

She started moving immediately, leading the way inside.

John collected Lady Loresetter, who hesitated until she saw her niece's face. The three of them offered goodbyes to the Hartleys. Lady Caroline attempted to mask her tears, and John marveled at how much command and grace she exhibited, considering her angry outburst on the porch overlooking the garden. He expected her to do something brash, but somehow, she remained perfectly amiable on the surface. Amiable but silent.

Only when they had been alone had she not been in control. Clearly, he brought out the worst in her.

As they walked across the gravel, he gently took her by the elbow. "Let us speak with Mrs. Horne before we go."

Her eyes shot wide. "Oh, I forgot," she said in a hushed whisper, and she stopped moving. She searched his face. "I can't speak to her like this. You must arrange for her to meet us at our inn tomorrow. I am sure Lady Hartley would not mind her leaving for an hour or so."

"Of course." He noticed her look past him, back toward the dancers. The happy Lord and Lady Hartley had made it back to the head of the set.

When he returned, she and Lady Loresetter waited silently inside the carriage. John dared look at Lady Caroline's eyes again. This time they resembled the flickering gas lamps he had just passed: full of fire, with darkness hiding behind them.

�֍ �֍ ✖

John sat up alone for several hours that night, various images vying for his attention, first among them Lady Caroline's treatment of the girl from the ragged school. Was it possible she really did think herself better than everyone around her? Many a wealthy person claimed superiority, but she gloated over her status with disgust for anyone below her station. He marveled that she had been so angry at another's happiness. If only she understood what blessings fortune and good health were. She could have been like Isabel, too poor for good treatment and in constant pain. His sister, at least, still sought for the good in life.

He stood and walked to the small fire. His mind shifted to the dance. Miss Elisabeth Felwig had been lovely, and taking the floor with her must have done something to his brain. Why had he pursued Lady Caroline for a dance? He paid her too much notice, and he understood what happened when a man gave attention to a lady—things became complicated until eventually the lady severed all hope for a future together. He would not allow himself to be interested in Lady Caroline's success. A pretty girl wouldn't ruin him again.

Yet he had reached for her hand, and she hadn't withdrawn it immediately.

Why had he done that?

Taking his candle down from the mantel, he noticed the wax dripped at an angle. He felt the urge to fix the simple contraption. He watched the flame dance for a moment before blowing it out. By the light of the low fire in his hearth he trimmed the wick and bent the holder back into place. Better. He loved mending things in a world where so much around him was broken. If only he could mend his sister. If only he could mend Lady Caroline. The embers of his dying fire kept his room warm, and yet he shuddered as he settled into bed.

Lady Caroline was cold to everyone, especially him. So why did he feel drawn to her? He ought to be able to attend to the task at hand with little personal investment. After all, he was merely accomplishing a wish of his father.

Yet, for that one moment as they'd prepared to leave her former home, she had looked at him, really looked at him, and something had been different. Beneath her chain mail of haughty superiority lay . . . something.

It was that something he would endeavor to discover. She was hurting, but like the candleholder, her damage couldn't be permanent. How could he help her find happiness? How could he fix things for her?

There had to be something he could do. He had seen her smile when she danced—he recalled her radiance. That was the real Lady Caroline. Everything else was a mask. At least, he hoped it was. He searched for the courage to find out.

CHAPTER FOUR

CAROLINE WRUNG HER HANDS AS she sat next to Aunt Ebby on a couch and listened as the housekeeper was ushered into the inn's small sitting room. Mr. Charleston had declared he'd join them after their meeting.

With a poised curtsy, Mrs. Horne entered silently. A kind smile washed across her face. It was laced with the happy wrinkles Caroline remembered fondly, though her gray hair was a few shades lighter. Caroline had forgotten just how much she loved this woman.

"I am so sorry you had to meet me here," she said by way of greeting. "I would have spoken to you last night, but I was feeling . . . out of sorts."

"Oh, it was for the best," Mrs. Horne said as she settled across from her. "The cook and a maid were having a disagreement, and let me just say it has been a very full two days."

"It was a lovely party," Caroline responded. She could not meet the housekeeper's eyes.

"You thought so?" Mrs. Horne spoke loudly for Aunt Ebby's benefit, and Caroline could feel the dear housekeeper trying to catch her gaze.

"Well . . ." Caroline tried to let Mrs. Horne's omnipresent calm restore her, but her nerves only rose, and she considered turning haughty and aloof and donning her usual facade. She suspected Mrs. Horne would expect such behavior, for Caroline had assumed the habit during the last year or two at Elbury House. But today she felt weary, and her perfect posture sank.

Mrs. Horne placed a hand on Caroline's. "Take a breath, dear."

Caroline tried to master her jittery fingers. She swallowed hard. "The truth is the whole house felt different. It felt like it used to, before Mother died, before Father shut me out of his life . . . such lightness! I enjoyed myself. For a moment, I didn't worry about my father, the role I had to play, how much money I represent, whether someone's class was high enough, or what people thought of me. I felt . . . happy."

Mrs. Horne's chin dropped in understanding.

Caroline's eyes at last braved a look at the housekeeper but quickly narrowed her gaze in frustration. "And then, when I realized how good it all felt, I became so angry—at Father, the house, the garden, the books . . . everything." Caroline grasped at her skirt, twisting the fine trim. "I shouldn't care. That house, those people— they are all in the past." She jutted out her chin, barely realizing her tone shifting to superiority. She nodded toward her aunt. "I have an excellent situation in London. I want for nothing. What a simpleton I am to dwell on Elbury at all." She rose to her feet, angling toward the window that looked over the street. "Perhaps we ought to go."

Aunt Ebby placed a reassuring hand on Caroline's arm. "Sit down, dear girl. We have something to tell you."

The worn bits of brown brocade on the couch seemed to devour Caroline as she sank back into them. "We?" She looked skeptically at the two women, who both nodded.

Mrs. Horne spoke again. "Your father made me promise to wait until you had received the first letter from Mr. Charleston."

With sober hesitation Mrs. Horne withdrew a note that looked just like the letter from Mr. Charleston, but this one was sealed.

"Another letter?" Caroline said.

Again both women nodded.

Caroline took it, now distrusting them. Hurt, betrayed, and nervous, she unfolded the page.

> *My Dearest Caroline,*
>
> *Greed and grief ruined me. But I pray it is not too late for you. When I first met your mother, things were simpler. My focus was so different and, in so many ways, much clearer. It is not money that makes one happy.*
>
> *I know because I used to be happy. Happy—and poor.*
>
> *My steward, Mr. Charleston, who has no doubt brought you here, lives a much simpler life than you or I have led. For you to visit his family, experience his ways, would be a magnificent opportunity. Stay with his family for a time. He is one of the only men who extended kindness to me when I least deserved it, and you will be well taken care of. One week with his family is all I ask. To this end, I've made this trip a requirement for you to gain your full inheritance. Our family's solicitor is aware of this addendum to the will.*
>
> *I pray your visit will open your eyes to what happiness life can hold. You live in a state of wealthy ease. I made sure you could want for nothing. But I now know that focusing on your monetary possessions will not garner you true happiness.*
>
> *Your father,*
> *Jacob Morleigh*

Caroline kept her eyes on the page. "I must go or forfeit my inheritance?" Her scathing whisper echoed off the cold walls. "And I don't understand"—she glared at each woman in turn—"Why not send me to Mr. Charleston's in the first place? Why did he send me here first? Did my father know what I would have to endure returning to Elbury?" Her father had never cared about how she felt, yet the words of his letter spoke otherwise. She sought a real answer and waited for either woman's explanation.

Aunt Ebby grasped Caroline's hand, and her voice softened, more than it had for the whole of the journey. "Caroline. He wanted to explain all of this to you, but the onset of his illness was so quick. When we told him you probably wouldn't arrive before he died, he began furiously writing letters. He said you would ask questions, but I think he hoped if you came back first, you might be reminded of the wonderful parts of your childhood."

Mrs. Horne smiled at Aunt Ebby. "He also feared you would not go with a stranger unless someone else you knew vouched for him. And I do vouch for Mr. Charleston, my lady. He was admirable in every respect. I am sure his son is every bit the same."

Hardly. So far, he'd been pushy and irritating. Except there was that moment when he had touched her hand, offered his handkerchief, and given a kind word.

In the moment she'd least deserved it.

She pushed the thought away. "His son cannot possibly be as much of a gentleman, I assure you. I cannot visit there. The son of a steward? Imagine how people would talk." She drew her mouth tightly into a pout, like a child.

Aunt Ebby brought her face near her niece's. "Caroline," came her raspy voice, too loudly, "for the sake of your inheritance, you must go. Mr. Charleston is an excellent gentleman. I think such a visit will be to your benefit, and of course, I plan to stay with you the whole time, so you needn't worry that people will talk."

"Everyone expects it? Even Mr. Charleston?"

The door to the sitting room opened then, and Mr. Charleston's form filled the doorway, almost like a summoned apparition. When her eyes narrowed toward him, he gave a solemn nod. "I came to see if you were finished, but since I overheard, I must admit my father warned me this might involve me a bit more than

I expected. Though I was *not* informed explicitly that it would include a trip to my home, it would be a great honor to have you as our guest. Will you accept?"

He appeared to be all kindness, and his voice sounded genuine. It was too much.

Caroline looked from Mrs. Horne to Mr. Charleston. She held his gaze a long moment, while the other women's eyes bored into her. She cast a moue toward her aunt, then let out a long sigh. "I suppose." She shook her head. "Thank you for your time," she said to her beloved housekeeper. It was exhausting to be so angry at everyone, and she really did love the old woman.

Mr. Charleston stepped toward Mrs. Horne. "May I escort you back to the carriage?" The housekeeper nodded and embraced Caroline before she exited.

Aunt Ebby waited until Mr. Charleston was gone before speaking. "Do not berate me with those eyes of yours." She tried for an easy tone, but Caroline did not budge. "Everything will turn out splendidly. Mr. Charleston is harmless, and if you ask me, he has a good head on those shabby shoulders." A wry smile met Caroline's drawn face.

"We have known him only a matter of days."

Aunt Ebby shrugged. "I knew his father. I watched my brother wield tyrannical power over him all those years, and Mr. Charleston took it with the nobility of a knight. His son is no different. There is goodness in his eyes. Have you not noticed?"

Caroline looked down at her slippers. "I hardly expect goodness from anyone."

"Perhaps it is time to seek it," Aunt Ebby said, unaffected. She pulled Caroline into a tight and nearly awkward hug, but there was something pleasant about it.

They stayed until Aunt Ebby at last broke away and grabbed her cane. She stopped and leaned over it in the doorway, lifting a bushy brow at her niece. "You can't run away forever."

❋ ❋ ❋

After John escorted Mrs. Horne to the carriage, he returned to the inn to find a resigned, agitated Lady Caroline and a very pleasant Lady Loresetter. He offered an arm to Lady Caroline, but she clenched her jaw. "I don't . . . I don't need any of this or any of these people or you."

John winced as she strode on ahead, eventually gripping the edge of the carriage door for stability as she climbed in.

Lady Loresetter, however, accepted his offer and leaned on John's arm. She walked slowly and clicked her tongue. "That girl." She shook her cane slightly toward the carriage and lowered her voice. "Now, Caroline may put up a fuss, but pay her no heed. I trust it will be just lovely visiting your home. Where did you say . . . ?"

"Thornton Heath," he said as he helped Lady Loresetter into the carriage. "Less than a day's ride from here."

Lady Caroline glowered at them both as he and Lady Loresetter discussed plans. It was settled that they would all ride together back to London. Once there, John would travel directly to Thornton Heath while Lady Caroline prepared her things in London. The next day she and Lady Loresetter would take the new train line to Thornton Heath, where John would collect them. At least he would have time to prepare for them that way.

Not many words passed between the three during the ride back to London, but John's thoughts kept him engaged. He had known he'd be involved with Lady Caroline's letters but not to such an extent. Worry, dread, and inconvenience pulled at him. His father had instilled in him that he must be kind and do the right thing above all else. He would do his best to live up to that expectation.

Lady Caroline would think his sisters far below her status, of that he was sure. Not to mention the meager circumstances of his home. When she inevitably scoffed at it all, she could blame her own father for John's family's poor circumstances. Not once in the thirty years they had worked together had the man paid a fair steward's salary. The meager income, coupled with Isabel's medical expenses, had left the Charleston family ever struggling to have enough.

At last he broke the silence with slow, deliberate speech. "Lady Loresetter, I have been thinking it over, and the town of Thornton Heath is quite full of ash and soot this time of year—not enough rain or snow to clear it out—and the weather could have an awful effect on your health." He cleared his throat and looked at Lady Caroline. "If you do not wish to make the trip currently, I understand. The spring might be better."

Lady Loresetter's bushy brows screwed up into a wary, knowing scowl. "I may be hard of hearing, Mr. Charleston, but if I catch you insinuating that I am not able to make some journey or another, I will seize this carriage and suffer you to walk yourself back to London." She finished with a large huff and placed her hands on her cane.

Lady Caroline must want for an excuse. Now that he had given her one, perhaps she would weigh in and second him. She clutched her aunt's arm and said with a full voice, "Of course you are able. How dare Mr. Charleston assume such a thing as bad health."

Simpering long lashes beat toward him. She was playing him now, just to vex him. These two dastardly women saw right through him and had for once banded together. Lady Loresetter must have some kind of pull on her niece, for Lady Caroline did almost always give in to the old woman.

But her tone. He had been able to deal with Lady Caroline's harsh tone, but add her female wiles of flirtation and coquetry? She was far too pretty, and she knew it. "Although," she continued, her voice silky, "perhaps you don't have quite the hospitality of a gentleman. True gentlemen feel no qualms when inviting anyone to visit, regardless of how little time they have to prepare."

This was the second time she'd accused him of not being a gentleman. He'd heard her complaining about him to her aunt when they met with Mrs. Horne. He was sure his manners were what they ought to be and were much more developed than those of this shrew before him. He had never met a woman who vacillated more quickly, fully aware of her effect. She was like reading a weathercock in a storm, and now, not for the first time, she had insulted his pride. His house was not as fine as hers—nothing of his ever would be—but he was proud of his family. They loved each other, and that, he thought, might be something worth seeing.

※ ※ ※

"Are you really on your way to the train so soon?" Timothy said as he paced his room that evening. "So much for your visit to London. You have hardly been here two days together."

"I never could have stayed long anyway. I still seek better options for Isabel's care. I will go tonight, and Lady Caroline and her aunt will travel to Thornton Heath tomorrow. I hadn't expected a weeklong house visit . . . it will take us almost to Christmas!" He rubbed his arms for warmth. Timothy always kept a window cracked, regardless of temperature. "She wasn't the sort of cold I expected to encounter this season. But I gave my word. Best to prepare Sophie, don't you think?" John gave a wry smile.

Timothy clicked his monocle against the hearth of the fireplace. "Certainly. I daresay Lady Caroline will eat them all alive."

"Sophie won't be eaten," John replied.

"That is true. Your sister can most certainly stand her ground. But I do hope Lady Caroline is compassionate to poor Isabel."

"I hope so as well. It is a good thing Lady Caroline is so high and mighty about her gowns, or I wouldn't have been able to give my sisters even this much warning."

Timothy shook his head. "You've really got yourself into a scrape with this one . . . maybe worse than the last."

"That is impossible," John said, wincing. He pressed his eyes closed. Timothy was too dramatic, as always. This time, though, his reaction seemed unfortunately applicable.

"You are sure you do not care for me to accompany you? I know Lady Caroline loathes me, but I would come to help you." Timothy held out John's coat and gave a smile.

"I know you don't wish to be subjected to a miserable time. I couldn't ask that of you. I shall suffer alone."

"Suit yourself," Timothy said as John walked toward the door. "Yet why go through with all of this?"

It was the same question he had asked himself many times since yesterday. He had come up with several answers, though none fully satisfied him. The letters demanded it. His father and Lady Loresetter expected it. He was a man of his word. He felt two main emotions: obligation to his father and, somehow, to Lady Caroline's father, whom he had never met. And . . .

"I suppose I like a challenge," John answered as he turned through the wrought-iron gate and onto the sidewalk.

He glanced back as Timothy smiled and shook his head incredulously.

It wasn't the challenge of a beautiful woman; it was the challenge of an idea—the hope that people could change.

※ ※ ※

"The problem, John," Sophie said, "is that I have scheduled a few different events for next week, which we can't change. We have a dinner with the Winters family, an appointment with Isabel's doctor, and the church fete, where I am hosting a booth."

"Good heavens. If you weren't such a social butterfly, Soph! Must all those things happen this week? I especially wished to be absent when you invited the Winters family, and now . . ."

John eyed his sister, her light-brown hair pulled back neatly with a few curls in front, like always. With her dark eyes and hair and her ivory skin, she looked so much like their mother. She moved closer to him in her worn-out dress, once altered already, and gave a curt nod. "It is rather bad timing. I am sorry." She tried to hurry past the moment. "Really, John, how bad can this Lady Caroline be?"

He raised his hand and commenced ticking off each item with his finger. "Well, she has a rather scrutinous eye. She has no problem speaking harshly. She is terribly judgmental. She pushes people away like she's afraid of them. She's as solitary as an oyster, and she has the bark of an angry dog. And the combination of her with the new Mrs. Winters and her awful husband . . . I don't know if I can bear it. All three think themselves superior to everyone."

Sophie's eyes widened. "Not exactly a glowing account."

John chuckled and patted his sister's hand. "But I am not without hope! Where she is dismal, I am merry. Where she is morose, you are happy. I do wish her to have a pleasant time here, just not at the expense of my friends."

"Then, the only thing left to do is be our drab selves." Sophie fingered her limp dress with a smile that twisted her mouth to its best shape. She stepped toward him and took the hat he had been crumpling from his anxious hands. "You are enough," she whispered.

It wasn't true, or Anna—*Mrs. Winters*, he corrected himself—would've been his.

Sophie put a hand on his shoulder. "Oh, come now. I haven't seen you this worried about anything in a long while." She swallowed and looked directly at him, then raised an eyebrow. "Is it possible that you care for her? You went to London to do your duty, and instead you now have . . . feelings for Lady Caroline, despite her bad tendencies?"

The great bounding laugh, which John hardly ever let escape, came running out of him. "Oh, Sophie, no! Not in the slightest. I am only doing the duty Father gave me. I promised I would, and frankly, I had no idea that delivering that letter would become so completely consuming." He sobered and added, "You know I am not seeking attachments to anyone—ever again."

"But people will talk. If you have a visitor coming from London—"

"Do not remind me. We will refer to Lady Caroline as an old friend of Father's who is just stopping through."

Sophie sat on the larger of the two couches in their sitting room. He had never noticed how thin the upholstery had worn. Now he wished he would have remained ignorant of its shabbiness.

"And she travels with her aunt, you said?"

"Yes, who is partially deaf and takes her role of chaperone quite seriously."

"That is perfect, then," Sophie said, her eyes sparkling. "We must simply emphasize that the aunt is visiting. She is your main charge. If anyone asks, we can say that perhaps she wished her niece to meet you."

"Now, Sophie," John said, "I can assure you neither Lady Caroline nor Lady Loresetter has any intention of ever connecting themselves with our family. If it weren't for the letters—"

"Yes, yes," Sophie said as she gestured for him to sit down. "That is no matter. That is just how we will phrase it."

"For the good of everyone, I suppose." John sank onto the cushion.

"Let us only hope she sees what we have to offer."

John tilted his head. "And what is that?"

"A happy home, made warm by love and friendship. Even some wealthy people don't have that, you know."

John's shoulders relaxed for the first time since arriving. His sister was wiser, kinder, and cleverer than seven women combined. "I suppose you are right. Hopefully, she'll take you and Isabel as examples."

CHAPTER FIVE

"If Mr. Charleston were half a gentleman, he would have offered a carriage to bring us from London." Caroline shook out her skirts and stomped her feet on the boardwalk of the train station, her maid, Edith, alighting from the train to join her on the platform.

Aunt Ebby shifted her weight from side to side and laughed. "I completely disagree. I hear all modern women travel this way now, and I found it invigorating."

Caroline didn't even attempt to withhold her scoff.

Her aunt beamed at her, undeterred. "Of course, Mr. Charleston was not trying to impress you. He doesn't enjoy your company; he just wishes his business finished." She looked down the wooden platform and brushed her hands for effect.

He did seem to be a matter-of-fact gentleman. Not that Caroline wanted his company, but it hurt to hear Aunt Ebby say it so bluntly. She had always been a little too eccentric and far too honest. It would be best to change the subject.

"Am I completely covered in soot?" Caroline turned to Edith.

"Not in the slightest," the maid answered quietly.

Caroline looked to Aunt Ebby for a second opinion just as another train screeched to a stop.

"What was that?" her aunt asked loudly.

Caroline gestured to the whole of herself. "Do I look as dirty as I feel?" she nearly shouted and hoped the exaggerated hand motions would help.

"No, you look perfectly poised, just as you always do." Aunt Ebby stepped closer and lowered her voice, studying her as if she were a bug, and said over the gusting of the train, "But will you act the part? Remember who you are—a lady—and please behave accordingly." Caroline glared. How dare she!

Aunt Ebby seemed to realize the effect of her words and placed her hand over her heart as she added, "For my sake, dear. You are too high and mighty, and your tone is too harsh. Give it up for the week and try to enjoy our visit, will you?"

Caroline felt the color in her face rise. How could her aunt chide her so openly, in front of her maid, no less? She had half a mind to increase her haughty performance just to spite the old woman. Then she remembered her aunt's will.

Aunt Ebby was Caroline's only relative, and she had always made sure to write, visit on holidays, and send her gifts. The old woman had perhaps become a bit senile, deaf, and crazy in her old age, but Caroline would try to honor her wishes. She gulped down her white-hot anger. "Yes, Aunt."

From far down the platform, Mr. Charleston strode briskly toward them. He looked exactly as he had the day before—wearing a well-tailored but worn suit and shoes, his watch fob hanging neatly from his pocket, his hair the color of warm chocolate.

This time he held a robust bouquet of hothouse flowers—white roses. It seemed an overly cordial peace offering. Perhaps he was more of a gentleman than Caroline thought.

"Good afternoon," he said with complete affability as he stopped in front of them. A servant following behind him spryly picked up their traveling cases and left the group.

"Good evening," Caroline and her aunt said simultaneously.

"These are for you," Mr. Charleston said as he extended the flowers.

Caroline prepared her most stoic face as she put out her arms. She would not give him any satisfaction from the offering, though she *did* like the idea. She hadn't been sent flowers for a long time—not since Lord Hartley.

Then she realized he was not reaching for her but for her aunt. She clasped her hands behind her, attempting to tamp down her embarrassment at the snub.

"Why, thank you, Mr. Charleston," Aunt Ebby said with a wide smile. "They are beautiful."

"I figured that after such a train ride, you deserved it."

At this Caroline grew even more enraged, for Aunt Ebby had borne the train ride perfectly, whilst Caroline had nearly lost her breakfast. One glance toward the shrewd eyes of her aunt, however, kept her tongue in check.

"Let us be going, then." Mr. Charleston extended both arms for them to take.

The servant from before had already loaded their belongings onto a rather small hackney carriage with two unimpressive cream horses that waited at the edge of the station. Mr. Charleston helped Caroline and Aunt Ebby up, and Caroline's maid followed. The four of them were quite snug on the ride home, Mr. Charleston's knees constantly brushing Caroline's.

"My sisters are rather eager to meet all of you," he said.

"As are we them," Caroline said. "Are your housing accommodations as snug as this coach, Mr. Charleston?"

Caroline felt a quick jab on her ankle from Aunt Ebby's foot. Her lipreading must be better than Caroline realized.

Mr. Charleston tugged on his cravat. "It is all a matter of perspective, Lady Caroline. We have given the guest room to your aunt," he said loudly, "and I hope you shall find yourself comfortable sharing a room with my youngest sister, Isabel. It is the most advantageous room in the house, for it has two large beds and bright windows that overlook the best part of the garden."

"It sounds . . . idyllic." Caroline couldn't imagine sharing a room with anyone, let alone a stranger, but she smiled.

"I hope you think so. My sister has had a poor constitution for the last several years and hardly leaves her room. I think she will be excited to have a friend . . . a visitor, I mean."

Did he truly think she could be his sister's friend? Unlikely. Part of her loved to do exactly the opposite of what stubborn young men predicted she would do, and since it would positively shock him were she to truly befriend his sister, maybe she could like Miss Isabel.

When they arrived at Mr. Charleston's home, Caroline gaped as she entered the tight entryway. The small space was quite tidy, though every curtain and wall hanging in the house looked worn. She might have called the family middle-class if she were being generous. They could have used at least two more servants, but she doubted they could afford them. Whatever salary her father had given Mr. Charleston Sr., the steward ought to have managed it better, if the furniture were any indication.

"Do come in," a pleasant voice said.

"Lady Loresetter," Mr. Charleston said as they entered a small parlor that also doubled as the entryway, "allow me to introduce my sister two years younger than myself, Miss Sophie Charleston."

"It is a pleasure to meet you." Miss Charleston spoke with a calm, confident voice as she curtsied gracefully, and Caroline noticed her glowing face and thick light-brown hair. She was lovely.

"And this is Lady Caroline Morleigh, daughter of our father's longtime employer, Lord Marchant." Mr. Charleston did a fine job of the introduction, for not being a true gentleman. He turned toward a low padded settee, where a young girl with a crutch cumbersomely rose to her feet. "And here we have my beautiful sister Miss Isabel Charleston."

She leaned on her crutch and gave a wavering curtsy with some effort, which was admirable considering her feebleness. A small twinge of sadness tugged at Caroline. Isabel couldn't have been older than seventeen, but she appeared so frail. There was something in the girl's face that was truly—just as he said— beautiful. Perhaps it was the way her eyes turned up pleasantly or the small smattering of freckles that played across her cheeks. All of it gave her a genuine feel. She was not the striking porcelain doll her sister was but was somehow easy and likable.

"I understand you and I are to share a room," Caroline said, letting a smile emerge before she realized it.

Miss Isabel returned the smile. "Yes, if that is to your liking, Lady Caroline."

Caroline could feel Mr. Charleston and his other sister watching her, listening to every word.

"I would be delighted." She ignored the questioning brow the elder Miss Charleston sent her brother. "And, please, call me Caroline."

"Thank you," Miss Isabel said, her voice airy. "And you must call me Isabel, for I do hope we will be friends."

Miss Sophie Charleston then came to her sister's side and spoke loudly. "We none of us stand on ceremony here." After giving Caroline leave to use her Christian name as well, she said, "Might I show you to your rooms, Lady Loresetter and Lady Caroline?"

"Thank you," Aunt Ebby said.

Mr. Charleston joined Isabel, whispering to her and then helping her settle again on the settee.

As Caroline ascended the stairs with her aunt and their hostess, Sophie said, "We have supper ready, if you wish to take it downstairs once you situate your things. Tomorrow we have a dinner planned with some dear family friends. We do hope you will join us in all of our activities this week."

"Of course. We wouldn't miss it," Aunt Ebby said.

"Actually," Caroline said, her voice superior, "do not wait for me to begin supper. I must make sure my gowns are attended to in just the right manner."

She walked past Aunt Ebby and into her room so she could oversee her maid's attempt to air her dresses. She always doubted her servants' competence, most especially when traveling.

After twenty minutes, Caroline walked slowly to the banister and paused, glimpsing a small dining room just around the corner from the parlor that was at the bottom of the stairs. Aunt

Ebby was already seated, and the whole group was eating. The unfailing energy and efficiency of her aunt astounded her.

The group was laughing, so Caroline checked the corridor to make sure she was alone and tucked herself against the wall behind some musty curtains so she could observe them without being seen. She didn't wish to join the lively group yet.

"For heaven's sake, John, pass the bird. Do you intend to eat all of it?" It was Sophie who spoke, and again Caroline noticed the buoyancy of her words. Her voice resounded with pleasure—and Caroline envied it.

"Of course not, Soph, but it isn't every day we have a goose for supper. I am guarding it so Lady Caroline can have at least a bite."

"Perhaps we should be guarding it for her instead of you," Isabel teased quietly as her brother chewed on a large bit of poultry from his plate.

Mr. Charleston turned toward Aunt Ebby. "Please ignore my bantering sisters, Lady Loresetter. Now, what else can I hand you?"

"I'll take another pass at the carrots. It is all excellent. You did not need any extravagance for us, truly. We do not want to inconvenience you."

"We wished to impress our guests," Sophie said. "But thank you so much for putting us at ease. I am confident we will enjoy your visit immensely."

Mr. Charleston cleared his throat. "Yes, we just wish to appease—I mean please—as much as possible," he said with a grin as he looked toward the stairs.

Aunt Ebby smiled, catching the joke. What a traitor she was to so openly agree with his antics! Caroline marveled at how he so easily sat in the good graces of everyone around him. Everyone, that was, except herself.

Mr. Charleston drank from his glass, his smile wide and so free it would have been handsome on any man but him. "Sophie, how do things with Mr. Baker come along?"

His sisters' hands immediately shot to their mouths, both trying to stifle a laugh. Aunt Ebby sat back in her chair, her hands clasped, as she studied them.

"I . . . don't think I'll see much of him after what transpired last weekend," Sophie managed.

Mr. Charleston rested his index finger on the side of his face. "Oh? But the chap was trying so hard to win you. I liked him. Too serious, maybe, but an adept farmer."

How could he condone his sister marrying a farmer? Caroline watched as he turned to Isabel, who still couldn't suppress a giggle.

"What is it, Isabel? Lady Loresetter is going to think us nothing but gossips and ninnies. I promise you, ma'am, usually—"

The quiet, wispy voice of Isabel then piped in. "Bless the man, but he had a run of it. It started when he let the pig out on purpose!" She giggled again. "On purpose, so that he'd have an excuse to come through the back fields and find Sophie while she gardened. She beheld him, and the pig, mind you, coming the whole way. That was when poor Mr. Baker stepped right into a fresh pile of . . . the, um . . . horses had been there recently, you see, and the cow—"

"Yes, Isabel, they understand," Sophie said, patting her sister's napkin.

"And his foot sank so deep in—" Isabel continued.

Mr. Charleston's nose wrinkled as he chuckled.

"It was quite up to his calf, I am afraid," Sophie added with a playful grin.

"Did he notice it?" Mr. Charleston asked, clutching his belly as he nearly rolled off his chair. At least his laugh was a good, pleasant one—hearty, healthy.

The story *was* amusing—such lighthearted conversation would never have happened in Caroline's family.

"I am not so sure he did," Sophie answered, "for he let the pig prowl around our garden patch for well over a half hour as he insisted on continuing to speak." She winced. "It took everything

I had to continue a polite conversation with him for such a *strenuous* amount of time."

Caroline found herself completely enthralled in the recounting, and a stifled laugh escaped her lips. She thought she saw Mr. Charleston look up the stairs, but she pushed farther against the wall.

"So you aren't interested in his pursuing you?" he said as he brushed a tear from the corner of his eye.

"He was never my first choice, and this episode made that tragically more apparent."

"Ahh," Mr. Charleston said with a nod. "Another disappointed lover falls to the siren call of our dear Sophie."

Sophie shook her head.

Perhaps the family wasn't so awful after all. Not to mention Caroline's stomach growled with hunger. She drew a breath, wondering if she could find a place among such an amiable set of people. She descended the stairs quickly and tried for a quiet entrance.

"So glad you have joined us," Sophie said, and Caroline felt like she meant it.

Isabel gestured to the open chair next to her. "And I saved you some of the goose, despite my ravenous brother."

"How good of you." She smiled and quirked a brow. "Thank you for having my aunt and me."

As the dinner progressed, Caroline offered a few pleasantries and complimented the food—though it was a very small goose, in truth—but mostly stayed silent and basked in the interactions of these delightful sisters and their stodgy brother. A few times when something was mentioned that sparked her interest, she ventured into the conversation. She learned that she and Sophie agreed on new trends for lady's fashions. Of course, Mr. Charleston disagreed heartily with them both, but she paid him no heed. Isabel had even read a few of the same novels she had as a girl.

The evening passed pleasantly and quickly. It was strange. Caroline did not feel like her usual self—had definitely not acted like her usual self—and was not even sure what her usual self was at that moment, but it was enjoyable enough to be among them, and no amount of gamey, thinned-out goose could make her feel ill at ease.

Mr. Charleston excused himself and left the ladies to their conversation. By the time they finished, it was quite late, and Aunt Ebby announced that she wished to turn in for the evening. Just before Caroline walked up the stairs with her aunt, she noticed Mr. Charleston analyzing something on the bookshelf in the parlor.

"I shall be right there," Caroline said to Aunt Ebby, who seemed to miss that her niece lagged behind.

If her aunt had better hearing, she might have been spooked by the loud creaking floorboards as Caroline turned toward the parlor and the blustering winds outside. The eerie noises and the darkness of the night almost made the house feel haunted by spirits.

But Caroline had no fear of anyone, let alone ghosts. She walked right over to Mr. Charleston and waited for him to notice her. He had just pulled a volume from the shelf and was searching its pages.

Caroline found she could wait no longer and broke the silence. "I must know exactly what you told your sisters about my coming here. They received me so warmly."

He did not look up from his book. "They think we are madly in love, and therefore, I told them they *must* like you."

Caroline could not dislodge the shock from her face. She was rendered momentarily speechless.

He lifted one eyebrow, and a laugh escaped his lips. His expression boasted a smirk.

Her eyes narrowed, and her shoulders lowered. If he wanted a harsh rejoinder, she could surely provide it. At this moment, however, she could not see past the subject of his joke.

"You cannot be serious." Caroline pressed her lips into a small line.

"Of course not." He closed the book and slid it back onto the shelf, then looked at her folded arms. "If you really want to know, we have decided Aunt Ebby is our esteemed guest, and you just happen to be with her."

She blew a gust of air in his direction. "May I remind you, Mr. Charleston, that I happen to be with her because you just happened to bring me a letter."

His becoming laugh rolled out. "I did seem to bring this upon myself, didn't I?" His eyes glimmered in such a way that Caroline couldn't trust herself to look at him anymore.

"I underestimated you," she said.

"What do you mean?" She stole a glance in Mr. Charleston's direction long enough to observe his brows pulling tight. Shrugging, she reined in her cheeks so she would not smile and said, "You orchestrated it all to suit your explanation of our visit—hence the flowers." She was one shade closer to amused by his clever plan.

"Hence the flowers," he agreed with a mischievous smile.

She tried to ignore his inviting countenance. "Well then, as my aunt's poor ward, you should be warned that I am determined to be kind to Isabel, attentive to Sophie, and awful to you." She curtsied, took her candle, and made to leave.

"I suppose that is the best I could hope for." He laughed as he turned and pulled out another one of his old books.

Caroline attempted to forget Mr. Charleston's laugh as she approached Isabel's room. She called for her maid and then snuck quietly through the open door to find Isabel reading by candlelight. Upon Caroline's entry the sickly woman closed her book and set it rapidly on the nightstand. As soon as Caroline's maid had helped her out of her things and left, Isabel spoke. "I didn't know how late you'd stay downstairs, but I'm glad I'm still awake."

"Oh, um, yes. Just stopped to ask your brother a question."

"And which mood did you find him in?" Isabel's chin angled to the side.

Caroline frowned. "He was . . ." She wanted to say "cunning" or perhaps even "charming," but she divagated instead. "Does he have many moods?"

Isabel's braid shook as she nodded. "We Charlestons all do, I'm afraid." Her voice carried a sadness, a weight, and Caroline yearned to understand it.

"I am sure you have your reasons." She moved to sit on the spare bed.

"We are, generally, a jovial set." Isabel twirled the end of her braid in her fingers and didn't look up. "But Sophie now has the weight of all the household on her, I have reduced health, and John—well, he feels responsible for us. For everything. Since Anna, he's never been the same."

The room's heaviness hung so thick that Caroline didn't dare venture more questions, though she wondered who Anna was.

"Forgive me," Isabel said as she extinguished her candle. "We have much to be grateful for."

Caroline pulled the covers round herself in the dark, marveling that Isabel was able to be grateful under such meager circumstances. "Well, thank you for letting me be in your home."

"Of course. I am glad you came," Isabel answered softly.

CHAPTER SIX

JOHN HAD HARDLY SLEPT THE night before. He'd lain in bed as the early-morning light crept into his room, utterly astonished that Lady Caroline had not been completely awful during her first evening and day with his family. She'd been fairly quiet, and when she did speak, she was quite pleasant. It amazed him, confused him, relieved him, frightened him. For once, he did not know what she was thinking. He knew enough about Lady Caroline to expect her to reveal exactly how she felt, most likely at his expense and in front of others. He only prayed she wouldn't tonight.

The last person he wanted to be further embarrassed in front of was the newlywed Anna Winters and her husband, who would be coming for dinner in a matter of moments. Mrs. Winters would likely patronize him enough without Caroline making additional comments. There would be far too many opinionated women in one room, and John thought of a hundred different conversations that could end in fire and brimstone.

"You look haggard," Sophie said as they finished their preparations for the evening.

"I hardly slept for fear of this dinner," John answered.

"Oh, come now. I am sorry they are coming, but Anna *was* my best friend, until she broke your heart. To cancel their visit would have looked like cowardice and would seem inexcusably rude." Sophie made sure they were alone as she continued. "I really should have invited them sooner after their marriage, but it has taken me some time to forgive her."

"Lady Caroline will make a laughingstock of me in front of her, I know it. And then Anna—I mean Mrs. Winters—will feel even more justified in her actions."

"I have more faith than that in Lady Caroline," Sophie said. "She has spoken only a little since her arrival last night and has laughed at least twice."

"Exactly. You haven't seen anything yet," he said. Sophie left to confirm with Cook that all was ready, and John walked into the dining room to check the placement of the name cards.

Lady Caroline leaned into the doorway of the dining room. "Checking to make sure you are seated far enough away from me, are you?" she said in a silky, challenging voice. The house was small enough that one was almost always close to the dining room.

"Oh no," John said, ruffling his hair. The oblong table didn't have enough corners to secure him far enough away from anyone.

"You ought not do that." Lady Caroline gestured toward his head.

"Excuse me?"

"Your hair. You oughtn't rumple it so."

He dropped his hand quickly.

"I am sure you want to look your best." Lady Caroline stepped farther into the room and gently touched the hem of one of the napkins, her eyes intently studying the tablecloth.

"What is it about Isabel?" Lady Caroline said as she continued to gaze downward. "I must admit I feel so . . . comfortable around her. Her room seems to hold a sort of magic."

"It is not the room," John said. "It's Isabel herself. There is something special about her. She is filled with so much goodness."

Lady Caroline looked away and cleared her throat, and then she was gone. That was strange. She had seemed almost . . . genuine.

"Excuse me," the housemaid said, coming in where Lady Caroline had just left, "but Mr. and Mrs. Winters have just arrived."

John took a deep breath and exhaled slowly before walking into the parlor.

Sophie stood eagerly waiting as the couple entered and then hurried across the room and took her friend by her crochet-gloved hand. "It is so good to see you," she said quietly as John nodded to Mr. and Mrs. Winters. "Are these new?" his sister asked, eyeing the delicate gloves.

"Oh yes," Mrs. Winters said. "My Phillip dotes on me so." She simpered toward her husband, then made eye contact with John.

John's teeth clenched, but he managed, "Mr. and Mrs. Winters, welcome," followed by a curt bow.

"Thank you." Mr. Winters eyed John. "I trust London was invigorating?"

"It always is," John answered almost cordially.

Lady Loresetter appeared at the doorway then, wearing a pretty lilac dress.

"Mr. and Mrs. Winters," John said, "allow me to introduce a dear friend, Mrs. Ebby Loresetter, and her niece, Lady Caroline Morleigh, both visiting from London. Lady Loresetter is the sister of my father's close friend Lord Marchant, who is Lady Caroline's late father."

Mr. Winters nodded, smiling, and Mrs. Winters analyzed Lady Caroline from hair to heel. Lady Caroline wore an ornate rust-colored silk—not her finest, John assumed, but the sheen of the fabric set her apart from the rest of the party, informing them silently of her rank.

"Shall we dine, then?" he asked, not wanting the silence to last any longer than necessary.

He escorted Lady Loresetter and left the rest to follow, though he knew Sophie had already decided this ought to be a more informal dinner party. The small number of guests necessitated that John sit across from somebody, and he was glad it was Lady

Loresetter. To his left sat Lady Caroline, and to his right sat Mr. Winters, with his wife as far from John as the small table allowed. One more chair next to Sophie was unoccupied, as at the last moment Isabel had not felt well enough to join them.

Sophie had ordered a particularly large meal, again wanting to impress their visitors. John wondered how many more extravagances they would have to sustain over the week. They really could not afford it—any extra money should be going to Isabel's treatments.

As soon as the meal began, Mr. Winters began telling the group, in most animated terms, how he wished to divert his ample stream and move some trees around his property. The women at the table seemed quite engaged, for he was talking with excessive volume, but John could not stop himself from remembering a very different conversation with the man's wife less than six months before.

John had known Anna Lister since she was in braids. Sophie's increasing time with her as they grew had led to his increasing time with Anna as well. He'd asked her to dance once when she was seventeen and he was twenty-one, and one dance had led to another and another until nearly two years had passed and he was sure they would wed. There had been a loose understanding between them, and everyone had generally assumed them engaged. He had tried to officially ask for her hand, but with the passing of his father, she'd declared they ought to wait a few months. And then, just outside this very room, he had proposed marriage one more time.

"Anna," he'd said, for they had used Christian names for a year or so, "I have honored my late father these past six months. Now that I am out of mourning, I hope you will accept my hand." He'd offered a teasing smile, tilting his head toward her.

She had been light and giddy that night, like she was most nights, but in that instant her face shattered, her giddiness suddenly replaced with an unfeeling stone wall. She swallowed. "Oh, John, we have played at this silly game long enough. I cannot marry you."

John's mouth had dropped open before he'd managed to respond, "Why, if I may ask?"

"As of last week, I am engaged to another." Her voice had been so altered that he'd had to make certain he was staring at the same woman.

"Excuse me?"

"Yes," she'd said, sounding completely detached. "I met someone on my trip to London last week, someone who has made something of himself, and we shall be married at Michaelmas."

John's hand had flown to his eyes, shielding his wince as his whirling mind tried to make sense of her words.

"What . . . what happened between us? Did this"—he'd gestured wildly between them—"mean . . . nothing?" His voice had escalated, echoing his inner turmoil. "I thought we had an understanding . . . I thought you *loved* me."

She'd sighed and said, "I haven't felt anything for months, John. Our life would be full of scrimping and saving." There hadn't seemed to be even an ounce of pity or concern in her eyes. "Phillip Winters is exciting, rich, dynamic, and so mature. You and I . . . it was all for play." A half laugh escaped her. "We were children dabbling at an adults' game. I didn't realize how juvenile I had been. I am a grown woman now, and a grown woman has a head on her shoulders when she chooses to marry."

John's jaw had clenched furiously. "This . . . this wasn't dabbling, not for me, Anna. This wasn't just some game. I am a grown man, and I thought I understood who I was giving my feelings to. Thank you for showing me so clearly that I have never been more mistaken in my judge of character. I am ashamed I bestowed my feelings in such a way." He had walked to the door and opened it. "I will send for our maid to accompany you home in our carriage."

"I had wished to see Sophie so I could tell her the news of my engagement."

He had stared at her. Did none of this cause her any pain? Had she any idea of her effect on him?

"I will tell her myself. Good night."

John shook his head, trying to forget that awful day and focus instead on the conversation at present.

Mrs. Winters spoke then. "Tell me, Sophie, what you will bring to the fete tomorrow. I heard my sweet unmarried friends have put together some kind of charity event to raise money for the poor."

How had Anna become so supercilious in only a few months? Perhaps she had always been that way and he had been blind to it.

As Sophie responded, explaining that she planned to sell Christmas greenery at the fete, John took a sip of his drink and stole a glance at Lady Caroline. She had remained quiet so far. Their eyes met, and it was almost as though she could detect the pain of his recollection.

He had assumed by now that she most definitely would have made some comment or two to draw attention to herself, but instead she offered to the group, "It seems like an excellent affair. I will make sure to bring my purse." She almost smiled then, and John couldn't help but realize her mouth was softer, fuller, and more breathtaking than any he had ever beheld.

Yet if Anna had turned out to be so two-faced, surely Lady Caroline was acting as well.

He had always believed people could change, but sitting in such proximity to these two women, he doubted the sentiment.

"How lucky for all of you," Mrs. Winters said, "that your wealthy London acquaintances will be in attendance to shower you with their charity."

Now she had really gone too far. John's eyes shot to Lady Caroline's, wondering if she'd believe they had brought her here just so she could donate generously to their cause. Lady Caroline's eyes grew wide.

"I assure you, Mrs. Winters, it is mere circumstance that brings Lady Loresetter and her niece here at this time." He continued with a crescendo. "The Christmas holiday has a way of bringing people together. Is that not why you have come to visit your mother? How is her health?"

His eyes implored her to change subjects, but Mrs. Winters circled quickly. "She is well. Alone in a big house, all by herself, always happy for visitors. I seem to remember a time when you chided me for seeking acquaintance with people of high Society. It looks as though you now subscribe to my line of thinking."

He would *never* align with her thinking. His hands balled into fists under the table. If he weren't a gentleman, he would demand she leave that instant, possibly throwing a fist into her stuffy husband's face on their way out the door.

But Lady Caroline interjected, all superiority. "I can assure you, Mrs. Winters, that you have absolutely no idea what high Society truly is. And let me also clarify that the connection between my aunt and the Charlestons is one of business. Do *not* insinuate otherwise."

Sophie stood and bestowed a tight smile in all directions. "It seems we are all very well satisfied with our meal. Might I suggest we go through to the drawing room?"

A dear girl, that Sophie. She really was a diplomatic hostess. If women were ever allowed in Parliament, his sister should be a prime member.

John watched an interesting exchange then between Mrs. Winters and Lady Caroline—neither of them used words. Eyebrows and half-masked glares conveyed volumes.

❋ ❋ ❋

This Mrs. Winters was ridiculous. What background story existed between that woman and Mr. Charleston, Caroline clearly did not understand, but she imagined it was disastrous.

To insinuate that Caroline was connected with him in any personal interest . . . the woman must be daft. Mrs. Winters's awfulness may possibly be the only thing on which Caroline had ever seen eye to eye with Mr. Charleston.

Caroline had meant it when she'd chided him for rumpling his hair before dinner. He shouldn't do such a thing. It made him too likable, too genuine. He ought to keep annoying her instead. She found herself standing now, watching him place his napkin on his plate and push his chair back.

Suddenly, from near the door, a male voice boomed, "I'll be the first to admit that we are rudely disrupting a perfectly pleasant and poised party."

A female voice giggled, and everyone turned to see the round, cheery face of a man escorting a young woman.

Who in their right mind would employ such impropriety and barge into a dinner like that? Upon closer inspection, Caroline realized she knew the man—Mr. Timothy Lennox, the elder brother of her old friend Eliza Lennox. They had been at several of the same social functions, though Caroline knew the Lennoxes' station to be significantly below her own. She had even spoken to Mr. Lennox at the governor's ball a month earlier. How he had risen to such a station to warrant an invitation to the ball she couldn't fathom. She recalled having put him in his place in the social hall.

It had made her blood boil, she remembered, when she'd learned just how much his family had earned in trade in the last five years. Father had banned Caroline from Eliza's companionship, and Mr. Lennox's too, because the Lennoxes were too poor. But now they had risen to the highest circles. One more horrible way her father had dashed her happiness.

Mr. Lennox continued, ignoring everyone except Sophie and Mr. Charleston. "I know it's quite untoward to come bashing in here, but we just arrived, and if you'll allow me . . ." At this he squared up to his squatty but full height and introduced his friend. "Miss Edgeworth has a widowed aunt in Thornton Heath who has graciously opened her home to us for a few evenings so we might join Sophie's fete tomorrow." He stared directly at Mr. Charleston. "After depositing our things there, we thought it would be a great joke if we joined your evening!" Mr. Lennox erupted into laughter until he noticed Mr. Charleston remained silent, and finally took stake of the room. Surely Mr. Lennox ought to be able to feel the tension.

"That aunt," Mrs. Winters said, eyeing Miss Edgeworth, "is my mother. Good to see you again, Clara." She curtsied an inch and gave a tight smile. "As you and your rambunctious friend have freely descended on my mother, I feel it incumbent for Mr. Winters and me to excuse ourselves to assist her in preparing whatever fortifications might be necessary to encamp you." She huffed a sigh. "Sophie, thank you again for the invitation. It has been so long since we've been together. You have certainly done your duty to our friendship." She did not even cast a glance at Mr. Charleston, but she took a slight look at Caroline, who returned her glare with a curtsy, though the woman did not deserve it.

An audible breath escaped Mr. Charleston's lips once the Winterses left. "Do make yourself comfortable," he told Mr. Lennox. "I am afraid most of the pork is gone, but I am sure we can procure something else."

"Oh, do not worry about us," Miss Edgeworth said sweetly, "for we had quite the full supper just an hour ago."

At least they'd had the propriety not to expect to be fed. Mr. Charleston's shoulders relaxed. "We just finished," he said. "Shall we go to the drawing room?"

He offered his arm to Aunt Ebby, and Caroline fell into the wake of people who came behind him into the small room.

As soon as Aunt Ebby was settled, Mr. Lennox clasped his hands together and began. "Now—I think I may speak for all— might we have some jolly good fun? What say you to games? Blindman's buff, anyone?"

Mr. Charleston's eyes shot toward Aunt Ebby as he crouched down next to her. "I will tell you this corner chair is the most comfortable we have, and I pray you'll be the farthest from Mr. Lennox's antics."

"I can watch out for myself, you know," Aunt Ebby said in her raspy voice, but she gave a bushy-browed wink.

"What about you, Lady Caroline? Are you familiar with blindman's buff?" Mr. Lennox asked as Miss Edgeworth started to secure a handkerchief over his eyes.

Caroline directed her gaze to Mr. Lennox, who could see her with one eye until the handkerchief tightened. "I do know several party games, naturally. However, blindman's buff is of an uncivilized variety—I must abstain." She walked to the other side of the room and perched delicately on a cushion.

"Serves you right to be first, Lennox," Mr. Charleston said, and immediately the game began.

Caroline tried to act disinterested, but the whole of it proved quite amusing. Oh, the way they stumbled over each other! Mr. Lennox rumbled to and fro in the small space, his thick form never touching anyone, unless it was Miss Edgeworth. After Mr. Lennox grabbed her hand for the third time, Caroline seriously wondered about the opacity of the kerchief. When it was Mr. Charleston's turn to play, he verified the unsuitability of the blindfold, for he seemed to take delight in finding only the females of the party and grabbing their hands in equal turns, vexing whoever he might while feigning blindness. For one brief moment jealousy tugged at Caroline. Why hadn't she accepted their invitation to join them?

The group continued happily and without pretense. For all the anger Caroline had harbored toward Mr. Charleston and Mr. Lennox, they certainly appeared amiable among friends.

"Have we had enough?" Sophie smiled after her brother's turn. "How about some letters of the alphabet for the group?" she said. "Surely you have played this one, Lady Caroline, and would wish to join. It is much more civil."

"I have heard of it," Caroline said. She hesitated, for it had been years since she had played games with anyone, but Sophie's emphatic pat on the sofa finally drew her in.

"Do you remember our game last winter?" Sophie asked Mr. Lennox, who had been careful all evening to ignore Caroline's gaze. It was a good thing, too, for she did not wish to speak to him. "I drew you an unfortunate lot. *Q*'s and lady's hair accessories!"

"Oh, that was awful." Mr. Lennox laughed. "Let us not play that silly alphabet game! Instead, shall we try our hand at yes and no?" His friends nodded their agreement.

"Capital!" Mr. Lennox exclaimed, wedging himself onto the couch next to Miss Edgeworth. He certainly knew how to make his intentions clear.

The next half hour was spent in guessing and answering what one person was thinking of—once it was a knight's lance, another time a monkey, and then a pair of men's trousers. Caroline found herself occasionally guessing too, despite her stoic resolve. She felt the unusual pull of a smile at her cheeks and then remembered herself, remarking under her breath how daft Mr. Lennox had to be to choose whatever it was, and then she settled back into the couch. Part of the way through, Aunt Ebby declared she must turn in for the night and left the room. Caroline stayed behind, actually enjoying herself among people who almost felt like friends.

As the night continued, she caught Mr. Charleston observing her every few minutes.

After the third round, she couldn't take it any longer. This was how friends were supposed to act, and she had none of her own. She rose, and the men quickly sprang to their feet as she declared, "I must turn in for the night."

It wasn't that late, but she gave no excuse.

"But the fun has just begun," Sophie cried.

No one else protested, not even Mr. Charleston. Clearly, her presence wasn't necessary. "If you will excuse me," she said mostly to Sophie, with only a quarter curtsy. She was at the stairs in a moment and looked over her shoulder. Mr. Charleston had come to the edge of the room, frowning after her, but then he turned back to the game.

"Well then," Caroline heard Mr. Lennox say, and she paused just outside her room, encased in the darkness of the corridor. She could still hear some of the game if she strained her ears.

"I have a hard one for you," he said, his voice bubbling with amusement.

"Oh, let me start!" Miss Edgeworth cried. "Is it an animal?"

"Yes," Mr. Lennox said.

"Is it larger than a bread box?" Miss Edgeworth asked.

"Yes."

Caroline, curious as to what he chose, returned to the top of the stairs to listen. She would not manifest her true enjoyment below but now smiled as she thought of possible answers.

Voices rose with excitement. Eventually, she learned it lived in London but not in a menagerie. It was not a pig, a dog, or a cat. Not even a bear. It was known sometimes to be quiet and at other times to screech at people but was not an owl either. At times its eyes seemed like glowing knives, and it often tried to snarl. At this Mr. Lennox laughed, though he did try to keep his voice down.

Caroline listened, as confused as the rest of the party.

Miss Edgeworth finally put it together, for her voice came with excitement. "I think I have found it out!"

"Have you, smart girl?"

Caroline could just imagine Mr. Lennox's balmy smile and lovesick eyes as he spoke.

Her voice dropped so that Caroline held her breath to hear her. "I think . . . is it . . . Lady Caroline?"

There was a small gasp, she guessed from Sophie, and several bouts of laughter.

"Perhaps I should have said yes to the bear question," Mr. Lennox said.

Caroline couldn't listen anymore and hurried to shut herself in her room. None of them liked her. Not many people did— she had heard someone say so once, but to be the object of such a joke while in the same house—how dare they!

Not even Mr. Charleston or Sophie had stood up for her.

She wondered . . . if she asked those two siblings, would they say it wasn't kind of Mr. Lennox to stoop so low and joke so openly, or would they agree with his antics? She slunk against the closed door, crumbling. Her jaw clenched, and she pressed her lips together as her whole person filled with the hate, despair, and shame that came from such an insult.

Eventually, she grasped the handle and rose. It took all she had not to fall to pieces as she climbed into bed, not bothering to ring for the maid. As she lay in the dark, her mind could not evade the unsettling realization that perhaps she deserved such censure.

CHAPTER SEVEN

"You slept in your stays and all?" Edith said the next morning. "Seems mighty uncomfortable. I would have come, my lady, no matter how late."

"I assure you it was actually quite early, but I felt indisposed, for the food was awful. And what I do is my own concern. I do not need suggestions from you," Caroline said.

"Yes, my lady." The maid bowed her head.

Caroline stayed upstairs long enough to miss breakfast, feigning an upset stomach, and came downstairs when she was sure everyone had finished. She made her excuse to Sophie, blaming last night's meal.

"I'll be sure to speak with Cook," Sophie assured Caroline. She turned to her sister, smiling. "Isabel, how well you look. I trust you slept well?"

"Quite well. I imagine I fell asleep before your party even started. I need to do some Christmas shopping, and with both of you as my legs, I was hoping you might find a few things for me."

Sophie nodded. "Surely. Just tell us what you need."

Caroline noted a sadness in Isabel's eyes, guessing she wished to come along but had not the strength. She could only come, however, if they hired a carriage, and no doubt Sophie knew they couldn't afford it.

"If I pay for a carriage," Caroline spoke up, "would you wish to come, Isabel?" Her eyes darted between the sisters. "My aunt mentioned she wished to stay inside today, but I'd like to make a day of it."

Isabel's face flushed with gratitude. "That would be lovely. I think some fresh air would do me good."

Caroline knew the feeling of being lonely and cooped up for far too long. "We can look at the shops' displays from the carriage windows. Sophie, you and I can make sure she remains comfortable." She and Isabel looked at Sophie with raised brows.

"Of course," Sophie said.

Two extra blankets plus a fur for the hired carriage were procured, and the three set off. Caroline could not help but wonder what life would have been like with sisters.

"Now what for John?" Isabel asked.

"He's looking a mite tattered, I'd say. Never buys anything for himself," Sophie answered.

Caroline thought he looked a bit more than a *mite* tattered, but she kept her mouth closed.

Isabel counted some coins out from her purse for Sophie. "A handkerchief, and I'll embroider it later. And, if there is enough, a new stickpin."

Oh, these dears, wanting to help their brother but barely having the pence to do it with! Maybe Caroline could convince at least these two that she was *not* a bear.

"And what about getting him a fine new white shirt?" Caroline offered. "I will pay for it, of course, as a token of appreciation for letting me stay with you."

Isabel shook her head. "We couldn't accept that! It would be far too much—"

"I insist," Caroline interrupted. "You know his measurements, I presume, Sophie?"

Sophie nodded slowly.

"Then, you go ahead." Caroline handed her an additional three shillings. "That ought to do it."

While Sophie walked into the shop, Isabel lowered her eyes and leaned in. "I've been saving this last six months. I want to buy something quite special for Soph. Will you go into the next shop?"

"Of course," Caroline said, realizing then how easy it had been to speak with the sisters all morning. She had almost forgotten last night. "What would you have me buy?"

"She would never say anything, but her boots are so worn. She wears them nearly everywhere, and I think if she had a nice pair of slippers for more genteel occasions . . ."

"Yes, of course."

Caroline entered the women's shop and ordered the slippers. She also picked out a turtle-shell comb for Sophie's thick hair, a canezou for Isabel, and a new muff for each. She gave the store-keeper a few more coins, and he promised to have the gifts delivered before Christmas.

"They were nearly out of everything," Caroline feigned with an apologetic shrug when she returned to the carriage. "But they said they will deliver the shoes before Christmas."

"I hope not for an extra charge?" Isabel's eyes grew.

"Certainly not," she lied, blinking quickly. "Said it was their fault."

"Bless you." Isabel looked through the window as Sophie rejoined them, and the carriage passed farther into town. Then Isabel drew in an awed breath. "Look at those boughs! The berries and the ribbons—Soph, you should make some like that to sell at the fete!"

"Oh, that *is* a splendid wreath. I shall. Let us all commit it to memory, and I'll get started as soon as we get home!"

They took a late lunch when they returned, and Mr. Charleston strode into the dining room. "Are you sure you are feeling up to tonight, my dearest Isabel?" he said.

"Yes, our outing this morning has invigorated me. I have Lady Caroline to thank for making it happen."

Color spread across Caroline's face. She had done nothing; it had been Isabel's idea; she'd merely paid for the carriage. Mr. Charleston gazed at her then, lingering just a moment, his eyebrows bunching together as he cocked his head. His face then relaxed, and he smiled. The feeling that suddenly overcame Caroline warned her to look away.

For the next half hour, she said nearly nothing but sat observing the three Charlestons, who spoke unencumbered by any guest.

"I can tell you, you did not miss much last night, Isabel. Mrs. Winters seemed . . . well." He raised an eyebrow toward Sophie.

"How was she ever my dearest friend? So altered . . ." Sophie said.

Mr. Charleston cleared his throat. "Then Mr. Lennox came, and he was in his highest spirits. He almost trampled us all."

He *had* trampled Caroline, but she tried to forget that whole conversation.

"Well, at least the food you sent up was delicious," Isabel said. "A perfect coupling of sage and onion, I daresay."

"Perhaps you should be the cook," Sophie said, teasing.

Mr. Charleston laughed. "Oh, I think not. Remember that Christmas, years ago, when Isabel wished to make the pudding with Mama? How it crumbled all over her as she carried it in? Purple juice spilling everywhere?"

The three of them burst into laughter, and Caroline wished she could have witnessed that scene and so many other happy ones they alluded to.

It was a wonder the way they all teased and none took offense, the fact that none of the food was actually all that impressive but they thought it utterly delectable, and the way no one seemed to stand on ceremony. They weren't savage, by any means—quite appropriate and kind—but so completely at ease with each other. Could a family really, truly behave like this?

Absent were the stoic nods, the civil inquiries, the necessitated and expected pleasantries that had so completely defined Caroline's relationship with her father. Never once had she felt with him the way they were now—at least, not since before her mother died. She sipped a bit of her punch, wondering if they had such an expensive drink only because she was there.

A faint memory pulled on her then. Once she *had* felt and behaved the way these people did now. It was the spring before her father's death. Her cousin Julia had come to collect her the day before their tour of the north country, and they had laughed over tea. It had been so pleasant and comfortable. Caroline had not seen Julia for nearly a twelvemonth, but they had acted as though they'd lived next door. Eliza and Timothy Lennox had stumbled upon the cousins in the garden, and the siblings had been easy and kind. The four of them had walked together, even floated boats made of sticks and leaves down the stream. In the moment, Caroline had thought the activity may be too juvenile and beneath Timothy, who was seven years Caroline's senior, but he had not seemed to mind.

Caroline had left with Julia the following day for their trip, and when she returned to Elbury, it had not been soon enough to see her father alive.

She had clung to the happiness of that memory for months and slowly distanced herself from her cousin—Julia had married quickly someone of little consequence. That was when Caroline had ceased talking to the Lennoxes as well, clinging to her father's dislike of the family. Perhaps her father had been right about them, after all. She'd not soon forget Mr. Lennox's awful treatment of her last night.

She realized the table had gone quiet; all three of the Charlestons were smiling at her. She scanned their faces but had absolutely no idea what they had been speaking about. The sisters kept their bright smiles, but Mr. Charleston's expression dimmed a little when he caught her gaze.

"I am ever so sorry," she said. "What were you saying? I seem to have been . . . thinking."

"It is no matter," Mr. Charleston said quickly. He probably thought her completely rude, not even paying enough attention to answer. She hadn't been trying to be evasive, not this time;

she'd just been completely absorbed in a past that should have been happy.

※ ※ ※

An hour later, John thought back on their discussion at lunch, when he had asked his sisters what they were excited for regarding Christmas and they had somewhat cryptically smiled toward Lady Caroline. She, however, had not even been giving any attention to their conversation.

Across the room, Sophie and Lady Caroline now took over the parlor, arranging and rearranging boughs for Sophie's booth at the fete when a fit of coughing came from Isabel's room. She had retired a few minutes earlier for a quick nap, but now John heard her gasping and even letting out small yelps of pain.

He and Sophie stood and ran to their sister's room. "I will fetch the doctor immediately," John said as he grasped the doorframe.

He pushed past a stunned Lady Caroline, who stood at the parlor table, as he hurried out the door.

When he returned with the doctor, he tried to ignore Lady Caroline's unimpressed appraisal of the physician as he walked the man upstairs to Isabel's room. The elderly man's jacket showed some wear, an old bloodstain darkened his sable sleeve, and he smelled of tonic, but he was the only doctor around, and they couldn't afford to take Isabel to Town.

The doctor's slow, thumping feet syncopated down the corridor, and John followed nervously behind. Again the hacking cough of Isabel echoed through the house. Sophie remained at her sister's side.

The doctor felt Isabel's forehead and then wrist before looking at John. "I think we ought to let her blood."

A small scream escaped Isabel.

"I fear such a course will weaken her," John challenged.

The man paused. "I suppose, though her cough has moved to the lungs. This kind of infection is difficult to fight. This liniment may help." He pulled a small glass bottle from his bag. "Apply it daily."

"Thank you, Dr. Ford," John said.

"I shall check on her tomorrow. If she worsens before then, let me know." The doctor clicked his bag closed, and the two men walked back down the corridor, stopping just before the door.

"Is there anything else we can do?" John whispered.

"I fear she is much more reduced than a month ago. I know of no solution. As I've said before, perhaps a doctor in London, with access to more advanced medication, would be able to help. I have done everything I can, but at this rate . . . she won't live to see spring."

Tears filled John's eyes. "Surely there must be something."

"If I knew of anything else, I would have tried it."

The physician bowed and exited.

※ ※ ※

Caroline watched from the parlor as Sophie and Mr. Charleston descended the stairs, halting on the last step. They turned and held each other's forearms and spoke in low, anxious voices. Caroline shrank into her seat, pretending not to listen.

Mr. Charleston spoke first. "I can't let Isabel die. We can't lose her too."

Oh, Isabel! Such a dear, wonderful girl. She was too good to die.

"But what is there to do?" Sophie wiped tears from her eyes.

"I could go to London. Tomorrow. Sell Father's land. That should give us enough for a few appointments with a doctor in Town."

Caroline did not dare to raise her head. For several moments, neither sibling stirred. In their grief they seemed to forget she remained in the room.

A fast knock came at the door.

Sophie dropped her hands from her brother and, with a furrowed brow, moved mechanically to answer the door.

A bent-over young woman in a gray work dress and a tattered apron stood in the doorway. What an awful time for such a visitor.

The young woman cleared her throat. "Please, miss, I just come from the ragged school, and I 'ave a bit of skill in the kitchen. You wouldn't be needing an extra hand for a few days until I can find m'self some employment elsewhere, would you?"

Sophie's large, beautiful eyes shot toward her brother. The young girl looked utterly pitiful. Surely he wouldn't accept. Not now, when he needed every penny for Isabel.

Mr. Charleston stepped closer to the girl. "Come to think of it," he said, looking around the room, "we have some extra visitors this week. Perhaps one week, say fourpence a day of good work?"

At this the wispy, unkempt tendrils of the girl's hair bounced vigorously as she nodded. "Yes, thank you, sir. I will do my best, sir."

It was far too generous a wage for someone he had not observed working, especially considering he could barely pay the physician. His goodness was suffocating.

Sophie gave her brother a wan smile and led the young girl to the kitchen.

Mr. Charleston wrung his hands together, then rested them on the mantel. He seemed mesmerized by the flames and still did not notice Caroline.

She stood and walked a few paces toward him. "I want to help. I will pay for the doctor," she said.

Mr. Charleston startled, and then his brow softened. "You would do that?" His eyes locked with hers, a small smile gracing his lips.

His penetrating eyes searched her own and nearly undid Caroline. She chided herself for feeling so vulnerable. "Why, of course," she said evenly. "Isabel is a wonderful girl and deserves the best. I would be happy to help." He continued to look at her, smile at her, and she had to glance away from him to slow her heartbeat and check her voice. Clearing her throat, she added, "Assuming you can guarantee that my money goes to helping her and not toward hiring unknown poorhouse beggars."

His unencumbered smile shattered into a stoic frown. "Of course you would disapprove of such a kindness. Of course you would put parameters on your own generosity."

"Well, if you must know, hiring her, even for a week, was completely foolish—especially considering your circumstances."

He shifted his shoulders and said in a low growl, "You would have turned her away, then, for the surplus population is not your concern?"

Caroline froze, a lump rising in her throat. He had heard—and remembered—what she had said to the girl who had begged her for work back in London. And now he'd used her exact words against her. It was too cruel a trick, especially when just moments before he had looked at her with such kindness . . . as though he might care for her.

It was the caring that had unnerved her, sent her into a panic, really. Her hands had begun shaking, her thoughts had raced into hopeful possibilities that she had immediately contradicted. She didn't know how to respond when someone showed such true and exposed emotion, even if it had been for only a moment.

"If you'll excuse me," Mr. Charleston said. His eyes bored into hers.

She attempted to return the feeling with a glare of her own—after all, he had used her own words against her—and such resolve almost worked, until she remembered again the tender look he'd given her when she'd offered to help Isabel. Then guilt from her unfeeling reaction forced her gaze shamefully to the floor as Mr. Charleston said nothing more and hurried away from her.

CHAPTER EIGHT

When evening came, Caroline wanted any excuse not to attend the Charlestons' poor country fete. She did wish to support Sophie, but Mr. Lennox would be there, and after his game last night, she never wished to see his face again. A tiny bit of her thought she ought to make an effort to apologize to Mr. Charleston, but she ushered the thought into the recesses of her mind.

"Isabel," she pleaded as they sat talking in Isabel's room, "I shall stay with you. That way Sophie and your brother can be at peace knowing someone is with you."

"I cannot let you," Isabel said with more resolve than Caroline thought her fragile frame could handle. "My coughing fit has subsided. Truly, I desire only solitude and darkness to shoo away this headache." She folded her slight arms. "Our servants look in on me constantly anyway." Her stern look proved she would not be swayed.

Caroline then sought out her aunt, who had stayed in her room most of the day. She might appeal to Aunt Ebby to stay. "I think we should forgo the fete," she said loudly. "Perhaps we could have the carriage take us directly to the train station."

"What's that, dear?" Aunt Ebby said, craning her neck.

"Let's not go to the fete," Caroline tried again.

"Let's all go indeed! I rested all afternoon so that I might enjoy tonight. Aren't Sophie and Mr. Charleston already waiting in the carriage I called for?"

Caroline pressed her fingers to her temples. The old woman's hearing seemed particularly bad this evening. "No, let's *not* go, I said."

"Yes, yes, let's all go." Aunt Ebby smiled, pushing Caroline toward the front door.

Caroline shook her head and set her lips in a tight line. Her aunt could be so exasperating.

As they walked into the large rented hall after their arrival, Caroline could not hide her surprise. The decorations were quite tasteful, with festive greenery and an abundance of holly tied to the doorframes. The room, which she was sure usually held an assembly of dancers, felt intimate due to the tables that formed a semicircle on one side of the room. Each table created its own booth, boasting beautiful wares, from table decor to baked goods to cloth embroidery and other items. One or two well-dressed and elegant women stood behind each one.

Aunt Ebby watched Caroline. "See? It isn't so bad."

"You understood me before, didn't you?" Caroline furrowed her brow.

"What was that?" Aunt Ebby scanned the room distractedly, her eyes stopping on a table full of artisan loaves.

"Oh, never mind," Caroline said, shaking her head. She led the woman to the bread table, purchased a baguette, and settled her aunt in a chair along one of the walls. She then came to Sophie's booth.

"Your arrangement is even more regal than the display in the store window," Caroline said. "I am sure everyone will love to buy your decorations."

"They would not have looked half so well if you hadn't helped make them," Sophie said. "I don't know how to thank you. I only wish Isabel could be here to enjoy this party."

Caroline nodded and offered a half smile as she searched the room. "Where did your brother go?" Her conscience nudged her about a needed apology to Mr. Charleston. The drive over had been more than uncomfortable.

"I saw him go through those doors at the back of the hall, toward the patio."

Caroline wondered what Sophie would think of her chasing after Mr. Charleston alone, but she would not let herself dwell on it. She knew what she needed to do. She excused herself and went directly out to the frosted garden, where the air hung with a chilly dampness.

She hoped to find Mr. Charleston right away. Their last conversation had been eating at her for hours. After a brief search, she found him walking slowly along the hedge outside the back doors.

She waited a minute, letting him come closer. When he was near enough, she stepped to the side and coughed slightly to give him warning.

His eyes shot up. He didn't smile, but at least he didn't cringe.

"I . . . came looking for you," she said, standing on the edge of the walkway. She studied him, the twilight lighting up his face. She smiled bashfully and continued. "I need to apologize. I shouldn't have said what I did about your servant."

"Lady Caroline," he said, his eyebrows pulling together, "you are entitled to your opinion."

She shook her head and tried to formulate the right words. "Yes, but I ought not speak so. If only my mouth could realize before I open it how often it wounds my friends."

He narrowed his eyes and looked askance at her. "So we are friends? Or are you referring to my sisters?"

"Perhaps it is too bold to say." She pursed her lips.

Mr. Charleston's face changed as he glanced down, paused a moment, and then gently shook his head. "It is not too bold. I am honored you would consider me a friend." He met her eyes and smiled. "Apology accepted. Shall we go back inside? You must be freezing."

How could he forgive her so easily? Could he really mean it? His eyes darted back and forth, and finally, he extended an elbow, and rather than turn away as usual, she decided to take it.

"Friends," he whispered with a smile.

They made it back through the door, and Mr. Charleston spoke again. "I realize you think it's rather a poor country party, but if you just get to know everyone, I know you'll enjoy yourself. Mr. Lennox's acquaintances are from London; surely they are refined."

She bristled at the mention of Mr. Lennox. She would never agree that he and Miss Edgeworth, and the few more who joined him now, were refined, even if they did generally reside in London. She glanced toward the group. "I am familiar with several of them" was all she managed in response.

"Perfect. I will rely on your prowess with fine society." Mr. Charleston said it in such a way that she wasn't sure if it was meant as a jest or a jab.

"I know all three of the gentlemen," she said to Mr. Charleston in a low voice. "Lord Fotheringham and Mr. Dralling were both acquaintances of my father, though neither of them was shrewd enough with their finances to come recommended. The other is Colonel Lennox, Mr. Lennox's brother."

Mr. Charleston raised one eyebrow. "He is the only one I know. I will apply to him to be introduced to the rest of the party. They look harmless enough." He smiled.

"No one intimidates you." Her lips twitched as she remembered their first meeting.

"Just handsome young women whose reputations precede them," he said quietly.

Caroline started, unsure how to reply. He hadn't seemed the least bit frightened during their first meeting.

Mr. Charleston and Caroline walked over to Mr. Lennox. She tried to hide her nerves as they moved toward the crowd and John requested an introduction to his friends.

"You remember my brother?" Mr. Lennox said.

Caroline fought the urge to fiddle with her skirts as the rest of the introductions were made.

"I am sure you will feel at home here, Lady Caroline, for you all have much in common." Mr. Lennox gestured toward the group. "If you'll excuse me," he said and clapped Mr. Charleston on the back, "John and I will be just a moment."

Caroline froze, suddenly left to the group, devoid of Mr. Charleston. Where were they going? The ladies seemed rather reserved toward her, and the gentlemen continued talking among themselves. Why could she not at least make pleasant conversation? She knew vaguely of these people and should be able to insert herself into any conversation, yet she felt alone, isolated. She couldn't even think of a friendly way to begin speaking with any of them, fearing how they would perceive her.

After several minutes of standing in silence, she excused herself to retreat to Sophie—no one had even tried to speak to her.

Once there she relaxed at Sophie's table with a glass of punch and watched Mr. Lennox, Miss Edgeworth, and Mr. Charleston return to the London set. Mr. Charleston was soon munching on a lemon cake as he sat across from Mr. Lennox's friend, a Miss Katherine Dale. She was a pretty girl with deep dimples. Caroline wondered what she had said that made Mr. Charleston smile in such a way.

Not that she ought to care. He was nothing to her—and she was nothing to him. He was a man doing his duty to his father and her own. For a moment she wished she had been the one to entice him to buy a lemon cake and smile so freely. In her distraction her fingers drummed on her glass.

She had success and money as her allies. Many here had ignorance and want. Surely she could entertain one of the young London men as easily as Mr. Lennox's friend had Mr. Charleston. At the very least, she ought to try to be civil and carry on a conversation with them, even if they were Mr. Lennox's guests.

She resolved to try again. She clutched her glass like a chalice of courage and walked to the punch table. She filled her cup, trying to think of the most engaging ways to begin a conversation with Lord Fotheringham, when she saw a few of the party, backs to her, draw their heads together.

"I have to admit I am in shock that Mr. Lennox moves in circles so close to her," one of the young ladies said in a low tone. "Do you remember how she berated him at the governor's ball?"

The other two girls nodded, and the men drew closer.

As soon as Caroline realized they were speaking about her, she pulled back behind a large vase of flowers to hide. Her heart pounded. She ought to turn away, but she wanted to hear just a bit more.

Lord Fotheringham spoke next. "It is not his fault, you know. He's been friends with John for years, and John's father was Lord Marchant's steward. I heard there wasn't a more miserly employer in all of England. Poor Charleston Sr. didn't receive fair wages for nearly thirty years."

Caroline's hackles rose at the comment. Her father surely paid a fair wage. It must not be true.

Miss Dale's little sister, Johanna, spoke next, whispering to Lord Fotheringham. "And what of the daughter? She seemed rather quiet a minute ago."

"Oh no," Mr. Lennox's brother said. "She was quiet only because she thinks herself so much better than us all."

That hadn't been the reason. Caroline just hadn't known what to say.

Colonel Lennox continued. "But it is no matter, for we knew better than to engage her in conversation. She is twice as bad as the old man. Won't even speak to anyone unless he is a lord or has fifteen thousand pounds. She is even more miserly with her father's money, to the point of pushing away anyone friendly or genuine. People say she thinks every young man is out to steal her inheritance."

These were the rumors circulating about her? Caroline *did* care about her inheritance, but still . . .

Miss Katherine Dale then spoke. "But she is here, at a country party, with Mr. Charleston. Perhaps he wants her money."

Caroline's color rose as she adjusted herself nearly into the corridor, still watching them.

Lord Fotheringham shook his head. "No, indeed. John Charleston is the best of men. He would never ask for her money, and she would never condescend even to talk to him had their fathers not been connected."

"I don't understand why she has come," Miss Katherine Dale said.

Lord Fotheringham looked around but not quite far enough to see Caroline. "I am not apprised of the particulars, but John Charleston has been given some type of business from his father that he must discharge with Lady Caroline. He's just beginning as a financial solicitor, so I'm certain it has to do with the will. Seems like an awful task, if you ask me."

"I couldn't do it," Colonel Lennox said. "Not for two hundred pounds." The group looked at him, several with raised eyebrows or inclined heads. "Besides Lord Marchant's sister and daughter, only Charleston Sr. attended her father's funeral, which is a credit to Mr. Charleston's father. I heard Lord Marchant spoke so poorly of the fellow that even if he had sought other employment, no one else would hire him as their solicitor. Nearly ruined him with so little income. Lady Caroline is just like her father, destroying those around her. Did you hear the way she mocked Miss Lewyton on account of her dress at her first coming-out ball?" The colonel clicked his tongue, and Caroline found herself unable to stop staring at him. "Surely you recall, Lord Fotheringham, how she also slandered Lady Markum's reputation? It was all hearsay, but now Lady Markum's family has disinherited her completely. Lady Caroline will be lucky if *she* has a single mourner when she dies."

Caroline had heard enough. She nearly spilled her punch down the front of her gown as she tore away from her hiding place toward the back door. Tears pooled in her eyes. How could people speak of her so? Her father had been cold and unfeeling; that she knew. To say that she was twice as bad as him . . . Had she really let herself become so calloused? Why had she been so cruel to Mr. Lennox, Miss Lewyton, Lady Markum?

This was humiliating. Infuriating. She must leave now.

Caroline scanned the room, noticing that Mr. Charleston had just left Sophie and walked toward Colonel Lennox. Aunt Ebby sat eating a dessert, surely delivered by Mr. Charleston from Miss Edgeworth's sweets table. He stood close to the party of Londoners now but wasn't quite inside their tight circle.

His eyes met hers, and she knew.

He had heard the group's every word.

If he hadn't been sure of her awful nature yet, now he had several witnesses and verbal proof.

He strode over to her with a wildfire in his gaze. "Is it true what they say? Surely they must be wrong."

How she wished they were.

"I knew you were . . . particular, exacting, but this? Can you deny it? Tell me you can."

She wished she had never come to Thornton Heath. "Mr. Charleston, I . . . my father . . ."

"I am aware of your father's lack of kindnesses. My family and I feel the effects of it every day—especially Isabel, who has needed better medical attention for years—though I did not know he sabotaged my father's ability to gain a better situation. I know Miss Lewyton's family, and everyone has heard of Lady Markum's circumstance. I have always believed her to be innocent, but I did not know it was you who circulated those lies." His jaw clenched and his chest heaved as he drew deep breaths. "I had not expected such an awful report as slander and mockery." He inched closer, and his eyes pleaded with her. "I had hoped you were different from your father. Tell me you are."

She tried desperately to keep her feelings in check, but her cheeks burned red, and tears flowed down her face. How had she become this?

She and Mr. Charleston stared at each other for a long, agonizing moment. She shook her head in defeat and then gathered her skirts in her hands and fled. She could never come back here, no matter her father's wishes.

※ ※ ※

"What happened to Lady Caroline?" Sophie asked as John came toward her. His body trembled, and he winced at her question.

Lady Loresetter joined them, leaning heavily on her cane, and craned her ear toward them.

"She overheard Timothy's guests talking about her. They should not have been speaking so openly. They knew of her past, of her . . . tendencies to be cold-hearted. I saw her face. I wanted to disbelieve them, but she could not deny it."

He replayed the conversation in his mind, recalling how her beautiful countenance had fallen by degrees into a hard, icy one of ruin and hatred. Then the pain on her drawn, tearstained face came back to his mind, and he felt for her, even though he could not believe she could be so cruel. "I think I ought to follow her."

Sophie nodded. "Yes, I fear we have done her a great disservice having her come here."

How could he even care for her after all that was said? She was just like Anna. Some people didn't care how they hurt others.

He thought of Lady Caroline's apology earlier that evening . . . the way she'd taken to Isabel . . . the happiness he'd seen in her eyes at the Hartleys' dinner in her childhood home. She had several less-desirable qualities, that was certain. But he thought that maybe, a few times, he had broken through her haughtiness and seen the true Lady Caroline.

"I need to make this right. For Father." He looked at his sister and then at Lady Loresetter, wondering if his desire to help was only because of his promise to his father.

Or was it for him too?

※ ※ ※

"Where is Lady Caroline?" John demanded of his servant as he exited Timothy's carriage. It had taken far too long to find Timothy, who had ventured to the patio with Miss Edgeworth, and then procure the man's carriage.

"Headed to the night train, I am afraid," the servant said. "Only stopped here to give direction as to where to send her things."

John had thought she would have just come back, perhaps retired early. But she'd left? "Fetch me my horse."

He rode as fast as he could, but by the time he reached the station, the train and Lady Caroline were nowhere to be seen. He returned home, dejected. Clearly, Lady Caroline did not wish to speak to him.

John was unable to sleep that night and roamed his frosted garden, alone and pensive, well past midnight. The moonlight shone as he meandered, trying to figure out how to fix everything. He ignored the cold air and touched the ice-laden tips of the leaves with his fingers.

As he passed the nearly frozen river at the edge of his property, he wished he were a boy again. If he were, he would break a twig from a half-dead tree, fashion a leaf around the stick, find a small bit of wood, and float a boat down the stream.

He snapped a twig in two. It was winter—there would be no floating boat races now. How he wished it were the almost-spring kind of winter, not the just-past-autumn variety. Things had been easier in the spring of his life, without human nature turning everything cold, frozen, and complicated. Oh, to be a boy again.

Too soon the copse of trees ended, and John made up his mind. He ought to escort Lady Loresetter home—the poor woman had been abandoned by her niece. He would accompany her to London, sell the deed to his land tomorrow, and use the money to find a better doctor for Isabel. The family would be forced to rent a smaller property until he could procure a few new clients, but it would be worth it if Isabel improved.

He thought again of Lady Caroline. Knowing the pain and humiliation she had suffered, he thought perhaps he ought to see how she fared while he was in London.

No. He shook his head. He could not worry about her any longer. Now that his duty to his father was discharged, helping Isabel was paramount.

He went directly to his study, withdrew the lease to his property, and packed it into his satchel. He paused, then walked over to the bookshelf—he knew exactly which spine he sought, its title worn, the volume looking especially unremarkable in the light. He wasn't sure why, but he added it to his luggage as well.

CHAPTER NINE

CAROLINE STAGGERED HOME IN A tearful blur, sobs wracking her body until she fell motionless onto her bed, where she remained the whole night.

When she awoke, she possessed an awful fever and pulled the bell to ring for Edith.

An undermaid carried a breakfast tray to the small table beside Caroline's bed. The mere sight of the food made her stomach roil. The scared maid handed Caroline a letter.

With bleary eyes Caroline opened it. Edith had apparently had enough and had taken her leave as soon as they'd arrived home.

Caroline swallowed back her horror. "Have the housekeeper come see me," she croaked at the girl.

The maid's eyes shifted. "She too has given her leave. Ran off with the butler while you were at Thornton Heath."

Caroline's head pounded as she processed this report, an angry growl rising in her sore throat. "We are without a housekeeper, a butler, *and* a lady's maid?" Caroline struggled to pull herself higher in her bed, incredulous, her eyes wide. "Get . . . get out," she hissed, nearly upsetting the teacup on the tray at her bedside as she batted her hand at the girl.

The door snapped shut, and Caroline sank down into her covers, crying bitterly against her pillow, her hair matted around her.

In the distance she heard the church bells chime, a more joyful and boisterous tolling than a simple ring of the hour. In three days, it would be Christmas, she realized, and the bells sounded in festive lays. She drew her blanket around her so it engulfed her in darkness. No housekeeper, no butler, no lady's maid, not a single friend, and no plans for Christmas. Nothing but a sore throat, a fever, and a terrible headache.

How could she be so utterly friendless? And at this time of year, when all good Christian people ought to be caring for one another—the sick and the needy. She *was* the sick, if not precisely the needy. And yet several of her staff had abandoned her!

She thought then of Aunt Ebby, whom she herself had abandoned. How had Caroline fled from the party without a single thought for her aunt? How abominably rude. She hadn't even remembered the old woman until she and Edith were on the train.

Recalling her aunt caused Caroline to mull over the days since Mr. Charleston had shown up at her door. Why had she ever consented to read his letter? To travel with him? To allow him to take her to Elbury and Thornton Heath? To be in the presence of his horrid friend? Far too many times she had said yes, given in, allowed him entrance into her life, and now—look at all the problems he had caused.

Never, never, never again could she let someone into her life like that. She had her prestige, her family name, her wealth, her superior reputation to stand behind, and that would suffice. She did not need anyone.

She was independent. Wealthy. Beautiful.

And oh, so alone.

❀ ❀ ❀

Caroline's fever raged, and she spent all night falling in and out of fitful half dreams, most of which seemed to portray her future.

First, she was cold, thin, and alone and wore a perfectly tailored gown as she tried to direct those around her at some lavish party. Her mother and father walked by but did not notice her. Then Sylvia Hartley and Eliza and Mr. Lennox. Then Mr. Charleston. Each one passed by as though they were deaf. They enjoyed each other's company without even acknowledging her existence.

The moment faded, and another dream started, in which Caroline hovered, disembodied, in a churchyard. One moment a clergyman spoke over a casket, standing alone with no other mourners present, and the next the scene flashed forward to an earth-covered grave and a beautiful headstone. Caroline drew closer to it, discovering large, masterfully carved words. With horror she read her own name. She waited above her grave for what felt like days, even months, as grass grew over the dirt and the seasons changed. Not once did a visitor lay a flower there or pause to pay their respects. Some who entered the cemetery walked around the plot, and others muttered to their companions awful stories of the terrible Lady Caroline Morleigh.

She awoke with a start, jolting to a sitting position in her bed. Cold sweat dripped down her temples, and her damp hair obscured her vision, though nothing could block out the nightmares.

It could not be so. She wished, hoped with every part of her that this would not be her ending. She had to do something—anything—everything to change the trajectory of her future.

But how?

She could not start with her aunt. Who knew if Aunt Ebby would ever allow Caroline to speak to her again? All hope of receiving her inheritance from her aunt would be gone now. Nor could she make amends with Mr. Lennox, and of course not Mr. Charleston—she could not even think of him. It hurt too much to think of her family and the people who had been, if only briefly, her friends.

Echoes of her superior, condescending tone entered her mind then. How many people had she yelled at, cast out, and belittled? How many servants and other people below her rank had she shunned? She ought to have been gracious toward those below her station.

And then she knew—she could start with the surplus population.

No matter how ill she felt, she must make her way to the poorhouse.

※ ※ ※

"I am here to beg your return, Edith."

Caroline's hair sat in a knotted mess at the back of her neck. She'd attempted to keep out the cold with a scarf as she stood across from her former maid in the doorway of the poorhouse. Edith had gone there yesterday, declaring in her letter that the humiliation of such a place was more comfortable than Caroline's presence. The young maid crossed her arms and stood firm.

"I am sorry, my lady, but I cannot subject myself to you again. I know it is bold to say, but as you are no longer my employer—"

"I've had a change of heart."

The young maid's mouth was set in a firm line.

"I promise." Caroline willed herself to speak without blundering or, worse, crying. "I know there is no reason for you to trust me." She wrung her hands together. "But do you remember that woman from the ragged school who came begging for work a few days ago? I've been trying to track her down all morning and have finally found her. I have decided to employ her as my housekeeper and have doubled her wages from her current situation."

Edith's eyes tightened, and she tilted her head toward Caroline. "You know Jess is my dear friend. Our mums grew up together."

Caroline's eyes opened wide. "I did not know that, but I will double your wages too if you'll only come back." She smiled and pleaded, "It isn't just because I desperately need a maid." She gestured toward her mussed hair. "It . . . it . . . it is because I wish to make things right between us. I'll pack all my own gowns every time we travel so I can't blame anyone but myself for any wrinkles. And I'll give you Christmas, Michaelmas, Twelfth Night, and any other holidays you want off."

At this Edith nodded once, her eyebrows raising in disbelief. "I . . . I think you're in earnest . . ."

"Yes . . . yes, I am." She stepped closer. "And you know all my faults, but I am going to change. I can and will be better."

Edith looked as though she'd warmed one more degree. "Good for you, my lady." She paused and then said, "Jess and I will keep you in line."

Caroline smiled. "I'll need it." For the first time in her life, she threw her arms around her servant. "Thank you for giving me a second chance."

Later that afternoon Caroline grasped a metal knocker in the shape of a man's face. Two taps and a long pause later, the butler pulled open the door.

"Has my aunt returned from Thornton Heath?" Caroline asked warily. She ought to know that answer, ought to have brought Aunt Ebby herself and assured her safe arrival. Caroline cowered sheepishly, clasping her hands in front of her, her eyes downturned.

The butler, whom she knew well, did not offer his usual cordial welcome. "She *has* returned. Please wait." He gestured to just inside the entry but no farther. He turned and disappeared into a nearby room, and Caroline could hear a muffled whisper. Then she heard a dress rustling and the sound of a cane coming toward her.

"Caroline. To what do I owe the honor?" Aunt Ebby's tone wasn't exactly welcoming. She had every right to be angry. Caroline had exhibited nothing but contempt and rudeness for years, not to mention her desertion after the fete.

"I came to offer an apology and beg for your forgiveness." The heat in Caroline's cheeks rose.

Aunt Ebby turned her pointed chin to the side, glancing deeper into the adjoining room, past a large shade that divided the space. Then she looked back at her niece with perched eyebrows and a stare that seemed to say Caroline's words weren't quite enough.

Caroline took a deep breath, willing herself to stay calm. "I am horrified when I think of how I have acted. I showed no respect to anyone, especially you, and my behavior was unpardonable. I thought only of myself. And just now you so graciously allowed me to come into your house, and I did not even thank you for accompanying me to Elbury and Thornton Heath in the first place."

Aunt Ebby stepped back and turned again toward the room with the shade, her eyebrows lowering a degree. "Your apology won't earn back your inheritance, you know."

Caroline felt the pain in her aunt's face. "This isn't about the money, Aunt." She spoke slowly, with a quiet tone. "I know I shall never deserve that, nor do I want it. I came only to apologize, with no other motives."

Her aunt drew her head back, studying her for a long, agonizing moment.

Caroline felt herself near tears now, her anxiousness to make everything right getting the better of her. "I shudder when I think of how I've treated everyone. You, Sylvia, my servants. I wish now I could make amends with all of them."

Aunt Ebby stood tall and tapped her cane regally on the floor. She clicked her tongue as she wagged her head from side to side. "You forgot Mr. Lennox," she said, her voice rising. "What of him? You treated *him* abominably."

Caroline's breath caught in her throat. She froze. If Mr. Lennox hadn't been at the fete, his friends wouldn't have pointed out all of her flaws. In front of Mr. Charleston, no less, who wouldn't have excoriated her publicly.

How could she forgive Mr. Lennox? He had exposed all the worst parts of her.

Her aunt's voice softened. "Are you not happier now?"

The question took Caroline completely off guard. She wanted to berate Aunt Ebby then and there for such a bizarre query. None of this brought her joy. Only pain and remorse. But then she paused, really listening for the first time in years, replaying the question in her mind.

Aunt Ebby was right.

Perhaps Caroline was not happier exactly, not yet, but she felt more peace. Somehow the humiliating scene at the fete had helped. It had caused her to recognize her faults, inspired a desire to change, led her to gain two faithful servants, and guided her to now repair her relationship with her aunt. She hadn't experienced reconciliation like that . . . ever. She hadn't conquered all her problems, hadn't addressed all grievances, but facing them a little at a time somehow felt . . . right.

Caroline lowered her chin and dropped her shoulders. "I am not sure I am happy, Aunt. Not yet. But it is a start." She sighed and tried to take courage, though she felt small. "I wish there were some way I could apologize to Mr. Lennox. He did not deserve my censure and disdain those weeks ago."

Her aunt's face lightened a little, a smile emerging. "Do you really mean that, Caroline?"

Caroline thought for a moment, searching her heart. "Yes."

"Then, come in." Aunt Ebby gestured behind the screen, and Caroline walked slowly, grateful her aunt would once again offer her a seat in her home.

Then she understood. No wonder Aunt Ebby had come out to greet her, had paused in the entry hall.

There, standing as Caroline came into his view, was Mr. Lennox.

A lump caught in Caroline's throat. She thought she'd meant what she said, but had she really?

She looked at him, truly looked at him. He was still the same portly, unremarkable man she'd known from her association with his sister. But his eyes searched hers, and nothing in them seemed to portray any guile.

"I shall call for some tea," Aunt Ebby said before removing herself from the room.

"Lady Caroline."

"Mr. Lennox," Caroline said simultaneously. "What are you doing here?" she asked, still astonished.

"I worried about your aunt, after the fete. Thought I should call on her. We've become fast friends these last few days."

"Oh," Caroline said quietly. How did this man she'd loathed have more decency and compassion than she herself had?

She really ought to say something else. She clenched the sides of her gown and summoned her mettle. "I . . ." Her voice faltered.

Mr. Lennox studied her face and raised his brows expectantly.

She cleared her throat and tried again. "I . . . am so sorry for the pain I've caused you. You and your friends spoke nothing but truth about me."

Mr. Lennox's countenance relaxed. "In truth, Lady Caroline, we should not have been so harsh, no matter what you deserved." He gave a wry smile. "I remember our times together as children. My sister Eliza adored you. Then, when I saw you again in London, I had hoped for a warm welcome as I came into a new circle, and you destroyed me, so utterly . . . fearsome." It was gracious of him to end the last sentence with a small chuckle, and Caroline echoed him with a hesitant laugh.

"If you can ever forgive me for the way I treated you . . ." She shook her head.

His furrowed brow smoothed as she spoke. "If you can forgive my imbecile remarks and impudent friends . . ."

She nodded. "Their words were brutally unkind. But was I any different to you?" She extended her hand as a gesture of truce.

Mr. Lennox's mouth pulled up to the side, and he shrugged. He walked forward and shook her hand.

"Friends, then?" she asked.

"Friends."

The tea was brought, and the two sat talking together with Aunt Ebby for another quarter of an hour.

Mr. Lennox's words had conjured the memory of her conversation with Mr. Charleston at the fete. He had said he had been honored to be her friend. Had he really felt that? And then she recalled their later conversation, when he had questioned her, begged her to deny her cruel behavior.

And she could not.

It pained her to think of what he must think of her now.

Again and again she recalled his kindness, his open manner. Even his laugh flooded into her mind as she went home. She had tried so hard to deny it, but John Charleston truly was the best of men, just as Lord Fotheringham had said. Besides being kind, Mr. Charleston was frank, honest, hopeful. Willing to give people a chance. She had thought herself so decidedly above him in the beginning, but in truth, he was above her in so many ways.

Not that such a realization mattered now. She doubted they would ever cross paths again.

CHAPTER TEN

AFTER DEPOSITING LADY LORESETTER AT her home earlier that morning, John busied himself by reading in Timothy's study. He desperately craved any distraction from the heartbreaking errand that awaited him tomorrow—Christmas Eve, of all days—but with such muddled thoughts, he could not focus. His eyes glazed over as he read the same line for the third time, hoping to finally comprehend its meaning.

His worn traveling satchel glowered at him from the corner of the room. The deed inside it was all his father had been able to leave John and his sisters, the house the only home they had ever known, and soon all of it would be gone. Tomorrow he would sell the land and make a doctor's appointment for Isabel. He shuddered to think what would happen if she needed even more attention after the money from selling the deed ran out. What would he do then? What would be left to sell?

He glanced at the fire and thought, yet again, about asking Timothy for help—but the man had just invested his surplus cash in a railroad scheme. John hoped the investment would do well, but he knew there wasn't any extra blunt lying around at Timothy's disposal.

Lady Caroline had pledged she would help, but that was before their argument, before his friends had humiliated her in public, before he had accused her to her face.

There was nothing else he could do, so at the first sign of morning light, John walked to the legal office to meet his buyer. He thought with shame of his father, today being one year exactly from his death. How had it come to this? On the corner just outside the office, he remembered the book he had put in his traveling satchel at the last minute. The one his father had handed him last Christmas Eve. Now, wanting to delay as much as possible, he leaned against one of the building's brick walls and, for the first time, opened the book. It was the only gift his father had ever received from Jacob Morleigh and had meant a great deal to him, though John could never understand why.

He was surprised to find that the old book was full of classic fairy tales—such a text seemed oceans away from what miserly old Lord Marchant would ever deign to read—and John was further astonished to see it appeared to be an original edition. He wondered if it would draw a price. He leafed through the pages slowly, admiring the beautiful full-color illustrations. He had never cared much for reading, but he remembered Lady Caroline's speech in the garden at Elbury House. Books had taken her to faraway lands, she had claimed. How he wished this book might take him away from the terrible task in front of him.

He thumbed through the pages, and when he reached the last one, he found a letter folded into thirds, with a crumbling wax seal. The look of the missive seemed familiar, the paper beautiful and the folds crisp just like the first letter he had delivered, and he debated opening it. He flipped the letter over to examine it and noticed a neatly penned message.

> *I trust you'll know what to do and when.*
> *A million thanks for doing what I ought to have done long ago.*
> *—Jacob Morleigh*

His father had mentioned this book, but had he forgotten to mention this letter because of his sickness? It contained no address; surely it was meant to be hand delivered. Opening it would be the only way to know to whom it was addressed, though he believed he could guess. He snapped the book closed. To open the letter would be improper and nosy. He walked down the street and, distracted, passed his turn to the seller's office.

One block later, curiosity finally got the better of him. With a trembling hand he opened the book, retrieved the letter, and broke the seal. It was written to Lady Caroline, just as he'd expected it would be.

He read the contents once. Then again. And again. The pain of it wounded his heart.

What if he had not thought to bring the old book? What if he hadn't opened it? If not, Lady Caroline would never have had the chance to read her father's last words to her.

He clamped his eyes shut and took a deep breath. He must finish what his father had asked him to do.

Though he suspected Lady Caroline hated him, he knew he must deliver the letter. She deserved to know what it contained, regardless of how she felt about him.

The emotions their last conversation had provoked flooded his heart and mind. A cold tingle shot up the length of his spine. The chance of her even letting him inside after all that had happened seemed nearly nonexistent.

He could mail it. That would save him time and trouble. Not to mention he would save face. But sending it so impersonally felt wrong.

He would be lying if he said he hadn't thought of her since the night of the fete. He'd nearly visited her yesterday evening to apologize, but he hadn't been able to muster the gumption. He had behaved badly and felt terrible that he hadn't made things right earlier.

John ran his fingers through his hair. Suddenly, the deed seemed less important.

He straightened and forced himself to focus. He would deliver the letter now, and afterward, when his conscience was clear, he would sell the deed. A sincere apology, a final delivery, and he would be discharged from all duties to Lady Caroline, Lord Marchant, and John's own father. Forever.

CHAPTER ELEVEN

Jess—or Mrs. Stone, as Caroline insisted everyone call her—came into the sitting room midmorning on Christmas Eve. "A visitor, my lady."

Caroline stood and smiled. "Show my aunt in. I am expecting her."

"It is not your aunt, Lady Caroline." Mrs. Stone bit her lip. "It is a Mr. Charleston." She dropped her voice lower and leaned in. "Edith has apprised me of all the grief he caused you. Should I ask him to leave?"

Caroline's body tensed, and her breath quickened. She had forgiven Mr. Lennox and made amends with her aunt and her servants, but could she see Mr. Charleston? He had been the start of all this, had reopened her deepest wounds, past and present. But it was she who needed forgiveness.

She released her breath and placed a hand on the bookshelf to steady herself. "Show him in," she managed as she rotated toward the open door and pressed her trembling fingers against the bodice of her dress. Could she remain calm? Kind? Would she be able to speak at all?

Mr. Charleston strode in swiftly, a leather bag hanging from his shoulder. He halted a safe distance from her and offered a polite bow. He wore the same faded suit and had the same becoming curl to his hair, but his face looked different, tired. It was thinner, the pigment gray. His eyes looked weary. It had been but a few days since she had seen him, but he appeared so altered.

How much had he dreaded coming here? For the hundredth time she berated herself. She had caused him too much pain.

"Lady Caroline," he began with a heavy voice, avoiding her gaze, "I have come, first, to ask most sincerely for your forgiveness for the misery I caused you. I should not have insisted on so many things . . . traveling, visiting your home, attending parties you did not wish to—"

"Please," she blurted out, louder than necessary.

He glanced toward her.

"I am . . ." She wished to say much, but tears started to flow. She attempted to swallow but couldn't manage another word. Embarrassed, she sat down on the little couch and tried to discreetly wipe away her tears.

So many thoughts, words, and feelings raced through her mind, but she could not control herself enough to convey any of them.

She wasn't aware of how much time had passed before she felt a hand on her arm as Mr. Charleston sat next to her on the couch.

"I . . ." She shut her eyes and tried to focus on her breathing.

The hand on her arm gave a little squeeze. "Take your time," Mr. Charleston said, his voice gentle.

"It . . . it is I who should be so terribly sorry," she managed to say. She looked at Mr. Charleston then.

His dark-gray eyes stared at her, his face filled with a little more color than when he'd first walked in. The tilt of his head and the furrow of his brow almost overcame her, as they seemed to convey tender, genuine concern.

She took a sharp breath as she registered how near he sat, close enough to touch her arm and now rest his other hand on her back.

His touch, she realized, had infused a calmness in her. He smelled slightly like firewood but clean as well, and she liked the combination. She took a deep breath and started again. "It is I who should be apologizing, Mr. Charleston. You . . . you were merely trying to help me and do your father's bidding. I know I was—I am—unpredictable and unpleasant." A pitiful laugh caught in her throat. "And yet that did not deter you from helping me." He rubbed her forearm comfortingly as she continued. "I am so sorry. Can you forgive my awful behavior?"

His hand stopped moving.

She knew she asked too much.

He removed his hand and created space between the two of them. "Of course, Lady Caroline." His Adam's apple bobbed as he swallowed. "I am sorry for Timothy and his friends. But mostly for my reaction to what they said. I should not have upbraided you, especially when you had been through so much. It was not my place. I feel so much regret . . . I wanted to write, wished to visit, but . . ."

Caroline shrugged and tried to catch his downturned eyes. "I deserved the censure. It has instructed me more than you can know."

The wrinkles around his face smoothed, but his eyes met hers with a heaviness.

She found herself leaning toward him, wanting to take away his troubles and lighten his load. "And on another account"— she tried for a pleasant tone—"you haven't spoken lately with Mr. Lennox, have you?" She couldn't help the smile that danced on her lips.

He shook his head. "No, he has been quite busy these last two days."

"I had no idea my aunt and your Mr. Lennox were on such amiable terms, but suffice it to say that I have seen him myself, and we are becoming friends."

Mr. Charleston's brows raised, his lips almost drawing into a smile. "How curious. I shall have to ask him all about it."

At least she could report that small example of her progress. She didn't want him to leave but also did not wish to keep him too long. "Thank you ever so much for your visit, Mr. Charleston. Can we part on better terms than we started on?"

Mr. Charleston nodded. "I believe *that* will not be too hard. But I did have one other reason for coming."

Did he really wish to stay longer? Caroline attempted to mask her pleasure. "Oh, goodness. I haven't even offered you any tea. My kitchen maid is on an errand, but I am sure she will return soon."

Mr. Charleston nodded, then hesitated before saying, "I noticed your housekeeper." He shifted toward her, raising his eyebrows. "She is quite young. I recall a woman with a face like hers calling here once, asking for work."

Caroline bit her lip, then said, "She is the very same. From . . . from . . . the surplus population." She cringed to remind him of her cruel words from before.

But a grand smile spread over his inviting face, and Caroline felt her breath catch in her lungs. Had she really done it? Had she made him smile? He still wore the shabby coat and he needed a new white shirt, but when had he become so handsome?

He leaned back into the couch cushions. "You . . ."

"Yes, Mr. Charleston?" She knew she shouldn't interrupt, but she didn't have mastery over her tongue with him gazing at her like that.

"You never cease to surprise me," he finished.

She wondered if she could ever be worthy of someone like him. He was so good, so selfless. John Charleston always thought of others first, even to the point of self-neglect, whereas she couldn't ever stop worrying about her own problems. If only she could be like him, then maybe he might consider her.

They weren't staying on topic. He had wished to address something, but she couldn't help but want to bring that smile out again and delay whatever conversation of business he'd intended to have.

"How are your sisters? I trust Sophie has stayed away from the pig farmer?"

"Ah ha!" Mr. Charleston slapped his hand against his knee and laughed, the sound full and unencumbered. His laugh brought her even more satisfaction than his smile had. "You *were* listening. I knew it! I thought I saw you tucked away behind the upstairs curtains."

"Oh," she said and hid her face in her hands. She felt color flood her cheeks. "Mr. Charleston. Again—forgive me. I loved every word I heard. I was wrong to act like I loathed it all."

"You are, of course, forgiven," he said. His hand came up toward her for a moment, but then he settled it back onto his kneecap.

Of course forgiven? How could he be so kind? Again he looked at her with that same smile. It made her feel like she should either dart out of the room or never surrender her gaze. "And how was Isabel before you left?"

Mr. Charleston's face fell immediately, and she knew she shouldn't have asked. All the cheerfulness drained from the room.

"She is much worse."

Caroline thought she saw volumes of pain behind his eyes and wished she could take it away somehow. "I am so sorry," she said, suddenly not knowing what else to say.

He cleared his throat and ran a hand through his hair. She thought again how he really ought not rumple it so, for he was far too becoming when he did.

"Lady Caroline, the other reason I came . . ." He swallowed. "At the risk of damaging whatever beginning of a friendship this is, I have . . ." He looked at her, his brow drawn.

"Please go on," she said.

"Our conversation has been so pleasant. I hope this doesn't destroy it." He flashed another smile, and she thought she could weather a great deal with that image to buoy her. He still seemed unsure when he reached past several papers in his leather bag and grasped something. "Your father gave this to mine just before Lord Marchant's passing. My father was ill for several years, and he must have forgotten the book's significance. It has been collecting dust on our shelves . . . and I felt I ought to bring it with me when I returned with your aunt." He withdrew a book from his satchel.

"My book," she whispered reverently. She would know that worn brown cover anywhere. "May I hold it?"

"Yes, of course." He quickly handed it to her.

Her fingers caressed the books' edges reverently. "You have no idea how much this means to me. I was sure he threw it away or burned it."

Caroline barely noticed Mr. Charleston's long pause until he cleared his throat. "I am glad it found its rightful owner. I must confess that as I perused its pages, I found this letter inside."

He leaned over and flipped to the final page. Her eyes widened, and he went on. "I wish I were the soul of discretion, but I opened it. The outside seemed oddly familiar, and . . . I think you ought to read it."

Caroline's heart began beating rapidly. Another letter? She took the letter and lifted the broken seal.

> *My Dearest Caroline,*
> *This is my third and final letter.*
> *Can you ever forgive me? I hope, in receiving this book and this letter, that you will feel of my earnestness. Read and then decide.*
> *I am sorry for so many things. My silence, the way I ignored you, my expectation of perfection, not to mention the contempt I demanded you maintain with everyone not of your station.*
> *Can you believe me now if I tell you I once loved fiercely? I loved your mother with my entire being, and she loved me enough to take me, despite my many faults: my pride, my anger, my disdain for the world. Her goodness healed me.*
> *Then, after she died, my bad tendencies crept back, vices of the bottle and of greed, and I did nothing to check them as she had once taught me to do.*

Just looking at you reminded me of her, of what I had lost. I ached for your mother and the happiness she carried, but that is no excuse for my behavior.

My deepest regret is that I did not tell you every day and with every breath, no matter how faltering it may have been, how much I gained by having you in my life.

You were such a ray of hope to everyone around you until I dampened your light. I know you can become that beacon again, no matter how you feel now. That light is inside of you still. The way you treat and love others speaks louder than any uttered words. Don't let contempt and hatred fetter you as I did.

All my love,
Father

She could not stop the tears that came to her eyes.

Her dear father—the one person she hadn't yet forgiven. How much pain had this caused him to write? How far *had* she strayed from the light he said she possessed? Could she truly get it back now? Trying to change for the better seemed the only way she could ever show him she *had* loved him. That she *now* loved him.

Could she break free of her anger? Let go of her own greed and pride as he had? Move into the future and prove that her darkest propensities wouldn't take hold? She wrapped her arms around her book of fairy tales and thought of her recent nightmare. She didn't want to die alone and have people whisper about her awful life as they passed her grave. She cradled her tearstained face in one hand.

She wanted to live with light, from now on and forever.

But oh, the pain of her past. Her present. Even her future, if she could not master it.

She finally dropped her hand, remembering poor Mr. Charleston sitting close enough to witness her sobbing. What did he think of her now? He had read this. He knew all her secrets. But his face seemed to hold only tenderness. Perhaps he felt sympathy because of the contents of the letter. She knew that look couldn't possibly be for her after all she had done.

As if to confirm her thoughts, he stood abruptly. "I . . . I had better be going."

She nodded. She didn't blame him for wanting to leave. How awkward this must be for him. He was kind, but surely he could never fully forget her rude actions, the abominable way she had treated him and others.

She forced a smile, still clutching the book to herself. "Thank you for my book and the letter . . . and for being so kind."

He nodded and showed himself out.

Caroline set down the book in an attempt to shield it from her continuous tears, her heart nigh to breaking. The book would always remind her of her father. And now of Mr. Charleston, whom she knew she'd never see again.

❀ ❀ ❀

John charged down the street at a near run, his emotions propelling him forward. He allowed himself only one glance over his shoulder toward Caroline's window—*Lady Caroline*, he corrected himself—and thought for a moment he saw her there.

In that letter she had been *dearest Caroline*. He was shocked to discover that to him, she had quickly become dearest Caroline too. It had been excruciating to watch her read that note. Had he been right to bring it? Did it cause her pain or healing? He hadn't been able to tell by her tears. He'd briefly thought he discerned that it gave her happiness. But he also imagined the pain the letter might cause, the self-reflection, the regret, the longing for familial ties now lost to her.

He had wished to pull her close, hold her while she cried, but after all that had happened between them, he was not naive enough to believe she would want that from him.

The beginning of their visit had been incredible. He couldn't have imagined it going so smoothly. Anna had nearly ruined him, nearly convinced him that people lived for only selfish motives. But he had been so wonderfully wrong. Dear Caroline—he found he could think of her as Lady Caroline no longer—had changed. *One should* never *give up hope.* His father had taught him that. Now he really, finally believed it.

He thought of Caroline's sincere confessions, at the fete and during his visit today. Did she know how beautiful she looked, even when apologizing?

She had asked about Sophie—had eavesdropped on them.

She had also asked about Isabel. Maybe he should have said more concerning his sister. He had hastily changed the subject, as that topic caused him too much pain and wasn't why he'd visited Caroline. Not to mention, he was too proud to ask for her help. He would be mortified if she ever thought he had sought to continue their acquaintance just to prey on her money.

He had walked nearly a quarter mile in the direction of the property office. Best to get this horrible task over with quickly. He hung his head and made his way into the office to meet with the solicitor and buyer. His bag was much lighter after having removed Caroline's large book of fairy tales, but his heart felt heavier than ever. Everything had changed. He no longer had any excuse to call on her. There would be no more letters, no more meetings. No more land. No more Lady Caroline, just when he wished, more than ever, that they could actually be something more than friends. He was destitute, or would be in a matter of minutes, as soon as he sold the deed. She would never consider him as a suitor, and he couldn't blame her. He shook his head and thought of what he did still have, at least for now.

He still had Isabel. And he had to help her.

CHAPTER TWELVE

Less than an hour after Mr. Charleston left, Caroline entertained Aunt Ebby. Mr. Lennox accompanied her, and Caroline couldn't quite believe just how humorous Timothy Lennox was on this Christmas Eve.

"My goodness!" she said, laughing. "I had forgotten how particular poor Mrs. Jensen was!" He had just finished recounting a tale of their old neighbor, her obsession with tabby cats, and her severe superstition about tea. "Thank you for bringing him, Aunt."

Aunt Ebby nodded. "I had doubts about him too, my girl, but he turned out all right." She winked at Mr. Lennox.

He laughed heartily, and Caroline continued. "I think we are close enough acquaintances now that I might ask you a personal question."

Mr. Lennox laced his fingers together over his belly and waggled his eyebrows. "Anything, my dear friend."

"Tell me about Miss Edgeworth. Are we ever to see her again? And are we ever to see her with *you*?"

His eyes twinkled, and he smiled. "You consider us quite close friends then, eh?"

Caroline sat up nervously in her chair.

"Do not fret, Lady Caroline. She promised to come up to Town for the Season. She shall be here in a matter of weeks. Tell me you'll come to every ball and keep her company."

Caroline regained her composure, grateful she hadn't over-stepped her bounds. "I will try. It still gives me nerves to think about greeting all those people who think so horribly of me. Perhaps, in time, they'll see I've changed. I would love to become Miss Edgeworth's friend, but I think it is you who ought to be keeping her company, don't you?"

"I should hope so." His cheeks reddened, and he snapped open his watch and closed it rapidly, clucking his tongue. "Forgive me, but I must be going. Another party awaits! I shall leave you two ladies to your gossip."

Caroline shook her head. She stood and curtsied as he bowed and left. "Now, Aunt," Caroline said loudly when they were alone. "I am ever so glad you have stayed, for I have a question I am most eager to ask you." She resumed her seat.

"Yes, dear, go on." Aunt Ebby settled deeper into her chair by the window.

"Mr. Charleston came here just before you arrived . . . with a letter he said he found in a book of fairy tales."

"Intriguing," she said, perching her hands on her cane. "Another letter from your father?"

"Yes. It was a very good letter. Exceedingly apologetic and quite tender. But I have to know, do you know how it came to be in the book of fairy tales? That book was one of my favorites . . . and Father gave it to Mr. Charleston's father—"

"Never mind the book." Aunt Ebby interrupted and held up her hand. "Mr. Charleston came to call on you? Surely *that* is a good sign."

Caroline clamped her eyes shut and quelled the urge to scoff. She did not need a meddling old aunt making comments suggest-ing matchmaking and attachments. Mr. Charleston had always been all business—even her aunt had reminded her of *that*—hadn't he?

"His visit had nothing to do with romance, Aunt. He apologized and then finished his father's bidding. I doubt I shall ever see him again."

"Is that so?" Aunt Ebby peered out the window. "I thought I saw more than mere duty in his eyes when you ran out on him at the fete." She tapped her cane on the floor a few times.

Caroline adjusted her skirts around her. Could her aunt be speaking the truth? She wanted to ask more about her observations but couldn't bring herself to.

Aunt Ebby watched her face. "How much do you know about his sister?" One of the old woman's eyebrows arched. It was curious that she'd turned the conversation to this.

"As much as you do, I imagine. You saw that she was in very poor health when we visited. Mr. Charleston told me this morning she is now even worse." Caroline was quite sad about Isabel, but Mr. Charleston had not said much, and she had not wanted to press the matter.

She eyed Aunt Ebby and noted a grin on the old woman's face. Why would she smile at such somber news? What was she hiding? "What do you wish me to know, Aunt?"

"I thought you'd never ask." The smile grew. "Do you care about him, Caroline?"

Caroline froze, aghast at the boldness of her aunt's question.

Aunt Ebby's smile never faltered, but her bushy brows grew serious. She cleared her scratchy throat and continued loudly. "What if I told you Mr. Charleston sold all the land he had this morning to pay for Isabel's treatments?"

Caroline gasped. "No. He loves his home in Thornton. Why did he not tell me? I am sure you are mistaken."

"He never wished to ask you for help. That is what you suspected him of, what everyone suspected. He is a man of too much integrity to do that." She let out a gust of air. "Did he seem distressed or distracted this morning?"

Caroline sighed and stood, pacing back and forth. "He did appear very weary, maybe even defeated."

"It is a shame," Aunt Ebby continued, turning again toward the window. "If only someone cared enough to do something about it. By this time, he's lost his land forever."

"I would buy it back myself if I could," Caroline said under her breath. She stopped pacing close to the window and fingered the lacy curtain, peering out.

Aunt Ebby pursed her lips. "I happen to know who bought it. I wager he would sell it again." She shrugged one shoulder. "The man was not really sure whether or not he should purchase it in the first place."

Caroline looked down at her aunt in astonishment. "How did you hear me?"

Aunt Ebby's stiff body creaked as she stood to clasp her hand on her niece's shoulder. Another wide smile cracked across her mouth. "It turns out, all I needed was a good ear cleaning. I read of an exceptional doctor and visited him, and after a few water treatments, I can hear quite well."

Caroline stared at her aunt.

"Being the old, deaf, senile aunt has its perks. You can understand everything and process it all while everyone thinks you are none the wiser. Not to mention my lipreading is exceptional after so much practice. As is my ability to watch the dealings of young men who are interested in my niece."

Caroline's eyes widened. She felt her cheeks redden as she clasped her aunt's bony hand. "What? You have been *spying* on Mr. Charleston?"

"No! Certainly not. I am just . . . observant." Aunt Ebby broke away and swatted absentmindedly with her cane at the ornate brocade armchair. "He hinted toward a few things. He *did* have the obligation of escorting me home after I was so rudely left behind. It made for some time together on the journey. I'm sure he thought I was dozing off when he reviewed his papers."

"Aunt. I cannot believe this. Of all the insane, interfering, meddling schemes—"

"Like I said, I rather prefer the role of mad aunt."

"I . . . I don't know what to say." Caroline paced toward the open door and then dropped, flustered, onto the sofa.

"Don't *say* anything. But you ought to go buy his deed."

"You cannot be serious." Caroline folded her arms.

"I thought *you* were serious, just then," Aunt Ebby said, pointing toward the window and then back at her niece.

Caroline *could* buy it, but then what? Her mind moved too fast. She would figure that out as she went. She knew she cared for Mr. Charleston and could not let him fall to ruin if she could help it.

"Oh, I am just as mad as you!" Caroline ran her fingers through a curl. "What is the name of the man who bought it, and where can I find him?"

"My coachman has his card and is willing to take you, if you wish. Edith said she would accompany you."

As though she'd been waiting there during this entire conversation, Edith suddenly stood in the doorway at attention, ready to hand Caroline her things and pocketbook.

"You hoped for this . . . planned for this." Caroline eyed her aunt suspiciously as she hastily took her gloves from Edith and donned her cape.

Aunt Ebby just shrugged and walked Caroline and Edith to the front door.

CHAPTER THIRTEEN

JOHN PACED WITH HIS BACK toward the window in the small study, which opened to the back garden. Mr. Lems had agreed in the settlement to allow them to stay in their home until after the new year. John didn't know how to break the news to his sisters, but he couldn't do it tomorrow—not on Christmas. He had roamed the garden most of the night, trying to find hope, trying to find happiness, trying to forget that he had just sold the home and the land he held so dear.

He heard a knock at the door then, and Sophie's voice of greeting. "Oh, hello!"

He looked over his shoulder. Through the doorway, he saw the silhouettes of two women enter the front room.

"It is so lovely to see you! Can I offer you some food? Tea, perhaps?"

"Oh, thank you, but I am not hungry." John thought himself mad or imagining what he hoped, for the woman sounded like Lady Caroline Morleigh.

Sophie continued in her most pleasant voice. "Do have a seat. Is everything all right?"

It *was* an odd, late hour for a visit, especially on Christmas Eve.

"I had hoped Mr. Charleston might be here. I have something I wish to tell him. He did return home, did he not? I won't take too much time."

John's heart stopped for a moment; it truly was Lady Caroline. Why would she possibly wish to see him?

"Yes, he is. He is just down the corridor there. If you could spare your lady's maid, I need to make arrangements with her so you might stay with us while you're in Thornton Heath. Would you come this way?" Sophie gestured toward the maid, who nodded and followed Sophie.

John smiled at his sister's scheming—she was always so clever—but he did not wish to meet with Caroline in the study. It would feel too confined, too intimate. He opened the back door and stepped down a few feet, enjoying the crisp air on his suddenly hot face.

He glanced toward the stream, noting the strong reflection of the moon in the water's surface.

He waited for the sound of Caroline's footsteps, afraid of too eagerly meeting her gaze.

When he was sure she had walked through the study and outside a few paces, he at last turned to face her. He had planned to greet her right away, but her dark hair and moonlit features twinkling with the glowing light rendered him speechless. Her light eyes caught his, and something in them nearly sent him stumbling down the small hill behind him.

He cleared his throat. "Lady Caroline, I did not expect you."

"Yes. It has been a most unusual afternoon."

He watched her gaze fall to the ground. She fiddled with her dress, seeming nervous. John's desire to move closer to her, to reassure her, overwhelmed him. He dared one step in her direction.

"I am so sorry to keep you, especially so late. I will be brief." She looked up at him, her eyes wide and vulnerable.

He couldn't stop himself. He stepped even closer and took her gloved hand in his. "Whatever it is, please take your time." He wished she would stay for days—weeks. But how could he even think that? He reminded himself that he had nothing to offer her now, and he had started with very little anyway. No, he had learned from Anna that he was not any woman's best option, and surely not Caroline Morleigh's. He tried to ignore the icy thoughts and resisted the urge to touch the twists of her low chignon.

"I understand you are moving after the new year."

She knew he had sold his land? And she'd still come? Why on earth . . . ?

"So I thought you ought to have this as soon as possible." She pulled her hand away and reached down into a bag he hadn't noticed against her full skirt. She withdrew a thin folder and handed it to him.

"Thank you," he said, confused and cautious. He removed the twine and the cover paper and passed his hand incredulously over the first page.

Caroline rushed to explain. "I know it is strange for me to come unannounced, so late, but—"

"This is the deed to my father's land." He looked at her with raised brows, and she nodded, those beautiful crystal eyes sparkling.

"How did you know . . . how did you get . . . ?" He paced away from her and ran a hand through his hair.

She took a step forward and smiled. "I happened to own your land for a few hours today, but do not worry; I had the attorney write it out again in your name. Happy Christmas." Her face lit with a soft smile. "I never did care much for sheep." She laughed lightly, and John wondered if he'd ever heard such a beautiful noise.

Then he let out a laugh himself. "You bought my *land*?"

"Only for a few hours. I just wished to tell you it's yours now."

His smile faded. "I can't accept this, Lady Caroline."

He analyzed her eyes, amazed at what looked like strength and tenderness. He didn't need her pity. He was a grown man, after all.

"No," she said firmly. "You *must* accept it. It's the only way I can make things right. You see, I bought it with my money— money that should have been your father's wages all these years. You must use the sum from your sale to help Isabel. Besides, I could not see you left to the poorhouse."

She looked from side to side and scooped up her skirt in her hands. "I promised I wouldn't take too much of your time. Edith is no doubt wondering where I have gone. I wish you the best with Isabel. I shall pray for you all." Then she repeated, "Happy Christmas."

She was nearly running toward the door like Cinderella, though he could see she still had both her dainty slippers.

"Don't go," he cried out, unable to conjure anything more eloquent to say. She stopped, and her beautiful profile angled over her shoulder. "Come back, please."

She tilted her head and remained still a moment. Then she carefully rotated back toward him.

"Would you care to . . . um . . . take a stroll with me? This little stream is very fine."

He watched her mouth draw up to one side. He offered a small shrug and outstretched his arm. She nodded and drew near him, lacing her petite arm through his and resting both palms on his forearm.

He led her down the slight hill. "As a boy, I loved streams. I'd often float little boats down them, crafted from sticks and leaves. I was always so hopeful they would travel far. I've always loved a challenge, I guess. See this?"

He picked up a twig and fashioned a little sail from a leaf and attached it onto another stick. It floated well for a moment and then became beached on one of the small rock jetties.

"It is stuck!" Lady Caroline said.

John scooped it up and brought it between them. "Yes . . . but I think if we do this and this . . . just remove some of this thick, protective bark . . . it will be our fastest ship yet."

He lowered it to the water, and it sailed past the trouble spot. John straightened and pulled her arm back through his. "Sometimes it just takes removing the outer layer to see the beauty within." He gave her a purposeful smile.

Caroline's eyes tightened, but her smile grew. "And you don't mind working with . . . with that kind of craft?"

"Not in the slightest. It is my favorite, for its true strength can't be seen at the first. It gives me something to hope for."

Caroline looked down. "You're talking about more than just stick boats."

He nodded. "I was alluding to a stubborn, beautiful, caring, young lady who is a *little* more complicated."

"Far too complicated, I fear," she said quietly and turned her head away.

He lifted his hand and gently raised her chin so she would have to meet his eyes. "Not in the slightest. I love fixing things. The young lady I speak of, though, fixed things all on her own. That is what makes her utterly remarkable. She chose to change."

"I still need to do so much, to be so much better. There are many people I need to seek out. To apologize to and care for . . ."

He drew her hands to his heart, bringing her close to his face. Her cheeks appeared especially rosy, her eyes sincere and steadfast. He glanced at her lips but tried not to linger there. Not trusting his stare any longer, he quickly spoke again. "There will be time for that. You have begun a beautiful change and proved you can do so. We must all become better, kinder, more selfless. Your past reminds me you aren't perfect, and that makes it easier to think that maybe, just maybe, you could care for a man as plain and imperfect as myself. But perhaps I suppose too much." He let go of one hand and nervously ran his fingers through his curls.

She drew a trembling breath, and he could feel her warmth on his skin. "I told you once to stop rumpling your hair. The truth is it makes you far too endearing when you do." She pulled his hand back into hers. "I am so grateful to you for the letters, for your willingness to find me." She paused and chewed on her lip before starting again. "You said I did this all on my own, but *you* have been here every step of the way."

She let go of his hands, bent down, and gently gave the small boat another push. She watched as it raced through the moonlight down the stream, then stood. "I used to run away from everything that scared me," she continued. "I set up walls and barriers and blocked everyone out. Now I feel I can do anything, and it's because of you. You showed me who I needed to be." She retook his hand and gave it a squeeze. "When you are close, I am calm; I am whole. Your touch chases away my fears. It's something I haven't felt in a long time." She sighed happily, stepping closer. He gazed down at her, and she raised up on tiptoe, bestowing a soft kiss on his cheek, then placed her face in front of his so their noses touched. "I . . . I love you, John," she whispered.

He slipped his arms around her, pulling her tightly to him. He lifted her chin upward again, this time weaving his hands into her hair, lowering his face to hers, and kissed her. Once, twice, and a third time. "One for each letter," he whispered.

She smiled back at him, looking shy and joyful through her lashes, then wrinkled her brow and gave a pout with her lips. "But my father said the third letter was to be the last. Does that mean—"

He pulled her close again, and this time their lips met for longer. "Definitely not."

Their soft laughter entwined, and they held each other again, staying in the moonlight as long as they dared.

※ ※ ※

Christmas morning brought a host of other guests to the Charlestons' home. At half past ten, Lady Loresetter and Timothy both appeared on the doorstep.

"We couldn't help ourselves!" Timothy cried as they came into the small parlor.

Caroline had just given out her gifts, which, true to the shopkeeper's word, had been delivered before Christmas, and the room overflowed with friendship, paper wrappings, and goodwill.

"Happy Christmas!" John said with a laugh. He looked at Caroline's hand in his. "I suppose I ought to ask you, Lady Loresetter, for permission to marry your niece. I would love your blessing."

Sophie stifled a squeal, and Isabel gasped in excitement.

The old woman tilted her head. "Ah yes. But not yet," she said, looking him squarely in the eye. She tsked her tongue a few times for emphasis.

John looked warily at the woman, then around to the rest of the party, took one step away from her, and pulled Caroline close.

"May I ask why you say so? I know I do not have a fortune, but I do have my land, thanks to Caroline. And I love her with all my heart—"

Lady Loresetter held up a hand, stopping him. "I just think you ought to have this before you ask her in earnest." She procured a small red box from her pocket and opened it. John stared.

"Mother's wedding ring?" Caroline breathed. "How did you know to bring it?"

"You . . . you wished for our future together this whole time?" John asked. He ran his fingers halfway through his hair before stopping himself and exchanging a look with Caroline. Still in disbelief at her aunt's antics, he shook his head.

A sly smile pulled at one side of Lady Loresetter's face. "Ebbeneze Loresetter, at your service." She bowed. "Always knows more than she lets on, rather like an apparition, don't you think?" She ended her words with a dramatic flourish.

"Yes," John said, exhaling loudly and rubbing his chin.

"I knew my niece's past, saw her present and yours, and wished for your future together. Her father and mother would most definitely approve of you, John Charleston." She grasped Caroline's hand. "Your father wanted you to have this when you were ready."

Lady Loresetter handed the box to John, and he deliberately withdrew the large ruby ring and slipped it onto Caroline's finger.

"You look just like your mother," Lady Loresetter said to her niece. "Full of the same light." Her bushy-browed eyes scanned the room in triumph.

Timothy applauded.

John knew everyone watched them, but he did not care. He pulled Caroline close and kissed her soundly.

ABOUT THE AUTHOR

SARAH L. McCONKIE STARTED HER writing career in the second grade with a thirteen-page magnum opus about dinosaurs. Although the plotline and penmanship lacked polish, Sarah learned she loved retiring to bed thinking of stories. On a good night, she still does the same thing. Sarah took up the pen several years later after tucking her own little dreamer into bed and now combines modern life experiences, a robust knowledge of Regency classics, and a passion for all things old-fashioned and proper to craft her historical romances. She costars with her own Mr. Right in the real-life romantic comedy she calls life as they raise their four darling children. Sarah believes creating thought-provoking and moral stories promotes literacy in a world that needs more readers.